THE FINAL CUT

STEVEN SUTTIE

The Final Cut

Cover design by Steven Suttie
Cover photo used under license from PA Images

Font type Calibri Light

P/B 1st Edition – published 27th November 2017
Kindle 1st Edition – published 27th November 2017

Thanks

There is a lovely author called Donna Maria McCarthy who retweets and Facebook shares my book adverts on daily basis, without being asked, or sent gifts. I would like to thank you Donna, for supporting me, and so many other indie authors, on a daily basis.

I hope my readers will head over to Amazon, and buy your excellent books. The Hangman's Hitch is brilliant.

*****

I got a little stuck on a technical policing matter whilst writing this story. I'm not a policeman, and as such, not 100% accurate on police procedure. (I've seen The Bill though.) I know some readers have mocked my policing knowledge in previous books.

Anyway, one day a few months ago, I met a very nice police officer, PC Graham Hartley from Accrington police station, and he put me right on a few points. Thank you very much, PC Hartley.

*****

I'd like to thank my wife Liz for her never-failing support, as we reach a pretty cool milestone this New Year's Eve.

25 years ago, aged 16 we became a couple, and almost every day since then you have let me off for annoying you.

I hope that I can enjoy the privilege of your partnership for another quarter of a century, at least.

I love you

Important Note

Although this is a work of fiction, the activities of the government, and their acts of war against the poor which makes up the heart of the story, sadly are not.

Most of the examples of deliberate cruelty against benefit claimants which feature in this story, are based on real events, events that have actually happened to real people. Each time you think "that's absolutely ridiculous" or "this is too far-fetched" as you read this novel, please just take a moment to remember this note, or better still, Google the event which seems so hard to believe. You will discover it as fact very easily.

Because I write books, some people wrongly assume that I'm loaded, and one person, another author in fact, accused me of being a "poverty tourist" for exploring the themes that this book is based around. I feel it's worth noting therefore that this book was written in the council house that I rent. I'd like to add that I have always lived in council houses, and I have lived in the areas of high deprivation which feature in my books. When I pointed this out to the very successful Edgar winning author who made the accusation, I was blocked by her on Facebook. I'll take that as winning the argument that I am not a "poverty tourist" but that I am in fact, a native. This is something I feel no shame about and I have been inspired to write this book because I know, and regularly come into contact with many people who are falling victim to horrendous treatment from the government, just for being poor.

If you are a passionate supporter of the Conservatives, I must point out that this is going to be a very uncomfortable story for you to read. But none-the-less, I hope that you do read it, and that it does make you feel uncomfortable.

This book contains swearing (including the worst one a few times) as well as some upsetting violence. If swearing, and/or violence is not for you, please choose a different book. Ta.

Prologue

John Smith had arrived for his signing-on appointment in plenty of time. He was sitting on the chairs at Ashton Jobcentre, patiently waiting to hear his name being called out.

The forty-three-year old had been unemployed for just over a year, since being made redundant from Tameside Council Parks and Gardens Department. John had worked for the council for almost twenty-five years, since leaving Tameside College. He had loved his work, which ranged from planting decorative flowers in the parks, to mowing the grass and picking up litter along the roadsides. It was a good, honest job. Not brilliant money, but he and his wife Sally and their two kids had managed to get by okay, making just enough to pay the bills and enjoy two weeks in the Med each summer.

But then in 2016, John became the latest victim of the "cuts" and his position had been made redundant. He'd left the council with a glowing reference, and the promise of a "call back" should the Town Hall's dire financial situation improve. But as another three years of "austerity cuts" of 26% of the council's spending power had just been announced, that situation didn't look as though it was likely to alter.

"Mr Smith?" said the young woman behind the counter. She sounded cold, and quite strict, characteristics which contradicted her youthful face.

John stood, and walked across to her.

"Morning," he said.

"Morning."

John passed the lady his job search diary, which itemised all his attempts to find work since he had last signed on. There were dozens of records of phone calls, letters sent, applications posted.

But the lady didn't look at it.

"Mr Smith, it says that you missed an appointment with your job coach on Wednesday last week?"

John looked shocked. He had to think for a minute. He quickly remembered what had happened.

"Oh, no, I was at an interview."

"A *job* interview?"

"Yes. For the caretaker position at Hartshead High."

She looked up at him with an inquisitive expression.

"I didn't get it." John looked disappointed about the unsuccessful application, but was more concerned that the computer was saying that he'd missed an appointment with his job coach. It was his job coach who had arranged the interview for him. It didn't make sense.

"Did you ring the Jobcentre to inform us that you would not be able to attend your appointment?"

"No. Well, I mean, it was obvious, if I was being sent on an interview that you arranged..."

"But Mr Smith, it clearly states in your contract that you must inform us in plenty of time if you are unable to attend an appointment."

"Well, yes, I know that, but, obviously, I..."

"I'm afraid that you've broken the rules of your contract Mr Smith. You will face a thirteen-week sanction."

John Smith smiled. This was clearly a joke. He'd heard about these sanctions, where your tiny bit of unemployment benefit was stopped if you didn't follow the rules. His wife Sally was so frightened of the sanctions that she always made double-sure that his paperwork was spot on, the night before each of his appointments.

"You guys told me to go to the interview. Chris, my job coach, he arranged it. Ask him, he'll confirm it. Even Chris knows that I can't be in two places at once!" John was still smiling, he knew that this was just an error. It would soon be sorted.

"Mr Smith, I feel we are going round in circles here. Did you phone the number on your contract, to inform us that you were going to be unable to attend your appointment?"

"Well... no, of course I didn't. I've just said..."

"And that's why we have no alternative but to take the action that we are taking. As a consequence of breaking the rules of your contract, you won't be able to claim Jobseekers for thirteen weeks."

John looked totally lost. He was beginning to realise that this wasn't a joke. He was starting to understand that this stony-faced young woman was being completely serious.

"I can't… I've got two kids, my wife… How am I going…"

"We can give you a leaflet about the process. It will include details of how to apply to the Food Bank as well."

John couldn't take this in. He sat, looking dazed for a minute. How the hell was he going to tell Sally that the money they couldn't get by on already, had been stopped. For three months.

"Wait, can I talk to somebody else? A manager. Please, get me a manager. This is just a mistake."

"If you read this leaflet, it will explain how you can appeal against this decision if you feel that you have been treated unfairly. But I must inform you that appeals cannot be heard until after the sanction period has ended." The woman sounded like a robot. She couldn't give a shit about John, or his family, or his problems. He took the pamphlet, stood, and walked out of there, unwilling to let her see the tears that were forming in his eyes.

They were tears of pure rage, of helplessness, and humiliation.

Chapter One

The mood within the Serious Crimes Investigation Unit was very tense. It was Tuesday morning, just after eleven, and DCI Andrew Miller had just interrupted his team, demanding that they step away from their work and join him in the incident room. He was breaking the news of a new case which had been handed to Miller's department only moments earlier. He had a stern, sombre look on his face, and his small team of detectives sensed that whatever he was about to announce was likely to be very serious.

Their intuition was spot-on. This *was* serious. Before going into any further detail. Miller informed his team that all of the department's current live investigations were being suspended, with immediate effect.

"There's too much shit, and not enough spades." Said Miller, as he broke the news. It was frustrating, and extremely rare for the detectives to be taken off their current cases. They were all desperate to learn what had come in.

"I don't know if any of you know about an attempted murder case that Stockport CID were dealing with last week… it made the news. It was reported as a random axe attack at a bus-stop." Several of the detectives nodded.

Detective Inspector Saunders interjected. "Yes, I was reading up on that case Sir. It was a lady in her fifties, wasn't it? Just minding her own business, waiting for the bus."

"That's right Keith. The victim had just finished work, and was stood, reading her Kindle. She was struck in the small of the back, just above the buttocks with an axe. The injuries that she sustained are life-changing, in the most tragic of ways. The axe penetrated her spinal cord. They don't think she'll regain use of her legs."

There was a moment of angry silence as the SCIU team considered the gravity of the seemingly random, unprovoked attack.

"Stockport CID haven't made any progress in identifying the attacker, but it's not for a lack of trying. The problem they face is that the attacker was standing at the bus stop as well, wearing a hoodie. He waited until the road and the pavement had gone quiet, before he launched his assault, so there are no witnesses who saw what happened. The few bits of CCTV that they've managed to grab offers nothing. There was no incriminating forensic evidence left behind at the scene. Most worryingly of all, the victim is a well-respected mum-of-three grown up kids. She's described as the pillar of the community, loved by everyone. So, as nightmare cases go... this one was right up at the top of the tree. Motiveless, cowardly, and totally inexplicable. Until today, that is."

Miller looked at his team, and smiled humourlessly as they all sat up a tiny bit taller. They were desperate to hear this next bit. Miller indulged them.

"I've just learnt that another, very similar attack occurred yesterday, in roughly the same area of Stockport. It wasn't an axe this time, it was a knife. A gentleman was walking home from work and was struck across the shoulder-blade with a large knife, we're still waiting for full details of the weapon, but what we know for certain is that it's a very sharp, very heavy one, quite possibly a meat-cleaver. The victim is okay, in that he is alive, but the attack has cut through his supraspinatus tendon." Miller lifted his hand and pointed to the back of his shoulder, demonstrating the area where the injury had been sustained. "The victim is in Stepping Hill hospital, undergoing surgery. But here is the thing, it is very likely that he won't use his arm again. This injury has pretty-much switched it off."

"Jesus Christ!" said DC Jo Rudovsky, looking around the incident room at her colleagues. They all looked thoroughly shocked and appalled by this news that Miller was delivering.

"The victim is a forty-four-year old dad of two under-tens. Boy and a girl. He too, is also a very well-respected member of the community, these are not the kind of people that usually get caught up in street-fighting, knife culture etcetera. In fact, they are both the total opposites of that demographic."

"So," said DC Bill Chapman, "we've got two very nice, perfectly ordinary people with life-changing injuries. What's the link between them?"

"What makes you think there is one?" asked DC Peter

Kenyon, spinning around to face his colleague. "The guy might be mental. There doesn't have to be a link."

"Nah, not in my experience," said Chapman. "There is something that connects these two, I'll bet you a pie."

Miller nodded. "Yes, I'll stop you there Bill, you're spot on. But the last thing you need is another pie, mate." Miller waited for a faint laugh at the familiarly themed joke, but it was not forthcoming today. His team wanted to hear the rest. "This has been fast-tracked to this team because there *is* a link between the two victims. A very, very sinister one. They both work in the same office."

"Whoah. Flipping heck!" said DC Mike Worthington. He wasn't expecting that.

"Good grief!" commented DC Helen Grant, the team's newest member, and girlfriend of DI Saunders.

"So yes. It's not random, there is a motive of some description... and we need to get the sick bastard responsible in custody before he hurts anybody else."

"What's the plan Sir?" asked Saunders, leaning forward as though he couldn't wait a second longer to get stuck into this case.

"The plan is a very simple one. We are going to the office where the two victims work, and we start there. We find out who everybody is, who the office weirdo is, we try and establish a motive, and most importantly, we let them all know that there'll be no more injuries now that we're in charge."

"How many staff are we talking about in this office, Sir?" asked Rudovsky.

"The core team of staff is thirty-six, but others come and go from other sites as the workload dictates."

"Shit!" said Worthington. "Sounds like a pretty big office."

"Oh yes, it is. It's a government office, the Department for Work and Pensions. They employ eighty-five thousand people around the UK."

Chapter Two

Miller's team had been working on a number of high-profile jobs until this DWP case came in. The most significant one, in Miller's view, was the inquiry that he was personally investigating into the notorious Manchester gangster Marcus MacDowell, known better as "Marco". The inquiry was centred around MacDowell's criminal activities, primarily the gigantic cannabis farm that he was operating inside an old cotton mill, alongside rumours that MacDowell was responsible for the disappearance of several well-known criminals and their associates. Miller's objective was to find some damning proof of MacDowell's activities, and enough of it to lock him up and throw away the key. The police didn't want to mess about with charges against the cannabis farm, they wanted a list of water-tight charges, in order to see the back of MacDowell for a very long time.

It was an extremely sensitive inquiry, and Miller had been working steadily on it for a couple of months. He was disappointed that he would have to take a leave of absence from it now, in order to deal with these DWP attacks.

MacDowell had become a real pain in the arse for Manchester police since his release from prison eight years earlier. He had been an up-and-coming young star amongst the criminal underworld, prior to his imprisonment for murder in the late 1990's. At his sentencing, MacDowell was mocked openly by the judge and jury. He was described as "the Frank Spencer of the crime world" and at the time, he became something of a figure-of-fun amongst the city's gangsters, who always had comical stories about Marco MacDowell.

But that was then. Things had changed dramatically since that time. Maybe it was the fact that he was viewed with such amusement when he'd entered Strangeways prison in 1998, that he went on to become the most feared and respected inmate in there, and had managed to build an empire of power outside the prison walls, on the streets of Greater Manchester, from his prison cell. He went in as a joke, but he came out of there as a serious gangster. One who had made himself into a house-hold name in the region.

Today, MacDowell was running everything on the east side of Manchester. From Middleton to Mossley, and from Rusholme to Oldham, Marco MacDowell was the man who controlled the gangs, the drugs, the guns and the clubs. It was a hell of an empire, and one which he was extremely pleased with. He was more interested in the prestige of the title, rather than the wealth and the power. Going away to prison as the biggest joke in the north had been the making of him, he'd spent every single day since then, working hard to readdress the balance. His driving force was to make sure that everybody knew that he was not a joke, and he certainly wasn't to be messed with.

Marco MacDowell had started in the crime world by selling a bit of weed as a teenager, making just enough money to get by. But as the money came in, he began to realise that there could be more to life than simply "getting by." He felt that he worked hard selling the weed, and he was taking most of the risk, but he was passing most of the money on. His portion was tiny compared to the money he was passing on to his suppliers. He decided that he was going to cut out the middle-men, and grow his own. He saved up, and bought his first hydroponics set-up, making sure that with each new batch of weed from his suppliers, he was keeping the best seeds for himself.

That first set-up gave him enough cash to invest further. And so it went on, for a couple of years. If drug dealers and weed farmers had ever held an awards evening, Marco MacDowell would surely have walked away with an award for "up and coming entrepreneur."

As the nineties were drawing to a close, it was rumoured that Marco was supplying twenty-per-cent of the weed that was being smoked in Greater Manchester. And for anybody who has never smelt how much weed gets smoked around this part of the world, it's a lot.

But just when things were going so well, his success was to come crashing down. And it was all his own doing. Marco had turned his weed-growing into an industrial operation. Quite literally, he had taken over a small industrial unit close to the canal in Hyde, and cultivated almost a thousand plants, the flowers of which had a resale value of over a million pounds. But his success wasn't going unnoticed amongst the most serious gangsters, and word was going around Manchester about the new kid on the block.

Marco MacDowell had known what to expect. He was successful at what he did because he had studied and worked hard. He knew everything there was to know about the plants, and how to grow them to the highest standards. He was also very astute at developing a trusted network of wholesale dealers. He had recognised early on that dealing with other growers and dealers would be the riskiest part of the enterprise.

However, the way that Marco planned to sort this part of the business development strategy was about to end his emergent career, and land him in the big house for a ten stretch. Marco had been getting attention from the wrong people, as word of his little factory got out to other dealers and growers. The dreaded gypsy firm of Gorton, the Desmond family were sniffing about a bit too much, and Marco knew that it was only going to be a matter of time before they turned up mob-handed at his weed factory, to take it over. Traditionally, the only way to fight these kinds of people, was to have a bigger, braver, harder mob. But that wasn't how Marco wanted to play it. He didn't want to give all his cash away paying a gang of knuckleheads just to protect him and his investment. He was making a great success of things with a very small team, and now that the Desmond family were acting the goat, he needed to show them that he wasn't scared, and that he'd kill them if they ever tried to take one plant out of his factory. It was a simple case of kill, or be killed as far as MacDowell was concerned.

Instead of spending money on a large group of mates, who would ultimately let him down anyway, Marco invested his money on security. He had huge steel gates put up around his unit. He invested heavily in surveillance equipment, and he bought himself a gun, and made sure that everybody who needed to know, was fully aware that he'd bought it.

"Anyone wants to come and fuck with me, they'll rue the day!" He'd say to other underworld figures, mixing some aggressive street-talk with a phrase he'd borrowed from his nan.

The fact was, Marco wanted trouble. It was an integral part of his business development strategy. The bigger the trouble, the better. And the sooner it came, the better. To step up a division, you had to make yourself known.

It didn't take long until the Desmond family turned up, and tried to figure a way to get their three cars past the giant, expensive steel gates, and into Marco's yard.

Marco was standing on the roof, shouting down at them.

"What do you want?"

"We've come for a brew!" Shouted Danny Desmond. "See how you're getting on with the new factory!" he shouted over the giant gates. His gang were looking around the perimeter, trying to find a way in. But Marco had secured the place like a fortress. The steel, spiked perimeter fence had razor wire and barbed wire all around the top.

"No milk, sorry, and I'm out of biscuits. Phone me next time you're planning a visit, eh? I'll make sure I've been down the Kwik Save." shouted Marco. He took his phone out of his pocket, and started writing a text message. It took a few moments, this was back in the days of pressing the buttons a few times to get the correct letter you wanted. Back when Snake was the best game you could get on a phone.

After what seemed like a minute, he sent it.

Danny Desmond's phone vibrated in his pocket. He took it out, and saw that he had received a text message from Marco. It read "Go now, or I'm going to shoot you in the tit."
Danny laughed loudly, and shouted his companions around him. "Hee-ya lads, come and have a look at this. I think Marco's getting a bit fucking cocky!" Danny was shouting loud enough to be heard by Marco. His team were laughing loudly, mockingly.

"He must have been on the brave pills!" announced another Desmond brother, Daz. There was a roar of laughter, and the nine men were making a racket, acting like football yobs on the way to a game.

"Come on Marco, let us in. You know what's happening. You can't stop the sun from rising in the east tomorrow morning, and you can't stop us from becoming your business partners today. Now come down and open the fucking gates, you turnip."

The newest member of the Manchester criminal underworld pulled his handgun out the waist-band of his trousers, and opened fire, firing six bullets at the group of men. They absolutely shat themselves, throwing their bodies down onto the floor, their laughter had been replaced with a real fear, as the bullets whizzed by, inches away from them. How nobody had been caught was anybody's guess. As they lay there, hiding, wondering how to reverse their cars away without being shot, Marco was reloading his handgun with another six bullets.

He fired again at the huge steel gates, shouting "yee-haaaa!" as each bullet pinged off with a deafening bang. The Desmonds crawled away into the undergrowth, leaving their cars where they were. It was a humiliation that none of them wanted to speak about.

"And don't come back, you pikey twats!" Shouted Marco, firing his last bullet into the air, and shouting "yee-haaaa!" once more. He never did hear from the Desmond family again. Presumably they decided that this nutter was going to be more trouble than he was worth. They didn't even return for their cars.

The word soon started going around that Marco MacDowell was a maniac. And as long as it's the right people who are saying it, that is a very positive reputation if you want to be a major player. There were other scrapes and confrontations with other gangs, and MacDowell always seemed to outwit them, or just freak them out so they'd follow the Desmond family's lead, and just leave him well alone.

But Marco wasn't happy with that. In order to achieve his big dreams for his weed growing venture, he wanted his enterprise to be known as a total no-go zone. He felt that needed to kill somebody connected to the underworld, to state his claim as one of the city's "main heads." After a lot of thought, he decided that he would kill the ex-police detective, turned criminal-advisor, Geoff Walsh. Walsh was a rotten piece of work, and although he provided sound advice on police procedures to the people who wanted to learn ways around the system, there were suspicions that he was batting for both sides. All too often, a criminal who had sought Walsh's advice, and had paid him his fee, ended up in a police van not long after. It had happened too many times for it to be a coincidence.

It had taken Marco a while to decide that Geoff Walsh was going to be his best target. And once he'd set his mind on the idea, the more enthusiastic he became. The way he saw it, he would be doing the crime lords of Manchester a favour by eradicating a seriously weak link in the chain, whilst also bolstering his own reputation. It was an extremely good idea, and Marco decided that his legend status would be immortalised if he killed Walsh with his bare hands.

Marco began working on his upper-body strength, it became an obsession. He also became obsessed with watching Walsh, learning his routines, observing his domestic situation. Marco became fascinated by planning. When he did this, he was going to make a great success of it, he was going to tick every box, he was going to make sure that plenty of people knew that he'd done it, but there wouldn't be a shred of evidence that could prove it. He would kill Geoff Walsh inside his own home, throttling the dodgy, double-dealing bastard with his own hands, and then set fire to the house. He'd let it be known that Walsh had crossed him, in the hours before his murder was announced. It was all planned.

But the reason that Marco MacDowell went to prison as the biggest joke in Manchester was because he got his audacious plan wrong, in spectacular fashion. He killed Walsh, as planned, and dragged the body up the stairs, before laying the man's body out on his bed. He then set fire to the bedroom, and ran away from the property, wearing his balaclava, and laughing loudly as he did so, for added effect.

However, Marco could have had no idea that Geoff Walsh's house had a top of the range fire alarm installed, which included a sprinkler system. As soon as he'd left that bedroom, the smoke alarm had detected the fire, and it was extinguished, almost instantaneously. And unfortunately for him, Geoff Walsh's body lay there intact, absolutely loaded with forensic and DNA evidence from Marco MacDowell.

As he was sent down, the word began going around Manchester, and the jokes began about Marco MacDowell's ill-fated attempt at getting away with murder.

But in MacDowell's mind, in the grand scheme of things, that oversight, of checking whether Walsh had installed a state-of-the-art sprinkler system, or not - wasn't really the issue. He felt he'd been unlucky, that's all. He certainly didn't think that he was the biggest joke in town. He knew, deep down that everybody who was taking the piss, would be laughing on the other side of their face when he got out, and he dedicated every one of the three and a half thousand days inside planning it, and building his empire.

But now, eight years after he was released, Marco MacDowell was getting a bit too big for his boots, as far as DCI Miller and his superiors at Manchester City Police were concerned. He had built an even bigger weed factory, and he had made the building even more secure than his first. He had bought a huge old mill, which he had once again turned into an impenetrable fortress.

Miller had been making very good progress, following seven separate lines of enquiry, including extortion, kidnapping and murder. If these inquiries all worked out and turned up some incriminating evidence, this would turn out to be a very good piece of police work. Miller was gutted that he had to close this file for the time being, and lock it away in his cupboard for the foreseeable future.

But as he did so, he felt confident that he'd soon get this DWP business sorted out, and he could get back to it, and take Marco MacDowell off the streets of Manchester for good.

Chapter Three

At 2pm, Miller was standing in the sports hall of Manchester City police's HQ. He was facing a team of twenty-eight police officers. Some were in uniform, but most were not. These officers had been sent urgently to HQ, to assist with Miller's enquiry. It was an excellent result, the officers had all been surrendered by their senior officers, from police stations across the city.

"Okay, good afternoon, and thank you for making yourselves available, and getting here at such short notice." Miller looked out at the men and women who were all standing to attention, many of them desperate to know what was about to happen. DCI Miller was Manchester's best-known detective, he was always on the news, always caught up in the area's most talked-about cases. It was a thrill for many of these officers to be given this opportunity to work with the celebrated SCIU team. "Stand at ease." Instructed Miller, and the officers' spread their feet apart slightly, and clasped their hands behind their backs.

"Right guys, listen up. We are faced with a major challenge this afternoon. We need to attend an address in Stockport and carry out around forty, that's four-zero interviews with suspects in an office block setting. We need to be fast, and friendly, and most of all extremely considerate towards the people that we are interviewing, or else we'll have more complaints in, than we will have time to deal with. Okay?"

There was a loud chant of "Sir!" from the officers, the sudden burst of sound reverberated all around the gymnasium walls.

"Now, some background. We currently have two very seriously injured people in hospital, both have suffered life changing injuries in the past week. And both of them work in the same office. That's where we're going now. We need to figure out if the two injured parties have any enemies at work, do they have any rivalries or arguments with any particular colleagues? Is there anything at all that the staff know about their injured colleagues that could explain why somebody might attack them so viciously? One of the victims has lost the use of her legs. The other has been paralysed in his arm."

Miller saw that all of the officers, male and females, ranging in age from early twenties to early fifties were fully engaged in what he was saying. This pleased him, as you could sometimes get the worst dickheads sent over on these short-notice requests for support. But these all looked alright, which would be an advantage.

"I have produced a briefing memo for you all, so please pick one of these up and read it on the coach as we head down to Stockport. I want complete silence on that coach please, all I want to hear is you reading my memorandum, and revising the list of questions that you will be putting to each of these office-workers. We need this doing quickly, at the same time, before anybody gets the opportunity to collude with others. Okay, attention!" The officers moved their heels back together, the sudden sound clapped loudly with the echo around the room.

"Dismissed."

*****

Miller and his team travelled on the bus with the others. The seven-mile journey look just under half-an-hour, progress was slowed by the constant stop and start as the traffic lights halted their progress every two-hundred yards or so, as the coach meandered along Stockport Road through Ardwick, Longsight and Levenshulme. The silence that Miller had requested was being observed, every single officer had their head down, studying the paper-work which DCI Miller had produced for them.

Miller's small, but eternally productive team were glad of the extra bodies. Interviewing thirty-six potential suspects in a timely fashion was going to be a tall-order, especially when the suspects would be in their work-place, and attending these interviews in a voluntary capacity.

The big, white police coach was usually only seen when there was a big demonstration, or a major event taking place. It looked quite odd on Wellington Road, as it pulled up alongside the DWP building. "Okay, SCIU staff, come here," shouted Miller, standing at the front of the coach. "The rest of you stay put for a couple of minutes and await instruction."

Miller stepped off the bus, and was followed his DI, Keith Saunders, and then DC Jo Rudovsky, DC Bill Chapman, DC Mike Worthington, and finally, DC Helen Grant. Miller looked up at the building, Wellesley House, as he walked towards it. This seven-story office block on the very fringe of Stockport town centre was the place where the two victims of the violent attacks worked. It was an impressive, 1960's government building which looked out directly across the old, red-brick factory chimneys, and the impressive 27 arch railway viaduct which dominates the Stockport sky-line.

Miller's team gathered around him as he stood at the doors of the office-block. "Okay everyone, as we discussed earlier, you are each going to be in charge of a team consisting of four of the temp officers. The idea is to get this done as soon as possible, reducing the opportunity for alibis and stories to be manufactured, and so that all these people can leave work on time. The one thing we don't want is to get loads of flack. Now, remember, someone in there knows what's gone on with these two attacks. There's a pretty good chance the attacker is sat in there right now, so let's fuck his day right up. Okay?"

"Sir!" replied the SCIU team in unison.

"Right, Keith, go and alert the managers in there what's happening. This needs to be a big shock, the element of surprise should give us a lead. Let's go."

Saunders nodded and headed inside, he began talking to the security guard at the main desk as Miller walked back towards the coach, and jogged up the steps confidently.

"Thanks everybody for your patience. Okay, when you get off this coach, I want you all to head towards my officers over there in groups of four. Once there are four of you with each of my officers, they will become your team leader. Understood?"

"Yes Sir!" said the officers from their seats.

"Good. Now then, what I've just said to my officers is that the person responsible for these attacks probably works in here, and there's a good chance he's in there right now. So, as I have stipulated in your notes, if you have any doubts or concerns when interviewing your suspect, any suspicions whatsoever, you simply grab the attention of your team leader, and ask them for a pen. This will alert my staff that you feel we need another chat with this person. Does that make sense?"

"Yes, Sir!" came another enthusiastic chant from within the vehicle.

"Good. Right, does anybody have any questions before we go in there?" Miller was looking at all of the faces before him. Nobody raised a hand, which pleased the DCI. Usually, there was at least one bell-end who had to ask something stupid, just to hear the sound of their own voice. But these lot seemed pretty good, on-the-ball.

"Okay, excellent. Out you come then, go and stand by my staff, thank you."

*****

Five minutes after DI Saunders had entered the building, the entire DWP staff team from the fifth floor were assembled in the canteen. The fifth floor housed the department which dealt with benefit appeals from the local area. Other floors in Wellesley House contained other DWP departments, including the Jobcentre, Universal Credits, Child-Support and Pensions.

Miller did want his officers to speak to the other staff, from the other floors at some stage. But his over-riding priority was to speak to these people, those who knew the victims best, and would undoubtedly know something that would assist Miller's enquiry. Miller was patiently waiting for the DWP manager to stop waffling, as he made a big drama of everything to his staff, whilst introducing the police officers.

"So, as I say, this is the first we've been informed of this matter, but in light of the circumstances, I have taken the decision to allow the police to speak to you all, and that is my position at this moment." The manager looked a bit nervous, almost slightly overwhelmed. His staff were all sitting down at the various tables around the canteen. Miller thought that the manager guy had shut up, and stepped forward to speak to the confused-looking people. But the manager began to say something else. Miller decided to cut him short, rather than listen to anymore of his pointless bollocks.

"Okay mate, that's plenty." Said Miller as he stepped in front of the twitchy, nervous man, who looked mortified at being carved up like that in front of his staff. But Miller wasn't aware of that, as he got down to business. "Thanks everybody for dropping what you were doing, and please accept my sincere apologies for dragging you away from your posts. As you are probably aware, two of your colleagues are currently in hospital, after suffering very profound injuries."

There was suddenly a great deal of shuffling and whispering. Judging by the looks on their faces, this was news to them all. "Sorry, what's up?" asked Miller, pointing to two ladies in their forties, who were wearing the most obvious expressions of confusion.

"What's this about two members of our team? We knew about what happened to Kath, last week. But who else is there?" Asked one. All of a sudden, the canteen erupted into a rabble as the colleagues all searched each-other's faces and whispered questions and comments to one another. The gossiping continued, forcing Miller to hold his hand up and grab everybody's attention.

"Okay, my apologies. You obviously haven't heard yet, then." Miller grabbed his notes. "Last week, Kath Palmer was attacked at a bus-stop just up the road from here…"

"Yeah, we know about that. Who else has been attacked?" shouted one angry, stressed looking man at the back of the room.

"Well, last night, Jason Brown was violently assaulted on his way home…"

There were gasps, and hands were being lifted to mouths as a wave of urgent gossiping swept through the room again.

"Is he alright?" shouted one lady.

"No, not really," announced Miller, quite matter-of-factly. "He's been violently attacked with a knife, and surgeons are doing all they can to save his right arm." The noise began again. It was irritating for Miller, but quite understandable. He'd taken it for granted that these people would have heard about the violent attack the previous evening. He waited patiently for Kath and Jason's shocked and upset colleagues to calm down a bit. Once everybody had got their breath back a little, Miller continued to talk.

"Naturally, in light of what has happened, our first priority here is to ensure that you are all safe, and we will of course be putting procedures in place that will offer you peace-of-mind and protection while we figure out what is going on. But before we come to that, I'm sure you will all understand that we need to interview you all, and ask you some questions about what has happened, just to try and work out if you have any information that might help us to find out who has carried out these awful crimes against your colleagues. We have to ask these questions, and we apologise in advance for any undue distress this will cause you. We really want to take this dangerous person off the streets before he gets the chance to hurt anybody else, and you might know something that can help us, without even realising it."

The staff were much quieter now. Their initial shock and outrage was turning to fear.

"I can't believe this, I just can't believe what's happening!" said one lady who was close to tears. Her hands were trembling, and a colleague leaned across and comforted her.

"Now as you can see, I have brought a considerable number of police officers with me, so we can get on and do these interviews as quickly as possible. I just want you all to think hard about the questions that you are about to be asked, take your time and answer them with as much detail as you possibly can do. I have been on the CID in Greater Manchester for nearly twenty years now, and I can't remember dealing with a case like this before. It is totally unprecedented. But, in saying that, the fact that two people from the same office are involved, I'm sure we'll find a very quick resolution to this case. Okay, let's get cracking then."

Chapter Four

Half of the DWP staff had been made to wait in the canteen, under the watchful eye of several uniformed officers. Meanwhile, the other half were being interviewed by the detectives in various offices, rest-rooms and meeting spaces all around the building. It was crucial that every member of staff had complete privacy, particularly because of the nature of the questions. The police were literally asking the staff if there was any dodgy gossip about the injured people. It was a rather unsavoury way to conduct an investigation, but it was obvious to everybody why these awkward questions needed to be asked, regardless of how vulgar and inappropriate it all seemed.

Somebody in the canteen had spent the waiting time writing an account of this unexpected working-day development, and had posted it on the Manchester Evening News' Facebook page. The press had not been officially alerted about the two "random" attacks being linked, so the information that had been leaked, along with a couple of photographs of Miller and his army of officers quickly became the Evening News' lead story, which in turn spread across other local media channels, and was even being picked up by some of the national press as well. BBC Radio Manchester was the first radio station to report the story, and were soon followed by the other stations on their drive-time bulletins.

"It's 5pm, here's the KEY 103 news, I'm Fran Stentiford. And we start with a breaking news story this hour. Manchester police are currently quizzing all of the staff at Stockport's DWP office, as they search for an attacker who has gravely wounded two members of staff who work at the building on Wellington Road North in the town centre. The first incident was widely reported last week, when Kath Palmer was attacked with an axe as she made her way home from the office building. This was believed to be an isolated, random attack. However, we have today learnt that another staff member was viciously assaulted with a knife yesterday, as he made his way home from the same office block. Forty-Four-year old Jason Brown from Romiley is said to be in a serious, but stable condition at Stepping Hill hospital."

The news was met with shock and fear by the radio listeners, tuned in all across the city, in their cars at traffic lights, in barber shops and on warehouse floors. The strange nature of the story caught a lot of people's imaginations, and the gossiping and discussions began in earnest.

It didn't take long for the Facebook detectives to crack the case, as they announced their theories underneath the Manchester Evening News' story.

"They'll be having an affair, I'll bet you a tenner. Go and question both of their partners and you'll find one of them has done it. Case closed. Next."

"Find out who's been sacked from there recently and I think you'll find that's the culprit. Nasty, twisted bastard. Karma is yours now sicko."

Elsewhere, the usual trolls were delighting themselves by making sick and offensive comments on the news pages.

"What do you call a DWP worker with an axe in her back? Eileen! Eileen against the bus shelter 'til the ambulance arrives LOL!"

Within a couple of hours, the story was everywhere in the north of England. These kinds of stories carry quickly in the communication age of the internet. By the time that Miller's team were finishing up with their interviews at Wellesley House, he was shocked to hear that this was the main news story in the region, and that a couple of news crews were waiting beside the police coach to capture footage of the officers leaving the DWP building.

Miller was standing by the window on the stair-case, with Saunders. They were looking down at the press members. "How much do they know?" he asked his DI.

"They know everything apparently. One of the workers from here leaked it. We should have guessed that this was a possibility."

"Yeah, true. It doesn't really matter I suppose, it's just annoying. I didn't really want the attacker hearing that he'd got famous. Anyway, its done now. Is everybody back in the canteen now?"

"We're just waiting for one last interview to finish. But they are getting pretty impatient Sir, could do with letting them go home soon. A lot of them are emotional wrecks."

"I know, well, we're nearly there. So, has anything come up as far as you're aware?"

"Nope, not a single thread. The two victims really are quiet, kind, popular members of staff. The only thing that I can gleam from scanning through the interviews is that they are consistently referred to as the most popular and well-respected members of staff. So…"

"So, you reckon it might be a social outcast, slightly jealous of the victim's popularity?"

"Well, I wouldn't quite go that far, Sir. But I thought that it was odd that the two victims don't seem to have a single enemy. I mean, we've all got somebody who hates us, haven't we? It's not always our fault, it's just how life works out."

"Well, that's not true in my case, Keith." Said Miller smugly, looking out across Stockport, at the gigantic orange-brick railway viaduct and the bus station beneath it.

Saunders laughed. "Well, you keep telling yourself that if you want Sir. Most people I know think you're an absolute twat."

Miller pulled an expression of feigned hurt, which made Saunders laugh again.

"But no, seriously Sir, I'm surprised that we haven't got anybody offering us a bit of a lead. The people who work here are genuinely upset about it though, absolutely no two-ways about it."

DC Jo Rudovsky appeared at the door, behind her senior officers. "We're all done. That's the last one finished," she said.

"Oh Jesus, you shit me up then, Jo." Said Saunders, holding his chest. Rudovsky laughed.

"Right, nice one." Said Miller. "I thought you were making a night of it, Jo!"

"Nah, some of them can waffle on a bit."

"Have you got anything?" Miller looked hopeful.

"Nah, nothing. It seems that the two that have been

attacked are adored by everyone in here!"

"Yeah, that's pretty much what Keith's been telling me. Have you not come across anyone who might fit the bill? Somebody who looks nervous, sweaty, agitated, high-blood-pressure, an axe in their back pocket?"

"Nah, that's all I've been looking for to be honest Sir. Every single one of them has been checked-out by my beady-eyes, and not one of them seems remotely plausible as the perpetrator. They are all shitting themselves about the attacker, though – understandably."

"The plot thickens. Cheers Jo." Said the DCI as he stepped away from the window, and the pleasant view of the old industrial landscape. He walked over to the door and held it open for his colleagues. "Come on, let's go and dismiss them, and then we need to try and think of a plan B."

Miller waltzed into the canteen as though he owned the building. The mood was low in there, the atmosphere tense. The appearance of the DCI did seem to break the tension a bit, there was almost a sigh of relief. "Right, sorry everyone for taking up so much of your time. I bet you're all keen to get off home… but I just wanted a few minutes with you to try and reassure you that we are doing all that we can to bring this situation to a swift conclusion."

"Are we going to get some sort of police protection?" asked one angry, sad looking lady. Her question was met with "yeahs" and "well-saids" from around the canteen. All of the staff looked worried, and Miller understood the sense of panic and anxiety completely.

"That's a good point, and of course your safety is of paramount importance while we try and figure out what the hell is going on. So, let's all think of a few ways that we can improve our personal safety, okay?"

The workers nodded, and they looked as though they might just be starting to calm down a little bit. Miller started walking around the room as he spoke. He wanted these people to trust him, and believe what he was saying. He hated politician coppers who promised all sorts of nonsense to scared people, knowing that it would be other officers of lower ranks that picked up the flack when the promises failed to materialise.

"The first thing I want to point out, is that you all need to remember the term "safety-in-numbers" okay? This individual is the most cowardly type of person you can get, sneaking up behind unsuspecting people, using weapons on them, all in complete silence…"

Suddenly, there was a wail from one of the employees. Miller's blunt, tactless remark had reminded her of the mindless, life-changing violence that two of her work-mates had suffered. The horror was brought back to the front of her mind. A couple of the lady's colleagues moved over and tried to offer reassurance and comfort.

"Sorry, I apologise for bringing that back. But the point I'm trying to make is that the person is a total coward. So, my main advice is safety-in-numbers. When you come into work, when you go out of work, stay together in groups. This person will not approach you when there is more than one of you."

"Is that seriously the best you can do?" shouted one furious-looking man from the back of the room.

"Sorry what's…"

"I'm saying, there's a maniac out there attacking our staff and your advice is to tell us to stay in groups! It's nonsense, absolute nonsense." There was the sound of agreement as the staff muttered words of encouragement to their angry colleague.

"Okay guys, listen I know you're all extremely upset and stressed, but don't start taking it out on me, right? I'm trying to offer sensible, sound advice to reassure you all."

"We want police protection!" shouted another voice, and once again the room was filled with chatter and confusion.

DC Jo Rudovsky was becoming annoyed by the pointless heckling. She decided to give her boss a bit of back-up. She had been stood by the Coke machine, but decided to walk out into the middle of the canteen floor. She clapped her hands together as she walked, to grab everybody's attention, and snap them out of their disruptive mood. "Guys, guys, can you shut up? Seriously? Let DCI Miller speak, and you'll find out that he is leading up to something. Honestly, pipe down and let him talk. If you have any questions, wait until he's finished."

Rudovsky's straight-to-the-point attitude worked like a charm. The DWP staff looked down at the table-tops and the floor. For a small, friendly-faced woman, Rudovsky could be incredibly intimidating when she wanted.

Miller nodded his appreciation towards his DC, before continuing. "So, as I say, keep that safety in numbers thing at the forefront of your minds. In terms of police protection, I am already in talks with your local police stations in the areas that you live, and police presence will be greatly increased in all of your local areas. We will also be sending out crime prevention officers to all of your homes, and these officers will be able to give you in-depth advice and support about how to maximise your personal security. These officers will also be able to fit your property with special equipment, things like panic-alarms... so that if the worst did happen, and the attacker did come to your home, you would have a police car on its way round immediately."

This comment created a fresh surge of panic, and several of the DWP staff looked back at him in a state of terror. The idea of this attacker visiting their homes gave it an even more personal dimension, and the employees looked terrified. Miller felt sorry for them, these were just ordinary folk, who led quiet, drama-free lives. The shocking nature of what had happened to their colleagues was hard enough to take in, but now, with this graphic suggestion that any one of them could be next, it was all getting too much, and several of them were in tears. Miller felt it was time to wrap things up, and arrange for these people to get off home now, where they could be comforted properly with family and friends in the place they felt safest.

"Before I finish up here, I just want to let you know that these crimes have made it to the very top of the list of cases that Manchester City Police are currently looking into. My department, the Serious Crimes Unit have been ordered to drop everything we were working on, and focus on this specifically. We will throw absolutely everything into this investigation, and I want you all to know that we will get this person locked away as soon as we possibly can. Until then, I want you all to take extra care, and try not to do any activities by yourselves, such as jogging, or walking your dogs. I'm not saying lock yourselves away, but if you need to walk the dog, or go down the shops, take your husband or your wife along with you. Just remember what I have said about safety in numbers. The man behind these attacks is the archetype of cowardly, and cowards don't attack people in groups. This loser is going to know that you lot have got the biggest gang in the UK covering your backs, that's us, the police. So, I want to split the room in two now, everybody who walks or takes public transport home, come and stand on the left here."

Around fifteen people got to their feet and made their way towards Miller, standing where he'd suggested. The others remained where they were seated.

"Right, the TV cameras are outside, because somebody has tipped the press off about this. Somebody in here... so, all you guys who normally leave here on foot are getting on our big police coach, and we'll drive you all home. That'll send a bloody strong message to this coward, when he watches it on the news."

This remark brought about the first smiles and luke-warm laughs of the afternoon as the staff started to feel the sense of terror easing slightly.

"Alright, you lot over there, are you all driving?" Miller looked at them as they nodded. "And are your vehicles all here, in the car park?" The nodding continued. "Right, well my advice to you is to go home an unusual way, just for the time being, and keep your eyes peeled for any cars following. The best trick is to go around a block, left, left, left and if there's still a car behind you, it's time to hit 999 on your mobile. Come on guys, we can beat this person, whoever he is. Okay?"

"Okay," said everybody in the room, though it lacked much passion. It sounded like a church congregation saying "amen" after a particularly long and uninspiring prayer.

"Right, here we go, let's get you all off home, and thanks for your time."

Chapter Five

The extraordinary numbers of police officers filing out of the DWP building was remarkable to watch. It made gripping TV footage for the local Granada Reports news crew, who were filming as the officers and the staff were led onto the coach.

"If you use that, I want the faces blurring out," said Miller as he reached the crew.

"Yes of course, no problem." Said the cameraman.

"Can we get a few words?" asked the presenter.

"You can, after I've spoken to your editor. You cannot show those people's faces on the news, and I want it confirmed by your editor before I'll say anything to your camera. Okay?"

The news presenter nodded enthusiastically as he dialled his boss on his mobile. "Gaffer, its Tony, I've got DCI Miller with me, he wants a word." The Granada man handed his phone across to Miller. The deal was done in a matter of seconds, after Miller explained the position. Within moments of ending the call, Miller was doing an interview to camera, with the DWP Jobcentre logo just behind his shoulder.

"DCI Miller, how many attacks are you investigating against people who work in the building behind you?"

"At this moment in time, we have two very vicious, very serious attacks, that we know of. But this investigation is at a very early stage."

"What do you think is behind the attacks?"

"We don't know, as I say, it's too early to make any sensible comments about things like that."

"How are the staff coping with this news?"

"Well, they're very shocked, very angry, very upset. But we're working with them, trying our best to support them, and help them to cope with the shock. Listen, I'll have to get off now, I've a lot to do. Cheers." Miller stepped onto the coach, and closed the doors behind him. "Right, do we know which way we're going, dropping all these off?"

*****

An hour or so later, the DWP staff had been dropped home, and the temporary police officers who had been so useful for this unusual mass-interview, had been taken back to HQ and dismissed.

Miller and his team were in the incident room, starting a fresh inquiry wall. The huge sheets of white paper covered the cases that had been live until just a few hours earlier. Now, the wall was a big, blank space, with just two photographs on either side. Kath Palmer and Jason Brown's security mug-shots, from their door-passes.

"I'm shocked that there wasn't one weirdo in there today, out of what, forty people?" said Miller, to himself mainly, but everybody heard him.

"There were a few weirdos Sir… to be fair. Just not weird enough to stalk their workmates and bludgeon them." It was Rudovsky who spoke.

"I'm with you Sir," said DC Mike Worthington. "I was convinced our attacker would have been in that place today."

"And we definitely checked that no staff were off work today?" Miller was looking at Saunders, who nodded, looking quite embarrassed that such an obvious question was being asked. But Saunders knew as well as the rest of the team that Miller didn't believe in taking things for granted. It was a stupid question, sure, but it was absolutely necessary in the grand scheme of things.

Miller wrote STOCKPORT DWP ATTACKS in capital letters across the top of the fresh, empty incident wall. He exhaled loudly as he stepped back and considered how little information they had to pin on there.

"Okay guys, over to you… what are you thinking?" Miller walked away from the wall, and sat down with his team.

Rudovsky spoke first. "Well, from what I've heard today, these two have never crossed anybody in the work place, they've never stepped a foot wrong. So, I'm of the opinion that the attacks are random, and that it's just a mad coincidence of them both working in the same place, on the same floor."

"Bollocks!" said Chapman, with more scorn than good-humour. Rudovsky shot him an icy stare.

"Fuck off Bill. Weirder things have happened, look at Donald Trump becoming President."

Chapman ignored Rudovsky. He just sat there, shaking his head dismissively.

"Go on then, Bill. What's your theory?" asked Miller.

"Well I haven't really got a theory as such Sir, but I'm not buying this random attack bollocks. The odds on this being unconnected would be a lot higher than the odds of winning the lottery."

"Go on…"

"Right, well for a start, if it was random, then the person responsible would be mental, and as a result, they'd have been doing some bat-shit crazy things before, during and after the attack. For example, if there's ever a lunatic out on the streets, attacking people at random, there is always a trail of activity… an attempted attack, or a big argument or some event, before and after the incident we're called to attend. But that's not been the case in either of these attacks. He's slipped in silently, and slipped away silently on both occasions. That's not random, that's ice-cold, hit-man style behaviour. Organised, calm, composed."

The team were nodding, agreeing with the points that Chapman was making. He had more to say. "So, let's consider random attacks. Always, about ninety-nine per-cent of random violence is committed by people under the influence of alcohol or drugs. There's no suggestion that our attacker was under the influence. Both attacks took place at tea-time, again, not a particularly common time for seeing these types of violent attacks. And as I say, we can rule out any theory that this guy is mentally ill. It would take great control and discipline standing there behind Kath Palmer, silently, calmly waiting several minutes until the coast was clear to attack her, then sliding off into the shadows. It's not random, it's definitely, one-hundred per-cent connected with the attack on Jason Brown, yesterday."

Chapman stopped talking to take a sip of his brew, before concluding his point. "I don't know why it's happened, I don't know if it's over now, or if there's likely to be another attack. But one thing I do know, there is no way on God's earth that its random. So clear your fucking locker out Rudovsky, you're sacked!"

Chapman's quip got a big laugh from everybody in the team, including Rudovsky.

"Interesting stuff Bill, cheers." Said Miller, he'd stood and started jotting a couple of notes onto the wall. "Anyone else want to share their thoughts?"

"Not if it's going to get me sacked!" said Kenyon, mocking his partner.

"Well, I had a thought this afternoon, on the way over to Stockport," said DC Grant. "It could be somebody who has been given a sanction or something. It's in some of the newspapers all the time, the DWP have been stopping people's benefits for all sorts of petty reasons. Who's to say that the person responsible isn't somebody that its happened to?"

"Fair point," said Miller, "but it's a none-starter I'm afraid Helen. It's just a call centre and admin hub, the staff in Wellesley House are not "customer facing" so there's no way that it can be personal, down to something like that. If they worked in the Jobcentre, or the DSS I could see your point. In fact, it would make perfect sense and I'd make it our strongest line of enquiry. But as these people are totally incognito, I'm not convinced." Despite shooting Grant's theory down, Miller did turn around and write "Sanctioned?" on the white paper with his thick black marker pen.

"Any other thoughts?"

"What are *you* thinking, boss?" asked Worthington.

Miller thought about the question for a few seconds. Eventually, he answered. "Not really got a theory yet Mike. I was playing around with the idea that whoever attacked Kath Palmer may not have intended to cause such appalling injuries, and might have come up with the idea of attacking one of her colleagues, in an attempt to throw the investigation into chaos. I thought that the change of weapon might be significant, the axe used against Kath Palmer might be in the bottom of the River Irwell. Then I thought, you can buy another axe from B&M Bargains for four-ninety-nine. Trying to get hold of an axe isn't like trying to get hold of a gun, is it? It's pretty easy. But other than that, I'm just keeping an open mind."

There was a blank expression on all of the detectives faces. This was the frustrating part of any investigation, when there was just too little information available to make any informed suggestions or theories. It was all supposition, and it was bloody annoying for detectives.

Miller felt the familiar sense of low-mood in the room, so decided to try and end this on a positive note. "Okay, well, get yourselves off home, sleep on it. I'm off to visit the victims, hopefully I'll be able to learn something new tonight. See you in the morning, and we'll all start again with fresh heads and new information."

Chapter Six

Miller hadn't managed to shake Rudovsky off his tail, she'd insisted on coming along to the hospital and meeting the victims. Miller was becoming more and more impressed by Rudovsky. Over the past few cases, he felt that she was really starting to mature, and probably had an eye on promotion. He was glad, she was an excellent detective with an incredible intuition, but more than that, her people skills were legendary. He didn't admit it to her, but he was glad that she wanted to come along.

It took a couple of minutes of negotiating with the hospital staff before they would allow the detectives into the critical-care unit where Kath Palmer was being treated. Both Miller and Rudovsky were shocked by the sight which greeted them. Kath Palmer was clearly very unwell, the colour of her face was disturbingly pale. She was attached to lots of different machines, by lots of different wires and tubes. Her bed was unusual in that she was lay perfectly flat, staring up at the ceiling. Her head was being held straight in a kind of helmet which looked to be attached to something much bigger which went right underneath her back. Her eyes were moist, as though there were tears forming, but unable to roll down her face just yet.

"Hello Kath, I'm DCI Miller, this is DC Rudovsky. We're here to see how you are, and ask you a couple of questions. Is that okay?"

Kath tried to smile, and very faintly she said "hiya."

"Are you on lots of pain-relief?" asked Rudovsky, adopting her most tender voice.

"Oh yeah," croaked Kath. "Off my tits!" she smiled faintly, and one of the tears had built up enough momentum to roll down her cheek. Miller and Rudovsky smiled politely at Kath's hospitable attempt at making a joke, but they both felt desperately sorry for the woman. These kind of visits, as unpleasant and upsetting as they were might not unlock any new leads, but they certainly hammered home the distressing nature of the attack, and always filled the investigating officers with renewed determination to catch the person responsible.

Miller and Rudovsky were at that stage already, they wanted to get the bastard that had done this awful thing to this kind-hearted lady.

"We've read through the reports that we've got. We're just really struggling for a description of the man…"

"I didn't see him." Kath was struggling to get her words out, it sounded as though she was thirsty, her voice was croaking. "He was just a shape at the bus stop, I couldn't tell you if he was black or white, if he was wearing a tracksuit or jeans… nothing. I was just reading my kindle, and I was standing up because I've got a bad back. Mind you, it's a lot worse now…"

Again, the two detectives were touched by the generosity of this poor woman trying to make jokes. This was not a laughing matter, and the bravery that she was showing was extremely moving.

"I know this sounds really stupid Kath, but you've not had any altercations with anybody recently?"

"No, I've been racking my brain trying to think of something I might have done. I've even been thinking of things going back to when I was at school. My mind has been racing all week, since its happened. I honestly can't think of anything."

"Well, things have moved on significantly today. I suppose you've heard about Jason Brown?" Rudovsky was talking calmly and softly.

A new tear began forming in Kath's eye. "Yes, my husband was here, he's only just left actually. He told me about it. I can't believe it."

"Have you got any thoughts about it? Any idea why you would both be attacked?"

"No. None. He's a lovely lad Jason, do anything for anyone. It doesn't make sense." Kath's chin was quivering and tears were rolling much quicker now. She was genuinely upset, but what was most endearing to Miller and Rudovsky was the fact that Kath Palmer was only upset for Jason. She'd been making jokes about her own situation. They could both see quite clearly why she was such a popular and well-respected lady.

"Is it alright if we pop back in again and see you Kath?

Tomorrow at some stage?"

"Yes, of course, no problem."

"Can we bring you anything?"

"A new back, please."

*****

Visiting Jason Brown was not quite as distressing as the previous visit had been. Jason was on a ward in a different part of the hospital, it had taken almost five minutes to get there from critical care, where Kath Palmer was being kept.

Jason looked like he kept himself fit, and his up-to-date Manc-band hairstyle suggested that he took his image quite seriously. He looked like a pleasant enough bloke, under the circumstances. He was sat up in his bed, he seemed sad and confused, but his injuries were practically invisible compared to those of his colleague's, on the other side of Stepping Hill hospital.

"Hi Jason, we're sorry to intrude, but we just wanted a chat while things are fresh in your mind." Miller realised that Jason was a little bit out of it, and clocked a morphine drip was attached to his wrist. That explained the vacant expression, and relaxed manner.

"I can't remember anything." He was talking slowly, just like a heroin addict in the middle of a big hit. Miller was glad that the patient was getting excellent pain-relief, but it wasn't particularly helpful for his enquiries. "All I remember is leaving work, heading off up the road, not a care in the world. I was thinking about what to make for tea, trying to remember what we had in the fridge at home and then nothing, can't remember nowt after that. Next thing I knew, I was in here. Waking up after theatre."

"What are they saying about your arm?" asked Rudovsky.

"They say its paralysed. Useless. They might have to take it off, depends whether there's a healthy blood supply getting through." Jason glanced away, focusing his eyes on the bed opposite as tears began to form in his eyes.

These words were like bombs. It really was an unimaginable horror that this man was going through, but he looked fine really, in a physical sense at least. Once again, Miller and Rudovsky were hammered by the nasty, personal implications of these mysterious attacks. Rudovsky explained the situation as it was understood. She told him that the investigation is currently focused on trying to establish the link between the attacker and himself and Kath Palmer, other than the fact that they work in the same office. She ended her explanation with a couple of questions.

"So, what we are doing at the moment is trying to find out who the attacker is. We don't want to see another person injured. We started our search at your office, this afternoon. We interviewed everybody in there, they all have a solid alibi, none of them have anything negative to say about you or Kath. So, we're stumped, mainly because everybody says you and Kath are the loveliest people in the place!" Rudovsky smiled widely, and it forced a big grin from Jason, one which quickly became emotional, and his eyes filled up again.

Miller decided to change tack. "Can you think of any staff from the past who left under a cloud, or were sacked? Or even anybody who just seemed a bit odd, didn't fit in around the place."

"No... seriously, there's nobody like that. Past or present. Nobody leaves, once you've got a job with the government, you stay put. Its good pay, good pension, great prospects. I can't think of anybody who has left... not in the last five years anyway."

"Yes, this is what everybody is saying Jason. They seem like a really good crowd you work with there." Rudovsky was trying to keep the positive vibes going.

"Yes, it's all good. I don't think the person who did this has anything to do with the place, to be honest."

Miller and Rudovsky looked at one another and sighed silently. This was such a frustrating situation, having literally no idea what was going on. The frustration was mixed with anxiety. The longer they went without any clues, the better the chances of somebody else being attacked.

Rudovsky turned back to Jason, who looked like he was getting a fresh dose of his pain-killing medication. A faint smile crossed his lips, and he appeared to relax his upper body muscles.

"I know you can't remember anything of the incident Jason, you're probably still in shock mate. There's a good chance that you might start to remember something, little flash-backs. We'll come back in and see you in the next few days, if that's okay?"

"Yes, yes, no worries, its fine by me." Jason's eyes rolled into the back of his head, and his eye-lids closed slowly.

"I think that's your meds just kicking in Jason, we'll leave you in peace now."

"Thanks..." he said slowly.

The detectives left the ward, and marched down the long, spotlessly cleaned corridors chattering none-stop about the bizarre lack of a single lead from two horrific attacks. They talked about the victims, and how decent they were, how puzzling this situation was. Soon, they had crossed the hospital and were back in the car park, standing by their vehicles. As they said good night, and headed off home, both of them were filled with a burning desire to catch the sick bastard that had inflicted these evil injuries to these two very kind, pleasant, ordinary people.

Chapter Seven

"I was really pissed off before, in the team briefing," said DC Helen Grant. She was sat cross-legged with her bowl of pasta rested on her legs. She was staring at her boyfriend, and DI, Keith Saunders.

"I know, I could tell…" said Keith, without looking up from his phone. His tea was sitting in a bowl on the coffee-table.

"Get your tea dip-shit. It's going cold."

"I know, sorry, I'm just…"

"Put your flipping phone down or I'll throw it out of the window…"

Saunders laughed, and chucked his phone across the settee so it was out of arms-reach. Since the couple's city-centre apartment was on the sixth floor, it wouldn't do to risk it being thrown out of the window. Besides, Helen had just come through from the kitchen, where she had been cooking for him. He realised that he was being extremely bad-mannered, and he apologised.

"Sorry Helen. I was just…"

"Working…"

"Yes, well, anyway, thanks for this, smells gorgeous. Much obliged to ya!"

"You're welcome… now you've flung your phone. So, now it's all about me for a bit… okay?"

"'Til your heart's content. What's up?"

"I'm just really pissed off, with Miller."

"Get used to it. Sometimes it can be a fifty, fifty mix of being glad you work for him, and hating his guts."

"He made me feel really fucking stupid in the briefing. He just dismissed my suggestion, straight-off. I don't mind, you know, if there's a reason, but he just shrugged it off. Arrogant bastard!"

"He does it all the time. But in his defence, he doesn't mind if you argue with him. If you feel genuinely pissed off, and you think that he's dismissed a good theory, tell him."

"Shut up. That's not okay!" Helen laughed at Keith. She thought it was an absolutely ridiculous suggestion.

"What?"

"You, you're winding me up! You're trying to get me sacked!"

"I'm not. Don't be daft. Go in and see him in the morning, and just tell him that you thought he was too quick to dismiss your theory. He'll either tell you the reason he dismissed it, or he'll ask you to convince him. But one thing I will say for him is that he'll listen to what you say. He's not got one of those daft egos like some DCI's."

"I know, but, well, it's scary, going up to your boss and saying they're wrong about something."

"Well its more productive than coming home here and slagging him off. That's not going to sort anything out, is it?"

"I know…"

"Do you really think he's wrong?"

"Yes, I do actually. I think he's totally wrong."

"Well go and tell him in the morning. Trust me, he'll hear you out. And if he does think that he is wrong, he'll be buzzing with you for having the balls to tell him."

"Honestly?"

"Yeah."

"How's your food?"

"Lovely, you're the best at this, I love it."

"It's a microwave one from Lidl."

"Really? It's proper nice."

"It is nice, and a lot quicker and easier than pissing about cooking from scratch. Especially if your boyfriend is so thick that he actually thinks you made it yourself."

Saunders didn't reply, he just nodded with an approving look on his face as he chewed another spoonful of the pasta.

"I hate going in that shop though."

"Why?"

"Well, I only went in to grab something for tea, and I came out with a giant box of washing powder, two microwave meals, a set of oil-paints and a fucking step-ladder."

*****

The late-night talk show on Manchester's local station Piccadilly Radio was discussing the attacks on Kath and Jason. It was a very popular radio show and had been going for years, the presenter Alan Newton was always keen to wind his listeners and callers up. When there was a big news story locally, the phone-in show was always busy. The people of Manchester care passionately about the place. People don't just live in Manchester, they get involved with the place too. The shocking events in Stockport that had been on the news since tea-time was the only topic that the callers wished to discuss.

At one time, not too long ago, it wouldn't be that shocking to hear of such violence in the city. Manchester is a place that has been widely known for its social difficulties through the years, particularly the issues around gangs and drugs. There was a lot of money spent on regenerating many parts of the city, in an attempt to solve a lot of the problems of youths with guns.

In the late 80's and early 90's, the Moss-Side district of the city was a notoriously difficult place to police, and things had got badly out of control. Everybody agreed that something had to change drastically. So, the place was regenerated and new attitudes were fostered and developed between the community, the police, the council and various public service bodies. Large areas of council housing were demolished, and new homes were built, based on the needs and aspirations of the community. The old style of estate designing had a lot to answer for. Criminals knew every nook and cranny of the estate, and knew exactly how to escape the police should they get chased, whether that was on foot or bike, or more commonly, in a stolen car. The victors would usually set the car on fire on the school fields. These types of problems created serious difficulties for the police, who found the place to be a "no-go area" but the problem was worse for the residents, who felt isolated, let-down, and like prisoners in their own homes after dark.

But what happened, over many years, was a brilliant example of how it is possible to turn a lawless ghetto into a nice, positive, cheerful place. Ever since those dark days of the early nineties, Manchester has shown the world new ways to tackle inner-city social problems. Delegates come from cities all over the globe to learn more about how Moss Side was turned around so spectacularly. Nowadays, Manchester is not automatically linked to negative thoughts about guns and gangs, teenage murders and lawless streets. These days, Manchester is celebrated for all the positive things that is has given the region, and the country, and the world.

But today, with these awful attacks in Stockport, and the apparent "randomness" of it all, the city didn't feel quite as safe and strong as normal. Alan Newton was taking call after call, from scared and frightened Mancunians.

"Johnny in Stretford, you're on the air mate." Said Alan. "What's on your mind, Sir?"

"Oh, alright Alan, nice one for letting me on. I just wanted to talk about these vicious assaults, I'm in shock about it, I was in tears reading about the woman, Kath, she seems like a proper nice woman, and to think that someone has just done that to her for no reason, it's just..." The emotion was clear in Johnny's voice. "...I'm just so sorry, so gutted that something like this could happen around here."

"Well, I'm sure you speak for everybody there Johnny."

"And the other guy, Jason, he seems like a proper decent bloke as well. It's just, I don't know Alan, I'm just worried that this is something really sinister. I'm scared to let my wife go to the gym."

"Well, I take on board your thoughts Johnny, and let's just hope the police catch the sick bastard responsible as soon as possible."

"Totally."

"We're lucky in one respect, that its DCI Miller and his team who are leading the investigation. He's got a pretty solid record."

"Yes, well, I hope you're right Alan. I can't stand the thought of anybody else being attacked, and suffering such appalling injuries."

"No, you're absolutely right. DCI Miller is holding a press-conference tomorrow lunchtime, and we'll be covering it live from noon, so make sure you tune in for that. Okay on to our next call now, Ruth, in Hazel Grove…"

"Hi,"

"What are you on about Ruth?"

"Well, same as everybody else Alan, these shocking incidents. I've had a bad feeling that something like this was going to happen for a few years now."

"What? I'm sorry Ruth, you've lost me…"

"Well, these two people who've suffered these horrendous injuries, they both work for the DWP, don't they?"

"That's right…" Alan sounded confused, but also suspicious about where the caller was going with this.

"And what has the DWP organisation been doing to people for years? Under that Ian David Smythe, they've been stopping people's benefits, telling disabled people that they're not disabled enough, that they should get a job. They've been kicking them out of their houses with the bedroom tax. God, there have been people who've been passed as medically fit to come off benefits and start work, and they've died the next day."

"Well, I'm sorry Ruth, I think you're being a little bit hysterical there my love…"

"I'm not Alan. I'm telling you, there's a list as long as my arm of disgusting things they've been doing to vulnerable people for the last seven years. Well, I hate to say it Alan, but I've a feeling that somebody is trying to get their own back. And if I worked for the DWP, I'll tell you now, I'd be bloody petrified."

"Well, I am going to apologise on your behalf Ruth, because I think that is an absolutely outrageous thing to say,"

"No, Alan…"

"Shut up, I let you speak. Now it's my turn. I think you're bang out of order there Ruth, knowing that there are a lot of people who know and love Kath Palmer and Jason Brown. For you to come on here and try to make out that they deserve those devastating injuries is absolutely shocking, and you should be deeply ashamed of yourself young lady."

"That's not what I said Alan. I said that I've been worried about something like this happening. I know that the people involved are just ordinary folk doing their jobs. But I've worked with the people that have been affected by all these DWP policies Alan."

"What do you do Ruth?"

"I work for the Citizen's Advice. I try and help people get their appeals sorted out when their benefits are stopped."

"Okay, okay, I'll stand corrected. I'll give you the benefit of the doubt Ruth."

"It's alright. But you've got to understand Alan, this government has been at war with the most vulnerable people in society. They've behaved with zero compassion towards millions of people, and the people are in my office in tears, every single day, I'm sending them off to food-banks... people who can't stand up are having their benefits stopped and are told to get a job. Blind people have been told they're fit for work, and lots of them are delighted by the prospect, at first."

"How do you mean, at first?"

"Well, once they realise that there are no jobs for blind people, they feel humiliated, and lost. Its degrading, and it's downright bullying."

"That sounds utterly bonkers!" The DJ sounded furious.

"There was a report that tens of thousands of disabled people have killed themselves because of this DWP policy. These people are the easiest targets, and what has been going on will leave a dirty stain on this society for a very long time. Honestly, I've had an awful feeling that something was going to snap eventually. And it looks like it has."

"Well this is certainly an interesting point that you are making. I'm no expert on these benefit cuts that have been taking place, I'll be perfectly honest. I have no idea if it really is as bad as you say."

"Oh, it is Alan. It's worse than that. The DWP have adopted a policy of stopping everybody's benefit, and making them appeal the decision."

"For what reason?"

"They say it's to help people come off benefits, you know, cruel-to-be-kind type of thing. But that's nonsense. It's all in the name of manipulating the figures. If you stop somebody's benefits for three months, even in the knowledge that they'll win the appeal at the end of the three months, and you back-date the three-month's worth of money..."

"Yes?"

"Well even though it didn't save any money, the DWP managed to get somebody off benefits, and the unemployment figures go down. That's why they say on the news that unemployed people are at the lowest numbers ever. It's because they've been sanctioned. They don't exist in the figures."

"This sounds like rubbish, Ruth, in all honesty."

"I wish it was Alan. But it's happening every day, to thousands of innocent people up and down the country. The people who work at the DWP have targets to meet, they have got to stop a certain amount of people's money per week, or else they are put on a disciplinary scheme. It's well known that its going on, and it's all happening to weed out the few people who have been defrauding the system for years. The problem is Alan, you can't just come up with a one-size-fits-all solution to these kinds of complicated problems."

"Are you honestly saying that this is a realistic assessment of the situation?"

"Yes Alan. You must believe me. The government have this idea that lots of people are just refusing to work because they can't be bothered. It's simply not the case. There are a small number of people who are playing the system Alan, of course there are, just like there are a small number of motorists who don't insure their cars, and a small number of people who don't have a TV license. But you wouldn't fine every motorist in Britain a thousand pounds, because of the few who don't insure their vehicle. Would you?"

"Well, no."

"It's exactly the same principle. Most of the claimants are genuine people, with genuine problems, and they are being treated worse than animals. Disabled people are being told they are fit for work by ATOS, who take care of the DWP assessments. They over-rule claimant's doctors! Their own GP, a professional doctor, who knows the person, and knows that they are not fit for work, are being over-ruled by ATOS staff with no medical experience. As I say, this is the biggest scandal of our time."

"This is really happening?"

"Yes Alan, I'm saddened to say. Listen, think back a few years. Tell me what would happen if you didn't feed your kids, and your kids didn't have electric in the house, or clean clothes for school."

"Well, I'm pretty sure Social Services would intervene, and they'd be taken into care."

"That's right. Traditionally, the state would get involved, to protect the child's welfare."

"And rightly so..."

"But not now, Alan. It's the state that are making the kids hungry. It's the state that failing their own people, deliberately. One in four kids in this country are now living below the poverty line. This has been designed by the government, and I'm so angry because the Ministers and spokes-people go on the news and laugh it off. They deny it, they explain it using confusing jargon and quoting bizarre figures about how their disgusting policies are helping people. But it's not helping people Alan, its causing devastation to ordinary families that we should be helping and supporting. It's absolutely heart-breaking to see this unfolding, day-in, day-out."

"Well, I'm truly stunned by what you are telling me." The presenter sounded genuine, and it sounded as though he'd stumbled upon the biggest scoop of his long and celebrated career.

"The only way to describe it is this,"

"Go on."

"Remember when you were at school?"

"Just..."

"Well imagine that you and your classmates were all really excited about going on a school trip, say. Alton Towers, or somewhere really exciting like that. The whole class are absolutely thrilled for weeks. But then one kid in the class breaks the pencil sharpener, and won't own up to it. So, the teacher cancels the trip for everybody."

"Well, that would be harsh!"

"Exactly. That's the sadistic mentality behind these benefit reforms Alan."

"Okay Ruth, this is your world, I know very little about it, but I will use our little disclaimer here to remind listeners that Piccadilly Radio does not endorse the views of our callers."

"You can say your disclaimer Alan, but rest assured, nothing I have said is libellous. It's the truth."

"So Ruth, let me ask you, apart from the fact that these two victims work for the DWP, what else are you basing your theory on?"

"Well, it's rather simple Alan. Both of the victims have been made disabled themselves now, haven't they?"

Chapter Eight

Miller was in a meeting with his boss, DCS Dixon. They were finalising the details of the upcoming press conference. DC Helen Grant was watching through the windows, nervously waiting for her appointment to see Miller. When she had asked him "for a word" earlier, she had no idea that he was putting a press conference together, as well as having the morning's team brief to present. As bad-timing went, Grant's request for a few minutes of her boss's time was spectacular. But to Miller's credit, he had politely accepted the request, and advised to her "hang on a bit, we'll have a chat after I've got rid of Dixon."

Grant's nerves were jangling now. She was the newest member of the SCIU department, and she was also living with the Detective Inspector. Every day, she felt she was walking a tight-rope trying to fit in, and find acceptance as a decent detective. Her desire to pursue this matter with Miller was part of that objective. If he *did* agree with her, and they led the enquiry based on her suggestion, it would be a great day for Grant being judged on her work, rather than who her boyfriend was. Her nerves jangled further as she saw Dixon stand up. This was a nightmare. Her idea was to have a relaxed, informal chat about the line of enquiry that she wanted to pursue, it certainly wasn't to be chucked into a two-minute window on the busiest morning in weeks.

Glancing up again, she saw that Dixon was starting to shuffle about the office. Miller looked pretty pissed off. "Shit," muttered Grant under her breath as Dixon made to leave Miller's office. As soon as Dixon departed, Miller looked out through the glass, pointed to Grant, and waved her towards the office door. He still looked a bit pissed off, she thought.

Confidence! Thought Grant as she stood, and walked across the open-plan office floor towards the DCI's office.

"Sir, sorry, this can wait…" she said as she entered.

"No, don't be daft."

"But I had no idea you had so much on this morning… seriously, I can catch you later."

"It's fine. What's up?" Miller had a kind expression on

his face. Grant had no idea how to start this off with small-talk so she dived right in.

"Well, Sir, with all due respect…"

"Ha ha!" Miller laughed loudly, throwing his head back as he did so.

"What?"

"Oh, nowt. I just laugh when people start off saying "with all due respect," it usually means I'm about to get a bollocking!"

"Well, it's not… I'm not…"

"Come on Helen, what's up?"

"The thing is, I have been thinking long and hard about this DWP link, the fact is that the DWP have been doing some outrageously nasty stuff over the last few years. And now suddenly, two members of their staff have been targeted in horrific attacks. I really think that the motive for these crimes is linked to the hostile activities they're accountable for, and, well, I thought you were a bit quick to dismiss it yesterday." Grant sat back, her shoulders relaxed slightly. She looked like she was glad to have it off her chest, and Miller had been pretty cool about it so far.

"Okay, I accept your point-of-view. And I may have got it wrong to dismiss this idea so quickly."

"Thank you, Sir."

"For the record, Dixon has just told me that there are very similar conspiracy theories being passed about on the internet, and Piccadilly Radio sent us a recording of a call they received last night, which says pretty much the same thing as what you are saying. Wait up, I'll stick it on now…" Miller leant across to his computer and looked through his e-mails. Once he found the one from the local radio station, he started playing the clip.

Both Grant and Miller sat in silence as the caller "Ruth" explained her theory on the attacks to the DJ. Once the call ended, Miller looked up and across the desk at his DC.

"So, I think I owe you an apology. Get yourself a presentation together based on your theory, you can address the team with this line of enquiry. I'll e-mail that call across to you as well. We might as well play it to everybody. She makes some interesting points, doesn't she?"

"Yes, she does. Thanks Sir."

"No, thank you. I appreciate you pursuing it with me as well. Well done."

*****

Miller was trying to get ready for his press conference, but there was a minor irritation on the phone. It was the manager of Wellesley House DWP. He sounded like a drone, and despite the fact that he had only been on the phone a couple of minutes, Miller was gutted with himself for leaving his number behind.

"I cannot tell you how distressed my staff are. This is a situation that is completely unheard of, Mr Miller. Half of my staff have failed to arrive at work."

"Well, I suppose that it's understandable really, under the circumstances..."

"It may be understandable to you, but it is very far from understandable to me and my superior management quadrant. It is my team that are absent, and that is my failing as their immediate line manager. I would like to add that I hold you and your scare-mongering activities yesterday wholly responsible. It's completely outrageous. I am going to fail to reach my most basic of productivity indicators today, and as I say, this is your fault." The line went silent, and the furious DWP manager seemed surprised not to get a response. "Did you hear me?" he barked down the line after an awkward silence of ten seconds or so. There was another silence. It went on for an uncomfortable amount of time before the DWP manager snapped again. "Are you there? This is beyond anything I've...."

"Hello."

"Yes, DCI Miller, did you hear what I said?"

"No"

"No... what do you mean, *no*?"

"I haven't heard what you said. I stopped listening."

"You stopped... are you..."

"I went to make a brew when you started giving me jip. And now I've got my brew. Bye." Miller ended the call and looked up at the ceiling, making a loud raspberry sound with his lips as he did so. Time was getting on, and he had a lot to get through. He decided it was time to make a list.

*****

Just after 10am Miller left his office and joined the rest of his team in the incident room. The tight-knit group of SCIU detectives were once again joined by the support officers that had been seconded over from various divisions across the Greater Manchester area. The uniformed PC's and plain-clothed DC's were glad to be back on this temporary job, and there was even more of them today. Dixon had agreed to throw unlimited resources at this case, and although it was bad news for the local police stations who had lost staff to the SCIU, it was extremely good news for Miller.

Everybody seemed relaxed and eager to get on with some work, except for DC Helen Grant, who looked a little nervous. Miller smiled at her supportively as he walked past her. He was really pleased that she'd had the confidence to come and speak to him. In hindsight, he'd been a dick to dismiss her suggestion so quickly, and in front of the whole team as well. He decided he was going to make it up to her, as she smiled back at him nervously.

"Okay, morning guys. Let's start with a joke. What's a horse's favourite TV show?" Miller answered his joke with a ridiculously camp and over-the-top "nay" impression of a horse. "Nayyy – bours."

The newcomers in the SCIU office laughed. Some uncomfortably, some with genuine amusement. Some of them remained completely still and felt embarrassed. Miller's stupid joke received the standard amount of mirth from his team, although Rudovsky seemed particularly fond of today's shit joke. She had tears in her eyes, and Miller couldn't be sure if she was genuinely tickled by the shit joke, or if she was taking the piss out of him.

"Alright simmer down Jo, it wasn't that funny!"

Rudovsky was dabbing her eyes, grinning from ear-to-ear.

"Yeah, it really wasn't mate. Are you on spice, again?" asked her partner DC Peter Kenyon.

"She's after a promotion!" suggested DC Bill Chapman, to a wave of nervous laughter. Rudovsky was still laughing as she showed Chapman the two fingers he was most familiar with seeing.

"Right, let's just settle down, I've got to go and do a press conference at noon… who wants to come and do it with me?" Miller looked around his team who were sat in front of the support officers. Miller was looking high above their heads where their hands should be. But there were none raised.

"Right, well, I'll just pick one of you at random then! Okay, let's get cracking, back to this case in Stockport. Since I last spoke to you all, I've been to visit the two victims in hospital, and Jo came along with me." Miller walked over to Kath Palmer's picture and pointed at it, and repeated the same gesture at Jason Brown's mug-shoot. "Now, I know we heard it all day yesterday about how nice these people are… but for the record, they really are. Would you agree Jo?"

"Yes Sir, very nice, warm, genuine, down-to-earth people."

"And as you can probably guess, that's bad for the enquiry. If we found out that these people were involved with a bad crowd, or owed some loan-shark twenty-grand or summat, we'd be able to pick up a scent, and we'd no doubt have the personal responsible for these vile attacks locked up by tea-time. However, it's not looking quite as straight-forward as that. Now, last night, I shot down the only sensible lead that we have been offered for this enquiry. So, DC Grant, please accept my apologies."

Grant looked as though she wanted to die. Her pale complexion turned an instant shade of red, and she could feel the heat rising in her cheeks. She swept her long auburn hair over her shoulder nervously.

"But if you'll forgive me, I'd like you to come and speak

to everybody about your theory."

Grant stood up and nodded to the crowd of thirty or so colleagues, only six of whom she actually knew. She wasn't nervous about presenting her ideas, but it did look as though she was. It was just the embarrassment of Miller's cringe-worthy introduction that had given her the crimson complexion.

"Okay, thank you Sir. Good morning everybody. I just wanted to share some thoughts about this case. Once we started investigating these two crimes yesterday, I was reminded of the many news stories that I have read about the DWP in the last few years, particularly some of the nastier aspects of their activities. Now, without this becoming a political issue, I'll summarise what has been happening in as neatly, and as concisely a manner as I can."

Grant leaned forward towards the desk and turned on the projector, which beamed onto the wall behind her, onto the investigation wall which contained Kath and Jason's mugshots.

"Can you all see okay?"

There was a loud, enthusiastic response from the hopeful new faces in the incident room.

"Alright. In 2010, the new government launched a review of the welfare state in the UK. From the off, they introduced a number of unpopular policies, most of which you will have heard of, the bedroom tax, the sanctions, the removal of the disability living allowance, tax credits, it goes on and on. Basically, the DWP are the department who have been given the dirty jobs to do. The government, under the umbrella of austerity saw this as a brilliant opportunity to reform the benefits system. Now I can see, from many of the faces in here, that there is a desire to see a change in this regard. That is why I don't wish to make this a political issue. However, whether you believe that benefits need changing, or not, the main argument against the DWP is that they have acted callously, and without apology. There are no hard-facts, but there are many estimates from extremely respectable sources that hundreds of thousands of poor people have died in this country, lots were suicides, many were stress related illnesses, many more were drink or drug related deaths. Now, the people who are trying to argue against the way the DWP are operating are suggesting that the deaths were intentional. They are campaigning that poor people are being murdered by the state."

There was a shift of mood in the room, it was obvious that the people before her had different views on these matters. Grant looked up and waited for the team to refocus their attention. "The argument is not against the government, the DWP and other agencies revising benefits. The campaign is in defence of the people affected by nasty, humiliating, often brutal, in-humane treatment. The campaigners, who range from MPs to GPs, Headmasters, a TV news reporter and even a Chief Constable, say that these policies have been targeted at the most vulnerable people in our society. The sick, the disabled, the handicapped, the people with learning-difficulties, people with absolutely no self-confidence, or educational attainments. These are people who literally can't fight back."

Grant looked up again from her presentation on the projector. The wall contained bullet-points of the issues she was discussing. The officers all seemed to be following. "I am of the opinion that the person who carried out these brutal attacks against Jason and Kath, has carried them out in some misguided, ridiculous notion of getting revenge for those people that have been affected by the DWP's actions and sanctions over the past seven years."

Suddenly there was sense of disquiet in the room. Subtle moans and exasperated breaths gave the sense that not everybody was buying this.

"Stay with me guys, I'm getting the impression that this is sounding a bit crazy, but let me summarise the extent of what I'm talking about, with cold-hard facts." Grant put her first story on the projector screen. She showed newspaper clippings of several stories which had appeared in The Mirror, The Guardian and The Independent. The Conservative supporting papers such as The Sun and The Mail rarely reported on the issues. The newspaper clippings included the story of a paraplegic woman who had her disability benefit stopped, after being found "fit for work" by the DWP's arms-length assessors, and a report about a Hartlepool woman who was told her appointment for a work capability assessment was cancelled. She was then sanctioned for failing to attend the cancelled appointment, despite holding the letter which confirmed the cancellation, in her hands.

"So, to conclude, I'm of the opinion that our attacker is a man who is aggrieved by the DWP's activities. I went to speak to DCI Miller about this matter this morning, and when I did, he told me that similar theories were beginning to be passed around online. He also told me that Piccadilly Radio sent him a recording of a phone call that they aired last night. I'd now like to play this to you."

Grant was doing a great job, and Miller was beginning to think that she'd make a better politician than a detective. She seemed to have swung the group around to her way of thinking in a matter of minutes, and he had to acknowledge that she had swung him around too.

The police officers all listened to the recording of the late-night talk show call. Once it was finished, Grant stood again and addressed her colleagues.

"That's all from me. DCI Miller asked me to share this theory with you. I don't know where it will go now, if anywhere. But thanks for listening." Grant switched the projector off and sat down.

Miller stood and thanked Grant for her presentation, and her closing remarks.

"Now, before we go any further with this, we need to be putting any political viewpoints to one side, let's remember that we are police officers. We may not like guarding fracking sites, and we may have political views about it. But we do it, because we have to do it. It's our job."

Miller allowed a little room for chatter and muttering amongst the officers. They all knew that politics was an area that they had to remain impartial of. Regardless of their opinions or beliefs, a police officer's job is to uphold the law. Whether they agreed with it or not, they had a duty to be seen to uphold the law, even at demonstrations and rallies organised to get them better pay. They all had to participate in many arrests that they may or may not agree with, dealing with matters that they held strong opinions about. Such as locking up prostitutes, wasting court and police time dealing with cannabis offences, chasing mentally-ill people all around the town all night because the mental homes have been closed. The police have hundreds of complex matters to deal with on a daily basis, and a great many of them result from short-sighted, ideological political decisions.

"So, I want this suggestion to become a major part of this investigation. I want to know from local DWP offices, who are the biggest complainers? Who are the people that have been making the most noise? We will start to build a picture of who the most vocal demonstrators are, particularly at the Wellesley House building, but also at other DWP offices across the city."

The team looked happy, they sensed that the briefing was finally coming to a conclusion, and that they could now start getting on with some work. For every one of the temporary officers, this was an excellent opportunity to impress the best-known CID department in the city. Many of them felt as though this was an audition, and they were desperate to get to work and make a positive impression on the SCIU team.

Miller looked calm and relaxed as he thanked everybody for their support with the previous day's exhaustive interviews. "I'm going off to do a press conference now. At this point in time, this new line of enquiry which DC Grant presented us with is strictly confidential. This topic is not suitable for public consumption, not yet at least. I do not want to be accused of dragging party politics into day-to-day police work. So, not a word publicly about this until I give the say-so. Okay?"

The officers all said "Sir!" at the same time.

"Brilliant, okay, I'll hand you over to Detective Inspector Keith Saunders. He will allocate your tasks and organise todays investigations. Thank you all."

Miller breezed out of the meeting, and back towards his office. He tapped Grant on the shoulder as he passed her.

"Got a sec?" he asked, gesturing her to follow him.

Once they reached Miller's office, the DCI closed the door behind them.

"You did really well there Helen, well done."

"Thank you very much Sir." Grant began blushing again.

This was biggest the problem with being fair-skinned.

"You've managed to convince me anyway. We are living in pretty weird times, and yes, I don't think it is beyond the realms of possibility that some whacko would start maiming people to make his voice heard. Sorry I dismissed you so quickly."

"It's fine. Seriously..."

"Well, I'd like to make it up to you, anyway. You're doing the press conference with me. So, ring your parents and tell them to put Sky News on at twelve."

Miller laughed loudly at the shocked expression on Grant's face.

Saunders was looking over from the incident room, wondering what Miller and Grant were so jolly about.

Chapter Nine

The news regarding the attacks on Jason Brown and Kath Palmer was still the number one headline story in Greater Manchester and the wider North-West region. It wasn't quite important enough to make the national news headlines, mainly because it was a story which was occurring "up north." Most northerners are fully aware that national news only covers local stories if they happen in London. Put simply, if these attacks had happened in London, then the story would be massive.

However, this was just a local matter for the northerners, not many people had heard about it outside "Granadaland."

The local ITV subsidiary, Granada TV is so well known that the north-west has become affectionately known as "Granadaland," and is one of the country's liveliest regions, if not the most vibrant in the land. The region starts just north of Stoke-on-Trent, and covers parts of North Wales, all of Merseyside, Greater Manchester, Lancashire, Cheshire, parts of North Yorkshire and much of Cumbria too. That's a hell of a diverse landscape; from the breath-taking scenery of the Lake District in the north, to the magical* coastal resorts of Blackpool, Lytham and Southport, through to some of the wealthiest country piles in Britain. All of this is intertwined with emerging and exciting new developments such as Media City UK and Liverpool Waters, and the area contains several of the nation's best-loved football teams too.

But it's not all a bed of red-roses. Granadaland contains some of the poorest and most deprived areas in the entire country. The heavy industries lost since the regions cotton, coal and steel hey-day have never been replaced, and entire towns have been left to rot, their people left to try and get-by on state-benefits and very few prospects. Places that were once the richest on earth, towns like Burnley, Rochdale, Accrington and Ashton were in decline on an almost industrial scale. These places had boomed during the industrial revolution, the Abu Dhabi's of their day. It sounds far-fetched, but to demonstrate their wealth and power, the cotton-towns all built decadent town-halls which were like palaces during Queen Victoria's reign. But now, these places are struggling to keep their libraries open.

The region is also home to many of the country's best-loved celebrities and sports stars. The cultural and political contribution that Granadaland has had on the world's stage is unmistakable, starting with the Industrial Revolution, the building of a ship canal, the birth of the Co-Operative Society, the world's first railway, the invention of the computer, the music of the Beatles, the drama of Coronation Street, the comedy of Peter Kay and the glory of Manchester United.

The north-west really is a remarkable region, and one which is known the world-over for its people and their good-humour, friendliness and warmth to strangers. And those decent people from Granadaland were extremely concerned about these attacks. The way the news reporters were putting it, these were random attacks, totally unprovoked, and carried out on unsuspecting citizens, from behind. It was a terrifying situation, and there was a lot to be scared about, especially when the poor woman involved will never walk again, and the bloke has lost the use of his right-arm.

The people of the north-west were desperate to hear more information about these incidents, and the scheduled police press-conference at 12 noon which was being covered live by local radio, and was streaming online via local newspapers websites, couldn't come quickly enough.

The media centre at Manchester City Police HQ was reasonably busy. It wasn't jam-packed, as it had been so many times on previous cases of Miller's. But none-the-less, the local press were out in force, and Miller was glad to see them all. The more press that attended, the better the coverage would be in the area that mattered, which was Stockport, Greater Manchester and just a little beyond that. At this stage in the investigation, there was no need for national press interest. There was very little point in people in Brighton and Cornwall being bombarded with this news every five minutes. As such, Miller was not remotely concerned that the national media hadn't attended.

"How are you feeling?" asked Miller of DC Grant, as they prepared to enter the media centre.

"Fine, I'm really looking forward to it." Grant smiled confidently at her DCI.

"Good, let's go and do it." Miller pulled the door and started walking briskly to the front of the hall. Grant was surprised at the pace her boss had set off, and found herself speed-walking to catch up with him.

"Good afternoon guys, thanks for coming," said Miller as he stepped up onto the raised platform in front of the assembled cameras and sound recorders. After a few minutes of idle banter with a few of the more familiar faces from the press, Miller started to give them all a run-down on the events so far, starting with the attack against Kath Palmer a week earlier, followed by the attack on Jason Brown. His account lasted almost five minutes, as Miller tried to ensure that every detail was covered.

"So much of what I have just told you is already public, and has been for the past twenty-four hours, or so. I'm now going to hand over to my colleague Detective Constable Helen Grant from Manchester's Serious Crimes Investigation Unit, who has a little more information regarding our appeal for information. DC Grant and I will be taking questions after the statement. Thank you."

The redness started burning up again in Grant's cheeks, but she paid it no attention as she thanked the press and read out her statement. "Good afternoon, and I would like to expand on what DCI Miller has just told you. At this stage of the enquiry, we do not have a description of the attacker. Our officers are currently going through thousands of hours of CCTV video from the main roads, passing buses and all local shops in the area. This is a mammoth task, and it is made all the more difficult because of the very vague description that we have for the attacker. However, we do have this still footage of him, close to the bus stop where he attacked Kath Palmer last Tuesday evening. We are confident that we will soon have much more information regarding this individual."

A CCTV still image appeared on the media screen by the

side of where Miller and Grant were sitting.

"As you can see," continued Grant. "The suspect is wearing very generic clothing, consisting of dark trousers and a dark hoody, with the lower half of his face concealed by a scarf. We have not managed to get a clear shot of his eyes, they are concealed by the hoody. He is wearing gloves, so we have not been able to ascertain his ethnicity. However, what we can ascertain from this image is that the attacker is male, of slim build, and is approximately six-feet tall." Grant stopped for a moment and took a sip from her glass of water. The media people were writing on their pads, or checking their camera lenses. There was a tension in the room, and it seemed that the press staff wanted this bastard off the streets just as much as the police did.

"While I accept that this is not a lot to go on, our team are optimistic that somebody in the community will know, or recognise this individual. This is a very dangerous, very vicious person who needs to be apprehended before another life-changing assault on an innocent member of the public can occur."

The pens were still scribbling away, the press wanted to capture every word that was being said here.

"We may not have detailed information about the attacker yet, but what we do have is solid information regarding the times and locations of the two attacks. So, if you know anybody from the local area, who looks anything like the man in these images, very tall, very thin, wears dark clothing. If you have any suspicions about any violent people you may know, or people with mental health challenges, including psychotic episodes, please think long and hard about the times of these attacks."

The locations, times and dates of the two attacks appeared on the screen, alongside photographs of the victims. These weren't the "mug-shots" that were being used in the incident room. These were "real" images, of Kath Palmer laughing as her grand-daughter blew bubbles at her face, and a delightful shot of Jason Brown smiling widely, holding his new-born baby, with a tear in his eye. These photographs actively encouraged the journalists, and their subsequent viewers to see what ordinary, happy looking people these victims were, before the attacks. The images were intended to "humanise" the victims in the eyes of the public, and subsequently encourage the public to really think hard about the appeals for help in hunting down this attacker.

DC Grant continued with the prepared statement. "The times and dates of the attacks are on the screen, along with the locations where the attacks occurred. We are especially keen to hear from any motorists or cyclists who may have been in either location around the times that are listed. It's extremely possible that you might hold invaluable evidence in a helmet-cam, or a dash-cam device without even knowing it. Please, take a look at your devices, and if you have any recordings at all, from either of these places, at these times, call us urgently on 101 please."

Grant clicked her button and another image appeared on the screen. It was the grainy, dark footage of the attacker in his dark clothing again. "We also want to know if anybody saw this person, before he pulled his hood up and placed that scarf around his face." Grant paused again, and lifted her glass of water. She looked as though she was absolutely determined to catch this maniac, and the press members could feel her steely energy.

"If you do have any suspicions about a specific person, somebody that you feel may be capable of such madness, we would urge you to ask yourself these questions. Think about those times and dates. Can you account for that person's whereabouts on those days, at those times? If the answer is no, I would urge you to phone us as soon as you possibly can. Once again, the phone number is 101, and we will try to eliminate all names as quickly as we can. Somebody, somewhere will know the person who has caused these catastrophic injuries, and I am urging you, if you have the slightest suspicion about a neighbour, or a friend, an ex-partner, or he might even be a relative. Get in touch with us, and let's get this person the help that he desperately needs, whilst protecting innocent people from the potential threat he poses." Grant looked straight down the lens of the BBC North-West Tonight camera, pleading for the support of the programme's viewers.

"Okay, thank you DC Grant. If anybody has any questions for myself, or DC Grant, please put your hand up in an orderly fashion and we'll try and get around as many as we can over the next five minutes. Miller pointed to a familiar face from the Manchester Evening News. "Joe."

"Thank you DCI Miller. There is currently a lot of discussion taking place on the internet regarding these attacks, and a lot of people are claiming that they have worked out a motive for the..."

"Can I stop you there Joe, sorry mate. I'm aware of the same discussions and theories that are going around. But as detectives, we can only deal with facts, as you know. So, there's not much point in me sitting here and talking about theories. Like all investigations that my team carry out, we have to work off the cold, hard facts, and not wild speculation. This is why we are here today, to urge your readers to check their dash-cams, their helmet cams, to help us find evidence of who this person is." Miller pointed to another journalist from The Cheshire Courier. "Harriet."

"Thank you DCI Miller. Picking up on Paul's point... I just wanted to explore this theory about a motive for the attacks. Our readers will all want to know what the official line is, and what you know about the attacks happening to DWP staff. It may only be a theory, but it is crucial that it is discussed."

"I'm sorry Harriet, but today's conference is about the matters that DC Grant has raised, and the request for help that she has put out." Miller looked around the room at the reporters and journalists with their hands in the air. He spotted Tim Kenyon from Granada Reports and pointed to him. "Tim."

"Thank you DCI Miller. I'm sorry to go on, but I need clarification. Are you ruling out the theory that these attacks have come in response to the DWP's activities against the unemployed, the sick and disabled in recent years?"

That was enough now. Miller snapped. "Okay guys, I've answered that one twice now. I'm happy to take your questions, but not that one. Any more questions?" Miller looked around the room, but none of the reporters seemed to have any other questions. They'd all had their hands up a moment earlier, and Miller realised that the only thing they wanted to talk about was the DWP thing. He got a sinking feeling, as he realised that he'd not prepped well enough for that question coming up.

"Okay, we'll wrap it up at that point I think. Please, pass out the information we have shared, please print and broadcast the photos that DC Grant has shown you. Let's get this person into custody. Thanks everyone."

Miller stood and headed out of the press conference, just as briskly as he had entered. DC Grant found that once again, she was struggling to keep up with her boss. Miller seemed like he was in a mood, so she deliberately slowed her pace.

But beyond the doors of the media centre, Miller was waiting for her, his arms were folded across his chest. He looked annoyed.

"Well done in there Helen. You did a great job." He was smiling kindly, even though he looked as though he was ready to blow steam out of his ears.

"Thank you, Sir."

"This bloody conspiracy theory is going to become a pain in the arse, you know."

"Yes, I totally agree. That's all the press were interested in, Sir."

"I know, and now I've backed myself into a corner by refusing to discuss it. Nightmare! I've nodded in an own-goal there." Miller turned and started walking, at a much calmer pace towards the stairs, and the SCIU office. "I need to try and think of a way of reversing out of this. I'll have a chat with Dixon later, he'll know we can bullshit our way out of this."

Miller needn't have worried though. If there was still any doubt about the link between DWP staff being attacked at random, it was about to be confirmed in very grisly circumstances.

Chapter Ten

There was a 999 call. Police and ambulance were being requested from a mobile phone number located in Hyde town centre.

"Quickly, we need an ambulance, and he's… get the police as well." The caller sounded like she was in shock. Her voice was fast, but stuttering. "Seriously, he's going to bleed out, there's so much blood."

"What's happened?" shouted another voice down the line.

"What the fuck's going on?" said another, terrified sounding voice.

The phone was distorting with the chilling sound of a man screaming in pain. The emergency call handler was struggling to make sense of what was happening here.

"Hello, this is emergency services…"

"I know, we need to get an… here, you, grab my phone, I need to stop that blood, tell them we need an ambulance." The original voice went off the line, and was replaced by another woman, who also sounded extremely shook-up and agitated. The phone line was crackling and all the call handler could hear was shouting and noise from the scene of the call.

"Hello, this is the Emergency Services, can you please tell me what's happening?" The operator sounded calm, and totally efficient, despite the obvious chaos and terror that was happening on the other end of the line.

"Hello, I'm, God, I'm, I'm not sure, I've just come out of work, one of my colleagues, Gary has been stabbed we think, he's losing a lot of blood. "

"Is the patient conscious?"

"Is he conscious?"

"Yes, he's losing a lot of blood, tell them to hurry up."

"And what's your location?"

"It's Clarendon Street in Hyde, it's the Jobcentre."

*****

Miller and Saunders were on the scene within forty minutes of learning of this latest attack. Almost a week had separated Kath Palmer's and Jason Brown's attacks. Only two days stood between this attack, and Jason's. The location was different too, the increased police presence around Stockport was of no use here in Hyde, six miles away, in the Tameside Borough. The area had been cordoned off with police tape, and quite a crowd had gathered on the opposite side of the road, this area was the main thoroughfare between the town centre's offices, market and shops, to the bus station.

The familiar white and yellow forensics tent had been erected around the corner from the main Jobcentre entrance, at another entrance. The attack had happened directly outside the staff exit of the Jobcentre's building, Beech House. Miller was surprised to see that the building employed its own security guards. They hadn't been of any help on this occasion, it seemed.

Beech House is an uninspiring 1960's four-storey concrete and glass building which houses the DWP staff who cover the Tameside area. This is a large metropolitan zone with a population of almost 300,000 people. Miller was quick to notice the deafening roar of aeroplanes passing overhead every couple of minutes, as they made their way towards the Manchester airport landing strip. There was another source of thunderous noise too, and Miller quickly realised the M67 motorway was running by the location, just twenty metres away behind an abandoned, decaying old bingo hall.

"I couldn't work here with all this racket going on!" said Miller. Saunders didn't seem to notice the noise, he was speed-reading through some notes that he'd been handed from another officer.

"Come on, we'd better take a look," said Miller as he pulled back the door-flap of the forensics tent and gestured Saunders through.

Inside the tent, both detectives were shocked by the amount of blood which had been lost by the victim. The forensics officers were scouring the pavement, looking for any traces of contaminating evidence that might have been left behind by the attacker.

The situation started to become clearer as Saunders relayed the notes, and the forensics officers added their own assessments. In short, the victim had been hit by a large weapon across the back of his legs. At this early stage, it seemed most likely that the weapon was a large knife, or more likely a sword, similar to a Samurai type of weapon. The injuries sustained by the DWP employee were consistent with being whipped with great force across the back of both legs with a long blade. The weapon had penetrated both thighs, extremely deeply, just above the back of the knees. It was obvious that the injuries were life-changing, in so much as the blade had severed many of the victim's tendons, muscles and hamstrings. Miller shuddered as he listened to the forensic officer's opinion that if the victim survived, he'd never be able bend his legs again.

"Good God. This is like something out of a horror film." Saunders was talking to himself as he struggled to make sense of the amount of blood lost.

"They don't think he'll make it," said Miller. "The ambulance crew just threw him on a stretcher and shot off to the hospital."

"But there are witnesses?"

"There's a couple from here, they heard screams, and heard the loud footsteps of the attacker running off, down towards the bus station. There are a dozen or so who saw him legging it through the bus station. After that he headed off across the motorway footbridge. Nobody knows where he's gone after that. He's long gone though."

"And I thought I heard someone say he moved pretty sharpish?" asked Miller, referring to a comment that he'd heard over the police radio, on his way over. The comment was made by a witness, to the first police officers on the scene.

"Yes, he shot off like Usain Bolt, according to those who saw him legging it through the bus station. He was carrying a black-bin bag with something in it. One person thought it was a poster, rolled up."

"The blade?"

"Sounds like it. Anyway, he's gone right through the

middle of the bus station, which doesn't make any sense as you'd think he'd have run along the bus carriageway."

"Yes, that is odd."

"Its double-odd, because there are two motorway footpaths. One at either end of the bus station. He's chosen the one that is furthest away, but they both lead out to the same place, which is the opposite side of the motorway."

"So, he wants to be seen?"

"No idea. It's the same bloke though. The description is similar to what he wore in Stockport, he sounds tall and skinny. We're just waiting for a call from Transport for Greater Manchester who are reviewing all of the bus station's CCTV. Fingers crossed, we'll get a pretty good shot of him."

"You know what, it sounds like he wants to be on telly. Why else would you run through the bus station, which is totally lit up, full of witnesses and CCTV?"

Saunders shrugged. He didn't like to try and second-guess the motivations of people who were clearly mentally ill.

Miller's phone began ringing. It was Rudovsky and Kenyon at Tameside Hospital. He listened for a minute or so before replying. "Right, okay, nice one, keep me posted Jo. Cheers."

"What's happening?"

"He's alive, he's in surgery, they think he's got a chance."

"Fucking hell! Lucky bastard if he survives that!" Saunders looked again at the puddle of congealing blood which was setting darker around the edges.

"Right, well, I think we need to follow the path the attacker took to get away."

"Sir."

Miller and Saunders thanked the forensics officers and left the tent.

"Down here?" Miller looked along the street and saw the familiar M logo of the bus station. The officers walked in silence, scouring the pavement and the road for any obvious items that may have been discarded as the attacker launched into his sprint. Up ahead, Miller could see the first motorway footbridge, it started outside the boarded-up entrance to the derelict old bingo hall. The detectives crossed the road, and stepped into the modern, glass bus station. There were dozens of people standing around the various stands, a great many of whom were gossiping about all the blue-revolving police lights outside. Miller and Saunders walked through the building in silence. After a minute, they had reached the opposite end, and crossed the pelican crossing, which led them to the second motorway foot-bridge.

"So, instead of crossing that one, he's run all the way down here? That is fucking bonkers."

"It doesn't make any sense."

"It's to our advantage though, he's bound to have left summat behind." The two detectives started walking across the bridge. Cars were zooming beneath, the lights of thousands of speeding vehicles were heading towards Sheffield in the east, and Manchester in the west.

"We need that shrubbery searching," said Miller as they reached the other side of the bridge. There was an embankment of trees, weeds and long grass. "Good place to chuck the weapon, especially if he wants to get caught, which is what it seems like to me!"

"Sir." Saunders was making notes in his pocket book. He looked both ways once he reached the end of the footbridge. It was just a path, and a piece of wasteland. It wasn't very obvious which way the attacker would have chosen to escape.

"Right, we need to lock this entire area down, the motorway bridge, the bus station, the whole area between the crime scene and this location. I can't believe the local Inspector hasn't closed the bus station. We need a finger-tip search of every inch of this place." Miller was walking back across the bridge. He stopped halfway across and looked down at the steady flow of cars, vans and wagons. He was looking towards Manchester, and an endless stream of what looked like a million white car lights were headed his way. The view was matched with an endless flow of red lights of vehicles whizzing underneath, heading towards the city.

"Do you know what, we might need to close this

motorway and get those carriageways checked as well. If the attacker has deliberately chosen the route, and consciously decided to run through the bus station, then there's a good chance he wants to tell us something."

"Agreed."

"If you don't want to be caught, you go the easier, quicker, less populated route, don't you?"

"Under normal circumstances, yes, that's what usually happens."

"God, this one is a proper loon. We need to get this one locked up sharpish Keith, or our reputations are going to be hacked down as ruthlessly as these DWP staff."

Chapter Eleven

The BBC North-West editor had alerted the national BBC News desk about the latest attack. Until now, there had been a sense of confusion about the motive for the attacks in Stockport. Sure, there had been plenty of insinuation about the motives, and plenty of online debate and discussion. But there hadn't really been enough to make it into the definitive headline of the story.

Now, the information was coming in from Hyde, that another DWP employee had been attacked, in exactly the same circumstances as the previous two incidents, and right outside the DWP building, too. It was pretty conclusive that this was now a major story. This was no longer a local item just for the north, it was now of paramount interest for the national news networks.

Within minutes of the national BBC editors receiving the North West Tonight story, the BREAKING NEWS graphic was applied on its TV, Online and App services, breaking this sensational story in the most dramatic of styles. It was a BBC exclusive for at least fifteen minutes, before Sky News copied and pasted the story, and went live with their version.

*****

Outside Beech House, a number of media crews had assembled across the road, and a little further up the street. Local newspaper reporters from the M.E.N and the Tameside Reporter were there, along with the familiar faces from BBC and Granada, as well as a smattering of reporters from local radio stations Key 103, Tameside Radio and BBC Manchester. They were all reporting, photographing and filming the scene, talking breathlessly about this disturbing assault which had taken place less than an hour earlier.

The footage they filmed was grim and disturbing, as dark silhouettes of forensics officers on their knees inside that tent were illuminated by their floodlights. The slow, meticulous pace at which they were moving gave a clue as to how grisly the scene must be inside.

A similar number of reporters were beginning to gather at Tameside hospital, the location that it was believed the victim had been taken to. The A&E staff found themselves suddenly bombarded with members of the press trying to find out the condition of the victim.

All of the media crews knew that they were embarking on the start of a very scary, very disturbing news story. It was potentially so serious, so terrifying, that it was going to give an enormous boost to the viewing figures between now, and its conclusion. This thought filled most of the reporters with great joy and excitement.

*****

DC Grant was waiting close to the tent with a number of the seconded officers. DC's Chapman and Worthington arrived from around the corner just as Miller and Saunders got back from their site recce. Miller headed straight for the Divisional Inspector from Hyde police station, and began to discuss his requirements. The Inspector seemed quite happy to accommodate Miller's plans. It may well be a headache to shut the bus station, and close the roads, especially the motorway in the middle of the rush-hour, but DCI Miller was an extremely well-respected officer, and if that was what he wanted, the local Inspector wasn't about to try and negotiate or downgrade the plans. He got onto his radio straight away, and began demanding that his officers carry out the orders.

"Thank you, Inspector," said Miller as he turned and addressed his team. He allocated jobs to several of the support officers, and asked Chapman and Worthington to oversee the temp staff. Their main task was going to be interviewing the bus station witnesses.

"Okay, Grant, you and Saunders can go back to base and start working on the background checks on our latest victim. Stick him up on the incident room wall. Find out if he has any links to the other two victims, other than via their employment. I want to know if they all hang around together, or if they used to work in the same office? I think it's fair to say that there could still be a link between these victims that doesn't involve a random vigilante who is pissed off about benefits cuts."

Saunders looked surprised. "Really? I thought this was a full-gone conclusion now Sir?"

"It might be. But you need to prove it. If you come back to me and say that this person has never met the other two, that they've never even heard of each other, then I'll agree with your theory Keith. But until then mate, there's a distinct possibility that this could be a very personal, very private grievance about something petty, like buying the wrong brand of tea-bags in the staff room."

"I'll get on with it, Sir."

"Oh and Helen, please can you do me a report on any new releases from prison, say in the last six months, for violent crimes, murders, robberies, anything like that."

"No problem Sir."

"Okay, great stuff. I need to talk to these security guys and see what we can pull off their CCTV. We might have footage of this bastard standing there waiting for his victim."

*****

Miller struggled to get into the building, the press-pack were all shouting for his attention and standing in his way as he tried to get through the alternative entrance. The main doors were cordoned off now, and the staff entrance was covered by the forensics tent. So Miller had to try and get in via the fire exit.

"Why were you dismissing this question in today's press conference DCI Miller?"

"Do you think this could have been avoided if you'd been honest DCI Miller?"

"Is it true you were anticipating this attack?"

Miller kept a neutral look on his face as he struggled through the rowdy reporters. Eventually, he was inside the building and the security guard closed the door, shutting out the noise and the stupid questions. There was a very sombre, very shocked mood inside the building. Several members of staff were sitting on chairs, crying and sobbing, and most were being consoled by other colleagues. The security man looked as though he might be close to tears himself.

"Are you alright mate?" asked Miller.

"Yeah, yeah, just a bit shook up like, you know. It happened right in front of me. It was so quick, he just stepped out of nowhere, and bang, Gary was down, the blood was pumping out of his legs like they were water pistols."

"Did you see the attacker.?"

"No, not really, I mean, it was just a shape, a dark shape that appeared from behind the pillar. It was all over in about a second."

"Did he say anything? The attacker I mean."

"No, again, that's what was so weird about it. He was totally silent, just appeared, then swung his knife or whatever it was, and ran off. I tell you what though, he was fast on his toes. Probably a runner you know, he was that fast."

"Did Gary say anything?"

"Nah, he was screaming, everyone was. It was just a fucking nightmare. We started taking our tops off and were wrapping them around Gary's legs, trying to pull them tight to restrict the blood flow. That's all we were concentrating on, trying to stop this blood, it was like a waterfall, I've never seen nothing like that. We were tying our shirts around the wounds, pulling them as tight as we could, it was exhausting you know, the ambulance seemed to take ages to come."

Miller liked this guy, and he felt sorry for him, he was clearly very shaken. Miller patted him on the back. "Well, thank God you did that mate, or he'd have died right there within minutes."

"What, is he alright?" The security man's eyes had filled up with tears, and his voice was wobbling.

"He's in surgery. But they're doing their best for him. Here, look." Miller opened his text messages and found the one that Rudovsky had sent;

"Alright Sir, apparently, things are going well here. They are feeling confident."

"That was from one of my officers at Tameside General,

apparently things are looking good."

"Aw, honestly, I can't tell you... that's the best thing I've ever heard in my life you know." The security man sat down and began sobbing openly. "I thought he'd died," he said eventually.

"Nope, you saved his life."

It took a few minutes for Miller to console the emotional security man, but it was worth the wait. Once he had calmed down, he led Miller through into a tiny office with several CCTV monitors on the walls.

"I've not looked at it yet, but I know the camera on that door is definitely working because I was watching it this morning when a couple of kids were skinning up round there." The security man was messing about with his computer system. "Ah, here we go. What time did it happen?"

"16.30." Said Miller.

"Yes, of course, right okay, I'll start it at about twenty-five past and we can fast forward through."

Chillingly, as the CCTV footage began, five minutes before the attack had happened, the tall, darkly dressed character with the hoody pulled over his face was standing there, leaning up against one of the concrete pillars that hold the building up. He looked relaxed, casual, still. His body language didn't make any suggestion that he was about to carry out a vicious assault. Miller watched with his mouth open. His heart was thumping violently, high in his chest. He felt anxious, and distressed by the prospect of watching this ghastly attack on replay.

"Look," said Miller quietly, as the staff door opened and a woman walked out, and walked past the man in the hoody. The screen read 16:26. The man didn't move a muscle.

A minute later, the door opened again, and another member of staff stepped out onto the street and walked casually away from the building. The shadowy character didn't move, he just stood there as though he was waiting to meet somebody. Another person left the building, and walked past him, without giving him another glance.

"What the f..."

The clock read 16:28. Five separate members of staff

had left the building, and the man hadn't moved an inch.

At 16:30 precisely, the victim of this latest attack, Gary Webster wandered out of the building and started walking down towards the bus station. He had got no more than three metres away from the door when he was struck from behind. The CCTV coverage showed the attacker pull his weapon away from his side, extend it out and then snap it back with great power. The hooded man chopped the sword at the back of Gary's legs with as much force as he could muster.

"Fucking hell..." said Miller as he fought the urge to vomit. That really was a disgustingly violent act, made all the more horrifying by the complete unexpectedness.

"Oh Jesus Christ, that's... what the hell is going on?" asked the security man, the colour had left his face, he'd turned an unhealthy shade of grey as the sickening violence was replayed.

"I'm going to need this on a stick."

"Yeah, no problems. But what the hell is going on?"

Miller had a grave look on his face. The footage had had an overpowering effect on him, and he felt a swell of anger that he had never experienced before. "I don't know, but I'm not going to rest until I find this bastard and ask him."

Chapter Twelve
Thursday Morning

The story was national now, the "lone wolf" character appeared on all of the front pages except The Star, as they were reporting a Big Brother star's wardrobe malfunction. The Sun, Mirror, Mail, Express and Metro were all carrying the creepy photograph of the tall, hooded man standing outside the DWP office in Hyde. Miller had allowed the press to access the footage the previous night. He wanted them all to be as outraged and as shocked and disgusted as he had been on watching the seven-second clip of brutal violence.

It wasn't just the newspapers who were making this the number one news item. Breakfast TV, News TV and all of the talk-radio stations were leading on the attacks. There was no doubt left that the attacks were personal, and aimed at people who work for the government's DWP.

This was a primary news story, and one which brought lots of public opinion along with it. Radio station phone-ins were struggling to answer all the calls they were receiving. At Sky News, the reporters and presenters were trying to maximise the drama and expectation, with a tone of expectancy, and with blatant insinuations that the emergency services were anticipating another attack "at any time."

BBC News were replaying their footage of the previous day's press-conference with DCI Miller, repeatedly showing the part where he refused to ask the questions regarding DWP employee's safety. It felt a little bit as though the BBC news editors wanted to lay the blame for the latest attack squarely at Miller's feet.

One thing was clear. The story that had only been reported in the local area the previous day, was now the biggest story in the land. This could only mean one thing as far as DCI Miller's investigation was concerned. He needed to get this sorted sharpish.

*****

Despite all of the debate and discussion, Miller couldn't give a shit about what people were suggesting the attacks were about. It just wasn't relevant to the enquiry as far as he was concerned. The only thing that did matter was getting the person responsible for these unforgivable atrocities off the streets. He'd missed much of the media response and the debate that was taking place. His morning had been taken up mostly by meetings, the worst possible kind of morning for the DCI. All these meetings ever did was to shift the onus of blame onto another person or department or organisation.

Today, the outcome of the meetings was that the SCIU were the "fall-guys" and, any success, or failure would now be directly attributed to Miller and his team. That also meant that the press were going to be pissing him off no end until all this was taken care of.

Miller's office answer-phone was full of messages, the number was in constant demand from members of the press who wanted a "quick word."

The whole thing was a massive head-ache, and it was starting to irritate Miller that all of the news channels suddenly seemed to be transmitting vox-pops from people who claimed that "something like this has been inevitable for a long time."

To Miller, it was bullshit. The only thing that mattered to him was the positive conclusion, with the arrest of the maniac responsible.

"Good morning, and thanks all for coming in early." Miller wasn't in the mood for cracking stupid jokes or having any idle banter with his team today. He looked like he'd worked all night, his shirt was creased and stale looking, and he desperately needed a shave. "Welcome to those of you who are joining my team today, and welcome back to those who have been assisting with this enquiry over the past couple of days. I want to get straight down to business if that's okay? I want to start with an update on our latest victim, 31 year-old Gary Webster, who was attacked yesterday tea-time. I've been informed this morning that the surgery on his legs was positive, and he has survived the night. This is a miracle, as that boy should be dead right now. I cannot tell you how lucky he is to be alive. Now, to bring this crime into some kind of context, I want to show you this, its footage of yesterday afternoon's attack in Hyde. I must warn you, this CCTV is extremely graphic and violent. I've sent it out to the press last night, but obviously, they won't show it in its entirety. I must warn you all, this is about as violent as anything you will ever see, so look away if you want to."

Miller played the video footage. He wasn't watching it himself, he was looking at the team of fifty police officers and detectives that had been assigned to work under the SCIU's rule for the foreseeable future. The gasp echoed around the room as the officers saw the shocking footage with their own eyes. It had a profound effect on everybody in the room, and that was exactly what Miller was aiming for.

"Now I've been doing this job a long time, and I can't remember such a disturbing attack. I don't think I've ever seen anything as distressing or violent as this. The reason that it's so bad, is this."   Miller clicked the laptop mouse and the film started again. But this time, it was an earlier clip. "Now, watch closely. This is the attacker, standing very calmly, leaning against the pillar." Miller patted the projection screen, just to make sure that there could be absolutely no doubt who he was talking about.

"Okay, keep your eye on that clock. He has stood there for eight minutes, and watched ten different DWP staff leave the building, before he attacked Gary. Keep watching, I've fast-forwarded it up a bit for you. There, one, two, three-four." Miller counted each person as the door opened and they walked past the camera and off into the street. "Seven, eight, nine and, here comes Gary. Watch what happens now." Miller pressed the laptop again, and the footage slowed right down to slow-motion. The hooded man suddenly looks alert, stands up straight, pulls his left arm out at a right angle to his body, and steps forward with total aggression. Miller paused it before the sword was swung. He didn't think these police officers wanted to witness that footage again. He certainly didn't want to.

"So, this is where it gets totally confusing. He arrived at 16.22. He maintained that calm, care-free stance throughout, as nine DWP employees wandered out of that door, straight past him. What happens next... as soon as Gary Webster appears at the door, the attacker bursts into life. He was waiting for Gary specifically, its written all over the guy's body language. But why? This is the thing, as with the victims in Stockport, we're hearing nothing but lovely stuff about Gary. He is a pleasure to know, he'd go out of his way to help anybody, he's a real gentleman in every sense of the word. Why then, do these nice people from the DWP keep getting attacked in such savage and damaging ways?" Miller looked out across the sea of faces. They all looked disgusted, and angry. And that's how it should be, thought Miller, pleased to see that the officers shared his sense of outrage at these cowardly, unprovoked, and life-changing acts.

"Last night, we closed the motorway, after the attacker had run off over the motorway footbridge. We were confused by something." Miller pressed his laptop again, and an aerial view map appeared on the screen. It showed two big blocks. "Block A here, is the DWP office where the crime scene is." Miller then pointed to the other block. "This is block B, Hyde bus station." Finally, Miller pointed towards a thick blue line which ran across the map. "This is the M67 motorway. Now, follow me here for a few seconds. This motorway has two footbridges crossing it. Bridge one is here, at the north side of the bus station, less than twenty-five metres away from the crime scene. And bridge two is here, southside of the bus station, and almost two-hundred metres away from the crime scene."

Miller glanced at the officers, just to check that they were all following. They seemed to be keeping up. "Right, now, a show of hands please... if you had just attacked somebody here," he pointed to Block A on the map. "Please give us a show of hands if you'd escape using bridge one?"

Most of the police officer's hands went up without hesitation. It confirmed Miller's instinctive belief that choosing the first bridge, the closest one, was a no-brainer.

"Okay, you can put the hands down. Anybody think that bridge two would be a better option. There were a couple of hands raised. Miller smiled and pointed to the closest officer with his hand aloft. "Go on, why are you choosing the bridge that's further away?"

The officer looked slightly embarrassed, but answered the question anyway. "Sir, my first thought is that the second bridge offers more opportunities to get away on the opposite side?"

"Okay. That's a possibility. I could look into that suggestion. Thanks. You, why would you choose the second bridge?" Miller pointed to a young female constable.

"My beat is around there, Sir, and I know those bridges pretty well. The nearest one comes out on an exit slip-road from the motorway. It would be impossible to keep a getaway vehicle near to the first bridge. Whereas, bridge two has a couple of options for stashing a vehicle nearby, be that a motorbike or scooter. It would be nearer for a car as well, and no traffic-lights."

"So, you are saying that even though it looks like he ran the long way around, it would have made his escape quicker in the end?"

"Yes, Sir, that's my experience, Sir, yes."

"Brilliant, thank you, constable?"

"Kerry Fisher Sir."

"And that's your regular beat is it, Hyde and surrounding?"

"Sir. Hyde, Godley and Hattersley mainly."

"Okay, that's very informative, thank you Kerry, and I may want to ask you a few more questions about the geography around there later on, thanks very much."

Kerry blushed and looked down at her lap.

Miller averted his attention to the rest of the group as he continued talking, but he added an explosion of energy into his voice, in an attempt to make the police officers jump, and maintain their levels of concentration.

"I however, have my own theory, and it's a theory that has given me this stubbly chin and these big ball sacks under my eyes, because I've been working on it all night." There was a faint sound of amusement amongst the officers, many of whom were fresh into the room this morning and had no idea how to respond to Miller, the DCI who had become quite a celebrity.

Miller smiled, sensing the awkwardness from many of the new faces. Miller turned back to the map projection on the wall.

"You see, I started thinking that he has committed the attack here, at Block A, and then ran down through Block B, and over Bridge two in order to attract as much attention to himself as possible in the moments after the attack. Just remember how he was behaving on the CCTV. This is a man who was standing as still as he possibly could for the eight minutes leading up to the attack. Once it's done, suddenly he wants as many people as possible to see him."

Miller looked around the faces staring back at him. "I'll tell you why I arrived at this conclusion, okay." Miller clicked his laptop and brought up an aerial view of the location, taken from Google maps. "Now, this might help you to get a better sense of the geography. That big diamond shaped thing is the bus station. Now can anybody tell me what those big grey things are on either side of the bus station?" Miller patted against the wall, at the projected image.

"Bus lanes, Sir," said an eager sounding officer.

"Correct answer! Bus lanes. Why would you run through the middle of the bus station, which is full of CCTV and witnesses, when you could just whizz along this piece of tarmac at the side of the bloody thing?" Miller highlighted the journey with a smooth swipe across the image. "It'd be quicker to go along the tarmac, than negotiate the doors, and dodging the old dears inside. Plus, this is Hyde, this is not a soft place. What if a member of the public fancied being a hero and rugby tackled him down as he sprinted through? All these thoughts and ideas were making me believe that he has come through here for a reason. And I was right..."

Miller smiled at the expectation on the fifty-odd police officer's faces before him. This was the best bit in every briefing, the "I know something you don't know" section, where he held all the cards. The attention in the room was all his. "He deliberately went that way, so that there was absolutely no doubt which way he had gone. The reason? He left us a little something. He threw a piece of paper down in the bus station, we found it last night. We've reviewed the CCTV, and it clearly shows the attacker reach into his jacket pocket, and throw it down onto the floor. I'll show you the piece of paper."

Miller walked back to his laptop and changed the Google map image, replacing it with a photograph of a very normal looking piece of white A4 paper. The note had been printed onto the paper, and by the way the words were a little blurred on some sections, it looked like a cheap, home printer had been used.

"Here it is." The room went completely silent as the officers strained forward slightly to try and read the note. "To help those of you at the back, I'll read it out loud for you. Here we go. It says, "How do you sleep at night?"

Miller could see that this was a very interesting note. Every single one of the police officers looked absolutely mesmerised by it.

The press people were also about to be just as mesmerised, as the investigation started making some kind of logical sense. Things may be chaotic and somewhat scary, but Miller was happy about this note. It meant that his team could now set about investigating a very solid line of enquiry.

Chapter Thirteen

Hyde is a market town in the East of Greater Manchester, nestled halfway between Ashton and Stockport. The small town, with a population of 30,000 has been home to many great personalities including John Fontana, Ricky Hatton, Timmy Mallett, LS Lowry and the writer and journalist Owen Jones, among many others.

However, despite being the home-town of so many famous people, the past fifty years have not been kind to Hyde's reputation. The town is indelibly linked with the Moors Murderers, the sick crimes of Brady and Hindley were revealed by Hindley's brother-in-law, a Hyde resident, and subsequently the infamous child killers were arrested by officers from Hyde police station. The arrests were made at the couple's address in Hattersley, the gigantic 1960's built council estate on the edge of Hyde. In the years that followed, Brady and Hindley's council house on Wardlebrook Avenue was demolished. The reason was two-fold. Partly, it was because nobody from the local area wanted to take up the tenancy, and anybody from outside the area who did take up occupancy of the house, soon learnt what horrors had occurred there. The other part of the reason that it was demolished was because the property attracted lots of strange and ghoulish people who came from all over the country, in order to dance in the garden, or hold seances and perform acts of devil worship.

As time went on, people began to distance the crimes of the Moors Murderers with Hyde. But just as people were starting to forget, the town was to be linked with another of Britain's most infamous serial killers. In January 2000 Dr Harold Shipman was sentenced to fifteen concurrent life sentences for murdering fifteen of his patients, though the findings of the two-year Shipman Inquiry which followed, revealed that the true number of his victims was likely to be around 250 patients.

During his 21 year period as a General Practitioner in Hyde, Shipman was said to be the area's best known, and most popular doctor. Shipman always denied the criminal charges against him, right up to his suicide in Wakefield Prison in 2004.

And as though the area hadn't suffered enough, the town's notoriety was to be pushed to the limit a decade later, when Dale Cregan, the one-eyed drug-dealer from Droylsden murdered two female police officers, after they attended a report of a burglary in progress. Cregan made the call to police, intentionally setting up the officers. After killing the two young female PC's, Cregan handed himself into Hyde police station, and is now serving a whole-life sentence with no chance of parole.

And now, once again, Hyde was back in the national news for all the wrong reasons. The previous night's attack outside Hyde Jobcentre was accompanied with a stark reminder of this small town's troubled past. The media couldn't leave it alone, and they had even linked all three notorious cases in their reports about Gary Webster, the young man attacked so violently the previous evening as he left his work at the DWP, and headed home.

Miller had arranged for the press conference to take place directly outside the crime scene at 12 noon, precisely twenty-four hours after his last presentation to the media. Press invites had been sent out after Miller's team briefing, shortly after 9am. With the press invitation, Miller attached the latest press release, along with a photograph of the victim, Gary Webster.

In the cheerful photo, Gary was sitting in between his parents, looking very happy and relaxed at a family do. The press release also contained an image of the attacker fleeing through the bus station, his weapon chillingly wrapped up in a black-bin bag, and finally, a photograph of the "how do you sleep at night?" note that had been thrown down in the bus station.

The press conference had been arranged to take place at the scene of the crime, for one simple reason. Miller wanted the press to really understand that this was a real, life-changing attack, by making the press come and visit the scene, and smell, taste and feel the reality. He wanted them to hear all about the horror, right there, where it had taken place. Experience told him that the press took more of a sense of ownership over it this way. It made these cases feel much more real than if they were just hearing about it at the police HQ.

Once again, Miller wanted to hammer home the message about the victims, Kath, Jason and Gary, and remind everybody of the fact that these were just ordinary folk. By all accounts, they were lovely, very kind and well-respected people.

They were extremely nice folk whose lives had been changed beyond all recognition, through the horrendous injuries that had been inflicted onto them by a sick, evil bastard.

Miller was absolutely determined that the promises he made to Kath, and to Jason, would be kept. He still hadn't met with Gary Webster, as the third victim was far too poorly in Tameside Hospital's high dependency unit.

The discovery of the note was a game-changer, and the press were completely obsessed by the contents, and making assumptions about the attacker. In terms of the media coverage, it wasn't really about the victims now, it was becoming more about the attacker, and Miller began to realise that it had probably been an error to release it, because now, the note had unintentionally become the story.

But Miller was determined to turn-the-tables back. He was standing on the pavement outside Beech House's staff entrance. The forensics tent was still in situ, so Miller made sure that this would be the back-drop to his press-conference. It was a wet, windy and grey day, and the press conference location looked just as dreary and depressing as the vulgar and distressing subject matter. It was like a scene from a Morrissey song.

"Good afternoon, thanks for coming. You've all had our press release this morning, and you are all fully up-to-speed with the investigation so far. So, I have nothing further to add to that." There were some bemused looks amongst the media employees stood before him. He was teasing them, and they soon caught on with his next sentence, "so I've come along here today to tell you about Gary Webster, the third victim of the individual that we are currently trying to locate. Gary Webster is an extremely well-known and well-liked lad around this side of Greater Manchester. He is currently in a very serious condition

In Tameside Hospital. I'm pleased to report that his condition is no longer described as critical, so that is very positive progress that he has made overnight. However, he is still extremely poorly, and the very grim news is that he probably won't be able to stand up again, as a result of the horrendous injuries that he sustained right here, yesterday afternoon."

Miller paused for dramatic effect, allowing the media representatives to take in the grim, depressing scene behind his shoulder. The only source of colour in that black, white and grey scene was the vivid yellow from the forensics tent.

"Now, let me tell you a bit about Gary Webster. He is thirty-one years old, he grew up in Audenshaw, just a few miles up the road. After leaving school with excellent GCSE grades, he went to Ashton Sixth-Form College and did his A levels. Many of the tutors remember him well, and this morning, the principal wrote this message on the College's Facebook page. It reads;

"He may have left fourteen years ago, but Gary was such a memorable character, it doesn't seem that long to those of us who enjoyed his presence here. Many of our staff remember Gary vividly, he was such a lively and amusing member of the college community. He was always happy, always positive, and always eager to lend a hand. Our thoughts and prayers go out to his family and loved-ones at this distressing time, and we wish Gary a fast and full recovery from this appalling and unbelievable attack."

Once again, Miller paused, he wanted the reporters to soak up every word. He wanted them to really care about this young bloke, and the horrific thing that had happened to him. Eventually, the DCI started talking again, aware that Sky News and BBC News were covering the press conference live, along with many radio stations.

"Gary has worked in this building for almost ten years. I know that a lot of people from the local community of Hyde and Hattersley know Gary very well, and that he has been a positive force in a great many of their lives. I want to read you another statement, this was sent into this Jobcentre this morning, by a gentleman called Fred Barker, a local man who owes a great deal to Gary. The message reads, "I am so gutted to hear this news about Gary. That lad is a one-in-a-million, and he did so much for me when I was out of work. I got laid off from Wall's after twenty-three years there, and I couldn't get an interview anywhere, in two years. But Gary never gave up, he'd ring me up, telling me about jobs, even when I was down and I'd given up. I know he's probably not supposed to, but he booked a morning off work once, so he could drive me to an interview, practising asking me questions and really boosting my confidence. He sat outside for about an hour, waiting for me to come out, asking me all about it. He really cared, and because of him, I got the job, and I've been here five years now. He didn't have to do that, none of it. But he cared, and that was what you really felt like when he was talking to you. You couldn't find a better lad than Gary, and I've been in tears all morning. I just wanted to write this, and tell you what a cracking lad he is."

Miller looked around the press people, and he was glad that this tactic was paying off. It was clear on the faces before him that his message was getting through.

"Now I'm not exaggerating when I say that I could stand here all day, and read out similar messages about Gary, and about the other victims, Jason Brown and Kath Palmer. These people seem to be the most genuine, and kindest people around, and yet this unimaginable horror has happened to them. I really want you guys to make this your biggest story until we've taken the person responsible off the streets. I cannot bear the thought of hearing that another person has been attacked."

Miller paused again. He wanted these sections to stand alone, so they could be easily edited into news bulletins throughout the day, and hopefully into the evening too.

"Okay, I've not got much more to add at this stage, but I'm sure you will all appreciate that we are flat-out working on this, I have fifty officers on this already, and I've asked for more. For the integrity of the work my officers are doing, I'm not prepared to discuss individual lines of enquiry. However, I am happy to try and answer any questions that you may have about this case, on the understanding that they will not jeopardise any ongoing investigations."

Suddenly, the press rabble became extremely excitable,

arms were going up in the air and dozens of questions were being shouted in Miller's direction.

"Do you believe that all DWP staff are at risk of attack?"

"I'm not in a position to rule that out. Of course, but I would advise everybody to try and stay calm. We are going to be communicating with the agencies involved regarding security measures, and naturally, those conversations will be confidential. The Chief Constable is in talks with central government this morning, and I am in a meeting this afternoon with the key decision makers from the police, the DWP and other security services."

"It all seems a bit of a U-turn DCI Miller! You were trying to deny this motive yesterday!"

"No, I didn't deny it, I just didn't have enough evidence to pursue that line of enquiry. But obviously, that situation has changed now, quite tragically over the course of the past twenty-four hours."

"Have you got any more information about the attacker?"

"Nothing concrete yet, but thanks to CCTV footage we recovered from the bus station, we have a gained lots of information about the attackers personal characteristics, and these are details which will be invaluable to this investigation."

"What is the advice to any DWP employees watching this?"

"My advice is to stay calm, stay in groups, don't panic. This is the biggest priority across the Manchester police force, and I know that colleagues in neighbouring forces are paying close attention to what is happening as well, with a view to implementing their own security procedures across Merseyside, Lancashire and Cheshire forces. We will have comprehensive news about our plans which will be communicated to all DWP staff, later on today."

"Is that definite DCI Miller?"

"Yes, that's definite. I can assure you all that this is a matter of the most serious nature, and we will not stop until we are absolutely confident that we have the man behind these abhorrent crimes in our custody, but equally as important is the safety of DWP staff."

"What do you think about the reason for the attacks, as we understand them."

"I don't want to get involved in that type of discussion." Miller pointed to another reporter, but the man that he had just snubbed continued with the line of questioning.

"You have to!" He shouted. Miller wasn't sure what paper he was representing, but the man seemed extremely angry. "I'm sorry DCI Miller, but it's important that we understand that as the leading detective, you are aware of the facts of the case, aware of the behaviour of the DWP over the past seven years. These attacks are horrendous, sure, but the person responsible for them must feel extremely strongly in order to do what he's doing."

"What, maiming innocent people, just hacking at them from behind with weapons? Causing them injuries that mean they can't walk, or work again? Sorry mate, but I'll never understand that, and if you do, I suggest you go and have a word with your psychiatrist." Miller looked absolutely furious, but his opponent wasn't done yet.

"I'm not agreeing with the attacker, I think he's sick in the head. But I'm trying to point out that these DWP staff are not all sweetness and light. They are responsible for genocide against the weakest section of society. So please, take the rose-tinted spectacles off, and stop trying to paint them as lovely people."

"Sorry, but which newspaper are you representing?" asked Miller. He'd never known a reporter to behave so appallingly at a press-conference.

"I'm not with a paper. I'm just a man, a man who has had my own benefits stopped by these cunts, it took thirteen weeks to get them back. For thirteen weeks I was left with fuck all, and I didn't even get an apology when they realised they'd stopped them for no reason. Thirteen weeks without any money for food or electric, all because these arseholes who work in there have got to stop people's benefits."

"I'm sorry, but this is completely ridiculous," said Miller. His mouth was open, as though he was about to say something else, but the man in the press-pack still wasn't done.

"I'll tell you what's ridiculous, yeah, the fact that you and the media here are all acting so surprised by these attacks. This has been inevitable, for years. Keep kicking a dog, and then act surprised one day when he bites your nose off. There was always going to be a price to pay, the government knew that. Well, it looks like the fight-back has started, doesn't it?"

"I'll tell you what mate, you can come down to the hospital with me later and say all this to Kath, and to Jason. I don't know what you're trying to achieve here pal, but I'm this close to arresting you on the grounds of inciting hate."

"You won't shut me up DCI Miller. It's obvious what this man is doing, he's trying to show you, and these who work in here, that anybody can suffer a disability. Let's see these bastards stopping the payments for Kath, and Jason and Gary, stating some bullshit reason, like they need a reassessment. Look, these people have knowingly caused untold suffering to the people who need their help the most. It's disgusting, they are responsible for some of the harshest, cruellest decisions against people who can't fight back, and they know it. Every single one of them knows it. And, they've all done it because their boss told them too. I agree with what the attacker says, I don't know how they can fucking sleep at night either!" The man looked up at the big, grey concrete building and shouted at the top of his voice, "SHAME ON YOU!"

Miller turned and walked away from the TV cameras and reporters, heading for the DWP building's fire-exit, which was being used as a temporary staff entrance. Miller was absolutely seething, he'd had to walk away, or he felt that he was going to punch that stupid bastard in the face. As he reached a uniformed officer, he turned and pointed at the man, who was still shouting "shame on you," in the direction of the offices.

"Here mate, go and arrest that guy who's doing the shouting. He's disturbing the peace, inciting hatred and if you don't lock him in a van in the next two minutes, the staff out of here are going to murder the little prick."

"Sir."

Miller headed off, walking towards his car which was parked across the market, on Asda's car park. He was so pissed off. The idea of that press conference had been to humanise the victims, and point out how lovely they all are. Thanks to that knob-head, the point had been totally lost. If anything, feared Miller, the reverse was done, and the victims had been made out as arseholes on the national TV.

Chapter Fourteen

Miller's instinct about the press conference had been right. The media's reporting angle had been altered from the point-of-view that the victims were all innocent, lovely members of the community.

Suddenly, thanks exclusively to that one gob-shite standing in amongst the reporters and journalists outside Beech House, there was an unforgiving debate erupting about the DWP's activities; and the debate was fierce. It was starting to become clear to Miller that there was a massive conversation going on, and he had had absolutely no idea that any of this stuff even existed before he had been handed this case.

On radio, on TV news channels, on Facebook newspaper threads and across tables in pubs, the discussion was in full flow. Passions were flying high, as a shocked British public tried to make sense of what this attacker was trying to achieve.

BBC Radio Five Live's afternoon show was covering the topic.

"John in Kettering, you're on the air."

"Thanks, look, I just want to add my name to the growing list of people who are completely and utterly aghast at what this man is doing up in Manchester..."

"But,"

"Well, yes, there is a but, actually. The but is this, the man is using a disgusting, absolutely appalling way of getting his point across. But the fact is simple, as uncomfortable as it is, there *is* a point to me made."

"The point presumably, is that you can break a grandmother's spine with an axe to create a conversation?" The BBC presenter was not in the mood for the direction that many of his callers wanted to take the conversation.

"Okay, that's a very fair point, and as I said at the start of the call. It's disgusting. I've not phoned up to say anything in support of the attacker."

"So why *have* you phoned, John?"

"I've phoned because the government are hung, drawn and quartered here, they have created this situation, and they need to make it stop, right now."

The presenter sounded exasperated, and he exhaled loudly. "Okay, John, you seem quite frustrated about this. Are you on benefits yourself?"

"No, I'm not."

"What do you do, if you don't mind me asking?"

"I'm a support-worker."

"And how have you been affected by the actions of the DWP?"

"I haven't. Not directly, but I know plenty who have. Neighbours, friends, lots of my colleague's relatives."

"Okay, and I have to ask you why you think that the government should change their policy because one mad-man has started attacking innocent people?"

"With the greatest of respect, it's not just me who is saying it. The UN are saying it, the United Nations mate! They have described the actions of the DWP as a 'human catastrophe' but this arrogant, malicious government just ignore them. Did you hear about the father-of-three who killed himself last year after his marriage broke down due to the utterly contemptible behaviour of the DWP?"

"No, John, I didn't. But before you go any further, I must warn you that you are responsible for any libel that your comments may contain."

"There is no libel. These are facts, and they are well documented. As a journalist yourself, I'm staggered that you aren't very well informed on the matter."

"Okay, you can have that. Go on please John, I'm eager to hear about how the Department for Work and Pensions, a government body is responsible for the death of a father-of-three."

"They are. It's been to court, they admitted liability for causing unnecessary hardship, and for helping to create a situation that created his severe mental health incapacity."

There was a silence. Suddenly, the motor-mouth radio know-it-all had quietened down. John from Kettering continued. "The man was called Trevor North, he lived in Sheffield, worked as a steel-man all his working life. He was made redundant a few years ago when the foundry he worked at closed. His marriage broke down shortly after the DWP stopped his benefit payments. He lost his house, his income, his marriage. And in the end, it was too much. He took his own life."

"Well, that's a very tragic story John, but how can you lay the blame with the DWP?"

"I'm not enjoying your patronising tone of voice, but I'll carry on, despite it."

"Please do."

"It's not me who blames the DWP, it was the Coroner's Court. The blame is laid at the DWP's door because they stopped his money when he failed to show up at the Jobcentre to sign on."

"But what's the point in having these rules, if you are not going to enforce them? Isn't that the whole point of the rules? To carry out the deed which was being used as a consequence?"

"Yes, of course it is. But since the DWP had sent him on a training course at a time which clashed with his signing on time, he assumed that he would be excused. He went to the training course, as he was instructed. But his benefits were stopped for thirteen weeks because he missed his Jobcentre appointment."

The silence was there again. It was as though the radio host had been caught unawares.

"That's... that can't be true."

"It is true. Of course it is true. Put it into Google."

"Well, no, I'm sorry... that's not..."

"People have been trying to get this discussion on radio stations like yours for years, trying to highlight the way the DWP are treating people. But you guys never report it, because you are part of the problem, you're out of touch. You talk about matters that affect your cosy little lives, you talk about Waitrose biscuits, and John Lewis sofas, because you're all middle-class media lovies who have absolutely no connection to real people's lives. But look at what's happening today, you *are* reporting it, and I can tell by your voice that you can't believe your ears! So, there's a story about a married, family man who killed himself because of the DWP, and you lot would rather do a phone in about a faulty Rolex."

"I'm not sure I'll agree with that. We discuss all of the major topics in the news."

"Yes, but you also decide what's in the news. Tell me, did you cover the story about the lady who lost her benefits because she was in hospital for two weeks after being run over by a car. She failed to make her appointment, so she was sanctioned, lost her money for three months. There's plenty more. The lady who lost her benefits for nursing her dying Gran all night. The Jobcentre said she wasn't actively seeking work in accordance with her contract."

"Well, if these stories are true..."

"How many times do I have to tell you? They are true. What about the couple who had their benefits stopped because they hadn't replied to the DWP's letters. It turned out, the DWP had the wrong address. But that didn't come up until the appeal, and it still meant the couple had no money for three months. These stories are out there, if you look for them. It's about time they were discussed properly, and the DWP exposed for the nasty, vindictive bullying that they've been doing."

"You really believe that this is a deliberate activity?"

"Yes, I do. Hand-on-heart, I genuinely believe that it is. I'm amazed how blinkered you are. Do you not believe what I'm saying to you, that the DWP are deliberately targeting benefits claimants, and trying to make life as difficult as possible for them?"

"No, I really don't think that in a civilised country such as ours, that those kinds of things go on."

"Well why then, has every town now got a food-bank? Why has every Tesco and Asda got a trolley at the front door where you can slip a box of tea-bags in for the poor folk that are using the food-bank? We never used to have them, before this government came in. There were sixty foodbanks in the UK in 2010."

"Yes..."

"And there are two thousand now."

*****

The debate was raging everywhere. Despite the horrific injuries that had been sustained by the three Manchester DWP employees, it seemed that the lid was finally off the can of worms. Most of the press had completely ignored the story over the previous six years or so. But now that the story was finally in the news, suddenly every socially conscientious person was eager to take advantage of the opportunity. They wanted to make their point and highlight the tragedies that they had seen, personally, at the hands of the DWP's "war against the poor" as it was being dubbed. Many commentators were repeating the satirical theory that DWP stands for "Die Whenever Possible."

It was a very grotesque situation. Three people were lying in hospital beds with injuries that were going to cause them misery for the rest of their lives, whilst half of the British public were arguing that this was "inevitable" and "predictable."

The other half claimed that people on benefits were "idle" and "deserve everything that the DWP are doing."

Social media platforms were awash with people saying things that simply weren't true, or even remotely researched. Typical, made-up, off-the-cuff comments sounded like "those that were injured are the ones who took the benefits off them." Or, "my mate knows someone who used to work at that place, and he said that they all bring cakes in when one of the claimants dies."

Meanwhile, the other half of the population were talking about the fact that people who were on benefits "can't be that badly off if they've got their cigs, and their take-aways and their tattoos."

The Conservative supporting media had spent the past decade brain-washing the general public that benefit claimants were all "taking the piss" and "laughing at the workers who pay the tax, which supports them." It had all been going on for a long time, the state-owned broadcaster Channel 4 were the worst culprits for delivering "divide and rule" style broadcasts such as "Skint," "Benefits Street" and "How To Get A Council House" ever since the Tory government limped to power in 2010.

Each TV show was basically a voyeuristic look into the world of Britain's poorest people. In every frame, the poor person was smoking a cigarette, and they were usually talking about how hard it was to put food on the table. It was extremely easy to make these programmes, and also very cheap. And, as Channel 4 is the only TV channel which is completely controlled by the government, it was a very easy and convenient way for the government to hammer home their message that people who are poor are the very worst kind of scum.

And this has been the rhetoric from much of the British media, ever since the "austerity" years began in 2010. A long and bitter war had been waged against the poorest people in the UK, and it was all a huge diversion tactic. The public bought the "Benefits Street" outrage, and felt thoroughly disgusted that people were laughing as they blew all their benefits on a day out to the pub.

Meanwhile, the bankers in London who had crippled the UK economy by lending out more money than actually existed were saying "phew, that was close" as Joe Public's attention was taken up by getting angry about poor people having shitty tattoos. Not a single banker was jailed for their part in wrecking the British economy, a scandal of such epic proportions that it required an eight-hundred and fifty-billion-pound bail-out. Almost a trillion pounds was lost, and not a single banker was punished for their part in the scandal. Attention was switched from the gigantic cake, and focused instead on the crumbs that were being "wasted" on the poor.

People who were aware of what was happening believed that if the government run TV channels had been creating investigative documentary series about the banking crisis, things might have been different. However, they weren't. They were flooding the airwaves with programmes about poor people such as "White Dee" and how many cigs she smoked, at the tax payers expense, in the most disingenuous example of diversion tactics that we are ever likely to see.

Naturally, it worked like a charm. The British public were outraged that they worked hard to put food on the table, struggled to make ends meet, while these "scroungers" couldn't be bothered. These "losers" were having the last laugh, and it just wasn't on.

Subsequently, an incensed British public helped to empower the government's agenda, which was to clean up Britain's benefit mess, and get the scroungers into work, come-what-may.

Sensible people, most of them highly educated and with professional jobs, didn't realise that they were being duped. The anti-poor agenda was suddenly everywhere. It was in the news, on the front pages of the newspapers, it really was being played out as the biggest crisis of our times. Each story was framed to tell the reader that the joke was on them, that they were paying for these cigarettes, tattoos, pizzas and three-litre bottles of cider.

Of course, what the media weren't telling their readers and viewers, was that it would take weeks of trawling the poorest areas to find a handful of these people who were prepared to come on camera and make fun out of their relentlessly miserable lives.

The people who actually appeared on these shows had so little in their lives, not even a sense of dignity, that they did the interviews to camera. They mocked the people who worked, they infuriated people who had aversions to bad tattoos. And best of all for the TV production companies, it was all for a packet of twenty Richmond Super and a sweaty kebab.

Many people in Britain had realised what was going on several years earlier, and it was these people, the police officers, the teachers, the social-workers and the probation officers who started to argue that this demonization of Britain's poorest wasn't working. Stripping them of benefits wasn't achieving anything, it was just making matters worse for dozens of other government agencies.

In the end, they argued, it was a stupid idea, it was all costing more money, because the crime rates went up, and people took their minds off their miserable lives by becoming addicted to alcohol or drugs, and they turned to shop-lifting, burglary and street robberies to fund their self-destructive new habits. Many of the people who'd been made homeless deliberately, by DWP sanctions, got themselves put into prison, costing twenty-five times more than their benefits would have costed the state, per week. The homeless charities couldn't cope, the drug rehab charities were overwhelmed with new clients.

All in all, the anti-poor agenda was an unmitigated disaster which created more poverty, more job insecurity, and more health problems, both physical and mental health issues, than any other act of Parliament.

Not once had this matter been given the serious air-time that it needed. The work of the "Benefits Street" TV production team had been an overwhelming success, they had filmed a dozen people, people who were leading unhappy, difficult and chaotic lives, and turned an entire nation against everybody who was in receipt of benefits.

As a direct consequence, there was no appetite to hear about the hard-luck stories of the people affected by the sanctions and the changes to their benefits. "Get off your arse and get a fucking job!" would be the standard response. But unskilled, unqualified and inexperienced people who have low self-esteem struggle to find work. That part of the discussion is rarely mentioned, as it requires a far more complicated response than "get off your arse and get a fucking job!"

And now, Britain had a big problem on its hands. The attacker who had maimed three DWP employees had managed to get the entire nation discussing the matter. It was a disgraceful, unforgivable way to go about getting the subject discussed.

But it had worked. It would be of little comfort to the families of Kath Palmer, or Jason Brown, or Gary Webster. None-the-less, it had worked, in a similar way that "Benefits Street" had worked for the other team.

Chapter Fifteen

Barry Dyson was biting hard at his fingernails. He'd just about chewed them down as much as they'd go, but still the anxiety inside him kept him gnawing away, and he was going to end up drawing blood if he didn't cut it out. He was sitting in his conservatory, looking out across his garden. Where he could usually lose an afternoon sitting and relaxing, just idly watching the birds and squirrels or reading a book, or enjoying a doze, today all he could do was bite at his sodding fingernails.

Retirement had seemed a long time in coming, but once it arrived, Barry was absolutely determined to enjoy every last moment of it. His wife Sheila still had a couple of years to go before she qualified for the maximum civil-servant pension, and that was all she and Barry were waiting for. He had it all planned out, he'd planned hundreds of days out already, all around England. He had notebooks full of places that he wanted to take his wife of forty-five years once she had hit her milestone. It was the family joke, Sheila would complain that she'd be more knackered going on all these days out than she would if she carried on working.

The kids had grown up and gone now, making their own lives. The couple had grandchildren, and they loved having them over every other weekend for sleep-overs. On the one-hand, they enjoyed the little ones' company, but on the other hand, they liked the idea of giving their own kids the night off. It was the highlight of the grandkids fortnight, they were spoilt rotten by Granny and Grandad.

Life had worked out very well for Barry and Sheila, and now as the autumn of their lives was upon them, they realised that they'd been very fortunate. It hadn't been easy, at times it had seemed an impossible task, but they had persevered and brought up their family, did well with their jobs, and managed to stay cheerful along the way.

But now, this, it was too much for Barry to stand. He'd been listening to the radio. They were talking about the attacks on the DWP staff. There were people talking in the most disgusting terms about the DWP employees, talking as though the victims had somehow deserved it. It was barbaric, listening to these people, and it had upset Barry so much that he'd got up and turned the radio off. But it was under his skin now. He put the TV on, planning to simmer himself down with a bit of afternoon TV, but the television came on to Sky News, and they too were talking about the same thing, the DWP attacks.

"This is no good. It's bollocks!" Said Barry, as he hit the standby button on the remote control. The TV shut down, and Barry stood and walked across to the phone. He'd been putting this off all afternoon, but now, enough was enough.

"Hello. Can I speak to Sheila Dyson please? Fourth floor, Baskerville House, Disability Section."

There was a moment of silence as the call was being connected. All Barry could hear was his own heart-beat as it thundered inside him.

"Hello?" said Sheila. She sounded embarrassed to be receiving a personal call at work.

"Hi love, its me."

"Barry! Are you alright, what's up love? Everything alright?" Sheila sounded spooked, as though this was a bad news call. It wasn't like Barry to ring her at work.

"No love, I'm... I'm in a state. I can't have you working there with all this going on. I'm coming now to collect you. Watch out for the car. When you see it, grab your coat and come and meet me. I'll be waiting by the main doors for you."

"No, Barry... I can't just..."

"I'm not debating the matter now. We can discuss it properly when I pick you up love. But I can't sit here a minute longer while you are in so much danger. I can't do it."

Twenty-five minutes later, Sheila was met at the main doors of her workplace by her husband. He hugged her when he saw her, and she knew from the strength of the embrace that her man had been to a dark place in his mind.

"Barry... love..."

He was in tears, and the moment took Sheila by surprise. This just wasn't his way. He didn't cry, not like this. He was trembling.

"I just want to get you home now, out of harm's way."

"But Barry... I could lose my job!"

"It doesn't matter! Come on and get in the car."

As Sheila walked by her husband's side, she noticed that he was carrying a hammer in his hand. It was at that moment that she realised what an ordeal all this was for Barry.

In that split-second, as the shocking image of her husband carrying a weapon registered, she understood the torment that he'd been going through. This was a scary situation, and even though Sheila had been talking about it with colleagues all day, she'd had no idea how distressing it was for Barry. She felt a fresh swell of love for the man as she linked his arm, along with a fear for the repercussions when she went back into work.

*****

A similar scenario was happening at DWP offices across the UK. This was a terrifying situation, and for those who worked in the DWP, and for those whose loved ones worked there, it was an extremely distressing and anxious time. The DWP is one of the country's biggest employers, with a work-force of eighty-five thousand people. Every single one of those people had family, friends and loved ones who were stressed out and scared about what was happening in Manchester.

The concern and the worry was felt most keenly by the manager of each DWP department, especially in the Greater Manchester region. The managers there were seeing their departments in crisis. The amount of staff that had called in sick that morning was unprecedented, and the amount of people who had left work during the course of the day, many without even offering an explanation, was impossible to calculate. It was understandable, of course it was. Each DWP office was like a pressure-cooker, ready to blow at any moment, as the team-members wound each other up further and further, talking none-stop about the attacks, and wondering if anybody from their building was going to be next.

To make matters worse, some staff had started weird rumours about "being followed home last night" and "there was somebody lay down next to my car last week."

At times of worry and panic like this, you could always rely on a few dickheads to make matters even more concerning. Every single DWP manager was refreshing their e-mail folders, astounded that still, no official communication in how to deal with this crisis had been communicated from the top. The entire institution seemed to be at a loss as to what their official line was. The managers had no information to share with their staff about how they were going to deal with this extraordinary crisis.

DWP managers in Ashton were calling managers in Oldham. Managers in Bolton were ringing their opposite numbers in Rochdale, and Bury and Wigan. They wanted to know if anybody had heard anything? They were trying to find out the official line. They wanted to know, so they could say something to their stressed-out staff. But so far, there was nothing but a growing sense of fear, panic and total chaos.

The impact of so many staff failing to arrive at work was starting to show. Benefit payments were not being authorised, and it was clear to all of the managers and supervisors that there was another crisis unfolding.

Not only were their staff that *had* turned in, in a poor emotional state, they were also failing to carry out their duties. The benefit claimants were not going to get their payments on time. This was panning out to be a disaster from every angle.

*****

The problem was, nobody within the DWP hierarchy was prepared to take ownership of the crisis. No single senior staff member was prepared to step forward and become the "spokesperson" for what was happening. The reason was simple enough, the person who traditionally offers to be the face of any crisis is undoubtedly the person who is forced to resign over the situation, in the end. It's just the way the system works.

The simple reason that no DWP high-earners were trying to calm the ship, or reassure their staff, was because they wanted absolutely no part in this unfolding calamity. The Universal Credit, the benefit cuts, the sanctions, the disability capability reviews, the complete and utter shambles that had been the "benefit reform" was the government's baby. All of the nasty, unnecessary policies that were allegedly the motivation for these attacks had come from central government.

As far as the DWP top-tier of managers were concerned, there was absolutely no way that any of their careers were being de-railed because of this. The DWP message may have been silent internally, but one office was hearing the message loud and clear, the government's cabinet office. To the ministers, the message was deafening. "This was your creation, and it's your mess, and ultimately, it's your problem. Deal with it."

*****

Part of the trick that had been pulled in turning the nation against the poor was the demonization of council house tenants. Most of the UK's council housing stock was built in the years following the second world war. Hundreds of thousands of smart new council homes were built, the mantra at the time was "homes for heroes" as the government looked for new ways to create jobs, create affordable, good quality housing, and of course, provide nice new homes for the British people, as the old Victorian slums were cleared.

Council homes were, and still are, extremely good earners. They have all paid for themselves dozens of times over, and they provide excellent, self-sustaining income to their local councils. There is not a Town Hall in the land that would say that the local council estate wasn't a nice little earner. The vast majority of people who live in council housing are nice, decent, hard-working folk who go out to work and keep themselves to themselves, watch Strictly or X-Factor on Saturday night, and try and get away for a fortnight every summer, just like everybody else in the UK.

But as part of the war on the poor, the TV shows which incensed tax-payers about "their tax" going towards ciggies, tattoos, and 52" plasmas for the "lazy bastards," also set their sights on council tenants, tarnishing them with the same brush.

In historical terms, this is a very new thing, a brand new phenomenon, where factions of the UK media has tried to shame council tenants about the fact that they live in a council property. It began in London, where TV crews and newspaper columnists would show work-less families living in rented council accommodation, pointing out that young professional families were paying two thousand pounds a month in rent, for a place that wasn't as big or as nice. And these "scroungers" were living in better accommodation, and it wasn't fair.

In a relatively short time, between 1979 and today, the housing system has changed. At the end of the seventies, 42% of the population lived in a council house. Today, that figure is only 8%. Of those 8%, there are undeniable instances of "out-of-control" people who blight their local communities. But in the main, the media have succeeded in convincing the other 92% of people in Britain that council house tenants are up to no good.

Using rare examples of individuals who trash their homes, create anti-social problems, and who live chaotic, troubled lives, the establishment has managed to tar all council tenants with the same brush. It was utterly ridiculous, in precisely the same way that suggesting all British 1980's TV personalities were child molesters, would have been.

But, if you repeat a lie enough times, it becomes the truth. And as the UK struggles to find enough housing for its growing, ageing population, the fact is that millions more council homes will have to be built. Whether the UK's media will demonise all of the future tenants as they do today's tenants remains to be seen. But no other policy highlights and illuminates the government's complete and utter contempt for the poor than the "bedroom tax."

This policy was, in theory, a way of making better use of council housing stock. The stock was in short supply, as a result of the 1980's policy of selling the council houses off at discounted prices to tenants, in the biggest pre-election voter bribe that the world has ever seen. It won Thatcher another term in office, but it also wiped out the nation's council housing stock practically overnight as tenants bought their council property for a fraction of the market cost.

No more council houses were built, at least not in any serious numbers. The resulting demand on council housing waiting lists became overwhelming, and a new industry was born. Buy-to-let properties, where private landlords bought up streets and streets of run-down properties in the worst areas of town, in many cases from as little as £500 per house.

The "Victorian slum clearance" had gone full circle. There were some of these dilapidated houses which were sold for just £1 each, because of the amount of work which was needed to make the property fit for human inhabitation again. These new landlords were delighted with the deal. They could offer sub-standard houses to the local councils to rehome people into, for astronomically inflated rates, and without the restrictions of the usual rules and regulations which went with a secure council tenancy.

It was yet another win for the richest, and another blow for the poorest in society. The Tory idea to sell off the council houses, in order to gain working-class votes was the gift that kept on giving, and the fact that a third of the nation's MPs are private landlords today, and that 309 Conservative MPs voted against the "fit for human habitation bill" lays testament to this fact.

In 2010, the nation was waking up to the fact that it was facing a council-house shortage and consequently, the bedroom tax idea was born. The idea was simple enough. If you are on benefits, and you have bedrooms that you don't use, you would now have to pay an extra subsidy on each room. This meant that a sixty-two-year old woman living by herself in a three-bed house was now facing an extra forty pounds a week cost. The idea was that she would surrender the big house and move into a one-bedroom property.

The basic theory made sense. But there was a problem. There were no one-bedroom little properties available. There were just hundreds of thousands of poor people in big houses, being charged a ridiculous subsidy on spare rooms. There was no alternative accommodation for them to move to, they just had to stay put, and pay the extra subsidy, whilst the government blissfully ignored the gargantuan flaw in their plan.

Rather than show some humility, hold their hands up and admit that they'd got it wrong, they simply lied and lied about what a great success it had been, and carried on regardless. This policy was just another example of how disgracefully the government have treated the poor since 2010.

The roll out of the Universal Credit was said to be the "box-set" of benefits, a new simpler, easier to navigate system for the most-needy in British society. The small print however, is that from the date of registering for Universal Credit, which would cover unemployment, or disability, or income support, an applicant will automatically wait six weeks until their first payment.

Not only is that impossible to sustain human life, but it is also negative in trying to find rented accommodation as no landlord is prepared to wait six weeks until the first payment. As though this was all part of a sick joke, the government set up a phone number for Universal Credit applicants in need of an emergency payment, which costs 55 pence per minute to call. It all seemed like a very sinister, dark, satire sketch show based around rich people being deliberately cruel to poor people.

Sadly, this was no sketch show. This was the reality of life for millions of poor people, whose crime in the eyes of the state, was to be born with nothing.

Now, after seven years of this sustained, unforgiving and wholly unchristian attack against them, it was becoming clear that somebody out there had snapped. Somebody, somewhere, had had enough, and was kicking back. Whoever that person was, it seemed that he was so desperate to highlight the injustice of the war on the poor, that he was prepared to seriously maim the people who were at the coal-face of delivering the government's hatred.

This was a deplorable way of trying to attract support for a campaign, and even to those who had the greatest sympathy for the appalling way that the British poor were being treated, there was an insurmountable sense of disgust and anger about the attacks, and a steely determination that the perpetrator of these sadistic, cold-blooded crimes was not going to achieve anything by this, come-what-may.

Chapter Sixteen

Behind the shiny, famous black door of Number 10 Downing Street, the Prime Minister was chairing a cabinet meeting. The cabinet is the boring, old-fashioned name for the senior ministers of office. These people are considered the greatest minds in the land. Admittedly, that's only by themselves and their handful of ambitious hangers-on in the "Westminster Bubble."

None-the-less, they genuinely believe that they are the nation's most important people. The depressing reality is that this Cabinet room full of landed gentry millionaires, are the most ill-informed and out-of-touch members of society. Not a single one of them would know to buy the most expensive sandwich in order to make a supermarket "meal-deal" worthwhile.

But sadly, the privately-educated, born-rich people in this room who had never had a real job, were the people who made the very biggest, and most serious decisions that affect the British population. They are the people who are ordered to meet up at short notice to make it look as if they are doing something whenever something bad happens in the UK.

Today's cabinet meeting was being chaired by the PM, who was making the most of the Secretary of State for Work and Pensions' attendance. It was the born-millionaire Ian David Smythe who had been the architect of the welfare reforms. He was the shiny headed face of the government's zero tolerance approach to poor people. The great irony was that he looked like quite a nice, compassionate man. He was shaking quite considerably, as the cabinet ministers and senior officials grilled him about the DWP's policies, and tried to get him to find a solution to this absolute PR disaster which was unfolding, quite unexpectedly.

"Quite simply," said the PM, in a typically cold, robotic voice, "somebody is going to have to carry the can for this. The way that the press are portraying us, is quite preposterous, and we need to adopt a damage limitation strategy, as we announce our plans to combat this threat." The PM, renowned for being cold and heartless, looked every bit the part today.

"But Prime Minister, with all due respect," said Ian David Smythe, his voice uncharacteristically squeaky today, was pleading, "the police are dealing with the matter. The man responsible will be apprehended at any moment. I implore you, can we please just wait a little while longer?"

The PM did not make eye-contact with anybody. "The press are having a great time highlighting some of our most controversial policies. The longer this goes on for, the greater the damage will be done on our stronger society portfolio. I must make this abundantly clear, when this meeting is over, we must offer something to the press which will make this heartless Tory rhetoric disappear."

"Am I being told, or asked, to resign?" asked the distraught looking politician.

"You are being informed that you need to come up with something that will make this go away. If you want to fall on your sword, that's your decision. However, your replacement will only inherit the same policies that are causing so much consternation."

"Prime Minister, are you telling me that I have to do a U-turn on the Welfare Reforms Bill?"

"I did not say that. But you could prune it. You could remove the most toxic parts, such as the bedroom tax, the automatic disability assessment fails, the pressure on Jobcentre staff to sanction as many people as they can."

Ian David Smythe looked crest-fallen. This was a major humiliation, in this crowded cabinet room full of peers and colleagues. He had dreamt of reforming the welfare state for over twenty years. And here, in this packed room, he was being told to either dismantle it, or resign.

"And all this, because of one maniac with an axe?"

"No Ian. All this because we need to manage the public perception of our brand. Each hour of this poor-bashing talk is losing us votes with the swing voters. So, is it the policy, or is it you that is being axed? No pun intended."

There was a roar of laughter around the cabinet office. That was a good one.

Another minister spoke, once the humour had died

down a little. It was the plummy, educated accent of the born-millionaire, Chancellor of the Exchequer, Farley Rees Grosvenor. He was the man in charge of the nation's bank account.

"If I may, Prime Minister, I wish to advise caution. The public will see this as a knee-jerk reaction, and they'll assume that we don't really have any principles, if we announce a panicky u-turn."

"Here here!" said several voices in the room.

"I might add, that if we are seen to be so weak in the face of a single mad man's behaviour about one of our policies, we are in danger of placing ourselves in double-jeopardy with the rest of our unpopular policies."

"Quite right!" shouted another Ox-Bridge accent. "Some lunatic would try and save the NHS by shooting nurses!" There was another great roar of laughter around the room, even the PM gave a wry smile. Once the noise and humour died down a little, the Chancellor continued.

"My advice would be to reassure the public that all efforts are being made to arrest the culprit, and use the opportunity to rubbish the heartless claims, by inserting a sound-bite about how successful the Welfare Reforms have been."

"Yes, that's a great idea, thank you," said Ian David Smythe, looking and sounding like a man who'd been offered a stay of execution.

"There is only one problem with that strategy, however," said the PM. All of the ministers looked up at their boss. "There are no positive sound-bites about what a success the Welfare Reform has been, because it has been a complete and utter farce from the very first instance!"

"It's okay, Prime Minister, we'll make something up." Suggested the PR consultant.

"We need to offer a positive angle," suggested the Deputy Prime Minister, who was also born a millionaire. "We could say that our Welfare Reforms have been responsible for the deaths of forty-thousand scroungers, so far!"

The response received another huge wave of laughter. These people were really enjoying themselves, and thoughts of the injured DWP staff, who were paying the ultimate cost for having no alternative but to implement these cruel policies, couldn't be further from their minds.

"Okay, well let's make this as tidy as possible." The PM looked across at the Defence Minister. "What are we going to announce as our improved security procedures for DWP sites in the interim?"

"We have called on our troops to take up emergency strategic security activities outside all DWP buildings throughout the United Kingdom during operational hours, with the major emphasis on the safe entry and exiting of all DWP employees. As you will no doubt realise, this is a huge undertaking, involving twelve-thousand troops, looking after the security of over one thousand locations, which as we are all fully aware, contain some eighty-five thousand employees."

"And, what do we anticipate to be the overall cost of this exercise?" The Chancellor looked aghast at the announcement.

"I don't have the final figure, but I believe the sum will be significant."

"Probably more than the actual savings that the Benefit Reforms were designed to make?" The PM had a cold, steely glare.

"Significantly."

"And here-in lies our next PR disaster, if I'm not mistaken?"

"We'll get the first spin, don't worry," said the communications director out of the side of his mouth.

"You'd better. We can't afford any more catastrophes. We're responsible for the biggest crisis since World War Two with this Brexit calamity, and our austerity brainwave has crippled all of our public services. We really cannot afford to step another foot wrong, because it's beginning to look like the public aren't actually as stupid as we originally anticipated."

*****

The media were informed that a major announcement

was to be made outside Number 10 Downing Street at 5pm. This was a very big, and long overdue development in the story, and to be fair, it had been forced by the media.

The TV news, radio talk-shows and newspaper hacks and editors had been constantly hounding the press office, demanding to know what steps were being taken to protect their 85,000 DWP employees. The stories of Kath's, Jason's and Gary's injuries were horrific enough, but with the press involved as well, this had now become the biggest crisis on the government's ever expanding list of self-made disasters.

The Number 10 "exterior" press conferences were a relatively new thing, and were generally only staged when a story of major significance needed to be seen as the government's top priority.

At one minute to five, the Secretary of State for Work and Pensions came striding out of Number 10 and stepped confidently towards the lectern.

"Good afternoon." Ian David Smythe looked for a camera to train his eyes on as he read out the much-anticipated statement.

"Today the cabinet have met to discuss the appalling crimes which have shocked and saddened us all, in Manchester. Firstly, I would like to send our sincerest condolences to our government colleagues in the Department for Work and Pensions, who have been attacked, and I want to say that we wish them well with the difficult weeks and months of rehabilitation that they now face, going forwards. This is a despicable and cowardly act, and it is being carried out by an individual who obviously does not understand the role of our DWP colleagues, nor does he understand the excellent work that they do for their clients, and for society in general."

Smythe paused and stared down the lens of the Sky News camera. He wanted that last line to resonate with the attacker, but more-so, with the public.

"I would also like to send out a message to the press who seem to be taking sides with the monster who has maimed three innocent people. The Welfare Reforms *are* working. They

Might be unpopular, but most reforms are unpopular. It is certainly unpopular that a growing number of the working people who do get up in the morning, and do go out to work, end up taking home less income than those who do nothing. Something has to be done to address this, and address it we will."

There was another dramatic pause. "But let me get one thing perfectly straight here. The person responsible for these wicked, cowardly and unjustifiable attacks will never achieve his aims. We will overcome this appalling chapter in our history, and we will never allow violence to win." He stopped again, looking about as sincere as any other politician who was keen to get a message across to the TV viewers, many of whom were employees, or friends and relatives of employees, petrified about the safety of their loved one.

"As we leave the police in Manchester to get on with their investigations, our job as government is to try and guarantee the safety of our DWP colleagues until this cowardly individual is taken into custody. We aim to do this in a very robust, and a very visual way and we are finalising these plans presently with the Ministry of Defence. I would like to send a message out to all our colleagues, throughout the country. Please, go to work tomorrow as usual, and don't let the politics of fear win over the excellent work that you are doing on behalf of the British public. Thank you."

*****

"You're live with Sky News, and wow, that was a powerful message from the Secretary of State, he used the word coward three times in that short announcement. But there was very little more than that, in terms of substance. Ian Riley, our political editor joins me. Ian, your thoughts on that announcement please?"

"Thank you Sue, I think it's obvious to everybody that the only information that we gained from that announcement was that the government are standing by their welfare policies, and that they consider the man responsible for the attacks as, nothing more than a coward."

"He said that three times," added Sue.

"Yes, I think that there must be some kind of a psychological aspect to that. Maybe the government strategy is to try and make the attacker realise the error of his ways?"

"Well, I must say that my initial reaction was fear. I personally thought that Ian David Smythe was actively goading the man who has attacked the three DWP staff, giving them all life-changing injuries. It seems a dangerous game to play, doesn't it?"

"Well yes, I mean, if that is the case. But let's remember that this is a major ongoing police enquiry. The best detectives and officers of Manchester are working around the clock on this, so if it was a case of goading, then I'm rather confident that they will know exactly what they are doing."

"And, of course there was the rather vague announcement about robust and visual protection for the DWP staff. Any idea what that means?"

"Well, one thing that it doesn't mean is extra police. The government have cut the service down by twenty thousand officers, and as we are all acutely aware, the police service is stretched to breaking point. The rather vague announcement can only refer to one thing, Sue."

"And that is?"

"In a nutshell, it would suggest that the army are being drafted in to protect the DWP staff."

Chapter Seventeen
Thursday Tea-time

It was dark outside, and the Manchester rush-hour was in full-flow. The DWP staff at Othen House in Middleton had finished work, but were all staying-put, waiting for relatives, friends or loved ones to phone, to let them know that they were outside, on the Tesco car park, waiting to drive them home.

The staff had been discussing this contingency plan all day, under the leadership of their manager. They had all agreed that once all of the staff member's lifts had arrived, the building's two security guards were going to walk them all out to the supermarket car park at the rear of the three-story grey, concrete and glass building, and to the relative safety of their own lives away from the DWP.

The mood inside Othen House was just as angry and anxious as it was at all of the DWP offices up and down the land. The people working in all of nation's Jobcentres, DSS offices, Child Maintenance and Pensions offices were all feeling the same nightmarish tension, and it was an open-secret that most of the staff were planning to phone in sick the following day, and the following days after that. They were discussing it openly, the thought of another day amid this unbearable tension was too much for most of them. They knew better than most people how easy it was to get a sick-note for stress and anxiety, and a great many of them were planning to do just that, at least until this hellish situation was over.

There were seventeen staff members in the staff-room, each waiting for the chance to get out of this awful place, and this overwhelming, suffocating environment. Despite the high-friction, one or two colleagues were still keen to try and carry on as normal, and perhaps even have a bit of a laugh, if it was at all possible, just to break the tension. They were all standing around the TV, in their rest room on the second floor. The BBC News presenters were replaying Ian David Smythe's announcement.

"Well, what's that supposed to mean, guaranteeing our safety robustly?" asked one member of staff.

"It's just politician bullshit, it probably means they haven't got a bloody clue what they're going to do!"

"Ah, just wait a sec everybody, I think I know what he's talking about. Come over here." One of the colleagues, Margaret Wilkins was standing by the window. She was a portly, friendly looking woman in her fifties, and she seemed quite excited as she gestured her chubby hand towards the group gathered around the TV. They all walked across, eager to see what was so interesting outside.

"Jesus Christ! Is that the army?" shouted another lady, visibly shocked, and also a tiny bit thrilled by the sight of several armed soldiers standing beside three dark green Jeeps, as a huge green army truck reversed down the sloped street at the side of the building.

"Wow! Bloody hell, that's just made me feel a lot safer!"

"I know! Phew, I can't actually believe how much weight that's taken off my shoulders!"

The staff were all smiling and feeling the first sense of relief since this whole drama had been announced the previous day. It was a good feeling, and suddenly, there was laughter in the air as a sense of safety reassured them all. But it was to be extremely short lived, as the sound of frivolity in the room gave way to terror.

In an instant, while many of the staff were standing at the window, looking down at the soldiers and their vehicles, there was a bang, a smash sound and a scream. Margaret Wilkins, the lady who'd called everybody over to the window, fell to the floor, clutching her face.

There was panic and confusion, and nobody really knew what was happening. The screams and shouts for help only added to the terror.

"Get down! On the floor!"

"Margaret's been shot!"

It took a minute for the screams and wails of fear to subside, but as the staff crawled across to where Margaret was lay, it soon became apparent that the attacker had struck again, with a gun this time.

*****

The scene was one of utter confusion as the first wave of police officers arrived at Othen House, known more familiarly as Middleton Jobcentre. There were army vehicles, they looked like they'd been abandoned outside, and there were reports of one casualty, inside the building on the second floor. It was believed that the victim was suffering from gunshot wounds.

The ambulance hadn't arrived, and DWP staff were performing first-aid on Margaret, taking advice from the 999 call handler. All around, people were panic-stricken, most were lay down on the floor, frozen to the spot. The general consensus was that the gun-man was waiting for another opportunity to strike.

All of the DWP staff were in shock, naturally, but the shock wasn't normal. It was double-wave of shock and confusion, as they all tried to figure out why they had placed themselves in such danger in the first place. It had been all that anybody had talked about all day. Scary, paranoid discussions about "what if he attacked one of us." Now, it felt that the sick-joke was on them, and nobody felt any desire to talk about it.

Those that were tending to the victim were doing a great job under the leadership of the 999 official. Margaret had been shot in the face, and the wounds were made-up mainly of gun-shot blast and shattered glass from the window, which had literally exploded just an inch away from her face. There was a lot of blood, and a lot of burns, but Margaret was alive, and she was conscious, complaining that her "face felt like it was on fire." It could have been a lot worse, and there was a sense of relief amongst everybody in the building that Margaret hadn't been killed.

As each emergency vehicle arrived outside the Jobcentre, the place was quickly becoming illuminated with blue revolving lights, which brought a small sense of comfort and security to the staff members who were completely bewildered by this unimaginable horror.

Across the road there was a lot of shouting, and as each new police crew arrived on the scene, things started making more sense. It became apparent that the gun had been fired from the mill across the road.

Warwick Mill was a gigantic, abandoned old red-bricked Victorian mill. It had been derelict for some years now, and it seemed that it had created the perfect opportunity for the cowardly DWP attacker to sneak inside and take his indiscriminate shot at one of the DWP staff members across the road.

There still wasn't an ambulance in attendance, some twenty-five minutes after the shooting had taken place. The commanding officer at the scene was Inspector Massey from Middleton police station, who was waiting for his superiors to arrive and take over the madness. The soldiers reappeared, carrying their machine guns before them, creating even more confusion to the chaotic situation. Police officers weren't aware that the military had been drafted in, and looked surprised as the soldiers came back to report that the attacker had managed to get away via the back of the mill, and had then disappeared into a housing estate.

The situation really couldn't have been any more bonkers. After informing the police of their intentions, the army officers headed back out onto the crowded road, heading back towards the dark, imposing old mill which overlooked the Jobcentre.

Not long after the ambulance had finally pulled up, members of the press began arriving, starting with a reporter from the Middleton Guardian, whose offices weren't very far away. Then followed the BBC Manchester radio car, and Granada Reports, and they wasted no time in capturing the unfolding drama on their recording devices.

*****

Miller was in Middleton less than forty-five minutes after the attack. The scene which greeted him couldn't have been any more chaotic, as large crowds of people had gathered close to the police cordon line. It soon became apparent that many of the people in the line were relatives and friends of the

DWP staff, and they were frantically trying to find out what was happening. Plenty of rumours were flying about, but there wasn't any official news from inside the building, and understandably, the relatives outside were hysterical, and were becoming extremely irate with the police officers who were trying to keep the cordon line secure.

"What a fucking mess." Said Miller to Rudovsky, who had jumped into the car with him as he raced out of HQ.

There was a screech of tyres, and Saunders scrambled out of his own vehicle.

"What's happening?" asked the DI.

"Not sure yet, just got here. It's a nightmare though." Miller was standing in the middle of the road. This was Oldham Road, the busiest road in town, and it was usually grid-locked with rush-hour traffic in both directions at this time. This evening, it was just police vehicles, and the flashing neon blue of their lights.

"Look at all those smashed windows." Said Miller, pointing up at the Jobcentre's second floor window that had been shattered by the gun-shot. "That's where he's taken his shot. What a cheap, lousy bastard." Miller nodded up at the sinister looking mill that towered above them.

"How's the victim?" asked Saunders, as he looked up at the derelict old building which stood in darkness.

"They reckon she's been blinded. All her face is peppered with gun-shot so it's a rifle of some description, a cartridge that's gone off in her face. The ambulance crew are still in there with her now."

"Really?"

"Yes, they only got here a few minutes ago."

"For God's sake."

"Oh, wait a sec, I think they're coming out now."

Miller was right, the paramedics appeared in the doorway, with their patient lay on the trolley. Miller leapt over the traffic railings and started jogging across towards the doors.

"Hi, I'm DCI Miller, I'm in charge of the investigation. What's the latest?"

The senior paramedic stepped aside to talk to Miller as

the first-responder and the ambulance driver rushed the trolley past, on its way to the ambulance.

Several police officers were assisting the medical professionals as they made their way to the ambulance. A small number of media representatives were photographing and filming, but it was impossible to see the victim as a huge brace obscured the view.

"Hi, she's okay, she's in a stable condition, but we're very concerned about the wounds that she's sustained. There is a lot of gunshot residue on her face, the tattooing effect from the gunpowder suggests that this was a hunting rifle, the damage to her face looks like it was a birdshot load."

"Go on," Miller was intrigued.

"Well, we do a lot of training on gunshot wounds. It's so we know what we're dealing with when we get to a shooting job. I've never seen this kind of injury in the flesh before, but I've seen it on pictures. I'm pretty certain that it's a hunter's ammunition, a gunshot cartridge packed with thousands of small ball-bearings. It was fired to injure, not to kill."

"Wow, that's very interesting, thanks very much."

"It's alright. We think she's been blinded though. Definitely in the left eye. The surgeons might be able to save her right one."

"Fucking hell."

"Got to go, cheers." The Paramedic started jogging to his vehicle. Miller, Saunders and Rudovsky all looked at one another, and then across the road at that big, scary, dark mill.

"This is totally out of hand now." Said Rudovsky.

"Look at the size of that place," said Miller. "It's going to take hours, if not days to work out where he's taken his shot from. How many broken windows can you see there?"

"A lot."

"Precisely. And scenes of crimes won't bother going in there until daylight. Risk assessments will need doing, there's no way of knowing if the floor is even holding up in there, it looks like it was deserted years ago."

"What happened with the army? I heard on radio that they'd gone looking for him."

"Yes, they did. It happened just as they were just pulling up."

"I suppose that explains the random parking. Where are they now?"

"Not sure. The last I heard, they'd chased after the attacker, but it was at least a minute, maybe two after the attack. Ah, wait, here they come now."

It was a bizarre sight which Miller, Saunders and Rudovsky were met with, as six fully armed soldiers marched noisily towards the Jobcentre, their full battle uniform on, complete with combat helmets and machine guns strapped across their chests. It was like a scene from 1980's Belfast, not a suburb of modern-day Manchester.

"Hello," said Miller, walking towards them.

"Sir!" Shouted the first of the soldiers, he was a sergeant, Miller quickly spotted his stripes on his combat jacket.

"I'm DCI Miller, I'm heading up the enquiry."

"Okay, thank you Sir!" The sergeant sounded as though he was shouting, but Miller quickly came to realise that this was just how the soldiers spoke when they were on duty. As aggressive and over-the-top as it seemed, it was ordinary military conversation. "We were just arriving at the location when the shooting took place. It was a confusing picture, it took a moment or two to realise what was happening, and then once we had an understanding of the situation, it took several minutes to gain entry into the grounds of the mill."

"Did you see him?"

"No Sir, we did not see the individual, but we have identified the escape route he made, and we have also done a sweep of the building, and identified the location where he took his shot, Sir."

Miller was visibly impressed. "Wow, that is fantastic work. How did you find the location so quickly?"

"Oh, it was a gunshot blast Sir, you can smell those cartridges a mile away. We sourced the window where he took the shot, it's on the third-floor. You'll find it very easily, he's left you something on the window-sill."

"What.. really... what is it?"

"It's a note Sir, addressed to DCI Miller."

*****

"Welcome to North West Tonight, I'm Roger Thompson. We start this evening's programme with some breaking news, which concerns the DWP attacks. In the past hour there has been a fourth attack, this time at Middleton Jobcentre. Our correspondent Suzie Sands is there, Suzie, can you please tell us what has happened there this evening please?"

The news presenter looked edgy, and almost scared as he handed over to the reporter. She was standing in the dark at the police cordon line. Dozens of police vehicles were illuminating the buildings on both sides of the busy Oldham Road. The cameraman had the army jeeps and the truck in shot too. It looked like something from a TV drama show, not a news bulletin from Middleton.

"Yes, thank you Roger. The scene behind me is one of total confusion and terror. Just a few minutes after five pm, a member of the DWP staff here at Othen House was standing by the staff-room window, when that person was shot in the face, we believe from one of the windows in the mill directly across the road."

"Any word on the victim's condition?"

"No, I'm afraid that we have very few details at this early stage in the inquiry. We cannot reveal any information about the victim, as family members will of course need to be contacted by police in the first instance. But we have been told, by one staff member who was leaving with police officers, is that the victim is alive, and that the injuries which were sustained were not thought to be life-threatening. One thing that is very distressing though, Roger, the injuries were described to us as life-changing."

"And, just to remind our viewers, that is the description that has been used to describe all of the horrendous injuries that have been sustained by this attacker."

"That's correct. This latest incident is now the fourth

attack, each one has left behind horrendous stories of unimaginable injuries that these DWP staff have sustained. The first incident took place in Stockport, when DWP employee Kath Palmer was attacked with an axe. Almost a week later, on Monday of this week, the second attack took place, also close to Stockport DWP building close to the town centre. The victim of that violent knife attack was Jason Brown, a forty-four-year-old dad. Jason was stabbed in the shoulder, and then, last night, at practically the same time as tonight's attack, Gary Webster received horrific leg injuries as he made his way out of his workplace at Hyde Jobcentre. It's now Thursday, and we are here, at the scene of yet another serious attack against a member of the DWP staff."

"This is a very scary, and very worrying situation." Roger really did look shocked, and frightened by this story. His reaction was felt in the homes across the north-west, viewers sat with their hands over their mouths, saddened and confused by the sheer nastiness of these random, creepy attacks.

"Suzy, thank you for the update. We will bring you the latest information as we get it, but for now, we'll look at the rest of the stories that are making the news here in the north west this evening."

*****

The army sergeant led Miller, Saunders and Rudovsky up a cold, echoey staircase, right at the heart of the dark, smelly mill. The smell inside there overpowering, the type of whiff that sticks to your clothes. The aroma was an odd mixture of old, rotting buildings, mixed with dust and the nauseating, acidic smell of bird-poo on an industrial scale, with notes of stale human piss. Soon, they had made it up to the third floor. All were carrying torches, and their beams created endless light strobes which illuminated the depressing state of the interior.

Smashed up doors and windows, old toilet pots and sinks were strewn all over the place. There were random pages from porno mags all over the floor. Graffiti filled the walls, some which clearly had artistic potential, but most just of it was just random names and stupid remarks. All around there was lots of evidence of beer-drinking. The floor was quite literally covered in litter, and it was apparent to Miller that this place was being used for a number of illicit activities.

In no time, the odour of the decaying building gave way to an overpowering scent of gunpowder. All three of the detectives instantly understood how the soldiers had identified this spot so quickly. This was it, the precise spot that the sick bastard had stood and taken aim on a random face in the windows opposite. There, folded neatly was a piece of A4 paper. The name DCI MILLER was printed on it.

"This guy is getting brave." Said Miller, desperate to step forward and read the note, but cautious to disturb the scene. There could be a human hair, or a finger print, or a dried fleck of snot which could identify the attacker. Miller could never forgive himself if he was responsible for letting scum like this bastard get a head-start. He'd have to wait, as torturous as it was, to find out what intellectual wonders this latest note contained.

"None of your officers touched anything here, did they?" asked Rudovsky of the sergeant.

"No Ma'am, we know how to operate in a crime scene." He was shouting again, and it made all three of the detectives jump slightly, as the soldier's booming voice reverberated around the gigantic building.

"I think he's a bit deaf," said Saunders very quietly. Rudovsky smirked, and she couldn't resist raising her own voice to a shout and saying, "OKAY, THANKS!"

Miller opened his contacts list in his phone. "I'm just going to get CSI down here right now. I can't wait until morning to pick this up again." Miller started walking away from the crime-scene as his call connected. "Sir, hi, yes, he's left another note. I don't know, I've not read it yet. It needs CSI treatment first. No, it's just folded up there on the windowsill, addressed to me. Alright, brilliant, cheers."

Miller ended the call. "Right, forensics are on their way, top priority, there's only one section on duty. Cut-backs are everywhere, not just on people's benefits. Anyway, Dixon's going to force it through, so at least we'll have a photograph of that note within the next half an hour. Meanwhile Sergeant, any chance you can show us which way you reckon he went after this?"

"Yes, we're quite sure that he used the steel fire exit steps on the outside of the building, as all of the lower floor doors were locked when we first gained entry."

"So how has he got in here?" asked Miller.

"Pick a broken window… there are dozens on the ground-floor level."

"How did you get in then?" asked Saunders.

"We just shot the doors in."

Chapter Eighteen

Miller was back at the office by 9pm. He was tired, and pretty stressed out as the press had now made him their prime target, which meant his mobile phone was switched off and his office line was constantly engaged. The handset lay on his desk, half a foot away from its cradle.

Miller blew out an exasperated breath of air. The thing that was pissing him off the most was the total lack of useful information that he and his team had on the attacker. And now that the attacker's confidence was clearly so high, the risk of further attacks was inevitable. It was a nightmare situation, and Miller couldn't think of any other case that he'd investigated which compared to this one.

Until today, he had been convinced that the person responsible was suffering an acute mental health episode, a severe psychotic breakdown of some description. All the usual pointers were there, most strikingly the utter disregard for others, the total lack of empathy towards fellow human beings. But he was starting to retreat from the idea of a schizophrenic episode, mainly down to the amount of planning and organisation that would be required to carry out the three attacks in three days, and especially, with all of them passing off with perfect escapes, and clean forensic scenes. There was a distinct lack of chaos or spontaneity. The sheer skill level involved left him feeling very doubtful that a mental health condition was the catalyst. It may well be a factor, he wasn't ruling mental health as a contributing factor, but it wasn't the driving force, in his view.

The DCI was making notes on his desk jotter, as he went over it all in his mind. If the attacker wasn't mad, then he was bad. And if he was bad, there was bound to be some record of him in the police computer. The thought frustrated Miller, as he realised that the person they were looking for was holding all of the cards. The truth was, they were just waiting for the attacker to screw up.

Miller looked up, and out of the huge glass wall which divided his office from the rest of the SCIU floor. Saunders was beavering away at his desk, and one or two of the temp officers that had been drafted in were also staying late, trying to either make a good impression, or an arrest. Either way, Miller was glad. He wanted to shout Saunders into his office and have a chat about everything, but he could see that Saunders was in the zone, and it wasn't worth interrupting him when he was this heavily involved in whatever it was that he was checking.

Miller was distracted by the sound of an e-mail. His screen had gone off, so he wriggled the mouse, and saw that the photo of the note had finally arrived.

"You beauty!" he said under his breath as he clicked the e-mail and waited for the photograph to load up.

Within seconds, the image appeared on his screen. The font was the same, it looked like the same kind of printer ink judging by the magnified section. But the message was equally as short as the last one. It simply read "MAKE THEM STOP KILLING THE POOR!"

Miller was about to shout Saunders, he wanted his DI to see this, hot off the press, but as he looked up from the computer screen he noticed that Saunders was running towards his office. He burst in through the door."

"Sir, its DCS Dixon on the phone for you." Saunders extended his arm and handed his phone across the desk.

"Cheers," he said, looking surprised and confused by this peculiar interruption.

"Hello?"

"Andy, its Dixon. What's wrong with your phone? I've been trying to contact you..."

"Oh, its, not sure Sir... anyway, what's wrong?"

"There has been another attack, just after eight o' clock, in Shaw."

"Our man?" Miller sounded as if he'd been winded.

"It certainly looks that way, it was a bloke walking down to the shop with his dog. We've just discovered that he works for the DWP. He's used the axe again, Andy."

*****

Miller and Saunders arrived at the scene, it was a quiet little cul-de-sac made up of neat little bungalows in Shaw, a suburb between Middleton and Oldham. The familiar forensics tent was up, and the police line do not cross tape was flapping in the wind. A few teenagers were loitering by the police officers at the cordon, sat on their bikes and looking quite excited to be this close to a big police incident. A nosey neighbour was watching the events from her front window across the road, she was talking manically into her phone. Miller imagined that she was saying "you never imagine anything like this would happen in your own street, do you?"

Both detectives were in a state of shock. This latest attack was completely unbelievable. The two detectives explored each other's faces for a clue as to what the other was thinking. Luckily, the press hadn't had wind of this yet. The only people in attendance were a few members of the local community, and the police officers who were attending. The ambulance had been and gone over an hour earlier, and it seemed to Miller and Saunders that it had taken the initial presence of police officers a little too long to put two and two together.

The story seemed quite solid though. The victim, a fifty-one year-old DWP staff member called Stewart Grimley was walking home from his local Bargain Booze store with his Yorkshire Terrier Barney, he was almost home when he'd been hit in the back with an axe. He'd gone down immediately, shouting out in pain. Neighbours soon came to Stewart's aid, alerting police and ambulance crews within seconds of the attack. The dog, Barney, ran off after the attacker, and hadn't been seen since.

Miller was seriously disappointed at the shoddy handling of this crime scene. It had taken far too long for officers to associate it with the other DWP attacks. If one of the attending officers had made the link sooner, police dogs could have attended and followed the trail of the attacker, and Barney. Miller shook his head, this was becoming overbearing. This was an abhorrent case, and he could feel the pressure building.

"Rudovsky said earlier, that its getting too much, or

something. At the time, I thought it was a daft way to put it. But I can see what she meant. How the fuck can you do this kind of thing to another person? Some chap walking his fucking dog? It's beyond me."

Saunders nodded. He too was struggling to rationalise this extraordinary case. "Does it not remind you a bit of the Pop case, though?" Asked Saunders. He was breaking a rule, talking about the Pop case. The SCIU team had all agreed not to talk about it, as it brought up too much bad feeling, too many bad memories. Too much grief. It may have been a few years ago, but it was still very raw, and the wounds were still healing for several of the team.

"I thought we..."

"Well, it has to be said. Pop was the only person I can remember who targeted strangers, and did more than one attack at once. Different, but similar."

"No, I see what you're getting at, but Pop was after paedos Keith, not bloody civil-servants."

"Well, I know that, obviously, but I'm just trying to find comparisons."

"I know, I get it, but you're barking up the wrong tree. Pop had his reasons for what he did. And most of the country agreed with what he was doing. It's a far cry from what this psychopath is up to. A far cry."

"Look, Pop had his reasons, I accept that. But this attacker may have the same mental state that Pop had when he was going about his attacks. I don't think its..."

"Keith, mate, I know what you're thinking. But I'm not buying it. Killing a child-molester, so they can't abuse any more children is not the same as disabling people who work at the dole, because you don't think the cuts are fair."

Saunders went quiet, and Miller knew that he'd pissed his DI off by dismissing his suggestion. But as far as Miller was concerned, it wasn't a thought worth pursuing.

"Where's this fucking Inspector?" asked Miller, changing the subject.

"He's just in a house up there, reassuring an old lady who has had a panic attack. He knows we're here so he shouldn't be too long."

Miller turned and walked across to the youths by the police cordon. They were aged about thirteen, Miller guessed.

"Did you do it?" he asked the first one.

"Do what?"

"Attack that man." Miller was smiling. The three kids laughed.

"I'm not talking, right, I'm not talking 'til you've phoned my solicitor!" said the kid, which made his mates roar with laughter.

"Seriously though, do you know the guy?"

"Who Stewart? Yeah, everyone round here knows Stewart and Barney. He always used to give us all two-quid when we went carol singing, or trick-or-treating. Didn't he?"

"Yeah, he's well sound."

"Proper sound guy."

"Did you see or hear anything tonight?" asked Miller.

"No, no, we didn't know nothing about it until we saw all the dib... all the police cars flying about and the ambulance. That's when we came down."

"Tell you what then, if Stewart was always so nice to you lot, why don't you repay his kindness, and have a ride round looking for his dog, eh?"

"Barney? Why, has he escaped or summat?"

"No, Stewart was walking him, when he got attacked. The dog legged it, he's probably still got his lead round his neck."

"Right, come on." The three teenagers set off peddling, and within seconds, they were shouting "Barney" as they rode their bikes around the neighbouring streets.

"Nice enough kids. It makes a change, doesn't it?" asked Miller of the PCs who had been entertaining them.

"Yeah, they're alright. Give them another year."

It wasn't long until the Inspector returned from the old lady's house, and was available to speak to Miller and Saunders. He had a look of relief on his face as he realised that it was DCI Miller who was waiting to speak to him. He wouldn't have to run this crime-scene for a second longer, and he was glad about that.

"Hi," said Miller. "How is the old lady?"

"Oh, she's a bit shocked and upset. The victim goes for her paper every morning, and looks after her cats when she goes to her daughter's house in Bakewell. I've managed to settle her down, and it sounds like good news from the hospital, no serious damage was caused in this attack, apparently."

This announcement stunned Miller and Saunders. They'd just assumed that this was as "life-changing" as the others. It was great news, but it didn't really make sense. It was obvious from the look on Saunders' face, that he was trying to work out how it was possible that an axe swung into somebody's back hadn't caused any damage.

"Stewart Grimley had been extremely cautious tonight when he set off out with his dog, and its paid off. He shoved a plastic chopping board down the back of his pants, protecting the base of his back. The axe shattered the chopping board, but its only caused bruising, apparently. It hurt like hell, but he's over the worst."

"Bloody hell, that's a result!" Miller was overjoyed by the ingenuity, and the good fortune involved.

"That is absolutely amazing!" Saunders was beaming from ear-to-ear. "Just shows you the ferocity of the attack though. I mean, shattering a chopping board. It's no wonder that Kath Palmer's not going to walk again, if that's the kind of power he's putting into his swing."

"Right, well, shall we go off and see him? Ask him for six numbers between 1 and 59 as well?" Miller was feeling happy, for the first time today. This news had really lifted his spirits. Saunders looked happy too, but suddenly, he looked serious.

"Erm, well, if it's all the same, I'd rather go back to the office, I was making some good progress on something before this call came in. I wouldn't mind getting back to it, Sir."

"Oh…? Anything you want to…"

"No, not at this stage. But I might have something positive to tell you in the morning."

"Fair dos Keith. Alright, I'll go and say hello to Stewart, and see if he saw anything, noticed anything unusual. You never know, he might have had a fucking CCTV camera attached to his head!"

Saunders laughed, as did the Inspector.

"Alright, you get going Keith, take my car back to HQ. I'll head off to the hospital, I'm sure one of these panda cars will stand me a lift?"

"Yes, yes of course Sir," said the Inspector, though he looked a little bit pissed off by the cheek of Miller's request. Saunders got in the car, and reversed it out of the cul-de-sac, almost hitting one of the young lads who came flying around the corner on his bike.

"We've found Barney!" shouted the youth triumphantly. Miller laughed. It suddenly felt that as though things were starting to look up.

*****

Stewart Grimley was sitting up on the hospital trolley in the A&E corridor, he looked as though he was in high spirits. His wife was by his side, she looked considerably less pleased about things.

"She told me I was mad, shoving the chopping board down my keks. I must admit, I was only taking the mick, like. But I'm not complaining now!"

His wife looked like she was close to tears, and not in the mood for her husband's daft jokes. What had happened had really shook her up.

"I don't suppose you got a good look at him?"

"Nah, I was just walking along, coming back from the shop and Barney started growling so I was looking down at him, and then bang, I was on the floor. I went down like a sack of spuds."

"And was anything said?"

"Not a word. I was screaming and shouting, and all I heard was his footsteps banging on the floor as he legged it. My dog went chasing after him, for what good he'd do!"

Miller smiled. He couldn't help but warm to this bloke, and he was reminded of how warm and pleasant the other victims had been, too. They were all really nice people, he mused, which added an extra layer of suspense and intrigue to the whole thing.

"Well, don't worry about Barney, some young lads found him."

"Oh, thank God!" said Stewart's wife.

"They said you always sort them out on Halloween, so they went off searching for Barney. They picked him up in no time. He's with the old lady whose paper you deliver in the morning."

"Oh Hilda, God, she'll be boiling him up a chicken! He won't touch his pedigree chum after a night with her!"

"Well, I'm glad this has had a happy ending. It was a bloody good idea putting that chopping board down your pants."

"Hey, it was only a cheap one as well!"

"Yes, well, it's been harrowing visiting the other victims, and seeing their injuries."

"I know."

The jovial mood suddenly dropped.

"So, there was absolutely nothing you can remember about the attacker?"

"No, like I say, it was dark, I just heard the dog getting stressed, then a big bang, felt the pain in my back and went down. I made it sound a lot worse than it was, obviously. He just ran away, very very quickly."

"Well, thanks a lot. And I'm glad you're alright, and in such good spirits."

*****

"Welcome to Sky's Midnight News and our major, unfolding story this hour. The DWP attacks have continued this evening in Manchester, with another two DWP employees being targeted this evening. Sky sources have informed us that the victim of the first attack, which happened at around five o'clock at Middleton Jobcentre, has left a woman in her fifties blind. The second attack, which we believe happened at around eight o' clock in the Shaw district of Oldham, was much less serious and we are hoping to speak to the victim, Stewart Grimley in the next few minutes. But first, let's cross to our North of England Correspondent Paul Mitchell, who is at the crime scene in Middleton. Paul."

The screen changed from the newsreader's face, to the familiar looking reporter who was standing outside the Jobcentre.

"Yes, thank you, we have indeed seen another horrendously violent act here tonight. This disused mill on my right overlooks this DWP building. The attacker crept inside here as the DWP staff were preparing to leave for the evening and shot one member of staff in the face. We have since learnt that the lady, who hasn't yet been named, has lost her sight in this attack."

"And this happened as the army were arriving on the site to increase security, Paul?"

"Yes, that's right. The government's response to provide soldiers at the DWP buildings was tragically completely futile here this evening."

"Any updates from the police?"

"Nothing of substance as yet, although the Manchester Police Twitter account has announced that the Chief Constable, and the leading detective on this case, DCI Andrew Miller, will be holding a press conference at 11am."

"What can you tell us about the second attack that took place this evening, Paul?"

"Well, this is a very unusual situation, as the attack which took place at around eight 'o'clock, involved a DWP employee on his own residential street. He is named as Stewart Grimley and we have been communicating with Stewart, who is now back home after being checked-over at the Royal Oldham Hospital this evening. Stewart is the first victim of this attacker who appears to have escaped any serious injury. All of the other attacks have of course occurred outside or nearby a DWP building, so although the injuries are not thought to be very serious, it is still extremely concerning that this attack has taken place where it has."

"Well, if I can interrupt you Paul, we actually have Stewart Grimley live, via Skype, good evening Stewart."

The newsreader sounded quite excited to be interviewing the victim, just a few hours after the ordeal.

"Hiya, aright?" he said, he looked tired and pale but he was smiling.

"It sounds like you had an extremely lucky escape this evening, Stewart?"

"Aye, well, you can say that again!"

"Can you talk us through what happened please?"

"Yes, well, I went to the fridge to make a brew after Coronation Street and one of the bloody kids had used all the milk again, and not said anything. I was bloody fuming, and I said to my wife, I'll have to go down the shops when I take Barney out, that's our dog. Any road, my wife started saying I shouldn't go out on my own, you know, that's what work have advised because of these attacks. So, for a laugh, I got this chopping board." Stewart held up the white, plastic block to the camera. "As luck would have it, I shoved it down the back of my pants, to make the wife laugh. Anyway, look at it now." Stewart held it close to the camera and the Sky News viewers were shown the chopping board, and a crack which had split it down the middle. "That's where the axe hit it. If it weren't for this little piece of plastic from IKEA, I'd be bloody paralysed now. And it was only two-quid."

Chapter Nineteen
Friday

"Good Morning, Britain, I'm Piers Morgan!"

"And I'm Susanna Reid. In the spotlight today are the awful, shocking DWP attacks in Manchester. Today we meet one former member of staff, who warned three years ago that this was bound to happen." The attractive, dark-haired presenter had a very serious look on her face as she stared into the camera. Her co-presenter continued with the programme's introduction.

"That's right, this morning we are talking about the Department for Works and Pensions staff being viciously assaulted in the street, causing them devastating injuries. We are joined by Helen Heath, who worked for the DWP for fifteen years, but left three years ago when she realised that her job had changed. She says that under the current government her role went from trying to help people, to trying to persecute them. Good morning Helen."

"Good Morning."

Britain's most popular breakfast TV show had over a million viewers and this exclusive interview with the Jobcentre "whistle-blower" was bound to attract a few more this morning.

"So, you left your job in 2014 Helen. Tell us why?" said Susanna.

"Well, it's simple really. I was being told that I had to put as many jobseekers on sanction as I could."

"And to enlighten our viewers who are lucky enough to have never claimed Jobseekers Allowance... a "sanction" is the procedure of taking away somebody's benefit. Is that right?"

"Yes, it basically means that you stop their income which includes rent payments and council tax payments. Basically, you're stripping them of their money and their home, just setting them up for severe hardship, and more-often-than-not, it was for childish, petty reasons. I just couldn't bring myself to do it. So, I was put on a disciplinary, basically a warning. It was the last straw, and I handed in my notice that day."

Piers Morgan looked interested in what Helen was

saying. "Obviously, you must have felt very strongly about the situation, to take such drastic action."

"Yes, and, well I know a lot of my colleagues at the time wished that they could do the same but with bills to pay, mortgages to keep up with, it wasn't such an easy option for them. The thing was, as the new, nasty tactics were being brought in by the coalition government, there was a sense that the Conservative's partners, the Liberal Democrats would put their foot down. There was just a real sense that this nastiness wouldn't last very long, that it *couldn't* last very long. I know that a lot of my colleagues felt that it was only a matter of time until the government realised that they were making a mistake and things would return to normal. But I couldn't stand it, not a day longer, and I was very lucky that my husband earned enough to keep us both afloat for a bit. I managed to find another job within a few weeks."

"And what is it that you do now?"

"I'm a housing officer. It's a job where I get to help people, that's what I wanted to do in life, and that was what I really wanted to achieve with my work at the Jobcentre. And I did, I had so many clients that I helped and encouraged. It was such a wonderful feeling when they came in to tell me they'd got a job." Helen looked as though she was becoming slightly emotional as the memories of happier times at the DWP came flooding back.

"Now, this is such a difficult subject to report on due to the absolutely appalling injuries that the victims have suffered. It's been well documented in the press just how evil the person is who is carrying out the attacks. The over-riding priority is to catch the man responsible and the police up in Manchester are desperately trying to figure out who this crazy person is. There are reports this morning that the British Army are guarding the entrances of all DWP buildings in the UK. There are also reports that it's all a waste of time because after last night's appalling attacks in Middleton and Oldham, no DWP staff will be turning up for work this morning."

"Yes, I...."

"Sorry, but I was going to finish up by asking you

whether you might think that coming on here, to say 'I told you so' is just a little bit insensitive to those poor victims who won't be able to stand up again, or drive, or see?" Piers Morgan didn't care if he shocked and upset guests, in fact that was his primary objective.

"Well...I... you invited me on..." Helen had looked a little wrong-footed at first, but came back with a razor-sharp reply which left Piers Morgan stunned momentarily. Helen continued, she was used to talking back to gobby pricks, it was all in a day's work for the forty-eight-year old mum of three teenagers. "That's the stupidest question I've ever been asked. Am I insensitive because I agreed to do this interview when your producer rang me, and get in the taxi that you sent, accept a cheque for two-hundred and fifty pounds, and a taxi home, to talk about a subject that I'm an expert about? God, no wonder people think you're a doorknob, Piers."

Susanna decided to change the topic. "Helen, what do you think about the fact that DWP staff are refusing to go to work?"

"It doesn't surprise me, not in the slightest. I wouldn't want to go... if I still worked there, I'd be calling in sick as well."

"What kind of impact will this have on the DWP in general, do you think?"

"Oh, it will be massive, I mean, the nation relies on benefit payments to carry on, we spend one hundred and seventy billion pounds a year on benefits in this country. That is a lot of money, and it all has to be processed. There are eighty-five thousand people employed to do the various jobs involved in providing that sum of money. So, what we are looking at here, apart from an evil, pathetic psychopath with a misguided agenda, is a financial crisis which is unparalleled. If benefit payments are unable to happen because DWP staff won't go into work, this country will grind to a stop. No pensions, no tax-credit payments. No job-seekers allowance, no personal independence payments. The country will genuinely, totally, grind to a halt. Now, if you consider the vile acts of this government over the past seven years, the absolute hatred that they have forced DWP staff to deliver against the weakest and most vulnerable people in society, there should be resignations, from the head of the DWP, to the Secretary of State for Work and Pensions Ian David Smythe. Even the PM should go. This is a colossal cock-up, and now, the cat is out of the bag, and everybody is going to see what an unimaginable crisis these scumbags have created, by being nasty, horrible, faceless little bullies. Like Brexit, like the stupid snap-election, like the Tory conference shambles in Manchester, this too is going to come and hit them where it hurts, and I for one couldn't be more pleased about that fact."

Piers Morgan had recovered from letting in his own goal, and hit back with a new question.

"That sounds as though you are congratulating the attacker."

"In your ears, it may do Piers. But hopefully your audience are a bit brighter and have a slightly better grasp on reality. Anybody with half a brain will know that I haven't said that at all. I just called him a pathetic psycho. But you've got to try and twist it up to get it going viral Piers, I get it."

Susanna Reid laughed. She loved the confident manner in which Helen was handling her adversary, it was a rare treat to see Piers being treated rough.

"I'll tell you what though, this is how bad they are," Helen continued, "all these Jobcentres are closed, so people can't sign on. When they re-open, people will come in to sign on, and the DWP staff will say 'you missed your appointment last week.' And the claimant will say 'oh, the Jobcentre was closed because of that pathetic psycho,' and I'll tell you what will happen. They will be sanctioned. Because they didn't keep their appointment."

"Now, that's just utter dross!" said Piers, laughing dismissively.

"Is it really Piers? We'll see. I was told I had to sanction somebody, strip him of his benefits for three months, because he missed an appointment. Do you know why he missed? He was on the pavement outside the Jobcentre giving CPR to a man who'd just had a heart-attack."

Susanna Reid looked stunned by Helen's passionate

speech.

"He'd saved the man's life. An ambulance came and took the guy away, and the claimant came in looking tearful. He was shocked and weak and exhausted from doing chest compressions. We gave him a glass of water, and told him to calm down and take deep breaths. We'd all watched this going on for half an hour outside the doors, several other staff members were involved. And then, I was told by my manager that I had to tell him that he'd missed his appointment and he wouldn't receive any benefits for thirteen weeks. That was the day I left."

"That can't be true!" Susanna Reid really did look shocked and agitated by this extraordinary story.

"It is true, I resigned that day because of it. Why are people always so shocked about these stories? This is what is happening, right now in our country, to our people, just because they haven't got a job, or they have a disease that prevents them from working, or they are mentally incapable of working. They are being killed off by the government, and its high-time that it was stopped. But it's not being stopped, it's being lied about by the government and it is getting ignored by the public, because they just see programmes like 'Britain's Most Shameless Mum,' and they assume that everybody on benefits is taking advantage of the system. It couldn't be further from the truth, and it has got to stop."

"What exactly has to stop?" asked Piers, with a smug look upon his face.

"The terrorism that the government are committing against people who can't fight back. It has got to stop, just as hacking dead kid's phones had to. Eh, Piers?"

*****

"Good morning to everybody waking up in the red rose county. This is BBC Radio Lancashire. Our top story this morning is the DWP attacks. Big Jim in Clitheroe has an opinion about these shocking, disgusting attacks. Jim?"

"Yes, good morning. Thanks for having me on."

"You're most welcome. What are your thoughts, Jim?"

"Well, firstly I'd like to start off with a message to the attacker, if he's listening. Please stop. If you wanted to draw attention to the sanctions and what have you... well, you have done, the whole nation is talking about it."

"You can say that again," said the presenter.

"But violence is never the answer. It never has been and it never will be."

"Well said Jim. The news this morning is possibly of some comfort to DWP staff, as it has been announced that all DWP buildings will be guarded by armed soldiers until the attacker is apprehended by police."

"Yes, well, maybe it would have been an idea to keep that a secret. Maybe the soldiers could be hidden from view, and would stand a better chance of catching him. It would be better than simply deterring him."

"That's a very good point. Big Jim, I'm interested to hear your thoughts on the Welfare Reforms, the Universal Credit and what-have-you. It's a topic which divides the nation. What do you make of all of this?"

"To be perfectly honest, I'm dead against the welfare cuts, it's just lazy, backwards thinking."

"But let me play devil's advocate for a moment. We do have a growing number of working age people who rely on benefits, people who have slipped into the habit of taking hand-outs and are now in the precarious position of not having any work experience to put on a CV. The government's thinking seems to be that these people need a wake-up call and need to think of an alternative way to fund their lives."

"Yes, and that's all well and good if you were actually putting them into work. Listen, there would be far less of an outcry if people were given a training course rather than having their benefits cut. Why don't the government sanction people with free driving lessons? Sanction them with free college classes in brick-laying or plumbing, car mechanics, hair-dressing. The simple fact of the matter is that this is not a solution that achieves any results. All the government are actually doing is making matters worse for people who are already down on their luck. It makes no sense, the government are making fools of themselves and being made to look like the nasty party once again."

"So, let me get this idea straight. You're saying that instead of stopping their money, the government should be investing in ways of getting the work-less skilled up and ready for work."

"Well, yes. Teach them how to drive buses, coaches, trucks, trains. Pay for them to learn to be electricians, welders, chefs. Then, and only then will their job searches be a bit more fruitful. No employers are looking for people with no skills, no work-experience, and that's why there are so many long-term unemployed people. It's pretty simple really, you don't need to be Professor Stephen Hawking to work it out."

"But there will be people listening to this who think that these people should fund their own training."

"They can't, can they, if they are stuck in the poverty trap. So instead of tormenting them with nasty, vicious stunts like stopping their money, the government could empower them and get them off the dole and into well paid jobs and ultimately paying in taxes which will contribute to society in a positive way. Everyone wins then."

"A lot of people have paid a lot of money to be skilled up in these jobs. Wouldn't your idea anger them?"

"Why, why would it? Listen, we all need a leg up at some point. Wouldn't you feel proud to live in a country that helped its people, instead of stamping on them?"

"Well yes..."

"I bet you've had a few leg ups in your time, haven't you?"

"Well, ooh-er Missus, I'm not sure what you mean..." The presenter tried to make a risqué joke of Jim's question.

"What I mean is, you're a successful radio presenter. But you didn't just write into the radio station and ask for a show, did you?"

"No, I didn't. I had to work hard, I had to work my way up. I started off walking around hospital wards asking patients if they wanted a request on the hospital radio. That's how I got started."

"And if it's not too rude, could I ask you how you funded that?"

"How I..." The radio presenter suddenly sounded flustered.

"How did you manage to pay your bills and keep a roof over your head while you were volunteering at the hospital?"

"I, well, I was... I mean I was much younger then. My outgoings were smaller."

"That's not really answering the question. I'm guessing that your mum and dad supported you doing this unpaid work?"

"Well, yes, actually, they did."

"But not every person out there has a mum and dad that can afford to support their fully-grown children to take a chance on something like that."

"No, okay, I accept your point. I've been very lucky."

"It's not luck though. It's a leg up. So, you did your hospital radio. And then you got a show on Radio Lancashire?"

"Well, no... of course not! I had to answer the phones, make cups of tea..."

"Paid work, or was this also unpaid?"

"It was unpaid. That's how this industry works. Your first million hours are unpaid!" The DJ tried to make a quip but his caller was relentless.

"That's very commendable. But my point is that you had a good, strong support network behind you, enabling you to take the chance. Your mum and dad sound like great people. And I'll bet there will be plenty of other people who have given you a leg up along the way. People who've helped you, advised you, introduced you to right people, the people who've eventually given you your own show on the radio."

"Yes, I'm not denying it. There are a lot of great people who've helped me along the way."

"Well, you've demonstrated my point for me. If you came from a one-parent family and you had to do two jobs on minimum wage, then go and look after your Granny two nights a week, you wouldn't be where you are right now."

"No, no, I suppose not Jim."

"Just like you did, everybody needs a bit of help from time-to-time. These people on Universal Credit, all they want is a job, they want a good wage, a nice holiday, a tidy car. That's all they want. But while we continue to have this idiotic system where we try to alienate people, try to humiliate them, strip away their tiny bit of money, it's not going to achieve that. It's just a waste of everybody's time and effort. So why doesn't the government do something constructive about the issue? And, fair play, if the people don't show up for their plumbing course or their bus driving lessons - sanction them then, by all means. But we should at least give the unemployed something to aim at."

"Well I think that what you've suggested here is a great idea. Why haven't the government thought of this?"

"Because they are stupid, frankly. They are all born millionaires, all privately educated toffs who don't recognise the struggles and difficulties facing people who weren't born into money. They have been sheltered from the real world, real people, all their lives. It starts at boarding school aged five, then at the posh Uni in Oxford or Cambridge, and then in the corridors of power when they start their Parliamentary careers as researchers or PAs, until their political party parachutes them into a safe seat when one comes up."

"Wow, that's quite a cynical view of our political system."

"It's not cynical at all, its spot on. And that's why it's no big shock that these rich zombies in the government are so out of touch. It's like you or I going to try and blend in with the lost tribe of the Amazon."

"But despite the class differences, do you not think that the government *want* to help?"

"No." Big Jim laughed. "They just want to demonise, they don't want to help. They have no interest in solving the problem, they just want to cause as much misery as they can. They hate the poor, yet they have absolutely no understanding that most poor people are poor because they were born into it. It's the exact same as most of the rich people being rich, because they were born into it. The only difference is that the rich get richer, by keeping the poor people down. That's the way the system is designed and ultimately, it is why they came into politics. To get richer, and keep all the money amongst themselves by doing shady deals like selling the NHS off at a fraction of its value to their mates, or replacing government departments with private firms like G4S."

"Interesting points there Jim. Thanks for sharing them, and if you ever stand as an MP, you'll surely get my vote!"

Big Jim laughed again. "Well, that's another story. But I wasn't born a millionaire, and I didn't go to Eton so I wouldn't get on the ticket for any of the major parties. I wouldn't stand a chance of getting my message out if I stood as an independent candidate, and if nobody could hear my message, I wouldn't get any votes. That's how Parliament works in this country, and that's why most of the MPs we have are all in it for themselves. But thanks anyway!"

Chapter Twenty

"Jo, have you got a minute, please?" Miller was standing at his office door. He had his arms folded and he looked pissed-off. It wasn't his intention, but he sounded and looked as though he had summoned DC Rudovsky to his office for a bollocking.

DC Bill Chapman certainly heard it that way and couldn't resist making a comment. "Aw thank Christ for that! Jo's finally getting the sack. Where are you holding your leaving do, Jo? The phone box on Church Street?" The caustic, harsh comment received a bit of a laugh. It wasn't Chapman's greatest moment of bantering but several of the temp officers found it quite amusing, based primarily on the sheer nastiness.

"And to think, you were the best sperm out of a hundred-million others!" said Jo theatrically, as she stood and walked towards Miller's office.

Rudovsky's come-back got a much bigger laugh and Chapman's face turned bright red, as it always did whenever he became the butt of the joke, which was usually what happened whenever he tried it on with Rudovsky. She turned to give him a sarcastic smile as she reached Miller's door and decided to kill him off, for today at least. "Fucking hell Bill. Look at the colour of you. You look like you are quite literally having a shit, mate."

"Right, that's enough," said Miller as Rudovsky stepped into his office.

"He started it. He's such a dick, Sir. I've got a new fantasy about that fat, ugly bastard, you know."

Miller laughed, and everybody who was noseying through the glass, trying to see if Rudovsky was getting bollocked, saw the DCI's head fly back as Jo's first remark amused the DCI. She hadn't even sat down yet.

Miller had heard several of Rudovsky's "fantasies" where she gets Chapman back for getting on her nerves, using only her imagination.

"I've got to hear this," said Miller.

Rudovsky sat down. "Well, for some mad reason, in this fantasy, me and Chapman have been paired up, and we're working late at my house."

Miller roared with laughter, mainly because of the sheer silliness of the expression on Rudovsky's face, but also because of the thought of her and Chapman working together on a case. That would end in murder, without a doubt.

"Anyway, I look outside, and bugger me, it's been snowing! Poor old Chapman has been snowed in at my place. So, I do the right thing, and let him sleep the night, and then, in the morning, I take my revenge for having to listen to all his shit jokes and boring opinions for all these years!" Rudovsky did a very impressive cackle.

"What do you do?" asked Miller, desperate to hear what she does to poor old Bill Chapman in her fantasy.

"I hand him a tooth-brush in the morning. I say, "here you go mate," and he smiles and thanks me. Only he has no idea that I'd been up for hours, cleaning all the skids off the toilet with it, scrubbing under the rim, then round the back of the taps on the bath, getting all the pubes and mould and all that. Then I scrub the cat's litter tray out with it, paying particular attention to the dried-on turd marks."

Miller's eyes were streaming, he was laughing so much.

"I rinse it of course, before I give it him, get all the big lumps off. But it isn't a thorough rinse, like."

Miller's head flew-back again, and the sound of his laughter reverberated around the entire floor. It was quite apparent to everybody in the SCIU department that Rudovsky wasn't in there for a bollocking. And it certainly wasn't for the sack, as Chapman had suggested. A few seconds passed before Miller stopped laughing at Rudovsky's insane coping mechanism for dealing with her negative thoughts towards her colleague.

"What's up anyway," asked Rudovsky. "You sounded a bit severe when you shouted me in!"

"Did I? Sorry Jo. I'm just feeling a bit lost with this case. I wanted to get your opinion on something, before the team briefing."

"Go on." Rudovsky looked pleased, it meant a lot when Miller asked for her input, and he seemed to be doing it more and more recently.

"Well, this is the latest note the attacker left last night, at the mill in Middleton." Miller handed Rudovsky a photocopy of the document. She glanced at the message. "MAKE THEM STOP KILLING THE POOR!"

Miller sat quietly until she looked up and met his gaze.

"What do you think he means Jo?"

"What do I think that the message means?"

"Yes. I'm missing something, I can't understand what the point is. I get it that the DWP are being extremely harsh on their claimants and its pissing people off. I know people can be a bit dramatic... but it's not exactly killing them though, is it?" Miller smiled, more out of exasperation than anything.

Suddenly Rudovsky looked annoyed. "Sir, are you being serious?"

"What... yes, of course I'm..."

"You don't know how many people are committing suicide because of these arseholes bullying them out of their shitty little bit of dole money? How many die within weeks of being found 'fit-for-work?"

Miller shook his head. His expression suggested that ignorance was bliss. Rudovsky was starting to turn the shade of red that Chapman had gone a few minutes earlier. She still lived on the same council estate that she'd grown up on. She knew first-hand the misery that the government's austerity scheme was causing. She saw it every day, the zombie dads, the depressed mums, the alcoholic grandparents. Rather than "pull themselves up by the boot-straps" as the government had naively, simplistically imagined the poor would do under their vindictive regime, those at the bottom of the pile had just given up. All hope was lost. They still had the same shit prospects that they'd already had, only now they didn't have money for a stamp to post off a job application form, or the bus fare to get to a job interview, or the motivation and confidence for either. Rudovsky was a passionate campaigner against the cuts, against austerity, and the persecution of the poor.

"Sir, there are four million kids living in poverty in this country. There are over a million families using food banks. People are being treated criminally right now, in one of the richest countries on earth. Its fucking despicable mate. It really is."

"But there must be some reason for it Jo, surely?"

"Do you know what, if that was the case, I'd probably understand it. But there is absolutely no logic behind any of it. It's just creating bigger, more serious problems in society. I wouldn't be so incensed if we actually saw some sort of a payback for these cuts. It feels like sabotage, what they're doing. The fact is, there's absolutely no advantage, the debt is going up faster under austerity than it would if the government was investing in these people. Their idea is simple. Kill as many of the poor as you can possibly get away with. Preferably before they have a chance to breed."

"Jesus, Jo, it all sounds a bit O.T.T!" Miller laughed mockingly.

"Fucking hell Sir, please tell me you're taking the piss? Have you not seen the doorways full of homeless people all of a sudden?"

"Well, yes…"

"You've seen the homeless camp down at Castlefield, you've seen them all getting off their heads on Spice in the middle of town, they look like something out of a horror film. There's a dead one found every morning. Sir, these people are the best example of what the government are doing. They thought that if they took their hundred quid a fortnight off them, they'd go and get a job. But they didn't, did they? They got made homeless, they started living rough, they blotted it all out by getting hooked on Spice and cheap cider. And now they cost a lot more fucking money to sort out than just fifty quid a fortnight." Jo was getting herself worked up. For the first time, Miller was starting to see just how deeply she cared about this issue.

"What do you think happens when a family lose their benefits for three months Sir? In most cases, their whole world falls apart. The rent isn't paid for three months, so the council start trying to evict them, mum and dad start losing the plot, start fighting and arguing, probably start stealing and drinking to deal with the stress, the kids start seeing their lives in tatters. In a lot of these cases, they break up. The worst thing is, it can be over something as little as not applying for enough jobs."

"But if they…"

Rudovsky interrupted her boss. She knew about this stuff, and could answer his question, without hearing him ask it.

"They have to apply for a certain amount of jobs per week. But there aren't that many new jobs coming on each week. So, the DWP make you apply again for jobs you've already applied for, or worse still, jobs that you haven't got the skills, or experience, or qualifications that the employer is looking for. They are just like sadistic, nasty bullies, they are being spiteful and horrible for the sake of it, just because they can."

"Is this true, though Jo. It all sounds like bullshit, to be honest."

"Put it this way, if you treated me the way they treat the claimants, you'd be sacked, and I'd be given a six-figure sum in compensation, and a promotion. It would be labelled as institutional bullying, harassment, intimidation. It couldn't happen anywhere else, but it's encouraged in a fucking dole office. Honest, it makes my blood boil."

"God, I can't believe how bad it all is. I just thought it was a bit of bullshit, brought on by a few pissed-off claimants who were fuming about losing their dole."

"Well, the guy who is carrying out the attacks, the guy who wrote this obviously doesn't think its bullshit Sir, does he?"

"No. Fair point."

"It's not bullshit. Here, my uncle has a scrap yard in Walkden. He advertised for an experienced breaker to work there. It was good money, he was paying about four-hundred quid a week. He had over two-hundred applications. Out of those two-hundred, three of them had the experience he was asking for in the job advert. Only two of them had the right fork-lift truck license. So, my uncle had one-hundred and ninety-eight people applying for the job, with no experience, and without the correct license. And the reason is, the Jobcentre are forcing them to apply for jobs they can't even do."

"I don't believe you! Sorry Jo, but it just sounds too far-fetched."

"Seriously Sir, ring HR now, ask them how many applications they get to work here, from people who don't have the right credentials and stuff."

Miller appreciated Rudovsky's help. He decided to humour her. "Okay." He leaned forward and pressed the speaker icon on the phone on his desk, and dialled switchboard.

"Hello, its DCI Miller in the SCIU, can you put me through to HR please?"

"Putting you through."

Miller expected Rudovsky to laugh, or at least grin. But she had a deadly-serious look on her face. She was genuinely fuming about this issue.

"Human Resources?" said the voice on the line.

"Oh hello, its DCI Miller in SCIU. I'm just hoping you can help me with a query I have."

"I'll try my best."

"Cheers. I was just wondering what the last job was that you advertised for the police."

"Well, we had a job advertisement which closed last Friday, and that was for an experienced dog handler."

"Did you get many applications?"

"Yes, we had over five-hundred applicants for that position."

"And how many of those applicants were suitable, may I ask."

"None."

"None? Why not?"

"Because they didn't fulfil any of the criteria on the job description. They were just Jobcentre applicants."

"But that's just a massive waste of time. Why would anybody apply for a job if they don't have the necessary qualifications or experience?"

"Is this to do with the DWP attacks?"

"It is, I'm just testing a theory out that one of my detectives has put forward."

"Well, I can assure you that we waste most of our time sifting applications looking for suitable candidates. This dog-handler job has an application from a guy who has only ever painted cars, and he's allergic to dogs."

"So, what's the point in applying? It's insane."

"Because he'll have to apply for so many a week, or he'll lose his money."

"And do the Jobcentre ring up and check?"

"Yes, they do it all the time. They are just wasting everybody's time. We tell them, and they agree. They know it's nonsense, we know it is, the poor buggers who just want a job know it too."

"God, that's so depressing. Right, thanks a lot."

"You're welcome, and good luck catching the guy who's attacking them. They might be annoying buggers, but they don't deserve what's happening!"

"I know. Right. Thanks." Miller hung up the call and Rudovsky nodded in agreement with the HR advisor.

"This is so fucking stupid."

"It's the tip of the iceberg Sir. It's not just at the Jobcentre, they are making life difficult for everybody on benefits. It's even worse for people who are on the sick. Seriously, the government are deliberately being twats, and they are relentless with it. It's the biggest scandal of our time, people are killing themselves as a result. A lot of people!"

"How many?" Miller was starting to feel extremely uncomfortable about this. He preferred things to be straight-forward, and this was starting to sound like a weird conspiracy theory.

"Thousands, Sir. It's all being swept under the carpet, as you would expect. But deaths of benefit claimants following direct interaction with the DWP are through the roof. There have been plenty of cases publicised, just put DWP deaths into Google, it doesn't take long."

Miller leant forward and opened up the web browser on his laptop. He typed the search phrase that Rudovsky had suggested, and sure enough, the search yielded over 5000 results.

"Bloody hell."

"These people are the most vulnerable in society. They're out of work, they're skint, life's nothing but a struggle, and then the dole stop their money because they've not logged into the DWP computer enough times that day. It's no surprise that so many are finding that suicide is the best option. Do you know, they say you can tell how civilised a society is, by seeing how they treat their prisoners. Well, the fact is Sir, criminals, locked away for doing bad things, they have much better lives than people on benefits. But if you watch telly, the programmes are all about people on benefits going away to Tenerife, and telling all the ones who are working, who can't afford Tenerife, that they're the mugs. It's truly sick what's happening."

"Bloody hell Jo, you're really pissed off about this aren't you? I mean, really."

"Oh yes, I am Sir. I hate stuff like this, bullying people. But I'll tell you what worries me the most, Sir."

"What's that?"

"I'm really worried that if we don't bring him in, the government will have no alternative but to stop the war on the poor."

Miller looked confused. That didn't make sense, following the passionate speech that Rudovsky had just made.

"But surely that is what you want? Isn't that what you go on your political marches for?"

"Well, yes Sir. But we try to achieve things peacefully. What message would it send out to the public if peaceful protests don't work, but paralysing innocent members of the public does? If you don't like something, attack people in the street and force the government to do a u-turn. Shit, it would cause pandemonium."

"Yeah, good point Jo. I hadn't thought of that."

"If this guy managed to get the government to submit, it would open the floodgates for martyrs from every cause imaginable to follow suit."

"Right, thank you Jo, very insightful and informative as always. Now, I need to get on with this team brief, and then I've got another press conference to do at eleven."

"You love it!"

"With the Chief Constable."

"Oh."

*****

On Twitter, Facebook, and via various news websites, a letter was going viral. It had been written by a DWP Case Manager. But it wasn't the contents of the letter which had riled the public. It was the fact that this letter had been sent to the Daily Mail, from a DWP e-mail address, in the middle of the biggest crisis to ever engulf the service, and the Daily Mail had simply ignored it.

Rather than make the story go away, the newspaper's decision to ignore the letter actually became the story, as the author forwarded it to several other news agencies. This shocking disregard for such an informed opinion led to a barrage of accusations. In particular, that this exclusive communication from a senior DWP employee told a different story than the one which the newspaper wished to present. In short, the newspaper wanted to portray the viewpoint that the DWP activities against the poor were justified, and long over-due. The letter, however, suggested that the DWP staff were not from that school-of-thought at all.

"Dear Sir, I wish to remain anonymous for professional, and in the current climate, personal reasons.

I, along with all of my colleagues, observe the current activities against the DWP with horror, but a sense of wonderment that the public, the press, and the police appear to be so surprised that these horrendous attacks have occurred. We are all fully aware of the pain that the claimants have been going through, we see the tragic consequences, and we are threatened with violence, every single day. We are routinely sent for training courses on how to deal with aggressive, abusive customers, and to courses on how to help suicidal people, where other people, in other industries would be sent on first aid courses.

At present, there is some very sensational reporting, and a desire to paint DWP staff as the bad guys in all of this; I wish to present an alternative point-of-view.

Nobody within the DWP is taking any pleasure from the way that we are being ordered to work. Morale within the service is at an all-time low, staff sickness, prior to this week, has been at an all-time high, and in my thirty years of service, I have never seen so many staff leaving, and so few applications to join.

But, we have to do what our managers tell us, just like any other worker, in any other industry. If the government instructed us that we had to give claimants an all-expenses paid trip around the world, we would do it. We have absolutely no control over government policy, just like a taxi-driver has no control over a drunk vomiting on their back-seat.

The reason that I am writing, is to ask the nation's reporters to tone it down, and present the facts. What is happening is not down to DWP staff deciding to be cruel, it is not down to any ideas that we have had. We are not responsible for this in any shape or form, and we have absolutely no control over the benefit reforms, just as we have no control over any other government policy.

Please, I implore you to keep this fact in mind when writing your reports. If you absolutely *do* have to pin the blame on somebody, then that person is the Secretary of State for Work and Pensions, as you jolly well know."

This letter was being shared across the internet, all around the world. The motivations of those sharing it differed. Some were keen to call out the inexcusable way that the media controlled the "balance" of the news. Others were desperately keen to stick up for the DWP staff. Others were just interested to hear the views from inside the DWP, and happy to pass on that view to as many people as physically possible.

This latest, sensational development was to be short-lived in the public's collective psyche however, as the story took on a completely new angle.

Chapter Twenty-One

The media centre at Manchester Police HQ was full, as had been expected. Members of the press were out in force to cover this morning's update, which was being presented by the Chief Constable, Sir Stephen Foster. It was rare that the Chief held a press conference, and the fact that he was doing so today told its own story. This was a matter of the greatest importance to Manchester Police, but nobody who was gathered could have anticipated what was to come. Even DCI Miller, who was sitting next to Sir Stephen on the raised stage area, was visibly shocked by what the Chief Constable had to say to the journalists, and to the viewers of Sky News and BBC News who were watching the press conference live at home.

The Chief Constable just got on with it.

"Good morning. Thank you for coming along today. The purpose of this morning's meeting is to make a direct plea to the man who has been attacking people who work at the Department for Work and Pensions. I am talking directly to you, whoever you are, and asking you to stop this right now. You have made your point, in the most violent manner, and you have caused appalling injuries that will make life extremely difficult and uncomfortable for four innocent victims." The Chief Constable paused and took a sip from his glass of water. He seemed in no hurry to continue, as he calmly considered the next part of his announcement.

"I need you to stop this. I want you to surrender, and hand yourself in. But, before you do, I want to explain that I understand your activity, and while I cannot comprehend how you can act so violently, and so callously, I do want you to know that I can understand to a certain extent, the anger that you must feel, the anger which has developed into this atrocious situation. You obviously have very strong feelings about the injustices that you wish to publicise, and I can understand how anger can manifest itself into mindless violence. Most violent crimes that we deal with in Greater Manchester are caused by anger."

He took another sip from the glass. "But let me tell you,

you are not alone. There are many, many people who share your anger, and your feelings of unfairness. But they do not go around hurting other people, causing such shocking injuries like the ones that you have caused. Here at Manchester City Police, I am the person who has to manage our police force. I have to manage every aspect of our work, from making sure that we have enough police cars, to ensuring that all of our bills are paid on time. Over the past seven years, I have witnessed the most irresponsible, short-sighted and frankly, shambolic decisions made by this government..."

There was an audible gasp around the room. This was extraordinary. The most senior policeman in Greater Manchester was getting something off his chest, and it was in the most unorthodox fashion.

"Due to the completely incompetent way that the government has been slashing the budgets of all public services, I am the man who witnesses complete chaos every day here in my city, as a direct result. I know of very serious incidents, including stabbings and rapes that my officers haven't been able to attend, because there were not enough officers on duty. I know of a violent assault which took place just last week, and we couldn't get a police officer to take a statement, because we had none available, and the victim later died, meaning that we will never know what happened, or how, or why. We will probably never bring the person responsible to justice, either. That makes me angry."

The Chief Constable looked around the room. He wanted that to sink in with the media, and the other police staff in the packed-out media-centre. Most of all, he wanted the viewers at home to get angry about that statement. A man was dead, and the police haven't done, and cannot do anything about it other than feel anger. It was an incredible thing to announce. But the Chief Constable didn't seem phased. He continued, talking calmly and concisely.

"This is the second largest city in Britain, we have a population of nearly three million people and on our vans it says that we are fighting crime, and protecting people. Well, to be perfectly honest, I think we should paint over those slogans, as they are meaningless. If I had any budget, I'd replace that phrase on our vans and police cars with "Just trying to muddle through."

There was an embarrassed hush in the room, but the energy levels were reaching fever-pitch amongst the reporters and technicians who were checking their kit to make sure that this was actually recording. Nobody could believe what they were hearing. It felt strange, it was like watching somebody digging themselves into a bigger hole, and not having the courage to tell them to stop. Everybody was just watching on, wondering if it was really happening. It could be read from the completely expressionless face of DCI Miller, who was sitting beside the Chief Constable, that he felt just as perplexed by this as everybody else. Judging by Miller's face, this had not been in the script. He looked unsure about which facial expression this announcement required, so he'd opted for one that looked as if his batteries had run out.

The Chief continued with his address to the attacker. "The truth is, I can't guarantee anybody's peace of mind, and I cannot run this police service effectively. The entire organisation is in total chaos. Morale is at an all-time low amongst my officers, all of our targets are being missed and there is nothing positive to say. Poundland shops have more police officers than I do."

He took another sip of his water. DCI Miller suddenly glanced left at the Chief, and appeared visibly shocked by this incredible public address. He returned his face towards the crowd, and resumed the vacuous expression.

"Not only have I lost twenty-per-cent of my front-line staff, I am also seeing a larger work-load, as my officers have to plug the gaps in other areas of public services that are being decimated by the utterly futile cuts. For example, as a result of Mental Health Service cuts, my officers are now spending a lot of their time dealing with hundreds of Mental Health Service Users, protecting them from harming themselves, and others, chasing them all over the district and trying to return them to their inadequate living spaces, knowing they'll be doing the same thing the next day. As a result of the DWP cuts, my officers are now spending huge amounts of their time dealing with homeless people, and the effects of their drug and alcohol abuse. As a result of the cuts to Youth Services, my officers are wasting lots of their time chasing gangs of bored youths who are hell-bent on causing trouble in their local communities with anti-social behaviour. As a result of the cuts to North West Ambulance Services, my officers are spending time looking after people who have been injured in accidents and falls at home, providing first-aid, care and reassurance until the ambulance staff finally get to the job, sometimes four or five hours later. I could go on, I could tell you lots of things about the crisis that we face, directly because of the irresponsible, and downright stupid actions of the present government."

Again, the Chief Constable let it hang a moment. He wanted these hammer-blows to really cause damage. After a few, long seconds, he continued. "You don't have to be Albert Einstein to see that when all my officers are off using the majority of their time doing these other agencies jobs, it leaves very little time for any actual police-work. I wouldn't trust this government to run a bath, let alone run a country."

This was unbelievable. It could be read on the faces of everybody in the room, including the police officers and police staff, that the Chief Constable had shocked them all with this incredible address. The Chief continued, talking slowly, calmly, and it felt exclusively, to the attacker. He sounded totally genuine.

"But now you have started attacking people who work for the DWP, it now means that my police officers are spending most of their time looking for you. They can't help the mental health service users who have been let down. They can't help the vulnerable people who have been let down by social services, or reassure the elderly people who are waiting for ambulances. They can't stop the homeless people kicking seven bells out of each other as the effects of their legal highs wear off. What I'm saying to you, is that it's a constant struggle, it's a nightmare situation for me, trying to manage this police force. Why am I saying all this to you? Well, it's because I'm trying to demonstrate to you that I understand what you are feeling so angry about. I know first-hand that the DWP Welfare Reforms are a complete waste of time and effort, and I also know that the DWP staff feel exactly the same way. They hate the cuts just as much as you. These futile reforms have added an extra burden onto my police service, as our officers are called to try and clear up the mess, attend the domestics and suicide attempts when a claimant's benefits are stopped for trivial reasons. These reforms will cost many millions more than they'll ever save. I know what's happening, and I'm agreeing with you, right now, live on TV, that it is wrong, and it has got to stop. I have with me a letter which I have written this morning to the government." Sir Stephen held up the letter. The photographer's bulbs began hissing and popping as they illuminated the piece of paper with bright flashes. It was written on headed Manchester City Police paper.

"It reads, Dear Secretary of State for Welfare and Pensions, I am writing to you because of the horrific attacks which have been happening in Manchester, against members of your department's staff.

Be under no illusion. This is your fault, and you should take full responsibility for this unacceptable situation. I implore you to call an end to the deliberate and callous activities that your department is carrying out against benefit claimants, with immediate effect, before any more innocent people are hurt.

Furthermore, I believe that you should resign from your position, as this crisis in Manchester comes as a direct result of your completely deplorable conduct in public office.

We are not allowed to treat people in our custody cells the way that you are making DWP staff treat members of the public. If you were a member of the public, you would be arrested under section 146 of the Criminal Justice Act, for hate crimes.

Enough is enough.
Yours Sincerely"

There was another audible gasp in the room, and Miller wondered if he had been one of the people who had gasped too. This was such an incredible speech from the Chief Constable, and it was clear to everybody in the media centre, and watching at home, or listening on the radio, Manchester's top cop meant every word. He'd had enough.

"So, to recap. I am as angry and upset about the government's conduct as you are. But I don't want another person being hurt. If you really are doing this, to bring about changes, then prove it. I want you to hand yourself in, I want you to call it off, and I want to get you the help that you need. Now let's put an end to it. It is not the DWP staff that you are angry with, it's the government. Please, show how much you care, and end this before you hurt another innocent DWP team member."

With that, the Chief Constable stood, very calmly and gracefully, and walked out of the media centre with DCI Miller following close behind. If Miller's facial expression gave anything away, it was that he was just as surprised by that remarkable outburst as anybody else.

The media staff were just as stunned by the sudden, unexpected conclusion to this unforgettable press conference. They'd all been absolutely positive that the Chief Constable was going to end the statement by offering his own resignation. That was what it felt that he was leading up to, as each new bomb was dropped. But no, he just wandered out of there like a man who really couldn't give a fuck any more.

Chapter Twenty-Two

The media were going mad for this story. Nothing like this had ever happened before, certainly not in recent history anyway. Plenty of senior officers from the Army, or the NHS, or other police forces had made critical remarks about the government once they'd retired, or resigned. They generally did it to grab a splash of publicity for their autobiography coming out.

But never before had a serving Chief Constable gone on the record with such a vitriolic and scathing attack against the serving government. It was simply unbelievable, and the media centre at MCP headquarters was quite literally full of people who were a little dumfounded and shell-shocked by the remarkable press conference they had just witnessed.

"You're watching the BBC News Channel, that was a live broadcast, and I'm quite lost for words after that. Let's listen again to what the Chief Constable had to say." The BBC news channel started the press conference again, from the beginning, presumably to give staff a chance to catch their breaths, and to provide the opportunity to have a discussion about how the BBC were going to handle this, from a politically neutral standpoint.

"Well, that's escalated quickly," said the News Editor of the BBC News Network. "How the hell do we put that back in the box?"

"Do we have to?"

"Do we want the Media, Culture and Sport down here, slashing our budgets again?"

"They couldn't... could they?"

"Well they cut us by eighty million last time. Come on, you know how this all works. We need to spin this. Somehow."

"We could frame it as a stunt, maybe it was a stunt?"

"In what way?"

"Well maybe the Chief Constable is playing a trick, showing some pretend empathy in order to appeal to the attacker's own compassion?"

"Yes. Genius. We'll run with that. Grab a leading psychologist to come in and provide expert analysis."

*****

"Bloody hell fire! Put the news on. Manchester Chief Constable has just committed career suicide live on the air!" Said one Tweet from the popular Twitter political correspondent Theresa Larkin-Milne.

"Well, I think the Chief Constable might be visiting the Jobcentre himself soon, judging by that performance," tweeted the BBC's political chief Jennie Hills.

"The Chief Constable of Manchester just promoted himself to the level of Manc God! He can now stand proudly beside Eric Cantona, Anthony H Wilson and Jack and Vera as a truly God-like Manc." This tweet was published by the Channel 5 presenter Wendi Kaye.

Reaction to the Chief Constable's relentless attack against the government's austerity policy was everywhere. The video clip had gone viral instantly, millions upon millions of British people had been campaigning against the cuts and the austerity programme for several years. It was music to their ears, and it felt like a historical moment. It was an event which was definitely worth celebrating.

The system was so badly broken, so ineptly managed that now, in the wave of this scary, disturbing crisis caused by the cuts, a senior member of British society had decided that enough was enough, and made the decision to call it all out for what it was.

It was exciting, and many people felt incredibly enthused by the manner in which the Chief Constable had spoken. It wasn't a rant. It was a well delivered, well considered statement of fact. He'd been calm, collected, and it felt as though he'd been speaking to just one person. Although his intention had been to speak directly to the attacker; in actual fact, what happened was that every single person who shared the same opinion about the austerity regime, felt that the Chief was talking directly to them. It seemed that now, finally, something was happening. It really felt that a damaging blow had been delivered to the government. And there was an insatiable appetite for more. Where was the next, devastating strike against this cruel, austerity-obsessed government going to come from, though?

Celebrities from Manchester were congratulating the Chief Constable via their Twitter and Facebook accounts.

"Don't fuck with the Mancs. They don't have the same rule-book as everyone else!" stated the former New Order bassist Peter Hook.

"Like Tony H Wilson famously said. This is Manchester. We Do Things Differently Here." Added Steve Coogan.

"I like how the Chief walked out of there like he fucking owned the joint. Just wish he'd kicked the fucking table over though!" Former Oasis frontman Liam Gallagher's tweet managed to hit 100k likes within half an hour. This was going viral, and everybody in the land was going to hear about the Chief Constable ripping the Secretary of State for Work and Pensions a new arsehole.

There was a great deal of Mancunian high-fiving going on. The people really thought that the Chief Constable's extraordinary outburst against the government was a memorable moment in history. It certainly felt that way. But the beauty of this, was that it wasn't a cheeky little dig, or a sarcastic swipe.

This was a full-on, in-your-face statement based solely on facts. An earnest, "heart-on-your-sleeve" statement which was going to be extremely difficult for the government to simply side-step or make light of. It was all based on reality, and delivered by a man that you would expect to be telling the truth.

The Chief Constable had lit the blue touch paper, and now, the few media outlets that were not under Tory control were absolutely determined to make sure that the inevitable explosions would be spectacular and unforgettable.

*****

"Oh my God Andy, what the hell? I've not seen you looking that awkward since that gay bloke asked you to dance with him at Carole's fabulous 50th." Clare Miller laughed to herself as she sent the text message. That press conference had been excruciating for Clare's husband, she could tell by the way he just stared straight ahead, wearing a completely neutral expression. And it had been made so much more awkward by the sudden ending. The Chief Constable's unforgettable tirade had caused such a stir that everybody forgot to ask any questions of DCI Miller, the man who was leading the man-hunt for this vicious attacker.

It was bonkers, but also extremely amusing for Clare. She would be able to rib him for weeks on this one, she was already planning to adopt Andy's vacant posture, and stare impassively ahead next time her husband said something she didn't agree with.

Her phone pinged with a text.

"That was the hardest ten minutes of my life. I couldn't nod, couldn't smile, couldn't do anything but stare ahead like a bloody zombie! I felt like laughing at one point, I got this really weird feeling that it was a prank, you know, Game For A Laugh or summat! Anyway, I think we might be getting a new Chief Constable soon."

"Lol. See you later. Don't forget my mum and dad are round for tea tonight. Would be nice if you could make it, I bet they're starting to think you're avoiding them! X"

A minute or two passed before Clare Miller got a reply.

"I am. X"

*****

"This is YOUR fault!" screamed the front page of the Manchester Evening News. The headline was laid out next to a notorious photograph of the Home Secretary for Work and Pensions, Ian David Smythe, tucking into his infamous fried breakfast, the one which he later claimed almost £40 in expenses for.

Beside it was a photograph of a queue of families outside Salford Food Bank. These two photographs were being used as a contrasting example of how wide the gap between the richest, and the poorest people in modern Britain, is. This was now the main story in Great Britain, and the internet news providers were all over it. It was a bizarre moment, because the number 1 story had already been the DWP attacks, and the search for the attacker. But that aspect was now less important, the hot topic was the row which was breaking out between the head of the Manchester police, and the government.

"Who's going to be signing on next?" Asked The Mirror's website, using the same photo of the millionaire Home Secretary with his bizarrely expensive fry-up, which had caused so much controversy because it had cost almost ten times the price of a cooked breakfast at any normal cafe. Next to it was a photo of the Chief Constable taken minutes earlier, as he delivered his blistering speech.

The Tory supporting Mail Online had a much more sombre headline, "Chief Constable Claims Horrific DWP Attacks are Home Secretary's Fault."

The Express kept things simple with "Political Row Breaks Out Over DWP Attacks."

The Star went with "Big Bro Hunk's Five-In-Bed Sex Romps."

On TV, the news channels were making the most of the political angle that this story now seemed to have taken. All of the main broadcasters were jamming the switchboard of the Number 10 Press Office, desperate to get a quote in response, or better still, a big, dramatic statement read out by the Home Secretary on the steps of Number 10 Downing Street, defending the benefit reforms. Or even better still, the Chancellor of the Exchequer coming out to justify the cuts to public services. The very cuts that the Chief Constable had explained were having disastrous effects on his organisation's ability to adequately police the metropolitan city of Greater Manchester.

There was a holding message on the Press Enquiry page of Number 10's Website which stated simply, and frustratingly, "Response to Manchester Chief Constable's Statement to Follow." This was the difficult part of reporting on a story of this nature, as there was only one side to the story in existence. The most experienced news editors and journalists felt that the reply wouldn't be long in coming. They knew that the government had to act fast if any attempt at damage limitation was to be successful. The longer Number 10 left it, the greater the risk of the Chief Constable's views gaining traction, and causing lasting damage on the people the government feared the most. The swinging voters. It was crucial that the government came back ASAP and "set the record straight" and it was expected that they would.

But in the backs of the minds of several senior media commentators, there was an excitement stirring. This government had stumbled and limped, looking dazed and confused from one crisis to the next. Their self-made disasters of the austerity cuts, offering the catastrophic EU Referendum, and then losing a healthy majority in a completely unnecessary "snap election" in 2017 had made this government the laughing stock of the world. They were nick-named "weak and wobbly" in response to their utterly bizarre decision to brand their lacklustre work as "strong and stable."

There had never been such a hopelessly shambolic shower of twits, idiots and losers in power since the beginning of Parliament as we know it, in 1707. Even the Queen, who traditionally remains politically neutral, poured scorn on the "snap election" fiasco, by dropping all of the usual pomp, and opening the new Parliament period dressed quite unsubtly as the EU flag.

Judging by the eye-watering ineptitude of their bungling ministers, who car-crash every single fiasco which the government are tragically involved with, it was quite a reasonable suggestion that they'd make a pig's ear of handling this, as well.

This really was a delightful prospect for the left-leaning journalists and media bosses, and it looked like yet another amazing opportunity for the other political parties to take the piss, once again, out of the utterly hopeless, disturbingly inept, but ultimately nasty government.

*****

"I'm not happy with how this is all starting to go, Jeremy!" announced one angry caller on BBC Radio 2's lunchtime phone-in show. The daily current-affairs programme attracted over five million listeners, and it seemed that today, they all wanted to get on air and say something about the Chief Constable's unconventional announcement. Tony from Cornwall was the first on the line.

"What are you unhappy with Tony?" asked the presenter.

"Well, it's all getting a bit daft. This Chief Constable should be sacked on the spot for that nonsense he was spouting earlier!"

"How was it nonsense, Tony?"

"Well, its, of course it's nonsense. It's not the Chief Constable's place to..."

"I'm asking you how it's nonsense, Tony?"

"It's total nonsense, and we all know it is!"

"No, I'm sorry, I don't know if it is nonsense. I'm asking you to explain to me, how is it nonsense?"

"Because its, all these cuts, these are not being done for fun, it's because the country is skint!"

"But *is* the country skint, Tony?"

"Yes, yes of course, why do you think we're having these cuts in the first place?"

"Well its odd that we seem to have plenty of money for new roads, and new railways, and new nuclear weapons. There's also money there to increase MP's wages by over ten-per-cent. The refurbishment of Parliament itself has been given the green light, and is expected to cost seven billion pounds. The deal the government have just done to bung one and a half billion pounds to the DUP party in Northern Ireland doesn't really suggest that we are skint. But, none-the-less, the government keep telling us that there is no money, and it's so bad that we don't have enough to keep a battered wives refuge going in Doncaster, or a special needs school going in Plymouth?"

"No... that's... you can't."

"Tony, if I asked you to come for a meal and a pint, and you said that you can't really afford it, because you're skint..."

"Yeah?"

"But you came along anyway, and bought drinks for

everybody in the bar, and ordered the most expensive dish on the menu, and then offered to pay for mine, as well..."

"Yeah?"

"Well I'd start to think that you weren't actually skint at all. But that you were just saying it, for some reason."

"You're changing the subject. All I'm saying is, that the Chief Constable was bang out of order, and he needs to resign for poking his nose where it isn't wanted."

"But, surely people *do* want to hear his views, especially his officers, and the people of Greater Manchester, and the DWP employees who must be going through hell right now?"

"But to say all that, about the cuts. Its diabolical."

"Tony, I'm not too sure why you have come on air today, if it was just to say that we need the cuts, then I'm afraid that leading economists who know a bit more about these matters than you or I do, have gone on the record saying that the UK doesn't need the cuts, that the cuts have done no good, that they have just caused endless, negative problems throughout our society, and damage to the economy, which is the worst performing economy in the EU. Can you remember what the cuts were supposedly for, Tony?"

"Yes, because we had no money."

"No, it was because the government wanted to get rid of the deficit. They promised in 2010 that there would be five years of pain, but it would be worth it, because by the time of the next election in 2015, the books would be balanced, the deficit would be gone, and everything would be beautiful."

"Exactly, that's the point I'm trying to..."

"But, that's not happened Tony, has it? The deficit has doubled. People are beginning to think that they were all conned. So, rather than coming on here, trying to rubbish the very serious claims that Manchester's top cop has made, perhaps you should go and find out why we've seen such severe cuts to all of our public services, yet the bill that these cuts were supposed to pay for, has not been paid. In fact it's actually doubled."

"Er... well I still think he was out of line, saying what he did. He has to go."

"Okay thank you, Tony there in Cornwall. I think he's been at the Scrumpy, as he didn't seem to understand a word I was saying there. Sandra in Milton Keynes, good afternoon."

"Good afternoon Jeremy, and I just wanted to say that I'm really proud of what the Chief Constable has come out and said today. It's one thing all the politicians arguing amongst themselves... but I think you get real sense of substance when a professional person of the Chief Constable's calibre, gives you the facts, warts and all, based on his experience. Fair play, and now it's time to call time on these idiotic cuts, and start investing in our country."

"But where will you get the money?"

"Borrow it. Print it. This government has borrowed more than any other in history, at the same time as cutting public services harsher than any previous government. Let's imagine that they are looking after our household bills, okay. They say, 'we're spending too much, so we're going to eat pasta for the next two weeks to balance the books.' Then, after two weeks, they've saved thirty quid on the food shop, so they celebrate by going out and buying a brand-new BMW."

The presenter laughed. "So, what's your conclusion Sandra?"

"My conclusion is that they are mentally ill, Jeremy."

"Okay, well, I'm not sure I agree with your choice of words there, but I think we all understand the point that you're trying to make."

Chapter Twenty-Three

Miller was sitting in his office. He was watching the Sky News output on his laptop, and the more he listened and watched the presenter's expert analysis of that morning's press conference, the more that he realised that the Chief Constable's words had created an unhealthy conflict of interest as far as this inquiry was concerned.

Sure, the political aspect, the cuts and the damage they were doing was a very important topic. But Miller felt that this had completely skewed the public's attention away from the very nasty, and very real danger that the attacker posed. Miller was pleased that the army presence was going to make things seem a lot more secure, and it was a very impressive move by the government.

However, the bungled attack that had taken place in Shaw, the previous night was extremely troubling for Miller, as this one, albeit unsuccessful thanks to the IKEA chopping board, had taken place outside a DWP employee's home. It meant that what Miller had believed to be the random attacks against any old person coming out of a DWP staff door, wasn't so random after all. The previous evening's attack brought a disturbing, chilling new angle to the investigation; The attacker knew who he was targeting, and he had even managed to track Stewart Grimley to his home address, and had stalked him as he went to the shops. This new development meant that the army presence could yet prove to be completely futile.

Miller was wound up, not least because he was shattered. He'd only had a few hours sleep, due to the two incidents the previous night. He was also stressed about the Chief Constable chucking a great big diversion into the middle of the inquiry. He decided that he was going to try and put the real story back in the news. The real story was that four innocent people were lay in hospital beds with unthinkable injuries. Injuries which had either maimed, blinded or crippled them. This was the only story in town as far as DCI Andrew Miller was concerned, and he hatched a plan to get it straight back on the news agenda.

"They've got Question Time for politics, for fuck's sake!" said Miller under his breath as he closed the Sky News page and opened up his e-mail folder.

He searched out his favourite reporter from Granada Reports, Mike Johnson, and started writing an e-mail.

"Hi Mike,

Got an exclusive interview with the first attack victim, Kath Palmer, for you. Its lined up for 3pm at Stepping Hill Hospital. It's yours and yours alone. RSVP.

Cheers

Andy"

Miller clicked send, and smiled as the reply pinged in his inbox within a minute.

"Hi Andy, wow, that's so good of you. We'll be there with bells on.

Much appreciated

Mike"

Miller smiled, he loved treating reporters to good exclusives, it had earned him a good reputation amongst many of the local TV and radio reporters. The "you scratch my back, I'll scratch yours" strategy worked well, and when he was in a tight-spot, such as this one, Miller could guarantee himself some valuable air-time, at the same time as making the local reporter famous on the national stage for a few hours. Now all he had to do was check that it was okay with Kath Palmer.

Miller rang the High-Dependency-Unit at Stepping Hill. He asked the Ward Sister if it was okay to bring down a TV crew to interview Kath, at 3pm. The Sister agreed, and so Miller asked her to check that this was going to be okay with Kath. A few minutes later, the sister was back, and confirmed that the interview could go ahead.

"Brilliant! Cheers. I'll see you soon."

*****

The SCIU team was currently swelled to its highest capacity since it had been formed a decade earlier. Usually, the Serious Crimes Investigation Unit gets by with around seven or eight detectives. But in recent years, since the police cuts that the Chief Constable had publicised so well, the SCIU had been scraping by with the bare minimum of five operational detectives, under the leadership of DCI Miller. However, this was not an ordinary enquiry, and the SCIU had gone from famine to feast, with almost 50 operational police officers drafted in, working on a variety of different tasks. The complexity of this inquiry demanded a number of separate enquiries, all rolled into one. DI Saunders was co-ordinating the team leaders of each group.

The key lines of enquiry were written on the incident room wall. Each team consisted of around six to ten people, and each team leader was a member of the SCIU's full time staff.

Rudovsky was leading the biggest group. There were ten officers involved with her task, which was to contact all of the DWP offices in the area, and learn about the noisiest customers. She instructed her team to quiz as many front-of-house staff as they could, and ask them all to talk about any customers who made a fuss whenever they came in. By that, she meant the loud-mouths, the gob-shites, the kind of people that they couldn't wait to get rid of as soon as they walked in the door. But it wasn't just aggressive or noisy customers that they wanted the names of. They were also looking for names of anybody who regularly expressed any political thoughts during their visits to the DWP front counters. There were certainly plenty of names coming up, and the task of eliminating all of these people was going to require plenty more police officers involvement if it was to be completed in a timely fashion.

Chapman was overseeing a rather more serious, but equally time-consuming task of reviewing all of the appeals that had been rejected over the previous two-year period. It was assumed that the perpetrator of the attacks was a local man, based on the fact that the attacks had all taken place within the Greater Manchester region, and there was clear evidence that the attacker knows his way around the places where he had struck. The appeals that Chapman's team had to review, were in respect to benefits being stopped in the Greater Manchester area. It was hoped that within this list of people, was the name of the attacker. This was a mammoth job, as the DWP computer suggested that over 36,000 benefits claimants had had their payments stopped for one reason or another over the previous 24-month period. Chapman was stunned, as were the rest of his team of eight officers who would have to sift through the database, and build a new list of potential suspects. The method which was being used was quite rudimentary, and required lots of "common-sense" decisions to eliminate the genuine, perfectly legitimate cases of benefit stoppages, and those which were obviously petty. There was a hell of a lot of people included in this list who'd had their money stopped for the correct reasons. One typical example was a "single-mum" who had forgotten to "declare" that her boyfriend, who earns over thirty-grand a year, was living in the home and that she wasn't a single mum at all, but she was in fact, just taking the piss. There were also thousands who had been caught working, whilst claiming to be unfit for work. But in amongst the genuine ones, there were plenty of examples that Chapman's team were looking for. One man had his benefits stopped for three months because he hadn't applied for enough jobs that week. His defence, which was ignored, was that he'd been in hospital after being run-over by a car. He had his money stopped for three months, and was definitely a contender for Chapman's list of potential suspects.

Worthington and his team were looking over the various CCTV footage clips that had been collected at each attack, and were investigating potential new sources of CCTV coverage by mapping the attackers escape route from each incident, and building a picture of where he eventually went to. The work was frustrating, and involved many hours of going into nearby shops and businesses, explaining what they were doing, and then checking CCTV sources for the time leading up to, and following each attack. It was frustrating, because nine times out of ten, there was absolutely nothing. But Worthington kept his group focused, and positive, by promising them that there was a full face shot on a CCTV camera somewhere. It was just a case of finding it. And that's what kept them all at it, the prospect of finding footage of the attacker reaching his car, and seeing the reg plate, or catching a glimpse of him with his hood down, and with the scarf taken away from his face. It would be case closed within seconds of finding this elusive footage.

Kenyon's task was door-to-doors and witness interviews. He was overseeing the small team of support officers who were going back to the witnesses, and starting the whole interview process again, in the hope that they would have remembered something that could be useful in trying to find out who was behind these shocking crimes.

The team's newest member, DC Helen Grant, had been put in charge of the team who were researching Facebook, Twitter and Blog posts about the benefits cuts. There were literally millions of comments and posts about the various sanctions and benefit suspensions, the decisions to declare people fit for work, even when they were in a hospice, dying. There was a bottom-less pit of Blog posts dedicated to the topic, written by people who were absolutely horrified by the situation that they were seeing. The blog-posts ranged in quality, from exceedingly good, well-written, balanced articles, to angry rants that didn't really manage to get the intended message across. But regardless of the quality, there was a never-ending ocean of them out there, and Grant's task was to find out who was out there, what they thought they would achieve by slagging off the government, and ultimately, whether they were capable of carrying out these attacks themselves. The team were concentrating exclusively in the local area, investigating the people who were publishing regular posts, and regularly making anti-DWP comments on Facebook and Twitter. It was felt, amongst everybody in this team of nine, that the attacker would have started this campaign of hate on the internet, before actually taking it on to this disturbing stage.

Saunders and Miller were overseeing the various team-leaders progress, and offering support as and where needed. Saunders was also running a very small team of four, who were tasked with building a database of all the DWP staff who have been sacked, or disciplined, or made redundant in the past five years. This database was also looking at all DWP employees who had raised any kind of grievance since 2010, when the persecution tactics were first introduced. From that database, it was hoped that any ex or current employees with an axe to grind about the "benefit reforms" would quickly be identified. This small team was working in tandem with a much bigger team at the DWP, who had been put on this task as a matter of urgency.

The mood was very positive, and all of the DC's who were running their own little teams were sure that they would figure this puzzle out very, very soon. The added advantage was that every single one of the fifty additional officers wanted to be the one who cracked the case, and would hopefully be rewarded with a full-time placement in the SCIU. With this thought in all of the temp officer's minds, the mood in the SCIU office was competitive, focused and way more professional than usual. This case was going to be closed very soon, everybody was determined about it.

*****

"Hello, pleased to meet you." Mike Johnson had a well-known face in the north-west area, he was on the region's TV news most nights of the week. Kath Palmer seemed genuinely happy to see him, despite the look of pain and misery on her face.

"Hi," she said. There was a permanent moisture in her eyes, it looked as though she was crying, constantly. Mike Johnson felt an overwhelming sadness for this lady. She looked so nice, but so sad and she was clearly in a great deal of pain and anguish. It was a stark reminder to the experienced news reporter, that this story was very, very dark, and the implications for those affected were catastrophic.

"I really need the man who did this to Kath in the back of a police van as soon as possible, Mike. That's why I've asked you here. This crap that the Chief Constable started spouting today is not helping me to catch the bastard that did this to Kath."

The tear finally rolled down Kath's cheek. She looked so depressed, she genuinely looked as though she'd had enough. Miller handed Mike a photograph of Kath, taken just a couple of months earlier, when she'd taken her Grandchildren to Center Parcs in Penrith for their summer holidays. She was happy, beaming, full of the joys of life. And now, that light in her eyes was gone.

"Don't worry DCI Miller, I will make sure this interview will put the criminal investigation back in the spotlight."

"Cheers. I just want people to see with their own eyes, what this bastard has done."

Another tear rolled down Kath's cheek, as she stared up at the ceiling.

*****

By tea-time, the press had made such a fuss of Sir Stephen Foster's lambasting attack against the current state of affairs in the UK, that the PM had no alternative but to come out of Number 10, and defend the government's record. There were more than a hundred press representatives crammed on the pavement, all of them were eager to hear what the British Prime Minister made of the Chief Constable's remarks.

But it was quite clear from the off that the PM was playing this another way.

"Good afternoon. Our country is currently in a state of deep shock. We are proud that we live in a peaceful, law-abiding country which is the envy of the world. Great Britain is a wonderful place to live, work and play. But it goes against everything that we stand for, when one individual decides to attack the very people who help to make this country so special. I am appealing to every person in this great country, to stand together, and show this cowardly attacker that we will not be beaten. We will not be bullied. We will not succumb to violence."

The PM stared straight down the lens of the BBC News camera.

"These are dark days for our country, unquestionably, but by standing united, we can overcome the darkness. I would just like to thank the police officers in Manchester for the valuable work that they do, and congratulate them on the professional manner in which they conduct themselves. The man responsible for these abhorrent crimes will soon be arrested, and it will be thanks to those officers, who put their lives on the line every day, to protect you, the British public. Soon, once our fine police officers have detained this wicked, cowardly individual, every person in this great country will know that this type of barbaric behaviour will not be tolerated in our society."

There was restlessness amongst the press pack. They could see that this was a statement filled with waffle, and no real substance regarding the Chief Constable's scathing attack.

"I would like to offer my sincere sympathies to those who have been harmed so violently, and I give my word to all Department for Works and Pensions employees, we are doing everything we can to protect you. And that won't stop, until this is over. Finally, in response to the Chief Constable of Manchester, Sir Stephen Foster's comments earlier today. I would just like to say that neither I, nor my cabinet, recognise the picture of Great Britain that Sir Stephen paints. I will be calling for an urgent meeting with him to fully try to understand the concerns that he has, and at that meeting, I will also explain that by working together, by remaining united, we can, and we will, succeed. Thank you."

*****

"Holy smoke! What on earth was that supposed to mean?" PC Steve Mosby was sitting in the police van with his colleague PC Joan Williams. They'd been listening to the PM's statement on the radio, while enjoying a doughnut.

"Well, I'm no expert. But in a nutshell, to me it sounded as though the Prime Minister told the Chief to shut up, denied that the problems exist, and then said that he's being called in for a serious bollocking."

"Shit."

"Well, that's how I heard it, anyway."

"Do you think he'll get the sack?"

"Dunno."

"It was nice for us to get a mention though, eh?"

"Yeah, lovely. It's a load of hot air though, isn't it? I mean, I'd prefer a pay rise in line with inflation to be honest. Thank me with a decent bloody pay-packet. Truck drivers earn more than us!"

"I know."

"How do they justify that? How do they justify that in our jobs, we run after burglars, split up fights, tackle people with knives, deal with rapists, murderers, junkies, paedos, drunks and yobbos all day long. And we earn less than a wagon driver who sits down looking out of a window all day. It makes me sick."

"Chefs are on better money than us."

"The people who work for the DWP earn more than our starting salary. A personal advisor in the Jobcentre takes home twenty-eight grand."

"Fucking hell. Twenty-eight grand just to stop people's benefits and do their heads in. I might apply!"

"Nah, you're too nice. You wouldn't be able to send someone off home with no money for three months, just because they didn't write down their job search paper work neatly enough."

"Nah, you're right. You'd have to be a special kind of person to do that, and sleep well at night."

"You'd let them all come and live in your house with you!"

"Ha ha, I wouldn't go that far Joan!"

The two PCs listened to the radio for a minute, as the broadcasters tried to make sense of the PM's statement. After a while, PC Steve Mosby spoke again.

"So, everything the Chief said, about the state of policing, the state of the country, is just being denied?"

"Yes, basically. That's all they do politicians, don't they? How do you know when a politician is lying?"

"Their lips are moving."

"Exactly. Right, anyway, pass me another doughnut."

Chapter Twenty-Four

Miller was back in the office by half-five, and was looking forward to seeing what the Granada man had made of the report with Kath Palmer. Mike had text Miller to let him know that the ITV national news were taking the package for their lead story. This was great news, and it was exactly what Miller had wanted to achieve.

Miller was also feeling positive about the buzz around the office. He'd never known it so busy, and everybody seemed to be going about their work with lots of enthusiasm. He turned his laptop back on, as he sat down at his desk, and noticed Saunders wandering across the office floor, towards Miller's office.

"Don't bring me bad news, Keith! I mean it." said Miller as his DI entered the office.

"What? I'm..."

"I'm feeling positive for the first time in ages, so I don't want you pissing on my chips!"

"I'm not, Sir, in fact, I've got very positive news."

"Excellent. Go ahead."

"Well, all of the various enquiry teams are making great progress, we're seeing some very interesting results from the Blog team especially. I'll tell you what though, considering how little you hear about this DWP stuff in the news, it's shocking to discover how strong the feelings are on the internet!"

"Yes, well there's a simple explanation for that. Eighty-per-cent the mainstream media is owned by a few billionaires who are big pals of the government. Think of Richard Desmond, Rupert Murdoch, David Barclay, Fred Barclay, Jonathan Harmsworth. Between them, they control people's access to news. They refuse to write stories that paint their mates in a bad light, because the government do all sorts of sweeteners and deals that make their lives easier, and make them even richer, like not making them pay their tax. In return, the Tories get an easier ride in the press and on TV news shows."

"It's so depressing, how the system works. How is it possible that newspapers can manipulate the news? It doesn't seem right."

"No, well, it's *not* right is it? But it's all changing now, the internet has opened it all up. The total control they had a few years ago has been massively diluted. And not before time! That's why their character assassination on the leader of the opposition failed so badly in the election, people are starting to think for themselves. There are still a frightening amount of gullible people out there, who believe everything the Mail and the Sun tell them, though. But with the internet, most people are waking up to the fact that their political beliefs are based on what the newspaper editors told them to think."

"Yes, well, anyway, I've got a breakthrough."

Miller leaned forward. "Seriously?"

"Oh yeah. I've worked out the link between the victims. I know how the attacker is choosing them!"

"Fucking hell Keith! You come in here and start a dull conversation about the bloody media, and then drop that on me! Come on, tell me the rest!" Miller's face had lit up. He knew Saunders was about to pull a rabbit out of his hat, as he always did.

"Well, it's not water-tight, there's one victim that doesn't check-out in this theory... yet. But I'm still working on it."

"Go on Keith, mate. What's the theory?"

"Okay, well, you know how we keep hearing that the victims are all so nice, all lovely people?"

"Yeah..."

"Well, I thought it was a bit weird that nobody who is a bit of a bell-end has been attacked. That it's only nice people. I mean every workplace is like a pair of trousers, it has at least one arsehole in it, doesn't it?"

"No comment. Go on..."

"Well, here's the thing. Kath Palmer, and Jason Brown, the first two victims from Stockport are well regarded by everyone. It didn't stack up. But I did a bit of digging, and guess what I found..." Saunders placed a photocopy of a news article on Miller's desk. It was a Manchester Evening News story, which featured two very cheerful looking people holding a giant cheque. It was made out to RSPCA Stockport, and it was worth

£803.45.

"Is that…"

"Yes, Sir. Kath and Jason, the first two DWP employees who were attacked, and who also run their building's annual charity events."

"Fucking hell…"

"This is how the attacker has chosen them. That article was published two months ago, it was in the Manchester Evening News paper edition, and is still available online on the M.E.N website."

Saunders smiled at the expression on Miller's face, as he pulled a separate news cutting out of his folder, and placed it before his boss.

"The lad from Hyde Jobcentre, Gary Webster, presenting a cheque for six-hundred quid to Tameside Age UK." Saunders opened his folder once again. He placed another press cutting on Miller's desk. This one was the victim from the previous night, the one who'd had a lucky escape thanks to his IKEA chopping board, Stewart Grimley. In the photo, he was presenting a cheque to representatives of Dr Kershaw's Hospice. There were plenty of smiles, as Stewart handed over the cheque for £1,268.71.

"Holy shit." Said Miller.

"The only one that doesn't check-out was Margaret Wilkins, the lady from Middleton Jobcentre. She hasn't done any charity work, and she doesn't come up in any other news articles. I think he must have just thought that because she was standing in the staff room, that was enough."

"Jesus Keith, you're an absolute genius, you know you are! How do you do it?"

"Well, you know…" Saunders grinned as he began placing more cuttings on Miller's desk. Photo after photo, article after article of smiling, happy DWP staff members, with their names printed beneath the photo, handing over cheques to local charities.

"And who are these ones?" asked Miller, not quite grasping the point.

"By my calculations Sir, these are his next victims."

*****

Granada Reports broadcast the exclusive interview with Kath Palmer at 6pm, and it went national on the ITV national news at 6.30. The heart-breaking news package aired for seven minutes. In the hard-hitting report, and interview, the reporter Mike Johnson started the report with a warning. He said "viewers will find this report extremely upsetting." He had deliberately dropped the usual "some viewers might," warning. As far as he, and the Granada producers were concerned, this report, on this unforgivable act of evil would upset everybody who saw it.

The report began with footage of the merciless attack. CCTV images were shown of the attacker, and Kath Palmer at the bus stop. She was standing in the shelter, minding her own business, reading her Kindle. Behind her, about two metres away stood a man with a hood concealing his identity. He was just leaning against the glass.

Mike Johnson added his voice-over to the very normal looking CCTV feed.

"Last Tuesday evening, Kath Palmer, the mother, the wife, and grandma that you can see here, was standing at this bus stop, reading a book, when this man changed her life forever."

In the CCTV footage, the road suddenly became clear, all the traffic had passed by. There were no pedestrians in sight. The man stepped forward towards Kath, lifted an axe above his shoulder, and then swung it with incredible force. The TV screens in the Granada region faded to black, forcing viewers to imagine the next frame of the footage. The black screen stayed in vision for several seconds, accompanied by silence.

Eventually, the black screen faded into a much happier image, a photograph of Kath laughing with a friend, then, a few seconds later, another joyful moment was shown as a photo of Kath appeared, she looked happy, and content as she cuddled the family dog. A few seconds after that, another photo appeared, this time, Kath was dancing at a do, looking like she was having the time of her life.

The screen went black again, and slowly faded into video footage of Kath now, lay flat in her hospital bed, crippled by that stomach-turning, senseless act of violence. The lady looked thoroughly depressed, and beaten.

"Kath, it is so upsetting to come here and see you in this condition. How are you feeling?"

She had tears in her eyes. They seemed to be there permanently.

"I'm trying to stay positive. That's all you can do, isn't it?" She tried to smile, but it didn't look convincing, as a tear rolled down her cheek and betrayed her brave attempt to make it look as though she was coping.

"What are the doctors saying to you about your injuries, Kath?"

"Well, you know, they're trying to keep my spirits up, they're so lovely. But it's pretty obvious that I'm going to be lay down in this position for the rest of my life."

The reporter looked shocked. There was an awful, long, difficult silence. To his credit, Mike Johnson kept it in his report. It really hammered home that even a TV news reporter could be lost for words.

"What would you like to say to the man who did this to you, Kath?"

Kath thought hard about the question. She was staring up at the ceiling tiles. Eventually, she spoke.

"I'd just... I just want to say that, you need help, love. You need to get help. Please, just hand yourself in and the police, the authorities will be able to help you."

There was another heavy silence.

"And what are you focusing on now, Kath?"

Without hesitation, Kath replied. "The ceiling." She managed to smile at her wise-crack.

"I mean, what's keeping you going right now."

"Nothing. Nothing is keeping me going." Kath began openly crying, and she didn't look anything like the happy, fun-loving lady in the photographs that the programme had just aired. "The worst thing about this is, I've been saving up to take my grandchildren to Florida. They've been so excited, and I just can't bring myself to tell them that we can't go now. I can't."

Another tear appeared on the screen, but this one was Mike Johnson's.

*****

Miller had missed the ITV News and Granada Reports broadcasts, as he'd raced up to his boss, DCS Dixon's office to request extra officers as soon as Saunders had revealed his exceptional news.

"Andy, you're at your strongest capacity. There's literally nowhere else to seat additional officers!" Dixon was surprised by the request. Miller explained the newspaper cuttings to his boss. "We need twenty-four-hour police protection on all of these people. One of these people is going to be next, Sir."

This was a staggering development. The thought that the next victim was smiling back from one of the newspaper articles on Dixon's desk, was extremely disconcerting to both senior detectives.

"There are thirty-six people there. We need to work out an action plan of how we are going to guarantee their safety, whilst laying in wait for him to come after one of them. Now that the army are guarding the DWP buildings, and based on the fact that Stewart Grimley was attacked yards from his home, we have to make the assumption that he is going to be attacking them at home from now on. This is a massive head-start on that."

"Andy, I know..."

"But the big job is finding enough armed response officers to man thirty-six addresses, whilst staying hidden and discreet. If he gets a sniff of this, he'll stop, and disappear. We can't muck this up. We get one shot at this. And I need thirty-six armed officers on duty twenty-four-seven, until this evil little prick presents himself."

Dixon stared hard at the various pictures, then up at Miller. "This is going to be a big problem, Andy. I don't think we can..."

"Sir, I'm not having another DWP employee being hurt by this sick fucker. So, phone the Chief Constable, and tell him to arrange support. He can call in favours from neighbouring forces, if needs be. We'll be able to borrow some bodies from Cheshire, Merseyside, Derbyshire, West Yorks, South Yorks, Lancashire. Pretend it's the Tory party conference in Manchester again, we somehow managed to find thousands of extra officers for that, didn't we? I'll tell you now, Sir, there's absolutely no way we are playing Russian Roulette with a single one of these faces."

"Okay, Andy, I'll see what I can do."

"Well, I'm holding a team briefing in fifteen minutes time. I suggest you ask the Chief Constable to attend."

*****

Miller's team-brief started at 18.30. He wanted the entire team to know about this game-changer, at the earliest opportunity. He didn't want to wait until the following morning to share this momentous development. He was pleased to see that Dixon, and the Chief Constable had made it.

"Okay, guys, listen up, this is the breakthrough we've all been waiting for. And its Detective Inspector Keith Saunders who has worked his magic once again! So, without further a do, I'll hand over to our wonderful DI, and he can explain."

Saunders stood before the fifty or so colleagues, and felt a little nervous that the Chief was stood there, looking extremely pissed off. It took Saunders ten minutes to bring the entire team up to speed with his discovery. He began flicking through the file of potential victims, in front of the group.

"There are thirty-six people in here. One of them is going to be crippled, or maimed, or blinded by this sick bastard if we don't intervene. That's everything, for now. I'll hand you back to DCI Miller."

Saunders walked away as a round-of-applause broke out, instigated by Rudovsky and Kenyon. He looked like he was cringing.

"Top man Keith," said Miller as everybody settled

down. "Okay, well, this is a phenomenal discovery, and if we play our cards right, it's just a matter of time until we bring him in, and avoid any further attacks. I'd like, if I may, to ask the Chief Constable to let us all know what plans he has to staff this operation, as it is going to be massive."

The Chief Constable looked irritated by Miller's unexpected invitation to speak, but he stepped forward anyway.

"Yes, very good detective work there DI Saunders, very impressive. Now, as you'll all be aware, we are extremely short-staffed at present, and the pressure on our workforce is unprecedented, as we deal with our own work, and the resulting short-falls of other public service agencies such as social services, mental health and so on and so forth. This operation is going to take an enormous amount of resourcing, and that is what we are working on presently. My staff are currently in the process of contacting neighbouring forces to see if we can loan some officers. I have cast the net wide, between Scotland and the Midlands, from coast to coast. I will have more information tomorrow."

"Thank you, Sir." Said Miller, aware that he'd annoyed the Chief by dropping him in it, but completely care-free about the matter. Nobody ever gets anything from brown-nosing, except shit on their lip. "Our major head-scratcher now is regarding the thirty-six people that DI Saunders has identified as being at immediate risk from this attacker. I propose that before any of us leave here tonight, we contact each and every one of them, and explain the information as we know it."

"Sir, that's going to terrify them!" It was Rudovsky, predictably, who had shouted out.

"Yes, Jo, I know that. But I'd rather we are honest, and tell them, so they can make every effort to protect themselves, than to do nothing, and then try and cover it all up after they've been attacked."

"What are you going to say?"

"What are *we* going to say, you mean? We need to do this as a matter of the utmost urgency. So, you can all listen to me do the first one, and then a lot of you will have your own call to make."

Miller pulled the first article out, and held it up. "DI Saunders has even been on the DWP HR database and pulled up their contact details. Okay, everyone, gather round, and listen carefully to what I say to this potential victim." Miller held the picture up again. It was another charming photograph, with a huge cheque made out for £692.96 to "Child Action North-West." The cheque was being held by a very good-looking brunette in her forties, her name was Tina Mooney.

Miller's phone was on loudspeaker. He dialled Tina's number and it started ringing. She picked up after a few rings.

"Hello?"

"Hello, is that Tina?"

"Yes?"

"Tina Mooney?"

"Yes. Who's that?" She sounded very friendly and bubbly.

"Tina, my name is Detective Chief Inspector Andrew Miller, from Serious Crimes."

"Oh, I know you, you're leading the investigation, aren't you?"

"Yes. Yes, that's right. Well, that's what I'm ringing about, actually."

"Oh?" Her voice wasn't so bubbly now. There was a definite sound of fear creeping in.

"Well, are you sitting down?"

"Aw God! What's..."

"Are you sitting down, Tina?"

"Yes."

"Well, I'm afraid that there is some very important information I have to share. We are worried that you may be targeted by this attacker."

Tina broke down, understandably, and began crying and sobbing. A man's voice could be heard. "What's up? What's up, love?" The man sounded very concerned.

"Tina, listen to me, you're going to be okay. This is good news, because it means we can protect you. The only thing is, I can't..."

"Who is this?" shouted the man down the phone.

It made Miller, and several of his officers jump with fright.

"I'm DCI Miller, are you Tina's husband?"

"Yeah. What've you said to her, she's shaking like a shitting dog."

"I'm still in the middle of explaining it. Can you put her back on, please?"

The man could be heard comforting his wife. "Here, love, simmer down, eh? This DCI wants to speak to you. I'll put it on loudspeaker. You're alright."

"Tina?" said Miller softly. She still sounded extremely distressed.

"Yeah?"

"Can your husband hear me as well?"

"Yeah."

"Yes, I can," confirmed the gruff sounding man.

"Okay, listen to me, very carefully. Do you organise the charity events at work?"

"Yeah…"

"Well, we've just discovered, in the past few minutes, that the victims of the attacker are also the charity co-ordinators."

"Oh, for… what a sick bastard…" sobbed Tina. Her husband was comforting her, telling her that she was safe.

"But this is excellent news, because it means that we know who he is going to be going after, so we can protect those people, as well as arrest him the next time he attempts to hurt somebody." Miller thought that he sounded reassuring, but it wasn't him who had just been told that he was on the attacker's list of people to seriously harm.

"I can't believe this…"

"Now, listen, Tina, this is so important, so please listen to me incredibly carefully. Nobody can know about this. Just you, and your husband. You must not tell a soul, because if this gets out, and the attacker hears that we're onto him, then you will be in far greater danger."

Tina let out another sob, but her husband seemed to be agreeing with what Miller was saying, he could be heard encouraging her, and saying things like "makes sense," and "good idea."

"Now, the first thing that I want your husband to do is lock your doors, and close all the curtains in your home, in every room. Can you tell me when he's done that please?"

There was a couple of minutes of heavy-breathing and sighs of exasperation and fear. Eventually, a door opened and Tina's husband said "done."

"Okay, brilliant. Right, now you are going to have a plain-clothes police officer at your home anytime. They will be very discreet, and you won't know that they are there. I don't want you to answer the door, or step foot out of your house, until we say that it's okay. That goes for your husband as well, okay?"

Both voices agreed.

"Now, as I said, it's absolutely crucial that this stays a top secret. Please don't tell anybody, not even your mum. It'll all make it a better story for them anyway, once we've nicked this sick bastard. Okay?"

"Okay, yes, I think I understand," said Tina. "Just stay in, don't answer the door. Don't tell anybody. Until further notice."

"Correct, and stay positive, because this is the safest you've been since the attacks started. We're just going to wait for him to show up, and we're going to take him down."

"Okay, well, thanks..." Tina sounded completely stressed and confused.

"Save this phone number, and if you need anything, just call me straight back. Okay?"

"Okay. Thank you."

Miller ended the call, and looked around his huge team. "Right, let's get on with it. Write this down on your pads. Main points, number one, they have to keep this top secret. No drama on Facebook, no phone-calls to best friends, no mention to anybody except husband or wives...they need to be totally silent about it, or they are going to make matters worse. Number two, they lock doors and close all curtains and blinds, and they stay in the house, and they don't open the doors under any circumstances. Okay?"

"Sir, what if there are kids in the house, or teenagers?"

"How do you mean?" asked Miller of one of the new faces.

"Well, I've got teenagers. Asking them to keep anything quiet is a complete waste of time. If they hear about this, it'll be all over Snapchat and Insta and all the apps they use. They're millennials, Sir, they'll want to make it all about them."

"Good point. Okay, write this down. Kids must not be informed. The only people that are allowed to know are husbands and wives, stroke spouses. Really emphasise this point. Okay?"

There was a loud cheer of agreement.

"Sir, was it true about a plain clothes officer being outside?" asked another.

"Yes, well, I mean, it will be when we get one round there. But in the fullness of time, I mean within the next twenty-four hours, there'll be armed response officers guarding every single address. Any more questions?" Miller looked across his team, and smiled when he saw that there were none. "Okay, everybody who wants to make one of these unforgettable phone calls, come up and take a press-clipping, and don't forget to thank Saunders for also supplying their phone numbers. Great job Keith!"

*****

An hour later, the job was done. Every one of the thirty-six potential targets had been made aware of the situation. The responses had been overwhelmingly different from the employees. Some of the DWP charity liason staff had been very relaxed and calm about it all, grateful that they were now under police protection. Others were not so rational, and quite a number had required Miller or Saunders to get involved with the calls. Eventually, by 9pm, Miller dismissed his team, and thanked them for their excellent input today, and for also staying late to finish this task off.

It had turned out to be an extremely positive day, especially considering the difficulties presented by the Chief Constable's unhelpful comments. Miller was still incensed that the Chief had hijacked this ongoing inquiry to score a few political points. But it was done now, and the Granada and ITV news interview should by now have returned the public's attention to the sheer nastiness of the attacker, rather than the debate around the cuts.

Miller sent the list of the 36 names and addresses to Dixon, and the Chief Constable, to be distributed around each police station. Miller left the ball in their court, after ensuring that he had covered his arse for any future court hearings, saying "please make sure that all of these people, and their home addresses are given round-the-clock protection. I cannot stress highly enough that they are all in very, very serious danger at this moment in time. Many thanks."

Finally, this was coming together, and once again, it was DI Saunders who'd made the break-through.

"Right. Bollocks to this, I'm going home!" said Miller as he shut his laptop down.

But, he wasn't going to get very far, as news was about to reach him that the attacker had just been caught outside a DWP employee's house.

Chapter Twenty-Five

A 999 call came in requesting urgent police assistance at 9.32pm. The address was York Street, Glossop. Reports were sketchy, but basically, somebody had spotted the DWP attacker outside their home, and he'd been hit with a baseball bat. The call was being made amid great confusion, panic and adrenaline, and it took several minutes for the emergency services call-handler to calm the woman on the phone, and get her to speak slowly, calmly, and succinctly. It was worth it in the end, as the information became clearer.

The attacker had been hanging around in the shadows of a ginnel near the back-yard of a terraced property. He was wearing his usual disguise of dark clothing, and his hood was up, concealing all of his face and head. The home-owner, Kelly Taylor had been phoned, only an hour earlier by an SCIU officer, and warned of the danger she could be in. Thanks to the phone call, she'd been quick to spot the man from her bedroom window.

Her husband Mike, armed with a baseball bat, had sneaked out of the front door of the property, and had crept silently up the street, around the side of the houses, and around into the ginnel at the rear of the street.

"What the fuck are you up to, you sick cunt!" shouted Mike, as he ran into the ginnel.

The man had been leant against Mike and Kelly's back gate, looking at his phone. Upon hearing the sound of Mike's booming voice, the shadowy figure dropped his phone with fright, and began legging it as fast as he could. He was just a bit too fast for Mike Taylor, but Mike had managed to land a couple of blows with the bat, hitting the would-be attacker around the head, and on his back, around the rib-cage area. They were good, well landed blows, and Mike was surprised to see the guy carry on running. Mike managed to keep up with him for about twenty yards, determined to get another swing in, but once the attacker had gained a couple of metres distance, he started throwing wheelie bins over as he passed them, and Mike had to give up the chase. He was gutted, and instantly regretted the snap decision of shouting out as he'd ran into the ginnel. He had no idea what had made him do that.

The police presence on this normally quiet little street, in one of the quietest little towns in the Greater Manchester area, was unprecedented. The entire road was jammed with police cars, vans, tactical aid units, dog vans. The blue revolving lights certainly brightened up this normally dark, unremarkable little street. The entire back alley, or ginnel as the locals call it, was sealed off with POLICE LINE – DO NOT CROSS tape, and Kelly and Mike were being spoken to by specially trained officers.

Miller arrived just after ten pm, he'd raced to the scene in his car, mindful of the fact that his unmarked CID car was zooming up the very same motorway that he'd walked across a few days earlier, following the attack in Hyde. His Vauxhall Insignia was touching 100mph as the M67 motorway gave way to the A57 at Mottram, and he altered his speed accordingly.

Miller was absolutely delighted with what he found at the scene. The attacker had dropped his phone, which was still lay in situ. Miller had the feeling that this was all he needed to find out who the attacker was. The phone would most probably be logged into the attacker's Facebook page, too, if experience was anything to go by. It felt like a gift from the Gods, and Miller couldn't wait to see what delights the forensics team would come up with. Miller was feeling great, he was so hyped up about this unexpected, but brilliant development, mainly because the attacker had been given a good smack with the bat, and that the only damage done was the harm done by Mike Taylor's baseball bat, which was now being examined by forensics staff.

Miller went into the house, and saw the couple. Kelly was upset, she was trembling and talking really quickly to the police officers, and her friend from across the road, who'd come to sit with her. Mike Taylor looked like he was dealing with the after-effects of a massive adrenaline rush, his leg was bouncing up and down on the spot, and he was breathing heavily. He was getting on a bit, probably late forties, early fifties. Certainly a bit too old to be running around whacking people with a baseball bat. But Miller was glad that he had done.

"Now, who is it I have to speak to about carrying an offensive weapon?" asked Miller. He smiled widely, and it took Mike a few seconds to see that Miller was just having a bit of fun.

"Ha, shit, you had me going there..." said Mike. He smiled widely too, and stood up to shake Miller's hand. "You never know in this day and age though, do you?" he asked.

"No, you don't! But seriously mate, well done there. I think you've possibly cracked this case for us."

"No worries. I think I cracked his head open as well. I just couldn't believe he carried on running. He'll have a fair egg on his head, and I bet I bust a few ribs for him as well." Mike looked pleased with himself.

"Seriously. Did you hit him hard enough?" asked Miller.

"Oh yeah, you should have heard the clunk noise. He's definitely got an empty head."

"Well, that's brilliant. We'll hopefully be pulling him in anytime soon. This egg on his head, and the bruises on his torso will be extra evidence against him."

"Where do you think he's gone?" asked Kelly. Miller could see straight away that she was scared of him coming back.

"Don't know. The helicopters up, all of Manchester's police dogs are out, trying to sniff him out. But I know one place he won't be going again, and that's here! He didn't get a very warm welcome, did he?" Miller was trying to calm the DWP employee down. "So, quite an evening, eh? First we call you to warn you to be vigilant, and an hour later, your husband has given us our first decent piece of evidence!"

Kelly smiled, and looked admiringly at Mike. "I'm going to have to start calling you Bruce Lee!" she said to Mike.

"You mean Bruce Willis, you narner!"

* * * * *

Glossop is not the best place to try and escape from, when all of Greater Manchester's police officers are after you. The famous, bonny looking market town is the last stop before Greater Manchester gives up its boundary to Derbyshire and

Yorkshire. Glossop is the last place you can buy a Greggs before Sheffield, 25 miles away on the other side of the Pennines. The infamous, dangerous road which takes you there is called the Snake Pass, named as such for its dreaded bends and twists.

Due to its location on the very edge of the city's boundary, it was extremely fortuitous for the police that the DWP attacker chose this address out of the thirty-six. It was probably the stupidest decision since David Cameron called the EU referendum. There was a far greater opportunity of capturing this individual, based purely on geography. Manchester police had put South Yorkshire police on alert, requesting a road-block for all vehicles travelling into Sheffield from the west, so if he had gone that way, he was driving straight into a trap.

Similarly, road blocks were set up at the traffic lights at Mottram and on the various other B roads out of town. All escape routes from Kelly Taylor's address were covered. Put simply, if this man was driving, he'd better have had his toe to the floor, headed towards Manchester, from the minute he reached his car. Otherwise, he was bound to be caught up in a road-block anytime now. All cars, coming in or out of the area were being stopped, details of all occupants were taken down, the vehicles and their boots were checked. Each vehicle took several minutes, so it was extremely good that this had happened so late at night, the only time of the day that the traffic is calm going through Glossop.

Other officers, who hadn't been assigned road-block duties, were given the task of driving all around the town, checking all parked vehicles for occupants, looking underneath vehicles, inside and behind commercial bins, and inspecting all other obvious hiding places. Once a certain road, avenue or industrial site had been checked over, they were radioed through to the control room, and crossed off the list. If the attacker was still in Glossop, the Manchester police officers were determined to catch him. Every single one of them wanted to be the one who nicked this despicable individual, and receive the Queen's Police Medal for distinguished service.

This was a full-swing, major police operation, and nothing like this had ever happened in Glossop before. This normally sleepy little town was buzzing with people who were desperate to know what was going on with all these hundreds of police officers and vehicles zooming around. The police were checking all the streets and all the bins, lifting man-hole covers, and there was no escape from the roar of the helicopter circling above, shining its giant torch down on back gardens and all potential hiding places. It was very exciting stuff for the locals, especially the youngsters.

Members of the community were filming the activities on their phones, and publishing the footage to Facebook and Twitter and Instagram, and some were even sending theirs to the newspapers and TV news channels. Glossop was the last place you'd expect to find this kind of frantic police activity.

The problem for the local community was that nobody really knew what was going on. There were plenty of rumours flying around, and most of the rumours accurately suggested that it was connected to the DWP attacks. One or two in the know, realised that the hub of the activity was centred around Kelly Taylor's house, and that she worked at Glossop Jobcentre. But other than that, there wasn't very much more to say, and the rumour-mill was in overdrive. This was the worst thing, when major things were happening in the community, but there was no way of finding out what it was, so many of the community members resorted to that old northern saying. "If in doubt, make summat up."

Glossop Memories Old and New page on Facebook was bursting with comments and suggestions.

"Can't believe it, you know that Kelly from number sixteen, she's been stabbed in her feet."

"That sick bastard has just killed a girl from Glossop Jobcentre, I've heard."

"She isn't dead, I've just had a fag with her. They've caught the attacker as well."

There really was a galaxy of falsehoods and fake news, and many people from the local community were becoming extremely concerned. Somehow, one person managed to write a comment that pretty-much summed up the situation.

"I've found out what's what. This man who'd been

doing the attacks was waiting outside someone's house and he's been battered, but he's got away. All the police are looking for him now. DON'T APPROACH!" This comment got 76 likes, and once the word started to spread about this particular version of events, the excitement and curiosity began to turn to fear. If this was true, it basically meant that there was a mad-man, who cripples people, roaming around Glossop, injured. It wasn't good news by any stretch of the imagination, it was the stuff of nightmares.

The police presence seemed to grow and grow. There were literally hundreds of police vehicles driving around in convoys. It looked as though all of Greater Manchester's officers had been sent down to Glossop, with one job in mind. Bring in the DWP attacker. But as the time wore on, it started to become clear that they'd missed him. He wasn't here, he wasn't in Glossop.

Several hours passed with no news from the authorities, and tensions were really starting to reach fever-pitch in the small, close-knit former cotton and wool manufacturing town. Once the helicopter had retreated from the area, the deafening roar of the rotor-blades was not missed by anybody.

But despite the relative peace and quiet that the chopper's absence brought, the loss of the aircraft made the public feel even more vulnerable. The annoying sound, it turned out, had been very reassuring to the community.

It was turning out to be a very stressful, and scary night at the foot of the Snake Pass. Slowly, but surely the colossal police presence began to thin out, as other jobs and priorities came in, and the vans and cars were despatched to shouts back home in their own towns and on their own patrols around Greater Manchester. By 1am, it was all starting to look and feel like a massive anti-climax.

*****

DCI Miller had been back in the office since 11pm, his choices had been to stay in Glossop and co-ordinate the search for the attacker, or go back to HQ and see what he could find out about the amazing find of the attacker's phone. He learnt shortly after stepping foot in his office that he had made the right choice. He had the attacker's phone, which wasn't locked, as well as his finger-prints, all over the screen. It was even logged into the owner's Facebook profile. Saunders took enormous delight in showing these extraordinary exhibits to his boss.

"Tell you Sir, if this one had brains, he wouldn't have enough to blow his nose." Said Saunders, with a great deal of satisfaction and amusement present in his voice. Miller blinked and turned to his junior colleague.

"What, Keith, that doesn't even make sense?"

"What doesn't?" asked Saunders, scrolling through the attacker's Facebook page, seemingly oblivious to what his boss was saying.

"What you just said. About blowing your nose. Anyway, can't this guy just pop on a PC or another device now, and kick you out of his Facebook page?"

"Nah, I changed his password to TescoBigBoobs006. He's not guessing that!"

Chapter Twenty-Six

The mood was electric in all of the newsrooms up and down the country. As scoops go, this one was amazing, and none of the broadcasters or journalists on the night-shift could wait to get this sensational development out there. Britain's most wanted man was now, about to become Britain's thickest, dumbest idiot of all time.

Curtis Kennedy was the name of the man who had inflicted those absolutely abhorrent injuries on those poor victims. Kennedy's photograph had been published via a police press release, along with the details that the police had managed to gather from his phone, and especially from his Facebook profile page.

"Have you seen this man?" asked Sky News.

"This is the face of the DWP attacker. Curtis Kennedy, who police are seeking in relation to the horrific attacks in Manchester." Said the BBC News presenter. "In a dramatic new development this evening, police have recovered the attacker's phone from outside a DWP staff member's home in Glossop. It is believed that he was waiting outside the property, waiting for an opportunity to attack the home-owner. But the attacker had been spotted, and whilst escaping, Curtis Kennedy left his mobile phone at the scene. The advice this evening, is do not approach this man, as he is very dangerous and is believed to be armed. If you have any idea where this man is, or if you have any information about him, please phone the number that has just appeared on your screen."

*****

"Britain's Dumbest Psycho!" Screamed The Sun's front-page, alongside a photograph of the most-wanted man in the land. The police had deliberately chosen the least flattering image of Kennedy from his Facebook profile, to use as the official press pic. It was a picture of a pale, solemn looking youth, aged about twenty, looking like he was caned. He looked poor, and as though he had a bad attitude, and that he probably called himself MC Sick Rhymz or something equally as depressing.

Not to put too fine a point on it, the young man looked like any other generic chav, just another bland, paltry member of the idiotic Adidas North Face army. He certainly didn't look like a man who was running a perverse campaign of evil against DWP workers. He didn't look like the master-mind behind the UK's most audacious and callous attempt to make an extremist style political statement about justice and fairness.

Instead, he looked like the kind of person who limped along the street with his hand down his tracksuit bottoms, holding his genitalia, in the misguided belief that this bizarre, unhygienic spectacle made him look "gangsta peng." Indeed, the only impression that this extraordinary activity leaves on eye-witnesses is a strong desire to never shake hands with these imbeciles. Or use a door handle after them.

"This is the evil, cowardly piece of scum who attacks old ladies from behind, and yes, he's on benefits." Read the by-line.

The story had been absolutely massive prior to this extraordinary development. Now, there was nothing else to report on in the whole country. All TV, Radio, Online and Digital Media companies were tackling this development from every angle. At the heart of this journalism was the urgent need to uncover all of the information that they possibly could on Curtis Kennedy's background. The other key objective was spreading the word as far and wide that this man needed to be found, and stopped.

"If you see this man, phone 999" was the simple message, and in fairness to the press, it was everywhere. Smart-phones, Kindles, PC's, and basically any device that had an internet connection had pinged a message to its user about this "BREAKING NEWS" development. The key message was, get this evil little scrote off the streets.

Curtis Kennedy was born and raised on the gigantic council estate between Hyde and Glossop, called Hattersley. The estate was built to rehouse people from the slum clearances of Manchester in the 1960's. As row after row of rotten, decaying terraced street was pulled down around the city, these brand new, spacious council homes were supposed to be the perfect solution to solve lots of problems that stemmed from those damp, cold, miserable, crumbling terraces.

But it wasn't all plain sailing. Many of these new developments led to the "us and them" mentality which blights society today. The biggest mistake that the town planners made was to build these estates in the middle of nowhere. The feeling of isolation became a reality for many people, who had been ripped away from family and friends in their communities. The lack of jobs in the area and the lack of police resources so far away from the town, was a recipe for trouble here, and on so many similar "over-spill" or "sink" estates throughout the UK. It was the kind of place that people like Curtis Kennedy just fell into the world of petty-crime, anti-social behaviour and public self-molestation.

Within Curtis Kennedy's local community on the Hattersley estate, a mile or so east of Hyde town centre, the idea of this well-known young dickhead being involved with the most serious crime in years was met with a great deal of derision.

"Is this a fucking prank?" asked local resident, Chardonnay Bradshaw of her Facebook friends, when sharing the BBC News story. Her comments box went mad with similar expressions of contempt and disbelief from people all over the Hattersley and Hyde community. Curtis Kennedy was a little scumbag, nobody was prepared to dispute it. But this, this was just completely stupid. Riding stolen mopeds into the canal was more this guy's league.

"Not being funny, but I've seen this kind of thing before, they can't find the actual real person who's doing the crimes and that, so they just pick a random name out of the hat and stick it on them. There's videos about it on Youtube."

"I fucking hate Curtis Kennedy! But this is total balls mate, I'm not gonna lie."

Similar discussions were taking place more publicly on the Manchester Evening News' Facebook story. Dozens upon dozens of comments were making a mockery of the situation, and of Kennedy himself.

"Mate, this guy couldn't tie his shoelaces until he was

eighteen. Fuck off with this bullshit!"

"If Curtis Kennedy is responsible for those attacks, I'm Elvis Presley! The little fanny couldn't fight his way out of his duvet. You need to delete this off your page before he comes and eggs your Gran's house!"

"I used to teach Curtis Kennedy at Hattersley High, and I'm quite prepared to put my reputation on the line and state quite categorically that this is the most bizarre case of mistaken identity I've ever heard of. I'm so convinced by this, I've just phoned Manchester police and shared my views."

The staff at the Manchester Evening News, as well as other reporters and presenters from other local media organisations such as BBC Radio Manchester and Granada TV were beginning to see an unusual trend in these comments. It was extremely unusual for a story to get such a strong reaction from the community, in fact, it was unheard of. Something just didn't seem right with any of this. The M.E.N were the first to add an air of caution to their own reports, by suddenly adding phrases such as "it is believed by police" and "the information supplied to us by the police suggests," to the end of each paragraph.

Something just wasn't right.

PART TWO

Curtis Kennedy was a very well-known young man in the area where he was brought up. He had quite literally pissed everybody off in the local community. From authority figures such as teachers, council staff, social workers and police officers, to ordinary members of the public. As the streets of Hattersley became unsafe for him to roam, due to the fact that so many people wanted to kick his head in, he began roaming other districts with his day-saver bus ticket. He had become one of Tameside's best-known bell-ends, and was avoided by practically everybody who'd previously met him across the borough. He found the same reaction from people wherever he went, whether it was to Tameside's main hub of Ashton, or around Hyde, or Stalybridge, Dukinfield, Denton. He'd even started making himself known as a total melon in Manchester itself, his attempts at selling weed, and acting like a ten-quid gangster in Piccadilly Gardens had earned him a few more enemies to add to the never-ending list. Wherever he went, his reputation as a fucking nugget had reached unprecedented levels.

Around a month before Kennedy was linked to the DWP attacks, he made the biggest error of judgement of his chaotic, twenty-two-year life. He robbed a local dealer at knife-point outside Pete's Chippy in Hattersley. Kennedy had relieved the guy of his weed and a few hundred pounds, threatening to "chop your little fingers off." It wasn't much in terms of quantity, it was only an ounce or so, but the consequences turned out to be much worse than Kennedy could have ever imagined. The dealer was an old school associate of Kennedy's, and as this individual wasn't particularly "hard," Kennedy saw him as a soft target, somebody that he could make a habit of robbing. But the dealer's supplier had different ideas.

Kennedy was awoken that night by his mum's front-door going in. Two massive black men wearing all black outfits had taken the door off its frame in the middle of the night, and were calmly walking around the house, switching all the lights on, and saying "Curtis! Curtis!" in a really soft, almost playful way. It was terrifying. His mum was screaming, and his sister was kicking off, shouting all sorts of racist abuse at the two men. They were massive, at least six-feet-five tall, they were built like SAS soldiers, and they looked the part too, both were at least twenty stone of brick-shithouse. They were very scary men, and the fact that they were so calm, and were talking so softly made their presence all the more sinister.

"Curtis! Come on out mate, let's have a look at you," shouted one of the men, trying to drown out the noise of Kennedy's family. He had a broad Manc accent, possibly city centre, Moss-Side sort of area.

"You better get the fuck out my house now dickheads, or some real shit is going down, you get me?" shrieked Kennedy's older sister, Madison, standing at the top of the stairs in just her knickers and bra, wobbling her head from side to side.

"Not going nowhere Princess, not until we've had a word with Curtis." The calmness was totally unsettling.

Just then, Kennedy's bedroom door opened and he walked slowly onto the landing. Madison shot him an icy-look of hatred, before going into her own bedroom, slamming the door so hard that the whole house shook.

"Stop slamming my fucking doors!" shouted Kennedy's mum, obviously forgetting the seriousness of her front-door being lay in a heap at the bottom of the stairs.

"Yo, what's up mans?" asked Kennedy, using his black accent.

"Come down here, and we won't jump up and down on your jaw until its hanging off your face." The man was speaking so calmly, he made it sound as though he was asking for a light for a cigarette.

"I'm coming man, what's it look like I'm doing? Chill your bean yeah?"

"Shush now, or I'm going to push a cactus plant up your bottom."

The two scary intruders laughed loudly as they saw that Kennedy started pissing in his pants, as he walked down the stairs. His light-grey, fake EA7 joggies from Cheetham Hill were turning a shade darker around the groin area.

"What the fuck's up with this?" asked one as they high-fived. Both men laughed loudly. This was priceless.

"Go and get changed Curtis, you're not getting in the boot of my car with all that squish running down your legs man. Go on, hurry up."

"I'll go and stand outside, make sure he doesn't try and make his way through the window." Said the other man, quietly. The first one, who'd done all the talking so far let out a massive laugh again, as though he'd just witnessed the funniest moment in his life so far.

Kennedy's mum was now standing at the top of the stairs. She looked scared, and stressed, and frail. She was only young, late-thirties, but her life with Curtis Kennedy had clearly taken its toll.

"Don't hurt him. Please! He's special needs that lad. You can't hurt a window-licker, can you?"

"We can do whatever we want, when he's robbing our friends at knife-point. Didn't even wear a mask or anything over his face. I see what you mean about him being a not-right. Anyway, tell him to hurry up." The remaining black guy had really big, gentle looking brown eyes. He looked like a very nice man, and he sounded very calm and patient. But it was pretty obvious that he was a gangster, and that Curtis had messed up in a really big way, this time around.

"Oh, I'm going to bed. Can't be doing with this lot at three-in-the-morning!" Kennedy's mum turned and headed into her own bedroom. Kennedy reappeared, with another pair of pants on, they were filthy, and it looked as though he'd just raided the dirty washing basket to find them.

"What's all this about then blud?" asked Kennedy, trying to make this sound trivial.

"It's about you nicking our weed, and our money. So, pop your shoes on, so we can take you away and teach you a lesson, Curtis."

Kennedy began wailing, and screaming. It sounded as though he was being spun around the room by his ears. But he wasn't, he was just terrified. He'd heard of these two before, the Cole brothers. They looked after security for a number of high-profile people in the Manchester area. They were not the kind of blokes that you wanted to piss off.

The first black man grabbed Kennedy, hoisted him up in the air and onto his shoulder, then started carrying him out of the council house, and towards the all-black BMW. Once he reached the car, he pressed a button on his key-fob and the boot opened.

"Here, lie down in there. And don't touch anything."

"Fucks sake man!" protested Kennedy, but it fell on deaf ears. The man just slammed the boot shut, and moments after that, both doors were opened, then closed and the car pulled away. The Kennedy household was left in peace, but without a front-door.

*****

The Cole brothers had a great deal of fun driving their BMW around with Kennedy in the boot. They'd screeched around roundabouts, flinging him all around the boot. They'd built up speed on the dual carriageways, then slammed the brakes on, whooping with delight at the sound of Kennedy's skinny little body crashing against the metal work in the boot.

"Alright, fuck off now!" he'd shouted. His pathetic pleas for mercy were met with more explosive sounds of laughter. Kennedy decided that he just needed to put up with this bullshit until they got bored, and let him go. But the two massive black men had different ideas.

After around thirty minutes, the car pulled up, and one of the men got out. Kennedy could hear a big chain being pulled, followed by a heavy, metal, banging sound. It was like a girder being scraped along the side of the car, followed by what sounded like a heavy gate being opened. Footsteps came back towards the car, and the car door closed again, then the vehicle started moving again. And then it stopped, and Kennedy realised that the gate that had just been opened, was being closed, and locked.

Once it was locked up, the footsteps returned to the car and it pulled away slowly. Less than a minute later, the car stopped, the engine was switched off and the hand-brake was pulled on. Both car doors opened, and slammed shut. Kennedy was glad that this was finally all over, and he could go back home now.

The boot opened, and just as Kennedy was about to speak, he felt a bang in the face, and nothing else. He'd been knocked out with an expert blow to the temple. The two men pulled him out of the car, and one of them threw him onto his shoulder, whilst the other closed the boot. They walked across the car-park in silence, and into the steel, reinforced doors of an old red-brick cotton mill. Once they were in, and the doors were closed, they started talking.

"Are we just leaving him here then?"

"Yeah, Marco said just lock him in the dungeon, and he'll sort it tomorrow."

"Then what?"

"Then, I'm going to get a kebab roll, extra salad. What are you up to?"

"Nowt, if we're done, I'll get off. I'm ready for my bed."

"Fair dos."

After a short while, the two enormous blokes reached another solid steel door at the end of a long corridor. It took a few seconds to undo the gigantic padlock, but once it was unlocked, the door was pulled open to reveal what could only be described as a medieval prison cell. It was a small, cold, dark room. There were no windows, no toilet facilities, no lights. In the corner was a disgusting, damp looking mattress which looked as though it had dried blood stains smeared all over it.

The man who was carrying Kennedy on his shoulder stepped inside, and placed him down on the mattress. Before retreating out of the foul-smelling dungeon.

"Night night, sleep tight, don't let the bed bugs bite."

The big steel door was slammed shut, and the huge padlock was noisily reinstated.

*****

Curtis Kennedy seemed to have a very short attention span, and various doctors and teachers had tried to put his behaviour down to a combination of two factors.

The first of which was the condition commonly known as ADHD, attention deficit hyperactivity disorder. This condition affects a lot of people in society, and the severity of the symptoms varies from person-to-person. One person with ADHD may simply struggle to sit still and retain information. Another may be completely hyper all the time, and unable to control compulsive urges, such as shouting out at inappropriate times, saying inappropriate things and generally being "irritating" to others. Curtis Kennedy definitely suffered with the latter version.

But to make matters worse for him, Kennedy also has a condition called ODD. It stands for oppositional defiance disorder. Put simply, it's a compulsion to do the opposite of what you are told. If you tell a child with ODD that they must sit quietly and do their homework, then you can guarantee that they will make a lot of noise, and rip up their homework book, even if they had been really looking forward to doing the work. Even if the work had been their idea in the first place. An ODD sufferer has to take the opposite stance, and it always ends with the sufferer making life harder, rather than simpler, for themselves.

It was certainly the case with Kennedy, that he made life hard for himself. It was as though he had no concept of doing things in a simple, straight-forward way. Indeed, if he had carried on with the doctor's appointments, he might have been given some medication that would help him with this unfortunate combination of anti-social behaviour conditions.

But today, as he sat in this dark, smelly, scary room, the only thing on his mind was getting out of that place. There were no thoughts beyond that. He didn't have any great desire to get back home, or get away to a certain place. He just wanted out. He could hear a lot of activity, people walking around, laughing and joking. There was the faint sound of a radio playing. Every so often, Kennedy could hear a familiar song playing. There was beeping as well, every now and again, it sounded a bit like an alarm-clock. Kennedy's mind was racing with ideas and thoughts of where he was. His very first thought was that he'd been locked in an old disused electricity substation. The kind of which he'd climb onto the top of as a child, and win bravery kudos in the local community for jumping off, "stood up."

Kennedy drifted off into a light, anxious sleep, but was soon disturbed by the banging of a chain against the cold, steel door which was keeping him prisoner. A loud, heavy sounding lock was removed, and after a few tense, scary, nerve-racking moments, the door swung open. Once his eyes had adapted to the light, Kennedy was surprised to see who was standing there to greet him.

"Wakey wakey, rise and shine!" said a cheerful looking man. It was Marco MacDowell.

"Fuck…"

"Aw God, your breath stinks you smelly little scrotum!"

"Soz… I'm…"

"Is it true you had a little accident last night?" asked Marco. He threw his head back, laughing loudly.

"Well, I… yeah… pissed myself!" Kennedy looked petrified. He couldn't believe that he was being held by one of Manchester's most feared gangsters.

"That's fucking priceless! You rob one of my boys at knife-point, acting like Billy big balls, and then you piss in your pants like a toddler! Can't wait to tell everyone up on Hattersley about this!"

Kennedy just stood there. He looked humiliated, and in normal circumstances, he would give something back. He certainly wouldn't stand there looking down at the floor, trembling.

"Where's my money and my tu-sheng-peng?"

"Dunno…"

"Well, you're going to be gutted about that little stunt, aren't you? Because you're my little bitch now, and you're going to work that debt off, and it's going to take a fucking very long time you little dick nose. Do you understand?"

"Yeah."

"And the fucking Mayor of Hattersley will give me the freedom of the shit-hole for taking you off the streets for a wee while. So, in a way, you did me a favour nicking my drugs and my money. Do you agree?"

"Yeah."

"Good. Right, let me show you around. Do you see this room?"

Kennedy turned and looked at the cold, rotten room that he'd spent the night in. With the light coming in through the open door where Marco MacDowell stood, he could make out that it was a mouldy, damp old store-room. There was a tree growing out of the brickwork in the corner. The mattress was filthy, it genuinely looked like it had been involved in a death, or a birth. It was a very, very disturbing place.

"That's your living quarters."

Marco stepped away from the door and gestured Kennedy out. He stepped forward, but looked reluctant, as though he was expecting a good hiding. But Marco didn't touch him, he turned and started walking along the corridor. "Come on, follow me. I'll take you down to the stores and we'll get you some overalls. Can't have you working for me in those disgusting clothes. What size shoes are you, anyway?" Marco was just walking along, talking casually, as though this was just a new employee's first day.

"Sevens."

"No problem, I'll get some size seven work-boots ordered in for you." Marco pushed open two huge swing doors, and held them until Kennedy followed through. The sudden, pungent smell of skunk cannabis was overpowering. The heat in the place came as a welcome relief after that cold, damp room he'd just come from. "Right, here we are in the main factory. This is where you're going to be working off your debts."

The place that Marco was talking about was quite literally a factory. It was the entire floor of an old Victorian Mill, easily the size of a football pitch. It was set out with rows upon rows of cannabis plants, hundreds, if not thousands of them, all growing healthily under a very professional looking set-up of bright lights.

"You're going to need sun glasses on, working in here. This is the miracle of modern technology, LCD lights. Since these babies were invented, growing weed has become very cheap. That's why pretty much everywhere you go in Manchester these days smells it smells like Bob Marley's bedroom! It's all thanks to all these LCD lights, and my factory." Marco started walking along the first row of plants. He stopped and inspected the flowers of one. "Do you like a chuff yourself?" he asked.

"Nah. Makes me paranoid." Said Kennedy.

Marco laughed loudly. "Have you got ADHD?" he asked.

"Yeah, I think so. Summat like that."

"Yeah, that's the trouble with ADHD. Hyper people can't handle a drug that settles most people down. It makes them even more hyper in their brains, and that manifests itself as paranoia and psychosis and shit like that. I've been reading up on all this."

Kennedy wasn't sure how to behave around this guy. Not only was he one of the most feared men in the area, who Kennedy had just unwittingly crossed, in an extremely bad way. But he was talking to Kennedy as though they were old mates. It was very weird. Especially as he was famed for being involved in the disappearance of a lot of scary people. Kennedy started wondering if they were all in here, working for him.

Suddenly, a fork-lift truck came through some clear, plastic curtains, and beyond the curtains, Kennedy could make out that there was another factory, just like this one. The bleeping noise that had been driving him mad all morning had been coming from the fork-lift. Its driver was wearing a hi-vis jacket, and looked as if he was fully involved in his work. One thing was for sure, this was not a mickey-mouse grow house. This place was being run like a professional, multi-national company, complete with Health and Safety work-wear.

"What am I going to be doing?" asked Kennedy, after finally plucking up the courage.

"Glad you asked that. You're going to be my new watering assistant. What that basically means is…"

"Watering the plants?" asked Kennedy, growing a little in confidence.

"Bingo! You're bang on! Right, let's go and get you some breakfast, you can get a shower and freshen up. We'll get you some appropriate work-wear and then you'll start your training."

"Nice one." Kennedy was starting to think that he was going to like this new job.

"Oh, and seriously, if you make any mistakes, if you fuck a single one of my plants up, you'll be put to sleep and set in concrete that day, and then you'll become an upright support beam in the new town hall they're building in Ashton. Do I make myself clear?"

*****

Kennedy's first day in the role of watering assistant was exhausting. The constant, relentless heat in the factory was intense. The work was simple enough, all he had to do was walk up and down, constantly spraying a fine water mist over each plant. That was it. It was interesting for the first three or four plants, but soon after, the novelty factor began to wear off, and Kennedy began to realise that he had seriously fucked up this time. His mind was racing with conflicting thoughts and questions, such as how long will he have to do this for? How could he escape? Will he be stuck here forever?

His hand started hurting after the first hour. The constant squeezing on the spray bottle was giving him cramps. An hour after that his arm was dead, and his shoulder felt as though it was popping out of its socket. The only respite he got from squeezing that trigger was a trip to the sink to refill the bottle every five minutes. He had never felt happier than when another worker came over and told him to stop spraying.

"It's break time!" He announced, with a wide grin. Kennedy followed the other guy into a small room in the corner of the factory floor. Inside, there were three other men, and a KFC bucket meal.

"Two pieces and one chips. We share the gravy!" said the guy, opening a big bottle of Pepsi and then pouring it into the four paper cups. "It's the best day Thursday, KFC. On Monday and Tuesday its Farmfoods meals. Wednesday we get a chippy, Thursday a KFC, and Friday we get a McDonalds. It's always stone fucking cold though." The guy who was talking seemed alright, thought Kennedy. The other two were just silent, and they looked like they weren't to be trusted.

"How come you work here?" asked Kennedy, as he grabbed at the chicken and chips.

"Got involved in something that I shouldn't have. Turns out I was set up, selling things on Marco's streets. Been working in here ever since!" The guy took a bite from his chicken leg. Kennedy wanted to ask how long that had been, but he realised that he didn't want to know. He could handle the idea of working here for a short time. But he didn't want to know if it was going to be longer than that.

"What have you done wrong, anyway?" asked the other worker, once he'd swallowed his chicken.

"Oh, I robbed this dealer. I didn't think it through properly. Last night the Cole brothers came and took me mam's front door off."

"Knob head!"

"I know, yeah."

"Are you in the dungeon?"

"What's that?"

"Marco puts new starters in the dungeon for the first few nights. It's a freezing, stinking little shit-hole."

"Yeah, yeah, last night, I was put in there. It were freezing."

"Well, he'll let you come and sleep in the bunks in a few days if you keep your head down and blend in. But if you step one-foot wrong, you'll go straight back in the dungeon. He doesn't fuck about. There's no second chances or any of that bullshit here."

"Fucking hell. It'd be easier doing time."

"I know yeah. But Marco knows that prison doesn't work. He says he rehabilitates offenders in his own way, so they will never piss him off again."

The rest of the break time passed slowly, and quietly. It was nice to just have a rest from the heat and the smell of the growing room, as it was known. After around half an hour, a bell sounded around the building, and the three men opposite Kennedy jumped up and headed straight out of the rest-room.

"What's up?" asked Kennedy, worried that there was

a fire or something.

"Break time is over. Back to work. No more talking until next break."

"When's that?" whispered Kennedy as he followed the men onto the factory floor.

"Five hours. Beef and Tomato Pot Noodles. Now shush, if you're seen talking, you'll get a kicking you won't forget. If you're seen talking after that, you'll be part of a missing person enquiry that never gets solved."

*****

Curtis Kennedy had never held down a job before. Not a real job anyway. He'd done various stints doing community work for the Probation service as punishment for his anti-social behaviour. But he never really lasted, the Probation officers would let him go home as they couldn't be arsed baby-sitting him all day, and he just wound the rest of the group up with his negative energy.

"You can get off if you want, Kennedy," they'd say after half an hour. "I'll put you down for your hundred hours." It was a very polite way of telling him to fuck right off.

"Nah, I'm alright." He'd say, as he got on with walking along the canal tow-path kicking dog shit into the water.

"No, honestly mate, here's a tenner. There's a bus in five minutes."

Kennedy was an absolute nightmare to be around, and it was mainly down to his ADHD. But he was also a very antagonistic character, so it was a very unfortunate combination of characteristics, and it made him universally unpopular wherever he went. He had applied for a few real jobs, which actually paid money, but his applications weren't exactly conventional. By the age of 19, he'd given up on the idea of a job, and learnt how to get by taking other's people's stuff and selling it. Whether that was phones, trainers, bikes or drugs. He seemed to have no conscience about it, mainly because he blamed everybody else for the problems in his life. If somebody had a new I-phone, it was because they were a spoilt bastard.

So, he'd take it away, and punch the owner. It's worth pointing out that Curtis Kennedy never took anything off anybody who was bigger than him. He preferred to choose easier targets, young kids walking home from school, women with children.

Occasionally, he'd underestimated his target, and ran away crying after receiving a good beating. But most of the time, he ran away laughing as his victim picked themselves up from the floor.

This new job, working as a watering assistant came as a massive shock to the system for him. He had never stayed on his feet all day before, and he felt as though every bone in his body was ten times heavier, as that first, long day drew to a close.

"Do you think you'll like it here?" asked Marco as he walked Kennedy back to the room that the other guy had described as "the dungeon" at break-time.

"Yeah, yeah, definitely," lied Kennedy.

"You've done alright today, I've been keeping my eye on you."

"Cheers."

"You'll have paid off your dues before you know it."

Kennedy couldn't wait to get in that stinking, freezing cess-pit, and lie down. As soon as Marco opened the door and gestured him in, he lay down on that minging mattress, and closed his eyes. He was asleep by the time that the door was locked.

*****

The routine continued, day after day. It was a gruelling, relentless, monotonous cycle which saw very little change. But on the plus side, Kennedy's muscles were beginning to adapt to the physical demands of a daily, ten-hour shift. On the fifth day, Marco told Kennedy that he was going to give him a bunk, in the bedroom. Kennedy was beyond excited by this prospect, it really was the equivalent of winning the lottery for him. Instead of being walked down the corridor to the dungeon, he was led upstairs, to the third floor of the four-story mill, and shown into a room which contained seven bunk-beds, and thirteen frightened, frail looking men. They all stood up and looked down at the floor. It was like something out of a concentration camp.

"Going to see how Kennedy fits in up here. Anybody want to tell him the rules?" asked Marco. The sense of fear in the room was overwhelming. Not one of the men looked up in Marco's direction.

"Come on, how about you Frankie? Going to tell him the rules, or what?"

A very ill looking man, probably aged about fifty, cleared his throat before he started speaking. "It's not a holiday camp, we are here because we have upset the wrong person. In this room, there will be no talking, no wanking, no nothing. Just relaxing and sleeping."

"That's right. You see, if you hadn't been stupid little dick-chuggers out there, you wouldn't be in here. Would you not?"

"No Marco!" chanted the men. Kennedy began to realise that this was a bit of a ritual.

"This city is a nicer place with you horrible doggy-knobbers working in here for me. Isn't it?"

"Yes Marco!"

"What happens if you break my rules?"

"You break our bones!"

"Okay, well, I'll let you douche-noggins get your beauty sleep. You fucking need it, you ugly set of jizz-moppers. Night!"

"Night Marco."

*****

Life went on like this for several weeks. Motivated by an ever-present fear for his life, Curtis Kennedy had somehow managed to knuckle-down, and get busy following instructions, adhering to rules, and keeping his head down for the very first time in his life. The only conversations that the workers had took place over the two thirty-minute breaks that they were allowed each day. These conversations often centred around the things that had happened to previous workers who had stepped out of line.

Marco was a great believer in letting the other workers watch as he disciplined his workers. He had done many, many evil and wicked things to the people who had stepped out of line, such as whipping them, water-boarding them, beating them with sticks, and all manner of depraved activities. Marco would often laugh while he was delivering his punishments.

One of the workers described how hard it had been to watch one particular punishment ritual. It had been against a guy called Phil, he'd ended up in the factory after running up a debt with one of Marco's dealers. Phil had injured his back carrying some pallets up the stairs and he was struggling to carry on.

Marco wasn't happy, and he started giving Phil abuse, calling him a lazy bastard, and a useless bum noodle. Foolishly, Phil made the grave error of answering Marco back. It wasn't much, just something like, "oh leave off Marco, I think I've slipped a disc. My back is fucking killing." This had been a massive error of judgement on Phil's part, and Marco seemed perversely delighted that he had an opportunity to teach Phil a lesson. He left Phil sitting on the stairs, and rounded up all of the workers, making them follow him to the stair-well of the former cotton mill.

"Guys, look at Phil, he's twisted his back, he looks like he's in real pain!" said Marco with a nasty, sly grin on his face. "But he answered me back, lads. Can you believe that?" The workers were all standing there, dreading the punishment routine which was about to start, and scared about what might happen to Phil, who was a decent lad.

"Don't worry though Phil, I've got some Deep Heat spray here." Marco held out the can, and the eight or nine lads standing on the cold, mouldy stairwell seemed shocked that Marco was apparently about to show some compassion. They were about to change their minds though, as they watched Marco spray the liquid all over Phil's face, in his eyes, up his nose, into his ears. Phil started screaming, as the intense heat of the medication began burning his eyes, they were streaming with a heavy flow of tears, it was like water was pouring out of them. Phil was writhing in pain on the stairs, yelling out for help, pleading for somebody to do something.

But they all just stood, and watched. They did nothing, aware that it would be them next, if they stepped one foot forward.

Marco was laughing, and he started punching Phil in the face.

"You better shut up, you little pussy!" Marco was yelling in Phil's face, as blow after blow connected with the blinded young man who was shrieking for help.

Once Marco had satisfied himself, he told the workers to get back into the factory. They did, feeling relieved to get away from this horrific situation, but also weak and cowardly for not having the courage to try and help their horrifically injured co-worker. It was a wretched, horrible feeling of helplessness. Phil was never seen again after that, and nobody ever dared to ask Marco what had happened to him.

*****

A few weeks after being allowed into the bunks, Curtis Kennedy was asked to go up and see Marco in the office. He'd never been up to the office before, though he'd heard lots of scary things about events that had happened in there. The request terrified him, and as he made his way onto the stairwell, and began climbing the cold, stone steps up to the top floor of the mill, his mind was racing with thoughts of what he had done wrong. He paused as he reached the door. It took him ten seconds to pluck up the courage to press the bell. The door opened, and Kennedy walked through, and was amazed by the sight which greeted him.

The top floor of the mill was Marco's floor. This was where he lived, and worked. Most of the floor space made up Marco's sumptuous living quarters. This was a stunning place, and it looked like something out of a film. The floor was carpeted in an expensive, thick grey shag, and the furniture all looked brand new. Kennedy had never been anywhere so posh, apart from Sofology, where he'd made a nuisance of himself one day, jumping up and down on all the new sofas and beds, before being escorted out of the shop by security guards.

"Ah, alright Curtis, come on over here to my office." Marco was peering out around a door at the bottom end of the floor.

Kennedy gulped as he walked quickly in Marco's direction. What the fuck is going on, he wondered as he reached the office.

"Come in, come in, take a seat."

"Cheers," said Kennedy. He looked terrified and Marco laughed.

"Don't look so worried. You're not in any trouble. How's the harvest going?"

"Yeah, yeah, got loads done, about half already."

Kennedy sat down on a high seated chair, it was one of ten that was arranged around a huge, oval table. It reminded him of the table that he'd often have to sit around in the office at school, after being sent out of class.

"I have an errand I want you to do." Said Marco. "It's a job that comes with great privileges."

Kennedy was just sitting there, listening to Marco. He could hear his own heart-beat thundering away as well, and wondered if Marco could hear it across the huge table.

"I need you to do a bit of spying. Are you any good at spying?"

"Yeah, well, I bet I am."

"Good. Well, there are a few people that I need to know more about. I need to know their habits, I need to know their movements. So, what do you think about the idea of me letting you out of here for an hour or two, so you can do this job for me?"

It was obvious that Kennedy's mind was instantly filled with dozens of thoughts from this suggestion.

"Naturally, you'll be being watched yourself, so any attempts to do a runner will be viewed very badly."

This comment seemed to slow the young man's excitement, and his eyes suddenly focused a little more sharply on Marco.

"But the good news would be that you could get yourself a donner kebab or a pizza or summat, and just go and sit on a wall, and watch a couple of addresses for me."

"Yeah, yeah, definitely, sounds mint!"

"And you do understand that if you attempt to do a runner or anything, you'll be put in a coffin, and thrown in the Rochdale canal?"

"Yes, well, I wouldn't…"

"Imagine that. Being in a coffin, the lid screwed shut, and the water slowly leaking in, drip by drip, until you drown to death."

The thought made Kennedy want to cry. He was scared.

"But obviously, it wouldn't come to that, if you do exactly as you're told."

"Yeah, definitely. You can count on me!" Kennedy tried to smile, but he looked petrified.

Marco told Kennedy what he had to do. He gave him a phone, and asked him to log in to his Facebook account on it.

"You log in on that one, and I'll log in on this one. What's your e-mail and password?"

"Oh, er, DJ CK 95 at Hotmail dot com, password is on da sesh zero one."

"DJCK? That looks like dick." Marco started laughing loudly. "Dick 95! That's going to be your new nickname mate!" He laughed again.

"Right, its logged in," said Kennedy. He showed the phone to Marco. His hand was shaking with nerves.

"Cool, right, I've logged in on your account too, so I can see what you're up to. So don't try sending any messages or any of that shit to anyone. Remember why you're here, it's because you nicked my money and my cheeba."

"I know."

"You belong to me, until you've cleared your debts."
Kennedy desperately wanted to know if anybody had ever left here, having finished paying off their debts. All he'd heard of was people being seriously battered and tortured, and then disappearing.

"I don't send messages anyway. No one ever replies."

Marco laughed again, this daft kid was funny, without even trying. Marco started looking through his Facebook page, and then his messages. He was surprised to see that nobody had sent him a message to ask him where he'd been for the last five weeks. Not even his mum.

"Right, in five minutes, a car is going to come for you. The lads in the car will explain what you've got to do. You'll be messaging them, on this phone, and you won't be using it for any other purpose. Or you'll be going in that canal. Understand?"

"Yeah, I do."

*****

As sinister as it all was, it was rather an adventure for Curtis Kennedy. He was picked up at the front door of the mill, when Marco handed him over to two scary-looking blokes who Marco referred to as the "Chuckle Brothers."

"Listen Kennedy, these two are my best dealers. If you upset either of them, they have my permission to kill you. Got it?"

"Yeah, got it." He looked frightened, but also eager to prove himself. Prove he could do this.

"Right lads, take him. Tell him what he needs to do. I think he's a bit dim so talk slowly. And remember what we said, I want to know the habits of this guy you're going to watch. I want to know what time he comes in from work, what time he takes a piss, what time he goes down the pub. Every move he makes, I want it sending on a message from his Facebook. Understand?"

"Yeah, no problem."

Kennedy was led towards a Range Rover by the two men. They looked like serious gangster types, the kind who have been inside once or twice, but can handle themselves in there. One was much younger than the other, and Kennedy wondered if they were really brothers. They weren't doing much chuckling, and he couldn't understand the nickname.

The car pulled off, and Marco opened the first set of gates, allowing the car through. They were huge, steel gates, they were kept closed by a massive steel girder that Marco had had to lift off and place on the floor. As soon as the car was through, the huge gate closed, and Kennedy heard the banging of the steel girder being put back into the locking position. The car drove for about ten seconds before stopping. There was another set of gates, they were identical to the first set.

One of the gangsters rolled the window down and shouted. "Alright Dave, come and open it, you fucking clump." Suddenly a security guard with a massive dog walked towards the car.

"Soz, I was having a piss." He chained his dog to the fence, and then started removing the huge steel girder.

"What's that for?" asked Kennedy from the back-seat.

"It's the lock. No fucker is getting in here, unless they drive a fucking tank at it. Even then they'll have a job on. The gate-posts go underground three times their height. They're held in place by a piece of concrete the size of a house. This place is fucking impossible to get into, or out of, unless Marco says so."

It took Dave a minute or so to unlock the gate, and let the car through.

"Be back in a bit so keep an ear out. Cheers."

This excursion away from the factory where Kennedy now lived and worked, as he paid off his debts, was quite an education. It confirmed what the other workers had been saying. That there was no way out of this place. The universal advice against ever trying to make a run for it turned out to be very wise.

It didn't take long until the car arrived at a Spar shop. The older guy, the one who was driving had said nothing so far, suddenly he started talking. He had a broad Manc accent, and all of his words that should have ended in er, actually ended in or.

This guy definitely came from Manchestor.

"Hee-ya, see that street there, yeah, at the end of it is a little avenue of bungalows. The guy you're looking for lives at number sixteen. Where does he live?"

Kennedy looked surprised by the weird question.

"What?" he looked a bit scared, as the scary man

stared him out. He looked like a total psycho.

"God, you're not very sharp you. What's the address you're watching?"

"Number sixteen, of the bungalows."

"Good lad. Right, it's a quiet little avenue, full of Neighbourhood Watch types, so you need to make it very obvious that you're there. Sit on a wall facing his house, and if anybody asks you what you're doing there, just be nice and friendly, and tell them that you're lost, and your mum's coming to pick you up, and she'll be here in a minute. Yeah?"

"Yeah, sorted."

"The main thing we want to know is what time the guy gets home from work. We want to know if he drives, or if he's on foot. We want to know if he goes out anywhere. Every move he makes, you send us a message on this." He handed the phone to Kennedy. The Messenger app was open, and Marco had already set the conversation going. The contact that he was going to be communicating with was named "Irish Paddy."

As soon as the guy comes home, you message us. You just write "home." If he's walking, you just write "on foot." If he goes out, you just message us, saying "out." That's all you are doing, a complete moron could do this, so don't fuck it up."

"No worries, its safe mate."

"I'm not your mate. Call me mate again and I'll flush your head down the toilet."

"Right."

"What number house is it?"

"Sixteen."

"Good lad. Right, go on, get out..."

"Wait, er... Marco said I could have a pizza."

The two men laughed out loud. After a minute, they stopped.

"Listen, just get out, if you do a good job, we'll sort you out with a pizza on the way back."

Kennedy was disappointed. He'd eaten nothing but Pot Noodles and Farmfoods microwave meals for weeks, with the occasional cold McDonalds. He'd been salivating thinking about sinking his teeth into a red-hot pizza. He got out of the car, and walked across the road. He wished that he had the courage to just leg it. He could find a tram stop, get on the Metrolink, get to town and jump a train to Scotland. He could hide in the bogs. These lot would never find him in Scotland. His mind was fuzzing up with ideas of how to get out of this nightmare debt he owed. But he couldn't do it. Marco's words were still ringing in his ears, the stark warning about the coffin and the canal put his ideas on hold.

Soon, Kennedy was on the neat little avenue of bungalows. It was dark, and cars kept driving up the avenue, before reversing onto their driveways. Every single driver looked suspiciously at Kennedy, before locking up their cars and going into their homes. After about fifteen minutes of just sitting on the wall, looking down at the phone, the man from number sixteen arrived home. He was driving, and he reversed his vehicle onto his drive. As he did so, his headlights illuminated Kennedy as he sat there, directly opposite. But he didn't look up, he just stayed still, staring down at the phone screen in his hands.

"Home. Car."

The home-owner got out, grabbed a bag off the back seat, before locking his car and going into his bungalow.

"On his own?" Asked Irish Paddy via the messaging app.

"Yes."

"What's the reg."

"GM16 LPA."

"What sort is it?"

"Fiesta."

"Colour?"

"Silver."

The messages ended.

Ten minutes later, the man appeared at his front door, he had a little dog with him.

"Coming out. He's with his dog. Walking towards yous."

"Good. Stay where you are."

The messages stopped again. Kennedy just stayed put, aware that several neighbours were appearing at windows and looking at him. But they soon got bored and sat down to watch telly. Ten minutes passed before the man came back with his dog.

"He's coming back."

"Right. Come back to the car."

Kennedy put the phone into his pocket and started walking. The man with the dog smiled at him as their paths crossed. Kennedy smiled back, and felt relieved that he didn't have to sit on that freezing wall any longer.

Once he got back to the car, the two men were talking about football as he got in and sat on the backseat.

"Pass us that phone." The psycho guy took the phone and deleted all of the short messages that Kennedy had sent, before placing it in the glove-box.

"Can we get a pizza now? I'm starving."

*****

Kennedy got his pizza, and was driven back to the mill as he ate. Marco was waiting by the gates when he got out of the car.

"See you later lads, cheers," said Marco to the two gangsters. "Come here you, help me lock this gate."

Kennedy did as he was told, and grabbed one end of the steel girder.

"Did you enjoy your pizza?" he asked.

"Yeah, cheers."

"It's alright. You did a good job they said. You'll be doing the same thing tomorrow. You alright with that?"

Kennedy thought it was a strange question. It wasn't as though he had any choice.

"Yeah. Sound."

"Good, right, get back inside."

Kennedy went inside, and headed up the stairs to the bunks. As he walked, the taste of that delicious hot pizza still in his mouth, he had no idea that the following night's activities would end in completely different circumstances.

PART THREE

Chapter Twenty-Seven
Saturday

It had been an exhausting, yet exhilarating night, and the DWP case was looking remarkably close to being closed. Miller had arrived home just after three am, and decided to crash on the sofa, rather than wake Clare. He'd fallen into a deep, heavy sleep as soon as his eyes had taken their last, heavy blink of that long, tiring, roller-coaster of a day.

"Andy, wake up love," said Clare Miller gently, placing a brew on the table beside her husband.

"Eh? What... oh. What time is it?" he asked, pulling an ugly face as he realised his neck was hurting from the way that he'd slept on it.

"Its half-seven. What time did you get in?"

"Oh, about three. I could do with a bit longer."

"Yes, I bet you could. You're going to bloody collapse one of these days, and I'll be left with nothing but memories of you not being here."

"Aw come off it, you know I'm up to my nuts in this Clare. Don't go all Mariah Carey on me."

"I'm not doing, I just worry about these hours. I bet you ate nothing but crap yesterday!" Clare sat down beside her husband and started stroking his shoulder.

"I didn't! I had about three salads, and I had quinoa for my breakfast."

"You lie like Boris Johnson's Brexit bus."

"Anyway chillax, things will start to settle down now. We have a name for the attacker."

"No way! Aw, that's good news. When did all that come about?"

"Last night. I bet you're glad it didn't come on the news until you'd gone to bed, or you'd have been watching telly all night, and now you'd look as rough as me!" Miller started to tell Clare all about the developments in Glossop.

"I'm so pleased Andy, you needed a lucky-break on this one."

"Er, excuse me, it wasn't a lucky-break, you cheeky

cow! It was..."

"It was a lucky-break. Right, well, the twins will be up soon so I want five minutes quiet on my phone."

Miller sat up and leant round to grab the cup. "Cheers love. I'll make it up to you. I'll take you somewhere nice, sometime."

"Ooh, that sounds vague!" Said Clare as she slumped on the other settee with her brew in one hand and her phone in the other.

* * * * *

Miller arrived at the office just after eight. He looked dreadful. To his annoyance, Saunders arrived at the same time as him, and looked as though he'd just had a week off, followed by the best night's sleep of his entire life.

"God, you look like you've had more than four hours sleep Keith! How do you do it?" asked Miller, slamming his bags down on the floor outside his office door.

"It's because I'm only in my thirties Sir. Once I'm over that hill, like you... I might start looking grim. Like you."

"Nah. I'm sure there's two of you Keith. I'm absolutely convinced of it. If it ever goes quiet around here, I'm going to do some investigating into this. I'll find your body double." Miller unlocked his door and pushed it open with his hip as he picked up the bags. "Besides, I'm only forty-two, you cheeky bastard."

"Past it Sir!"

"Right, I'll get this laptop fired up and we can have a chin-wag about today's proceedings."

"Yes, no problem Sir. I'll sort the coffee."

Once Miller and Saunders had sat down and completed a brief recap of the previous day's developments, they were both reminded that the investigation had come a very long way in just twenty-four hours. It was easy to forget how much progress was being made, when you were right in the thick of it.

And now, with the chief suspect's name out there in the community, it should all come to a quiet, positive conclusion, anytime soon. That was certainly the way things usually happened in Saunders' and Miller's experience. It may take a few days, a week even, but once a known scrote's name has been released to the media in relation to a serious case, the scrote in question quickly discovers that they don't have any mates left, or any sofas to doss on. In their experience, it was now just a waiting game.

"How do you fancy doing a press conference this morning Keith?" Miller looked across the desk, and again felt a pang of annoyance at how youthful and fresh-faced his colleague appeared, despite the lack of sleep.

"On a Saturday?"

"Yeah. It's still the biggest news story in the UK."

"Well, yes, of course I'll do it. But why aren't you?"

"I can't do one looking like this."

"Fair point. I doubt anybody would come forward if you did it Sir. You look like Phil Mitchell during his crack phase."

"Right, that's settled then. I'll phone Dixon in a bit, I love ringing him on the weekend, it does his head in. Right, what do you suggest we get everybody working on now that we've got our prime suspect?" Miller really did look like shit. He started rubbing his eyes, before taking a huge slurp out of his cup.

Saunders thought about Miller's question for a bit. There had been an enormous amount of work done in this investigation, by a huge number of people working here in the SCIU, and also out in the DWP buildings, where staff were checking their own systems for details on recorded threats, and acts of violence against staff.

"Well, Sir, the truth is, I don't know. I've half a mind to suggest that we all work on locating the suspect, but we've far too many staff to justify that. And if we hand them back..."

"Yes, you're spot on. If we hand them back, we'll never see them again, and we might still need them in the coming days. So, I suggest we review what everybody is looking at, and we can deliver the good news in the 10am briefing." Miller was filled with positive energy, and was loving the blank cheque mentality regarding this case. Usually, he'd struggle to justify his tiny team's overtime. But today, the Manchester police were paying almost fifty officers to come in.

Miller sat forward and loaded Sky News on the laptop. They were repeating the comments that people from Hattersley had been making all night on social media. This was the first that Miller and Saunders had heard about this, and it intrigued them greatly. After a few minutes of listening to the Sunrise report, and a few of Curtis Kennedy's contacts from Hattersley being interviewed, Miller switched the news app off.

"What are they playing at now? We get our first decent lead, and Sky News are saying it's the wrong person. WE'VE GOT HIS FACEBOOK PROFILE! WE'VE GOT HIS PRINTS!" He shouted at the laptop.

"Dunno. Sounds a bit queer all this Sir. Why would Sky start reporting that we're looking for the wrong person. I've never come across this before. Maybe there's something in it."

"What do you mean?"

"Well, from that little bit we heard there, it sounds like the people who know Curtis Kennedy are all saying that its bollocks. Well, sorry Sir, but I can't recall a case where that has happened before. Can you?"

Miller thought long and hard. Eventually, he spoke. "No, I can't say I have, but times are changing aren't they, everything's going viral and all that shit nowadays. If this kid has got a lot of mates on Hattersley, it would be pretty easy for them to all start confusing the picture by talking shit about our only suspect, trying to throw us off the scent." Miller blew out an exasperated breath. "But, well, I think you'd better see what's behind this Keith."

"Right Sir, no worries. Are we putting the press conference idea on hold then?"

"Yeah, for now. I think we might fall in a trap here if we don't suss out the lay of the land. I'm not in the mood for us being made to look like dicks on Sky News."

"No Sir, fair comment. Okay, I'll see what I can dig up."

*****

It didn't take Saunders long to see why there was so much fuss about the suspect's involvement in this case. Judging by the Police National Computer, Curtis Kennedy was the typical ASBO. He'd had dozens of police interventions throughout his young life, and all of it for the type of behaviour that would be regarded as "silly" if it wasn't so stressful and infuriating for other members of the community where he lived.

He'd been in trouble for letting down all the car tyres on his street at the age of eleven, and since then, a decade of fuck-wittery of the highest order followed. Saunders smiled at some of the bizarre escapades of this ridiculous young man. One entry from the previous year caught his eye. Kennedy had burgled a washing machine from a charity shop in Stalybridge, and tried to get it home on a bus. Police were called when he started kicking off with the driver, who wouldn't let him on with such a bulky item. Officers were surprised to find him still standing at the bus stop, with the washing machine. Saunders laughed loudly as he read that Kennedy had stolen it, "because it was his mum's birthday, and hers is fucked."

In 2012, when Kennedy was 17, he was arrested for painting the panes of his next door neighbour's windows black. In 2013, he was sent to a young offender's institution for repeatedly kicking the wing mirrors off cars in the Hattersley area. In 2014, on return to the community, he was in trouble again, this time for setting the primary school's bins on fire.

By the time that Saunders had finished reading this depressing list of pointless criminal activity, he too was absolutely convinced that Curtis Kennedy was not the right man. He wasn't capable of the DWP attacks, it was quite obvious that there had been some kind of a massive cock-up here. The realisation frustrated Saunders, as he tried to figure out how this could have got so confused.

Miller arrived back from his meeting with DCS Dixon, and he appeared quite relaxed, cheerful even. But then he saw how pissed-off Saunders looked, and he knew straight away that this wasn't going to be as straight-forward as he had imagined. He could just tell.

"DI Saunders, got a minute please?" said the DCI as he stepped into his office.

Saunders stood and walked quickly across the SCIU

floor, which was a hive of activity with so many staff working so enthusiastically.

"What's up with you, Keith?" asked Miller as Saunders sat down.

"These people who are saying that Kennedy is not the man responsible for the attacks... they're right."

"You certain?" Miller looked dismayed.

"Yes, absolutely one-hundred per-cent Sir." Saunders leaned forward and handed over the PNC report into Curtis Kennedy's criminal history. Miller raised an eyebrow as he read. He sniggered at one part too.

"Fucking hell. This guy is a bit of a tool, isn't he?"

"He's an A-list bong-a-dong."

"Yeah. I bet the only way you'd get this one to wear a condom is to draw a Nike sign on the side of it."

"Oh, don't Sir. Have you got up to the bit where he got locked in the car he was trying to nick? It was the hottest day of the year, and he was screaming, banging on the windows for help."

They both laughed, but there was a real sense of disappointment present in the humour.

"So, come on Keith, I imagine that you've figured this out?"

"Not really. I've been thinking through few scenarios which might explain it."

"Go on."

"Well, he's done a bit of burglary. He was stood down a ginnel, in the dark. He might have just been casing a house to break into. Then, the lady from the DWP has spotted him, and we've all added two and two together and got seven."

Miller agreed. He was scratching his chin as he considered Saunders' explanation for the apparent mix-up.

"Yes. I think I agree with you Keith. He's wound up there on other business, probably about to set some fire extinguishers off or something, and it was a pretty insane case of wrong place, wrong time."

Saunders nodded. "Well, the fact remains, we're not going to know until we catch up with Kennedy. I thought we'd have felt his collar by now."

"It won't be long. But let's not go too far with explaining this to the team. We'll just tell them that we are keeping an open-mind, and continuing our investigations until further notice."

"What was Dixon saying about the DWP target list?"

"Oh, very positive news on that front. We're going to have armed police presence inside every one of the thirty-six addresses on that list until the suspect is in custody, regardless."

"That's good. Expensive… but it'll bring a lot of peace-of-mind to the DWP staff."

"Yes, it will. But it'll also drive them nuts having a load of police in their home twenty-four seven. The only thing that's going to make the DWP staff happy is the announcement that we've caught the bastard."

"Which presents us with a massive problem. We're going to pick up Kennedy at any moment. And when we do, and it's become public, the DWP staff will let their guards down, the armed officers will be stood down from the addresses, and we'll probably lose all these extra officers… even though Kennedy isn't the attacker." Saunders looked seriously pissed off.

"You're right. Shit. This is a pickle, isn't it?"

"Yes, we're snookered. What have uniform said about Kennedy's address?"

"Apparently, he's not been seen there for over a month. His mum and sister live at the address, neither have heard from him."

"Is that common?"

"Apparently so, it's quite normal for him to take himself off for a while. They don't seem like a very close-knit family, from the notes."

Miller looked deep in thought for a moment. "I think me and you should go down and speak to the mother. I'll be nice, you be a dick, let's see what we can uncover. What do you think?"

"Okay, I'll get this team brief nailed, and then we'll go and do Kennedy's mum's head in. But I was the dick last time, so you're doing it today. I'm in the mood for being nice."

"Fair enough."

Chapter Twenty-Eight

Miller and Saunders arrived at the address, just before noon. The curtains were still drawn in the front-room window.

"Is that a new front door?"

"Looks like it. It's not in keeping with the neighbour's front doors, is it?"

"They are tenants aren't they? I mean, they've not bought the property?"

"No idea. Shall I call the council?"

"Yes. Try and find out why they've had a new front door. There was nothing on the computer about us lot smashing their front door in. Do a bit of digging, see what info the council have about this family. I'm going to have a quick look around the street, and a peep around the back."

"Sir."

Miller got out of the car and had a walk along Sandybank Avenue, the neat, quiet cul-de-sac in which the Kennedy family occupied one of the gigantic estate's three thousand council homes. Despite Hattersley's "rough" reputation, Miller couldn't find fault with the place. It was a very nice street, all of the gardens were tidy, all the properties were clean and well presented. Most of the cars on the street were up-to-date models, and Miller realised that the place must have improved considerably since the last time he had reason to visit the estate, several years earlier, when putting a psycho loan-shark out of business.

The only house which looked deprived in this neat little cul-de-sac was the Kennedy residence. The paint work was looking tired, the front of the house had some "tagging" graffiti sprayed around the front-door, and one of the upstairs windows had a crack running all the way through it. The other window was closed, but had its curtain trapped, half-in, half-out. By the front door step was a bucket which was over-flowing with cigarette ends. It was the only property which had net curtains up, and the caramel shade of them suggested the occupants of this address didn't always go to the front door to smoke.

Miller continued walking up the avenue, passing a

couple of kids playing kerby. He smiled as he greeted a young mum pushing a pram. She was looking at her phone and didn't notice him. He turned off the walkway, and headed for the ginnel which ran along the back of the properties. As soon as he stepped into the ginnel, he heard shouting from one of the addresses. He hoped it was the Kennedy house, and he felt pretty confident that it was. Miller quickened his pace, he wanted to have a listen to the commotion. He stopped by the back-gate, and crouched down, pretending to tie his shoe-lace, just in case anybody wandered down here. There was a hell of a row coming from the Kennedy house, and it was easy to follow as all the windows were wide open.

"Well I couldn't give a fuck, he's not coming back here, so shut your trap Madison, keep your fucking stupid bullshit to yourself." It sounded like the mother, her voice was older than the other voice, and sounded as if several decades of cigarette smoking had deepened it quite considerably.

"It's family mum. You can't just turn your fucking back on fam. I know he's a bell-end. But, he's our bell-end."

"Madison, I couldn't care less. He's not stopping here. The police will be watching the house anyway, you barmy bitch."

"Well, if he comes here, I'm letting him in. So fuck off!" A door slammed loudly, and then the mother shouted, much more loudly this time.

"Stop slamming my fucking doors!"

Miller waited a minute, to hear if any other information could be gathered by listening to the row. But it seemed to be concluded for the time being. Miller was satisfied that Kennedy wasn't here, and hadn't been recently, from what he'd picked up eaves-dropping.

He stood up and headed back around to the front of the houses, walking casually back to the car. Saunders was in the passenger seat, talking on his phone. Miller got in and made a few notes in his pocket-book, passing the time while he waited for Saunders to finish up.

"Right," said Saunders, as he finished the call. "Just been onto the emergencies line to Peak Valley Homes, they manage the estate. The lady I spoke to checked their system, and she said that the Kennedy's had a new front-door fitted five weeks ago, the last one had been smashed off its frame. Mrs Kennedy hadn't offered an explanation for the damage, so they had to pay the costs."

"That was five weeks ago. And the reports you read from uniform last night said that Kennedy hasn't been around the address for about a month?"

"Correct, Sir. So, it would appear that he might have annoyed the wrong crowd."

"Looks like it. I was just ear-wigging at the back of the house, the mum and the daughter were having a bit of a barney. The sister is saying she'll protect Kennedy, if he comes back. The mum's telling her that that's not happening."

"Backs up the story that he's not there, then?"

"That's what I thought. They are very vocal, they sound like something out of Rita, Sue and Bob Too."

"Great film."

"It seems like one of those houses where the loudest one gets heard. It might be an idea to piss these off to the max, then go and have a listen at the back to see if we can gather any intel on Kennedy's location."

"Yes, well, I'm up for that."

"Come on then, let's get in there. And don't forget to wipe your feet on the way out."

Miller knocked out the familiar CID melody on the new front door. The two detectives heard a deep-voiced woman muttering some negative sounding words inside as she came closer to the door.

"Hello, Manchester Police," said Miller as a poor, tired looking woman appeared at the door. At first glance, she looked like an old lady. But after closer inspection, Miller soon realised that this woman was probably quite a bit younger than him, but had clearly had a much more difficult life.

"Aw for... we've already had yous round last night. He's not here!" She sounded desperate to be left in peace. Even when her son wasn't there, he still managed to bring stress and anxiety to his mother's door.

"Hiya, yes, I know. We've a few more questions, we

won't keep you…" Saunders was playing the good cop today. He liked that role much better than the bad cop. He always found that he got more information being nice.

"Come on then. I'm going to have me windows put in, they'll all think I'm a fucking grass or summat! Snitches get stitches!"

The smell of poorness hit Miller and Saunders as they stepped inside. Saunders smiled as he spotted a can of Oust air freshener by the front door, and decided that this lady must be very optimistic by nature.

"I know, it's a nightmare. We're just keen to speak to Curtis. We don't think he's got anything to do with these DWP attacks, but there's nothing we can do about that until we speak to him."

"I know, yeah. Well it's obvious that he hasn't done those attacks. He's a soft bastard anyway. Sit down if you want."
Saunders and Miller glanced at one another. Neither of them wanted to sit down, for fear of transferring the smell of stale nicotine and poor domestic hygiene onto their clothes. They had both spotted a very iffy looking stain right in the middle of the sofa. But they sat down, anyway, perching on the edge, as far away from the yellowy patch.

"Thing is, nobody seems to have heard from Curtis for at least a month."

"Yeah, I know. I've not… he's not been here. Not seen or heard off him."

"But that's quite common, isn't it?" asked Saunders. "He has a tendency to drift, doesn't he?"

"Yeah, he fucks off all the time. It's usually because someone on the estate is after him. He goes all over, he was living in a bail hostel in Skegness a few months ago. He's tapped. Always has been. Fucking head-the-ball."

"Mam! Who's at the door?" shouted an obnoxious sounding young woman from upstairs.

"It's the police again!"

"For fucks sake!" The sister came running down the stairs. She made no effort to be quiet and the heavy banging of her feet sounded like the end of Eastenders. She burst into the front room, looking angry. Her shocking blue hair really framed her pale, spotty face.

"If you think our Curtis has done that to them Jobcentre people, you're off your fucking tits!"

"Madison, shut the fuck up will you?"

"No, I will not shut up! This is prosecution!"

"We don't actually think Curtis is involved." Said Saunders, calmly. "We're more inclined to think that he was at that address for another reason, possibly buying some drugs or something. We need to speak to him, in order to eliminate him from our enquiries. That's what we were just trying to explain to your mother."

This announcement wrong-footed the gobby young woman who stood there with her hand on her hip. "So why are they saying it all on the news? The amount of shit I'm getting on Facebook because of all this is unbelievable."

"He was standing outside a DWP workers house last night, and some people have come to a rash conclusion. That's all." Said Saunders.

"For fuck's sake, so you've got him down for..."

Miller decided to shut this obnoxious little chav down, she was doing his head in, and she'd only been in the room for thirty seconds.

"Hoi you, shut your trap, it's your mum we want to talk to. It's not about you, so go and suck a gob-stopper."

"You what, who the..."

"Can you get her to leave please, Mrs Kennedy?" Miller looked hard at the girl's mother.

"I'm not going nowhere! Cheeky twat."

"Mrs Kennedy, if you don't get her away, I'll have to no alternative but to arrest you and speak to you down at the station. This is a very urgent enquiry and I haven't got time for drama queens."

This comment seriously upset the mum. She already looked like she'd had enough of life before Miller and Saunders had even stepped into this run-down shit-hole of a house. And now, her blood-pressure was through the roof again.

"Madison, please, just go upstairs while I sort it."

Madison looked at her mother with pure contempt, before pulling the door shut as loudly as she could.

"Stop slamming my fucking doors!" Shrieked Mrs Kennedy.

"Sorry about this. We'll be gone before you know it, we just need to ask a few more questions that our colleagues didn't ask last night."

Mrs Kennedy sat down and lit a cigarette. Her hand was shaking noticeably. Both of the detectives felt quite sorry for her. This was no life.

"When was the last time you saw Curtis?"

"About a month ago."

"Can you remember the date?"

"Nah, every day is the same in this house. Fucking shit."

"What about TV? Can you remember what was on that night?"

"Nah. I don't think so… Coronation Street probably."

"Where was he when you last saw him?"

"He was here, the last time I saw him."

"And was there a row, or anything? Did he say that he would be away for a while when he left?" Saunders was being really nice.

"No, just… I don't know. There's always a row about summat. But no, I don't think so. He was just… I can't really remember." Mrs Kennedy was being frustratingly vague.

Miller decided to spice things up a bit, and give her a judder.

"Roughly around the time that Curtis was last seen here, you had a new front door fitted. Are those two things connected?"

"What.. how do you mean… front door…" Mrs Kennedy suddenly started shaking violently, and the tiny amount of colour that she'd had in her anaemic looking face was completely drained now. She looked a ghostly shade, like a packet of Bernard Matthews chicken roll.

"You've got a new front door. It was installed on the fifteenth of October. What happened to your last one?"

"I'm, this is doing my head in, I'm not…"

Suddenly, the living room door burst open. Madison hadn't gone back upstairs. She'd stayed behind the door, listening in.

"Why won't you tell them mam? You're a fucking disgrace!"

"Madison, you'd better shut your trap you, or I'll shut it for you!"

"Tell them mam! Tell them why you've got a new front door that's costing you eight-hundred quid!"

Mrs Kennedy looked at the two detectives, then back at Madison who was glaring at her from the doorway. She took a long, hard drag on her cigarette, and blew the smoke out through her nostrils.

"Mam! Tell them, or I will."

"And then I'll have to move off the estate, you stupid bitch!"

"Good! It's a fucking shit-hole anyway!"

"Right, Madison, will you just pipe down a minute love? We really need to eliminate Curtis from this enquiry." Saunders was playing the nice guy superbly well. "All this shouting and kicking off is just delaying us. Mrs Kennedy, please just tell us what you know."

There was another delay as the boy's mother chose her words. Her hand was still trembling as she held the burnt-out cigarette butt.

"I've not seen him since the front door went in. He was taken away by two big massive black men. One of them carried him out on his shoulder, and shoved him in the boot of their car. That's all I know. I swear down."

Chapter Twenty-Nine

"Thank you for joining us on BBC Radio Five Live this Saturday lunchtime, I'm Susan Northwood. The suspect in the DWP attacker case has been named as twenty-two-year old Curtis Kennedy, a Greater Manchester resident, who is reportedly in receipt of Jobseekers Allowance, and it has been revealed, has previously been sanctioned by the DWP. It sounds like a clear motive, and there are reports this morning that Curtis Kennedy is well known to police locally, and has indeed served some time in prison. So, with this information at our disposal, we are trying our very best to get the message out there, and to tell the public to remain vigilant. If you suspect that Curtis Kennedy is around your local community, the advice is to call 999 immediately, and do not approach this man. Now, let's go to the phones, and see what our listeners have got to say about these dramatic developments. On line two we have Harry Webster in Lincoln. Good afternoon Harry."

"Good afternoon Susan, and thanks for having me on."

"You're very welcome Harry. Now, it says on my notes that you've got a theory for us?"

"Yes, well I have actually. I've been reading a few things that are being said about this kid, and it's becoming pretty obvious that he is not the person responsible for these crimes."

"Well, sorry to interrupt you there Harry, but, in the interests of reporting the facts, that is the name of the person that the police have named as their number one suspect. What makes you so sure that your theory is more reliable than that of the investigating officers?"

"Look, go online, and see what people who know Curtis Kennedy are actually saying. They think it's a joke. This person is more at home spitting on people from upper floors in shopping centres. It seems totally inconceivable that he has the intellectual ability to carry out these attacks, let alone plan them."

"Well, that is certainly an interesting viewpoint. But you'll appreciate that we have a duty to report the information that we are given."

"Yes, I understand all that. The thing is though, last night they were very excited about this, and today, it seems the mood from Manchester police is a little flatter. I'm guessing that they've realised that this young chav isn't the attacker."

"We will certainly find out if your theory is correct, or not, in due course. In the mean-time Harry, you sound like an informed kind of man. What do you make of what's happening with these attacks?"

"Hmmm. Good question. I just think it's yet another disastrous situation for the government, another self-made catastrophe. My mate and me were having a few pints and discussing it the other night. He said that if what was going on in this country at present was the plot of a film, you'd walk out of the cinema, or you'd switch the channel over. You'd just think it was total nonsense! Totally far-fetched garbage."

"Which part in particular?" asked Susan.

"All of it. Come on, you're a clever person, you know it's a shambles. It feels like we've asked the most idiotic people in the UK to cause as much damage as they possibly can to our country. It's like some conspiracy theory, to turn Britain into a joke!"

"Harry, I'm sorry, but you'll have to qualify those comments."

"I can qualify them. Take this DWP sanctions nonsense. They are spending more money on stopping people's benefits, than just paying them out in the first place. These sanctions cost an extra one-hundred and fifty million pounds a year to put in place, so let's just think about that. It is *costing* us tax-payers an extra one hundred and fifty million, every year, in an attempt to save money!"

"How does that work Harry?"

"I don't know how it works, but those are official figures from the office of national statistics. Go on line, look them up. Every person who is sanctioned has to appeal, and appeal again, and so it goes on. The extra admin and extra staff, court costs, etc it all adds up."

"But if it means that its getting people into jobs Harry, its surely a worthwhile investment?"

"What jobs? Zero-hour contracts down at Sports Direct, where you have to have a baby in the toilets on your lunch-break, because you're so scared to take a day off?"

"That was an isolated case. But I take your point."

"Look at what they are doing to disabled people, sick people, people with learning disabilities. They're signing them off as fit for work. Work where? A lot of them had jobs already, with specialist support workers and carers at Remploy. But this same government closed it down, turfing thousands of vulnerable people out of their jobs, to save money. Like I say to you, none of these policies make any sense. It would have *made* sense to expand the Remploy factories, to expand the amount of support workers and carers, and teachers, training these guys up to do valuable work, and improving their standard of living. But instead, they closed the factory, stuck them all in their houses, then took away their disability benefit, declaring them fit for work. It's just as illogical as every other disaster that these lunatics in Number 10 have created."

"Such as?"

"Oh, come off it, for heaven's sake! The whole situation in Britain is a complete joke. Just look at this mess that you see before you at the DWP up in Manchester, it is a perfect example. We've got the army working on security because there are no police. Ambulances are arriving half an hour late to a shooting, but even then, the A and E departments can't cope when the ambulance actually gets there. The DWP staff aren't turning in to work for fear of being attacked, I read a report that thousands of today's pensions are late hitting the bank accounts. It's a never-ending cringe watching this insane government going about their business. The issue that lies at the heart of these DWP attacks boils down to nothing more than good-old-fashioned nastiness. The people behind it are sadists, there's no other word to describe them. They cannot have a conscience. This diabolical, deliberate treatment against the poor costs more money than it saves, and the government are trying to pretend that their never-ending list of epic fails are good for the country. Seriously, from every single perspective of life in Britain, the government are failing disastrously. From Brexit, to schools, to health, public services. They lie of course, and tell you a different story. But people in Britain are not stupid. Everybody knows what's going on, they can see this country falling apart around them. Every single one of us can see the state of the place, the crisis of having no nurses, no police. We can see the mess they are making of schools, prisons, trains, the roads. One of the richest countries on the planet is being turned into a third-world country because born-rich morons who've never done a real day's work in their lives are running the show. Like I said, it would be laughable, if it wasn't so serious."

"I think you're painting a rather negative picture here Harry! Is it really so bad?"

"Well, you're paid to say that Susan. You're part of the propaganda machine, aren't you?"

"Well, um, if I am, I must have missed the memo about that one Harry, to be perfectly honest."

"You are, and if you don't believe me, let me ask you a question."

"Go ahead, I'll answer it if my government masters nod through the glass, oh yes, there they are, nodding. Go ahead."

"Very funny. They'll stop nodding in a second, when they hear my next question."

"Yes, yes, they're looking very worried now Harry." It was obvious that the presenter was having great fun taking the mick out of Harry.

"Ask them if they can see the sense in fannying about to try and save half a billion quid with these petty benefit reforms, when they could raise seventy-four times that amount of money, by simply raising the cost of corporate tax to the same level that it is around the rest of Europe."

"Sorry, I don't follow..."

"Didn't think you would. They are losing us thirty-seven billion pounds, every year, bungs to their super rich chums, whilst kicking disabled and sick and mental people in the balls."

"Come on Harry, we can't say things like that."

"Why? Because you're on a government radio station? Stop it. Imagine if I came into your studio now, and said that I want to donate some money to Children in Need, yeah?"

"Yes, go on."

"Well if I had 50p in one hand, and thirty-seven quid in the other, which would you choose?"

"The thirty-seven pounds, of course."

"What about if that was half a billion pounds, or thirty-seven billion pounds, which would you choose?"

"It's very obvious, I'd choose the thirty-seven billion, of course!"

"Well, go and ask your government masters why they're blissfully ignoring the thirty-seven billion, and snatching the half a billion off the poor! Poking the sickest, most vulnerable people in the eye while they do it!"

"Okay Harry, thanks very much! Another one who's clearly escaped from his hospital. Right, onto line three, Anne in Swansea."

"Hi Susan,"

"Hello Anne, I hope Harry hasn't made you slit your wrists?"

"Well, no, I wouldn't go that far. But he did make a few good points about the state of the country. It's a joke."

The presenter swerved Anne's observation. "It says here that you wanted to talk about the DWP attacks in a different light?"

"Yes, that's right. I know that a lot of people out there will agree with me, when I say that these welfare reforms that are getting everybody so emotional, well, I think they are long overdue." Anne sounded confident, and extremely nice.

"So, you're saying that the allegedly nasty activities of the DWP are acceptable?"

"Absolutely, I think they are spot on. I go out and work my fingers to the bone, and the money I make hardly pays the bills. As soon as I clear one debt, the car breaks down, or the washing machine blows up! I've not been on holiday for four years, and I work bloody hard. Yet there are people on benefits who haven't got a day's work in them, who are living a better life than me! I'm sick of it!"

"Yes, well, this is a point that comes up regularly. But surely the blame for that lies with your employer. Doesn't it?"

"Well, I don't know about that. If I get paid more, the costs of the business will go up, and then we'll lose customers who'll go to a cheaper supplier, and then I'll be made redundant. It's catch twenty-two."

"But it does seem quite harsh that you want people who are on benefits to suffer because your earnings aren't adequate for you to lead the lifestyle that you would like. That's grossly unfair."

"No, what's unfair is that I work, I'm sat in traffic for an hour before work, then an hour after work, I only have about two hours a day to myself after I've done my chores, and every penny I earn is spent before pay-day. Yet there are people who don't work who lead better lives than me. How is that fair?"

"But the point I'm trying to make is that the people on benefits are getting a very small amount of money. It's only enough to scrape by. It's a myth that people on benefits are living the dream Anne, you might see the very rare examples on Britain's biggest families on TV, but they are the exception to the rule. Quite frankly this idea that people are choosing a life on the dole is total codswallop, it's a tiny minority of illiterate racist thugs, who wouldn't get a job anywhere because they can't count past eleventeen."

"It's not, you're wrong. I see them on telly, they've got their fags and their booze and Sky TV, they're laughing their heads off at us, while their rent and council tax is being paid by me and all the other mugs who go out to work, and come home with less than them. I can't afford Sky, I can't, and it really makes me mad. So, I say to all these people who think that the benefit reforms are tight... come and live my life for a week, and see if you're still sticking up for the idle ones!" Anne's "nice" voice was starting to sound less so, a sharp, bitter edge had crept in.

"I think you're being quite outrageous Anne..."

"I'm not..."

"You can't just say that people on benefits are idle. People are on benefits for a variety of complex reasons. Take our regular caller Joe in Hastings for instance. A lovely bloke who had a stroke at the age of thirty-five. He can't work now, because he can't use the right-hand-side of his body. I know for a fact that he struggles to get by on his benefits, and I also know that he would give anything to be cured of his disability, and get out working again, back amongst his mates, not depending on meals on wheels to provide his lunch, which is usually stone-cold."

"Yeah, but, that's…"

"That's the fact of the matter Anne. What about people with MS? Should their benefits be stopped?"

"Well, no, but that's not what…"

"Blind people?"

"No, I'm…"

"How about people who suffer from mental health issues?"

"That's not what I'm…"

"Unemployed people then? Men and women who've been made redundant? What about the steel-workers in Port Talbot, the four-thousand that have just been laid off because of Tata steel closing? BAE are laying thousands off in the next few months in Lancashire. They're going to struggle to find new jobs at first, after all, their skills lie in making aeroplane wings."

"What's that got to do with anything?"

"Well, unless an aeroplane wing factory opens, they won't be working. So shall we refuse them benefits?"

"You're confusing the issue."

"I think that it is *you* who is confused Anne. But if we use your narrow view of the world, let me ask you a question. Do you know who the worst benefits free-loaders are?"

"No, but I'm sure you're going to talk over me again…"

"Pensioners. Those selfish old people, taking all our money, it's almost one hundred billion pounds a year that we dole out to these scroungers!" The presenter was clearly taking the piss, but the sarcasm was lost on Anne.

"Well, that's too much!" She sounded indignant, and it was clear that she felt that she ruled the moral high-ground regarding this matter.

"Oh, yes, definitely. Pay in all your life, taxed, taxed, taxed, your council tax, your VAT, even your petrol, booze, cigarettes, holidays, all being heavily taxed by the government.

And then selfishly, they live beyond the age of sixty-seven and need a bit back, about a hundred and fifty pounds a week, after wearing their fingers to the bone supporting the system for fifty years! You're as mad as a bottle of crisps Anne!"

"No... I don't mind the pensioners, that's not as bad, but..."

"But those battling cancer right now, those that can't work because they've broken their backs falling from scaffolding... those people deserve to get nothing?"

"You're twisting my words."

"Goodbye Anne. Wow, Anne there in Swansea, helping us to understand that there really are some very thick, bitter and twisted people out there in our communities. Here's Gabby with the weather."

Chapter Thirty

It had been a very interesting visit to Hattersley, and it had raised a series of important questions which needed answering as a matter of urgency. Saunders drove Miller's car back to the SCIU offices. Miller wanted to concentrate as he spoke to a colleague from organised crime. DCI John Barnes.

"John, hi, its Andy."

"Oh, alright Andy, how's tricks?"

"Busy as always, I'm on with this DWP business. We've got a real curve-ball with this. We've released the name of a suspect, but we've since realised that he's a complete fuck-wit. There's no way he's the culprit."

"Oh shit, it's all over the news. And now you need to reverse out of it. Nightmare!"

"Well not exactly, we still need to talk to the kid. The only problem is, he's been off the radar for the last five weeks. Nobody has heard or seen of him, but then he randomly turned up outside a DWP employee's home last night. So, I'm pretty confused by it all."

The line went quiet. It was obvious that John was struggling to see why he was being told all this.

"Oh, sorry, I'm waffling. I've just been with the mother, and we've managed to get it out of her that the door was booted in by two big massive black men, and they took our suspect and threw him in the boot. He's not been seen since."

"What sort of car was it?"

"A black beemer, massive rims apparently. The sister was singing like a canary. She said the two men were massive, looked like SAS soldiers, or heavy-weight boxers. Very scary men, but polite and well mannered! As well mannered as you can be putting a front door in, anyway.

Miller's opposite number in organised crime laughed.

"Sounds like the Cole brothers. In fact, I'd bet money on it."

"Who are they? I've not heard of them before."

"They're major league security, they started on the doors at Piccadilly 21's years ago, early nineties and they've built a bit of an empire from making people's problems stop happening."

"What like…"

"Well, if you were having a spot of trouble off somebody, you could make the problem go away by paying the Cole brothers to sort it out. I don't know their methods, but they're good at what they do. Well respected."

"Have they got any form?"

"Not really, no. They're very professional, very well respected. I'm pretty convinced that it'll be them that's taken your suspect away."

"What kind of thing do they get involved with? I mean, this guy is more at home with setting wheely bins on fire."

"Dunno. They usually work for the main heads, you know, club owners, dealers, gangsters. They looked after quite a few of Tony Wilson's problems at the Hacienda back in the day. So, it looks like your suspect must have pissed somebody off who is pretty high up the food-chain."

"How do you know so much about these guys?"

"Oh you know, their names come up from time-to-time. They're well organised though, it's not easy to stick anything on them. And to be fair, they never deal with any good people. It's only the scum of the earth that they have to sort out."

"So, they're a pretty good thing for Manchester then, eh?" Miller laughed.

"Yes, to be honest. Our job would be a lot harder without them. I'm pretty surprised that you haven't heard of them. There's a file on the classified database, tap in and have a look. But to be honest, the general consensus is to just leave them be, they're worth more to the community outside prison, than inside."

"Well, I might have to upset the apple-cart. I'm going to have to bring them in."

"It'll be a big job. Armed response, two addresses. I don't think they'll come quietly."

"That's not going to be my problem, that's why armed response earn their big wages! Nice one John, I might text you later if I need to know any more."

"You're welcome Andy. Hey, and it would be nice if you just phoned one time for a chat. I only hear from you when you want some free expert advice!"

"I might just do that one day! Cheers mate." Miller ended the call.

"Did you hear all that?" asked Miller.

Saunders looked at his boss as though he was taking the piss. "I'm sat right next to you! The call was on the hands-free system. I'd have been able to hear it if I was surfing on the roof."

"Alright, no need to be a clever-dick. Anyway, have you heard of the Cole brothers before?"

"Once or twice. Not for a while though, I heard more about them when I was in uniform, than I have recently."

"What did you hear?"

"Not much, just that they were the guys to be scared of. Nobody is worried about the police, because the police aren't a threat. But if you piss somebody off so much that the Cole brothers become involved, you're in serious trouble. The kind of trouble that makes you move to another country."

"God... I can't believe I've never heard of them! I wonder what this little knob has done to attract such esteemed punishment."

"Only one way to find out!"

"I know, I'm becoming more and more intrigued in this with each passing hour. Let's get back so I can read the file. I'm quite looking forward to meeting the Cole brothers."

*****

In the SCIU office, the work was continuing at the same enthusiastic pace that it had been doing over the previous days. Despite the fact that there was now a name for the attacker, DI Saunders had told the team to completely ignore that fact, and carry on regardless. There had been a look of great confusion at that remark, but Saunders quickly explained that there were more holes in that theory than there was in a tea bag. The announcement had lifted the spirits of the team again, and the mood was electric, especially as they had all arrived into the office that morning, expecting their over-time cancelled and their marching orders back to their regular police work. Each of the regular SCIU team members, who were managing their own small teams, were thoroughly enjoying the positive, productive mood.

Rudovsky was extremely happy with her team, who were quizzing DWP offices in the area, trying to build up a picture of who the biggest dickheads were that each office dealt with. It wasn't exactly throwing up any strong leads, there were one or two people who seemed like they might just possess enough hatred inside themselves to carry such appalling acts against another person. But they were very few and far between. Each time a name was presented, Rudovsky's team would carry out a deep investigation into their backgrounds, run them in, and carry out a very heavy interview with them. She didn't actually believe that the attacker was likely to announce his intentions to staff at the Jobcentre or on the phone to the Disability. But none-the-less, she and her team were relentless in their efforts. It was extremely entertaining work, hearing and reading about some of the clients, and the kind of things that they do when they are in front of DWP staff.

Each team was beavering away. Chapman with his team were reviewing the appeals, Kenyon's door-to-doors, Grant's social-media team and Worthington's CCTV researchers were doing a fine job, finding lots of new, still images of the attacker. They still hadn't managed to get a facial shot, but they all felt that it was only going to be a matter of time.

Miller and Saunders arrived back just after two pm. Miller went into his office, and Saunders walked around the office floor, getting updates from each team leader, and doing his best to keep everybody focused and enthused. At this stage, it was to remain a secret that Miller was planning the arrest of the Cole brothers, with the head of the armed response section.

But just as Miller was starting to plan the arrest, and was trying to come up with a few additional lines of enquiry which would keep the Cole brothers in custody for the longest amount of time possible, his phone rang. It was his boss Dixon, who was at home. He was ringing to let his DCI know that there had been a significant development, one which changed everything. Miller was informed that the body of a young man had been discovered in a suitcase. It had been thrown into a stream near Sheffield.

Miller was unsure where this phone call was going. But Dixon's next sentence sent shivers down his spine.

"We've not had a formal identification yet. But the body looks extremely likely to be that of Curtis Kennedy."

Chapter Thirty-One

Miller was transported to the crime-scene in the Manchester force's helicopter. He took Saunders, leaving the rest of the team to continue with their tasks at HQ. The flight had only taken twenty minutes, and as the Manchester helicopter India 99 reached the scene, it soon became clear that this was a major operation for the South Yorkshire police. The area where this grisly discovery had been made by a group of hikers was close to a tiny hamlet called Hollow Meadows, just beyond Ladybower Reservoir on the Sheffield side of the Snake Pass.

The whole area was littered with police cars, police vans and Range Rovers. A long line of police officers were searching the fields surrounding the crime scene. Sniffer dogs were leading their handlers along country paths, and as India 99 descended to land, the forensics tent came into view, it had been pitched beside a heavy-flowing brook with a stone bridge crossing it. Lots of dour looking forensics officers were standing around, talking.

Seconds later, India 99 had landed, and Miller and Saunders were walking across the field, towards the crime scene, the down-draft force from the rotor blades made them a pathway through the long grass.

The Manchester detectives were quickly brought up to speed. The South Yorkshire force had done a sterling job of containing the crime scene, and their officers had identified the route which had been made through the fields, up to the location of the suitcase. It had very quickly been established that two people had dragged the suitcase halfway up the field, a distance of almost a third of a mile. The grass had been flattened, and on either side of the track mark which had been created by the dragging of the suitcase, there were two sets of footprints. But then one set of footprints turned back, while the other set continued up to the location where the grim discovery had been made.

At the scene where the suitcase had been pulled from the water, the Sheffield pathologist was examining the body.

The Sheffield DCI explained. "The car which transported this suitcase pulled into a church car park at the bottom of the field, you can see where they threw it over the wall, and have then created a perfect indentation in the grass. It's clear that two persons have dragged it halfway up here, in the dark…"

"How do you know it was dark?" interrupted Saunders.

"There was a stray piece of stone in their pathway, you can see where one of them tripped on it, fell over, and flattened the grass. That person turned back at the point, leaving the other to continue the rest of the way alone."

"Oh, we'll have to have a look at that."

"Of course. Forensics are examining the scene right now. They're extremely confident that they'll pick something up there, a stray hair or some other vital DNA sample." The DCI pointed down the hill, at three white-suited colleagues crouching down.

"Go on," said Miller.

"So, the one who carried on has dragged the suitcase here, pulled it onto the bridge there, and thrown the suitcase over the side, into the water below."

Miller looked confused. "Why did they bother to drag a dead weight all that way in the dark?" He asked, not of anybody in-particular.

"Well, that's the most gruesome part. Looking at the state of the interior of the suitcase, and the fact that there were bungee cords attached to the outside, it looks increasingly like the young lad was still alive when he was chucked in the stream."

"Fucking hell."

"Precisely. My thinking is that whoever did this wanted to cause him a nasty injury before he drowned when the freezing water started gushing into the suitcase."

Miller and Saunders looked at one another as they considered this grisly suggestion, before returning their attentions to the DCI.

Just then, the pathologist wandered across to the three men. "Hi, I'm happy that he was still alive when that suitcase was thrown into the brook. He has died from drowning, the lungs are waterlogged due to inhalation. Had he already been deceased, we would not see that volume of water in there, if any at all."

"Time of death?"

"Good question. The body will have cooled at an accelerated rate due to the cold water. I'd hazard a guess that he's been dead for at least twelve hours, but no more than twenty-four."

"And do you think that it is Curtis Kennedy?"

"It looks highly likely. There is a rather amateur tattoo on his neck, looks like an attempt at some kind of a cannabis leaf."

"Yes, that's Kennedy," said Saunders. He'd seen the crude tattoo on the side-mugshot from Kennedy's last arrest.

Miller was confused. He started thinking fast. After a moment, he spoke, it sounded like he was thinking out loud.

"Right, so whatever he was up to in Glossop last night, he's been with two accomplices. They've driven him up here, then somehow tricked him into getting into the suitcase, chucked him in here. Then what? There were road-blocks all over this area last night."

"Two people in a car, they must have gone through the Sheffield side of the road-block."

"Yes," said the Sheffield DCI, traffic are just compiling a database of all the vehicles we stopped and searched. "If they came through, we'll have their vehicle details, along with the names and addresses of all occupants."

"Brilliant. That's brilliant." Miller felt that this was a very positive development.

"Unless they've stayed put. They could have parked up for the night, and headed back towards Manchester after the dust had settled." Suggested Saunders.

"Nah, doesn't make sense. They wouldn't have had a clue that we had road-blocks up. They couldn't have had any idea. What's he done wrong this lad, been spotted down some back alley and been chased off? No police force is going to chuck a road-block up for that, are they?"

"No, no. You're right, yeah. Fair point. So, there's a

good chance they've been caught in one of the road-blocks, either here, or back in Glossop. That's very positive."

"Right. Can we have a look at the body?"

Miller and Saunders were led down to the stream. The sight which greeted them was extremely depressing. The dead body was still inside the bright orange suitcase, but the lid was completely open. The corpse had no skin left on its finger-tips, and most of its finger-nails were missing.

"These injuries were sustained trying to rip his way out of the suitcase. You can see the blood and tear marks here. See?" The DCI pointed at the distressing detail within the case, but looked remarkably unaffected by the disturbing scene which lay before him. Maybe he had got used to it, now, assumed Miller. The suitcase was a large, plastic one. It had a handle and a set of wheels on the bottom. It had been locked shut using two snap-shut combination locks, which had been ripped off by the hikers when they made the grisly discovery at this quiet beauty-spot.

"Why would they have an old, retro plastic suitcase with them? It's not the kind of item that you carry around in your car, is it? This murder must have been planned." Miller couldn't make head-nor-tail of this sinister answer to the question of Curtis Kennedy's whereabouts.

"My bet is that he knew too much about something. So that puts his connection to the DWP attacks back on the table." Saunders looked away from the upsetting sight before him.

"Go on," said Miller, intrigued to hear his DI's assessment.

"We had him down as a coincidental by-stander. But maybe his presence in that ginnel *was* connected to the DWP worker's house after all. Whoever is responsible for this has taken the suitcase with them. There's absolutely no way they've nipped home for it, then driven through road-blocks, then convinced this poor bastard to get inside it. This had been planned, I'll bet you a fiver."

"God, you're such a tight-wad Keith. A bloody fiver!"

Miller's radio beeped. "Air Support to DCI Miller over."

"Miller receiving, over."

"We're due to return to Manchester, we're covering the Man City Arsenal fixture. Are you joining us, or making your own way back, over?"

Miller looked at Saunders, then across to his opposite number from the Sheffield force.

"Could do with getting back, to be honest…"

"You may as well. We'll send you all the updates, once all the forensic examinations are completed here."

"Where is the body going?"

"County morgue. The pathologist will need to do a thorough examination." The DCI talked in a matter-of-fact way which sounded as though he was talking about something much less serious, like having his loft converted.

Miller pressed his radio. "This is Miller. We're on our way, over." He turned to the DCI. "Thanks very much for your cooperation. We need to get back and put Kennedy's mum and sister in the picture before any of this hits the news."

"No worries. I'll send all of the necessary over in due course."

"Cheers. As a matter of absolute urgency, can you find out if two black men were caught in the road-block last night? Double points if it was a black BMW."

"I'll get on to that right away."

"Excellent. Alright, speak later."

Miller and Saunders started jogging back towards India 99, but were visibly struggling to make progress the closer they got to the aircraft, as the force of the blades was pushing them back. Once they'd stiffened their legs and fought the giant fan which was trying to blow them back towards the crime scene, they jumped in the aircraft, fastened their safety belts, and India 99 began to take off.

"Right, I'd better do a list." Said Miller, beginning to feel overwhelmed with the amount of tasks which would need completing now.

As the chopper began to elevate away from the site, Miller and Saunders literally got a bird's eye view of how far the killers had pulled the suitcase.

"Jesus," said Saunders. "It's a hell of a distance they've

pulled that suitcase."

"Yeah, it must have been a drag." Said Miller, completely without humour.

Chapter Thirty-Two

Miller and Saunders arrived back to the SCIU shortly after 3pm, and called an urgent team briefing for all of the officers working on the case. It took ten minutes to relay the facts that were known, starting with the doubts about Kennedy's involvement, to the discovery of his body inside the locked suitcase, and all of the information that they had gathered about the dead person in between.

There was shock and disbelief at how cruelly and sadistically Kennedy's life had been ended. There was disappointment that Miller and Saunders hadn't shared their knowledge about Kennedy, particularly amongst the permanent SCIU officers, Rudovsky, Grant, Chapman, Kenyon and Worthington.

But most of all, there was a feeling of utter confusion in the incident room. This did not make any sense, and almost every aspect of the recent developments generated dozens upon dozens of unanswered questions.

"Now, I want you all to stop what you are doing, and I want this department to focus on gathering every detail we can about every car that was stopped last night, on both sides of the Pennines. DI Saunders and I are going to go up to Hattersley, to break the news to Mrs Kennedy, and we also need to arrange specially trained officers, along with transport for her to go and identify her lad's remains. By the time we get back in this office, I need a map of the area on that wall, and I want visual details of all of the road-blocks, and with each of those road-block patrols, I want the details of every single vehicle and all of the occupants that were stopped and searched last night. Do we understand?"

"Yes, Sir." There was plenty of gusto and enthusiasm in the voices of the officers.

"DC Rudovsky, I'm putting you in over-all command of this task. I will alert South Yorkshire police that you are the main contact, and I will apply as much pressure as I can to make sure those road-block details are sent over as a matter of the utmost urgency. In the meantime, you have the Manchester side to look at, and I'll inform DCS Dixon to personally ensure that all of the information is supplied as soon as is physically possible. Okay, thanks guys. Oh, and just remember... I can pretty much guarantee that those car details will include the information that will lead us to the killers of Curtis Kennedy. Once we have that information, we will have a major piece of this puzzle, and the rest of the bits will come soon after."

*****

The drive back up to Hattersley was quiet. Both Miller and Saunders were locked into their own thoughts. Both were dreading this visit, and not because of the piss stain on the settee. It was never a pleasant task to deliver the news that a loved-one was dead, but it was all the more unpleasant when the death was down to murder. But she didn't need to know all of the grisly facts at this early stage. At least there was that.

Once they arrived at Sandybank Avenue, for their second visit within just a few hours, they both felt extremely tense and were eager to get this difficult task over with. They both got out of the car in silence, closed their car doors quietly, and walked respectfully up the steps towards Mrs Kennedy's front door.

The CID knock was quieter this time. After a short delay, Mrs Kennedy appeared at the door. She looked surprised to find the two officers stood there again.

"Oh... for f..."

It seemed like she was about to start ranting at them, but it was clear that she quickly read the sombre looks on their faces.

"No... aw, no..."

"Mrs Kennedy, can we come inside please."

Aw God, it's not... you're..."

"Can we come in?" Miller was using his nicest, most sympathetic voice.

"Is that the fucking dibble again?" shouted Madison, from upstairs. Her appalling manner really wasn't appropriate, and Miller began to feel sorry for Mrs Kennedy, who was standing there, looking as though her shitty little world was falling apart.

"Come in." She said, she swung the door open, and the DCI and DI were reintroduced to the odour of the Kennedy family's squalid home.

"Please, Mrs Kennedy, take a seat." Said Saunders, eager to assist his boss with this horrible job.

"Oh no, no, no no…" she said as she walked, dazed, to her seat in the living room.

"Madison, can you come down here a minute please?" Shouted Miller up the stairs, in as gentle a tone as he could muster.

It seemed that Madison had sensed the gravity of the situation too, as she appeared at the top of the stairs with a look of terror etched on her pallid, acne infected face. She began descending the stairs slowly, silently.

Once Curtis Kennedy's nearest and dearest were sat down, Saunders took the lead.

"I'm afraid we have some very bad news about Curtis. We believe that he is dead."

Those words were like bombs, and the explosive power of them ripped through the room.

Mrs Kennedy was weeping silently, her trembling had got a lot worse and she looked as though she was about ready to collapse with nervous exhaustion. Madison just stared directly ahead, and it was clear to the detectives that she didn't quite have the emotional capacity to deal with this information.

"Police in Sheffield discovered a body this morning. We've been over, and had a look. I'm afraid it does look like it is Curtis." Miller spoke softly and considerately.

"How?" asked Mrs Kennedy, staring down at the filthy carpet which had once been pink.

"We don't know… it's too early to…"

"But I mean, was it drugs, or booze or summat?"

"We aren't exactly sure of all of the details, but the suspicion is that he was murdered."

This detail opened the floodgates of emotion for the two Kennedy women. They both started crying and sobbing, Madison fell to her knees and shuffled across to her mother and they gripped one another tightly.

Saunders slipped through to the kitchen, to make them both a hot drink. He put the kettle on, but couldn't find any brewing tackle. The tea-bag caddy had nothing in it and there was an empty sugar bag lay on its side on the kitchen work-top. Saunders looked in the cupboards, but they were bare. He walked back through to the living room, and shrugged at Miller as the two women continued to sob together.

They stayed silent for a while. The only sound in that sad place was the sobbing, and the kettle boiling.

Miller left it a little longer before he spoke.

"I've arranged for specially trained officers to support you. They'll also drive you over to Sheffield, so that you can formally identify Curtis, when you feel up to it. They'll be here in about ten minutes."

This announcement caused a fresh wave of crying, wailing, sobbing and rocking.

"But one thing that I want you to know, is that I will catch the person who did this. You have my word on that."

Chapter Thirty-Three

"Fucking hell. They don't get any easier, do they?" asked Miller as Saunders reversed the car from its parking space, and pulled out of Sandybank Avenue.

"No. That was horrible. Couldn't even make them a brew. They've got no stuff."

"Shit. Is that what you were shrugging at?"

"Yes. It's tragic."

"Well find a shop, we'll have to get them a box of tea-bags."

Saunders and Miller returned to the address with a bag of tea-bags, coffee, milk and sugar, and a couple of packets of biscuits. Fortunately, the door was answered by one of the police officers who were now in charge of the Kennedy's welfare.

"Oh, right, cheers," she whispered to Saunders as he handed the carrier-bag over.

Saunders returned to the car and started the engine. Miller was on the phone. Within a few minutes, they were on the motorway, and headed back towards Manchester at 100mph.

*****

"Okay everybody, what have we got?" shouted Miller as he and Saunders entered the SCIU offices.

The team gathered around the incident room. The map that Miller had requested was on the wall, along with post-it notes situated at each of the road-block signs. Rudovsky stepped forward to present the team's findings.

Miller was impressed with how much had been achieved in the two hours that he and Saunders had been away.

"Sir, starting on the Manchester side of the Pass, we have identified that all roads in or out were locked down within eight minutes of the road-block instruction, which was issued at nine-forty pm. No traffic was allowed to enter the exclusion zone, the traffic lights just south of Mottram on the A57."

Rudovsky pointed to the map. "This action restricted all vehicular access to Glossop, and all vehicles coming out of Glossop were checked. The same action was taken here, here, and here." Rudovsky was pointing at other points on the map around Glossop, where other roads had been closed. "This was a very successful operation, and it resulted in a total of one hundred and fifty-nine vehicles being stopped, searched, and occupants details recorded."

"Is that all?" Miller seemed surprised that this operation, which had been in place until dawn, had such a relatively small number of vehicles on such a busy route.

"Yes, Sir. I have queried the numbers. The reason I am told, is that the word had quickly got around Glossop, via Facebook etc, that the town was in lock down. As a result, people just cancelled their plans. Most of the vehicles were recorded in the first two hours. After that, there was practically no movement."

"Just vital journeys?" asked Miller.

"That's right, Sir. People going to work on night-shifts, etc. Traffic from Manchester to Sheffield was re-directed through Tintwistle, and over the Woodhead Pass to Barnsley."

"Okay, that's good."

"South Yorkshire's operation took a little longer to set up, as their geographical logistics were a lot more challenging. But they are confident that from the time of Kennedy's discovery in that back ginnel at nine-thirty, and the time that they had closed the A57 at their end at ten pm, it would have been impossible for any road-vehicle to make the journey and get through."

"So, we got a total lock-down?"

"Affirmative, Sir. However, there is a small window of opportunity that they could have escaped the Mottram road-block if they'd headed for Manchester."

"But we know that they didn't, because we have Kennedy's body in a suitcase, here." Miller tapped the map at Hollow Meadows."

"That's correct, Sir. So, we might well have the vehicle's details in the two databases. We're working through them now, eliminating the obvious choices."

"And what is your elimination method?"

"We are concentrating on suspect vehicles only, Sir, for example families with kids present are being struck off, as are all of the pensioners and professional workers, such as teachers, nurses, police officers, etc."

"Good. Good. Keep going. Excellent work DC Rudovsky. Well done everybody."

Chapter Thirty-Four

Miller didn't know how to handle the press aspect regarding the brutal murder of Curtis Kennedy. He had half a mind to phone Detective Chief Superintendent Dixon, and pass the responsibility onto his boss. But something made him put it off. He wanted to chew this over for a few minutes, and make a decision after a bit of thinking time. He retreated to the relative peace and quiet of his office.

The SCIU floor was a hive of activity, as the detectives and support officers continued cross-referencing vehicles, names, addresses and PNC records for each of the vehicles which had slipped through Rudovsky's first short-list. The short-list totalled 55 suspect vehicles from the Manchester side road-blocks, and 31 from the east, around Sheffield.

Saunders was sitting at his desk, and he looked as though the tiredness was catching up with him, having only managed to grab three and a half hours sleep.

"Hey!" said DC Helen Grant.

"Oh, hi, you okay?"

"Yes, it's all getting a bit frantic now, isn't it?"

"Oh, yes I know, my brain's fried."

"You okay?" Grant knew that Saunders had been to see the body, and had also been to deliver the bad news to the dead man's mother. She didn't mention it, but she wanted Saunders to know that she was thinking of him.

"Yes, yeah, I'll be fine. My head is all over the place, got thousands of conflicting thoughts. None of this makes any bloody sense."

"I know. But we'll have identified the car soon, it's literally only a matter of minutes until we crack this. Stay positive." Grant touched Saunders' shoulder tenderly as she turned and headed back to her own desk.

"Hope you're right," muttered Saunders, who really didn't have a clue what was happening with this bizarre enquiry. He very rarely felt so disconnected from a live case. But this one was throwing up so many surprises and false-starts that he just couldn't find his usual mojo.

In the DCI's office, overlooking the rest of the team, Miller was hoping for one thing. He wanted the Cole brothers to come up on one of the vehicle checks. He knew that if that happened, he pretty much had the mystery surrounding the murder of Curtis Kennedy solved. But even with this positive thought at the front of his mind, Miller was still completely at a loss as to how any of this fitted in with the DWP attacks. The link between Kenyon and the DWP employee Kelly Taylor in Glossop was tenuous, to say the least. But despite the frustration of only having a small part of the picture, he was still feeling confident that something was going to turn up.

And he was right. Miller's phone rang. It was the Sheffield DCI.

"Ah, DCI Miller, answered on the first ring. You must be keen to hear from me?"

"Hi, yes, you could say that. Although desperate is probably a better word than keen!"

"Well, it's excellent news."

"Your officers stopped two black men?" Miller's voice was full of hope.

"No. I'm afraid not."

"Oh."

"But it's still excellent news. The crime scene has yielded us a DNA sample, some genetic material which in turn has matched up with DNA that's stored on the PNC. We've a positive ID for one of the people who was transporting the suitcase."

Miller pulled the phone away from his ear and stared at it for a moment. He was gob-smacked. This was way beyond any expectations he'd ever dared to have. DNA sampling usually takes seventy-two hours at least, and that's during the normal working week. Only four, maybe five hours had passed since Miller was at the scene.

"Are you there?"

"Yes, yes, shit. Sorry, you just took my breath away. That's unbelievable!"

"Yes, ha, I must agree it was a very lucky find. We've got the new integrated microfluid DNA testing system, it makes checking DNA blood samples almost as quick as a search for fingerprints. There was a sample of blood on the stone that one of them had tripped over. He must have had a harder fall than we had anticipated."

"Yes, shit. He must have."

"Well, you can go and ask him. His name matches up to a vehicle which was stopped in Sheffield. You've got him."

Miller wanted to punch the air. No, he wanted to drive over to Sheffield and kiss this DCI on the forehead. This was absolutely incredible.

"What, how…"

"How, what?" The DCI in Sheffield was smiling down the phone. He obviously found DCI Miller's reaction to this incredible turn-up extremely endearing.

"Wow, sorry. I was just about to bang my head against my desk… and now this. I can't believe it!"

"Okay, have you got a pen?"

"Yes."

"The man who has left a blood deposit on the rock is called Daniel Hart, he's thirty, and he's got a few convictions for assault, carrying an offensive weapon, witness intimidation. Reading between the lines, he looks like he's part of the gang world. His last known address on the system is 59 Whitehead Road, Gorton. Got that?"

"Yes, cheers."

"He was the travelling companion of Simon Wilson, forty-nine years old, he's served several stretches for nasty crimes. His last known address on the PNC is 411 Hyde Road, also Gorton. The vehicle is registered to him, at the same address, it's a Range Rover Sport, registration Foxtrot Papa Six Three, November Uniform Tango."

"Nut?"

"Yes, ha ha, I thought that."

"Aw this is top drawer, can't thank you enough."

"We've got the vehicle going through an ANPR camera leaving Barnsley, heading towards Manchester on the Woodhead pass. So, for all intents and purposes, it looks as though they've come up here for absolutely no reason, headed up to Barnsley, and then headed straight back in a big triangle. So, there's the blood at the crime scene, along with the vehicle with the two males inside. I think there's enough evidence to charge them on that alone."

"Ha! Try telling the CPS that. But hey, I really can't thank you enough there, you've done a sterling job."

"You're welcome. I'll e-mail my report over later."

"Cheers."

Miller shouted "YES!" as he ended the call.

The rest of the team heard him, and looked across at his office. Behind the glass, Miller was grinning from ear-to-ear, he was stretching out his arms as though his team had just scored the winner in stoppage time.

Saunders left his seat and walked across to find out what was going on. Two minutes later, he left the office holding the piece-of-paper that Miller had scribbled the details onto. Saunders had been told to dig up everything that he could on those two names. This was exactly the lift that the jaded DI needed. The lights were suddenly back on, and Saunders looked refreshed as he made his way hastily back towards his desk.

Miller phoned Dixon, absolutely delighted that his instincts had made him put the task on hold, because the conversation would have been about the best way of handling a disastrous press conference, the purpose of which was to explain that the principal suspect was dead, and that enquiries have found that he wasn't the attacker anyway.

Now, thanks to that astonishing phone call, the conversation was about pulling Simon Wilson and Daniel Hart in, at the same time as the Cole brothers.

*****

By 6pm, Saunders had delivered Miller a catalogue of information on the two men. They were both heavily involved in the gangland scene, and were both suspected drug dealers, working as middle-men for one of Manchester's biggest cannabis suppliers. There were many contradictory comments listed on the system about both men, gathered from several old investigations. But one unmissable detail was the consistent reference to Marco MacDowell.

Miller was baffled. The sheer coincidence of being forced to abort his inquiries into MacDowell, in order to deal with this DWP enquiry, and then for his name to come up within the DWP case, was bizarre. Not only was it a peculiar coincidence, but it was also completely puzzling. Miller continued to read the notes that Saunders had compiled, and scratched his head as he did so. He was absolutely convinced that this was the greatest coincidence of all time. He wanted to talk to Saunders about it, to bat a few ideas off him, but he had left for the evening, finally submitting to the need for a rest.

Miller continued to read through the gathered intelligence. There was no real proof, but there was plenty of suspicion and informant advice that Simon Wilson and Daniel Hart were major distributors for Marco MacDowell. There had been two swoops made against them, by undercover officers, but on both occasions, they, and their vehicle had been completely clean, and they were sent on their way. The last attempt at arresting them had been made six months earlier by Drug Squad, supported by an Armed Response Unit. Their enquiry was dropped soon after, due to funding cuts. It was clear from the case notes that the investigating officers were most dissatisfied that the enquiry had been dropped.

Miller was making notes. He cursed the fact that the rest of the team had gone home, and that the enquiries that he wanted them to make would have to wait until morning. He read through the case notes for a final time, before finally admitting that he too should get home, and get some rest. Tomorrow was going to be a busy day.

Chapter Thirty-Five
Sunday

Miller was beaten in to the office by Saunders, as usual. The DI was busy at his desk when Miller asked him if he wanted a brew.

"Yes, cheers." Said Saunders, without looking around.

A few minutes later, Miller placed the cup on Saunders' desk, and retreated back to his own office. He had a lot to get ready for this morning's team brief, and if possible, today was the day that he would be given the green-light to bring the four men in. But before that could happen, Miller wanted as much shit to throw at them as possible. The stakes were extremely high.

Miller was lost in his own thoughts in the office, compiling lists of jobs that needed to be completed today. When he eventually looked up, he saw that the office was once again brimming with activity, all of the officers were back in, taking advantage of the overtime, continuing with the tasks that had been assigned to them the previous afternoon.

By the time the team brief was about to start at 10am, the mood in the office was electric. There was a real sense of optimism in the air, once Miller and Saunders had shared the extraordinary developments from the past twenty-four hours with the rest of the team. The additional officers all knew that their time with the SCIU was about to come to an end, such was the confidence that the conclusion to this disturbing case was imminent.

"So, before we go any further, I'd like to thank you all for your excellent work on this frustrating case. Now, with a lot of hard work, and a little bit of luck, I think we are very close to finding out who the DWP attacker is, and putting this to bed once and for all. I have an extraordinary Sunday morning meeting scheduled for 11am, with DCS Dixon and the Chief Constable, and it is in that meeting that I intend to request the immediate detention of the four names that we have. Those individuals are," Miller pointed at each of the four mug-shots on the incident room wall as he spoke. "Lenny Cole, Linton Cole,

Daniel Hart and Simon Wilson." Miller took a deep breath before continuing.

"These men are responsible, in one way or another, for this." Miller pointed to the macabre photograph of Curtis Kennedy's body, folded up in the foetal position inside the suitcase. He pinned the disturbing image on the wall.

"After a lot of thought, I have reached the conclusion that this murder was planned, but that under the circumstances of Curtis Kennedy being spotted outside the property in Glossop, it was rushed, and thankfully for us, the perpetrators left behind lots of evidence. Why do I think it was planned? Well, I'm glad you asked me that. Where can you find an old, orange plastic suitcase at eight 'o'clock on a Friday night? If it was brand new, we could assume that it was bought at an all-night supermarket. But it wasn't, and there are no all-night supermarkets in the area concerned, anyway."

Rudovsky had her hand up.

"Go on, Jo." Said Miller.

"Sir, just a thought, but what if Simon Wilson had just come back off holiday? He might have had his suitcase in the boot, might not have unpacked yet?"

It was a thought. But Miller dismissed it quickly. "That's not a bad suggestion. But, look at it. Would you take that skanky old thing on holiday with you?" Miller had a point.

"Yes, shut up Jo!" said Chapman, unable to resist a chance to piss his colleague off.

"No, you shut up Bill, you fat bastard. I hope you get Crohn's disease."

There was a wave of shocked laughter at Rudovsky's vicious response to Chapman's attempt at banter.

"Alright, shush... there's lots to get through here..." Miller didn't look as though he was in the mood for any silliness today. Chapman looked embarrassed by Rudovsky's skilful rebuttal. He didn't learn from his daily mistake, and as such, few people had any sympathy for him.

The team were all quickly given tasks to do, and almost all of the tasks were connected to the Cole brothers, Simon Wilson, Daniel Hart or Curtis Kennedy.

DC Rudovsky was in charge of the team checking all ANPR logs of Wilson's Range Rover. The automatic number-plate recognition technology was an excellent new addition to the police's criminal investigations armoury. The brief was simple, build up a pattern of all ANPR logs of the vehicle, and firstly, see what, if any, the habitual geography of the vehicle was. Secondly, the exercise was to try and place the vehicle somewhere near, or around the attacks. There was a lot resting on these checks, and Rudovsky was determined to do a good job of enthusing her team.

DC Worthington was handed the task of checking CCTV footage again, this time looking for the Range Rover, and the Cole brother's BMW from the existing footage that they had gathered from around each crime scene. There was an added task too, to go and retrieve all CCTV footage from around the two domestic scenes, the first being Stewart Grimley's address in Shaw, and the second being Kelly Taylor's address in Glossop, where Curtis Kennedy had been spotted.

DC Kenyon and his team were handed the job of checking the four suspects financial details on the DWP databases, firstly to check whether they had any dealings with the DWP themselves, and secondly to investigate their financial situations using bank and Inland Revenue systems. The biggest anomaly in all of this was the fact that these four gangsters were highly unlikely to be signing on, and at the receiving end of aggro from the DWP. Miller wanted this clarifying.

DC Grant was paired up with DC Chapman, and their task was door-to-doors around the two domestic addresses. The simple thought was that the BMW and the Range Rover were distinctive looking vehicles, and Miller wanted to know if they had been spotted around either address.

DI Saunders was building on the file that he had started the previous afternoon, with special attention on the Marco MacDowell links. This was going to be the deal-clincher, once the four men were in custody.

Getting the four men into custody was Miller's job. He was planning dawn raids at all four of the men's addresses for the following morning, with support from tactical aid and armed officers. It was going to be a big operation, and he would prefer to move straight away. But due to the scale of the operation, and the huge numbers of tactical officers that needed to be involved, plus the fact that it was Sunday, and the police stations were operating skeleton crews, Miller had to concede that it would have to wait until the following morning.

But first, he had to meet with Dixon and the Chief Constable, then present a press conference, and update the press with the latest details.

He, and only he was aware that the press conference was going to be based on a pack of lies, in an attempt to completely wrong-foot the four men, and make them think that they were home and dry.

Chapter Thirty-Six

"Good morning ladies and gentlemen, and welcome to the Manchester City Police media centre. My name is DCI Miller, and this morning I would like to update you on the progress we are making in trying to detain the DWP attacker."

Despite the fact that it was Sunday, the media centre was packed, as this story was still the nation's major talking point. Rumours about Curtis Kennedy's murder had been circling, and all of the media representatives wanted to hear the facts.

"Yesterday, the person who had previously been named as a suspect in this enquiry, was found dead. The body of twenty-two-year old Curtis Kennedy, of Sandybank Avenue, Hattersley was discovered in Sheffield. We have no idea how he managed to travel the distance from Glossop, where he was last seen on Friday evening, to the place where his body was found."

The cameras were popping and flashing as Miller read out his statement.

"But one thing that we are now unclear about, is whether or not Curtis Kennedy was involved in the DWP attacks. Our initial investigations suggest that this was a very bizarre case of being in the wrong place, at the wrong time. There is no evidence that Curtis had any links to the DWP attacks, and we can only assume that his presence in the alleyway in Glossop was relating to other business." That was a loaded comment, and the journalists recognised it for what it was. Miller was suggesting that Kennedy was up to no good, but he wasn't sure what, and whatever activity it was, he felt sure that it was in no way connected to the DWP attacks.

"I'm sure you will all appreciate that Curtis's family would like to have their privacy respected at this very tragic time, and I would like to repeat that his presence in Glossop, outside a DWP worker's home, is *not* being viewed with any suspicion relating to this case, and we are leaving South Yorkshire police to pursue their own investigations into this tragic incident."

This was big news, and there was an outbreak of urgent

chatter amongst the reporters. They had been convinced that Kennedy was the attacker.

Miller allowed the press staff a moment to settle down before continuing.

"However, there have been a number of significant developments in this enquiry over the past twenty-four hours, and I would like to show you this." Miller held up a drawing. It was an artist's impression mug-shot sketch. The man had scruffy, wispy hair, his face looked hollow, the eyes were menacing, and the drawing looked exactly how you would imagine an angry, unemployed, psychotic, cowardly attacker to look. The only person in the room who knew that it was completely bogus was the man holding it up. Miller had pulled up a random photo-fit face from the system from a case a few years earlier, sunk the eyes in a bit and stuck a mullet hair-do over the man's shaved head, in a two-minute job.

"Do you know this man? We believe that this is the face that has been concealed behind that scarf, and that hooded top on the CCTV images previously released to the press."

There was another wave of excitement. The face looked scary, and the media personnel totally bought Miller's red herring. He hoped that the Cole brothers, and Hart and Wilson would, also.

"We need to speak to this person urgently, we believe that he lives in the South Manchester area, and we are appealing for anybody who recognises this face to call our incident room number on 0161 812 6767. Thank you."

*****

The trick had worked. Within minutes, the creepy looking, computer-generated black and white sketch was being circulated all around Greater Manchester, and beyond, as the instant online news channels released the photo-fit across their social media platforms. The picture of the man who didn't exist, was going viral.

"I know this guy, can't think how though!" Said one Facebook user who shared the image.

"Oh God, this guy gives me the creeps!" announced another.

"If you know this sad, pathetic individual, phone the police right now. Sick bastard!"

The image had become the story, and the sad loss of Curtis Kennedy's life was not even mentioned, which was all that Miller could have hoped for. That was a conversation for another day, under different circumstances.

By the time that Miller got back up to the office, he had to reorganise his staff, and put six of the officers on the phones, answering the calls from members of the public who recognised the man in the sketch.

Once he had checked that his team were making progress with their tasks, Miller went into his office to organise the following morning's dawn raids. During his meeting with Dixon and the Chief Constable, he had been given the highest level of support for his plans. The Chief Constable had said "whatever it takes Andy, the world's media are focused on us right now, and I want that to stop as soon as possible."

Whether he was genuinely keen to see an end to the DWP attacks, or whether the Chief Constable was talking selfishly about the non-stop press intrusion that he'd been experiencing since he had made his damning remarks about the government, Miller wasn't sure. He was just glad to be able to pursue these arrests with the necessary staffing and skill levels required for it to pass off safely.

Things were finally moving, and he felt supremely confident that this case was about to be cracked. He was absolutely desperate to get the four men in custody, and find out what the hell was going on. Once he had alerted the various departments, including numerous Inspectors whose tactical aid units he needed, and the various armed response superintendents, Miller settled down into compiling the interview questions for each man. He looked at his watch, and was filled with a warm glow, knowing that in less than twenty-four hours, he'd be grinning at the four men. The four men that he guessed would be laughing their heads off, mocking his total ineptitude right now.

Chapter Thirty-Seven
Monday

It was 6.05 am and Miller was feeling good. All four tactical aid teams had sent back positive reports from each of the addresses where the dawn raids had been carried out. The four suspects were all in police custody, under armed guard, and the two vehicles had been seized and were on low-loaders, headed for the forensics lab. This news excited Miller, and also put his anxieties to one side. He'd been nervous that something might go wrong, always a risk when dealing with people of this calibre. If any of the arresting officers had been hurt, or worse, he'd have to shoulder some of the blame, mentally at least.

But it had gone remarkably well. There had been no resistance, and all four had been home, fast asleep. It was as straight forward as these things could be. The previous day's stunt with the photo-fit picture had obviously played a blinder, and had conned the four suspects that the police weren't on their tail.

But they'd been spectacularly wrong, and now, they were all on their way to separate police stations for questioning. Miller was absolutely determined that they wouldn't be leaving the police stations any time soon, unless it was in a G4S truck, taking them off to their remand centres.

"Okay guys, positive news, all four detained, without incident." Miller was shouting across the office floor, towards his regular staff team of Saunders, Rudovsky, Chapman, Worthington, Kenyon and Grant. The elation was clear on Miller's face.

There was a cheer on the SCIU floor. That same, dreaded expectation of trouble had clearly been nagging at the rest of the detectives. It was time for a deep breath. The number of guns on the streets of Manchester, particularly in the hands of people like these four, didn't bear thinking about. It was a great relief to hear that this major operation had passed off without incident.

"Right, down to business. Lenny Cole is on his way to Ashton nick. Linton Cole is going to Swinton. Daniel Hart is joining the custody suite at Longsight and Simon Wilson is going to be looked after at Pendleton. As soon as they are checked in, our twenty-four clock starts ticking. Are we all ready?"

"Yes!"

"Do we know what we're doing?"

"Yes!"

"Is this a bit cringey?"

"Yes!"

"Okay, let's get busy. I've compiled a report for you all, relating to each suspect, and I've got a series of questions for you to take with you. Saunders and Grant, you're questioning Simon Wilson."

"Sir!"

"Rudovsky and Kenyon, I want you to look after Daniel Hart. He's the youngest, and his record has the pettiest offences, criminal damage, ABH, witness intimidation etc, so I think he's very immature. He should be an easy one for you to mess with Jo."

"Sir."

"Linton Cole is being interviewed by Worthington and Chapman."

"Sir."

"I'm going to be available via text message, so if anything crops up that you're unsure about, don't hesitate to contact me. I will be interviewing Lenny Cole, over at Ashton."

"Sir!"

"Now listen, before you go, I want you to all take a good look at this lad in the suitcase. Burn that image into your mind's eye."

"Sir."

"And I want you to look at these pictures of Kath Palmer, paralysed, and Jason Brown, lost the use of his arm, and Gary Webster, won't stand up again, and Margaret Wilkins, blind." Miller was touching the photo of each victim. "Remember these people, and the awful situation they are now in. I want to know why, I want to know what the fuck this is all about, and I want to know today."

"Sir!"

"Great stuff. Good luck, and don't forget these." Miller handed each of the three teams their reports. "Before you set foot in the interview room, I want you to know all this stuff off by heart, and backwards. Right, go on, speak later."

*****

Miller was the first to start his interview, shortly after 7.30am with Lenny Cole. It wasn't going well, Lenny Cole, a huge black man, built like a heavy-weight boxing champion looked completely impervious, he didn't seem remotely apprehensive about the interview. He just sat there with a huge grin across his face, displaying the whitest teeth that Miller had seen. He was unnervingly calm.

"No comment." Was his cheerful reply to every question thrown at him.

"Why did you take Curtis Kennedy away from his house in Hattersley?"

"No comment."

"Where did you take him to?"

"No comment."

"Was Curtis Kennedy a drug dealer?"

"No comment."

"Why was your vehicle spotted in Hattersley on the night Curtis Kennedy was abducted?"

"No comment."

"Is Hattersley a place that you visit frequently?"

"No comment."

Lenny Cole gave the same, confident, relaxed response to dozens of questions. If this man was worried about his involvement in the abduction and murder of Curtis Kennedy, he wasn't showing it. Miller wasn't getting frustrated, but he was disappointed that his interview was concluded just before 8am.

"Interview terminated at seven-fifty-eight. That's all of my questions for now, but I will have some further questions later. You will have to be locked up until I am in a position to interview you further."

"Yeah, no worries man, take your time. I'll get my head

down, not used to getting up so early!"

*****

At Swinton police station, on the opposite side of Greater Manchester, it was exactly the same scenario for DCs Chapman and Worthington as they interviewed Linton Cole, Lenny's younger brother.

"Why does your name keep coming up in relation to the abduction of Curtis Kennedy?"

"No comment."

"Are you responsible for the murder of Curtis Kennedy?"

"No comment."

It was clear to Worthington and Chapman that this big, massive guy knew the drill. It was not his responsibility to help the police by answering their questions. It was the police's job to prove beyond reasonable doubt that Linton Cole was involved, and that he was responsible for the abduction and murder of Curtis Kennedy. This guy obviously knew that answering questions would do nothing more than help the police to build a case against him. He was not commenting, that much was for certain, as his interview also ground to a premature conclusion after just twenty-five minutes in the interview room.

"Interview suspended at zero eight hundred hours. You'll have to go into a cell until we resume this interview later."

Worthington was visibly frustrated by Linton Cole's evasive interview technique. He really wanted something good to take back to Miller. But there was to be nothing good to report from this fruitless interview.

"Yeah, yeah, I know the score man. Just try and be quick though yeah, I've got badminton tonight."

*****

Saunders and Grant were a few miles up the road, at Pendleton police station, more commonly known as Salford precinct. They were interviewing Simon Wilson, the driver, and owner of the Range Rover that had been stopped and searched in Sheffield, just an hour and a half after Kennedy had been spotted in the ginnel behind Kerry Taylor's property in Glossop.

He was an old-school 'Jack-the-lad', the kind of man who had dozens of women on the go. It was obvious that he fancied himself a little bit. He had a twinkle in his eye for DC Grant. He was trying to exude his confidence, and presumably, this tactic was the reason that he had declined the offer of a solicitor to be present during his interview.

"Can you tell us why you travelled to Sheffield on Friday night please Mr Wilson?" Asked Grant.

"Yeah, my mate was feeling a bit upset, women issues, he wanted to talk, you know, needed a bit of a shoulder to cry on. Unluckily for me."

"Sorry, that doesn't make sense. Why were you in Sheffield?"

"I've just said, I was just listening to my mate's problems. I was just driving him around. Listening to his sob story." Wilson smiled widely at Grant. He seemed quite taken with her.

"That seems like a strange thing to do. Where did you start your journey?"

"At his house."

"And to confirm, you are talking about Daniel Hart?"

"Yes."

"What is your relationship with Mr Hart?"

"We're just mates."

"But you work together, is that right?"

"Well, work together, no, we just hang out together."

"What is the line of work you do?"

"Security consultant."

"And does Daniel Hart work with you in this role?"

"Sometimes. Look, he's just a mate who's been going through a tough patch. I can't really see what the issue is here?"

"Do you have any injuries on your body at the present time Mr Wilson?" asked Saunders, snapping Simon Wilson out of his cosy, pointless conversation with Grant.

"Any… what do you mean any injuries?"

"Well, it seems a perfectly reasonable question. Very straight forward."

"No...I'm, no I don't have any..."

"Do you know if Daniel Hart has any injuries on his body?"

The smug expression was starting to fade. "I don't know... you'd have to ask him about that. Look, what's this all about, I'm starting to get the fucking hump with all these stupid questions."

"Well, we are investigating the murder of a young man, and you seem to be linked to the offence. We're just going through..."

"Murder, are you having a laugh?"

"No. Not at all. I'm deadly serious."

"How the fuck am I linked to some murder, then?"

"Well, there are a couple of things, but your vehicle is currently being examined by forensics officers, so we'll probably have more to go on later."

"Ha ha, brilliant! You mean you've got fuck all to go on, and you're praying for me to make a confession to a murder I haven't done? Good one."

"Has Daniel Hart got an injury on his body?"

"I don't know!"

"Has he had a bleed that you know of?"

This question definitely rocked Simon Wilson's jowls.

"A bleed, no, I don't know of any bleed. Like I said, ask him."

Grant took over the questioning as Wilson looked as though he was becoming stressed.

"So, you drove over to Sheffield to listen to Daniel Hart's troubles..."

"Yes, how many times."

"You chose a peculiar route home."

"You what?"

"One of South Yorkshire's ANPR cameras picked your vehicle up, coming along the Woodhead Road, back towards Manchester. It just seems a funny route to take."

"We were just on a drive..."

"But I'm curious as to why you didn't come back the way you went? You added an extra thirty-odd miles onto your journey by going across to Barnsley, after you'd been stopped by police."

"I dunno... oh, it was because I didn't want to go through the road-block again."

"Why not?"

"Why... because I can't stand being mithered by police."

"But you told the officers who stopped you that you were going to pick your daughter up from Sheffield University?"

Simon Wilson was on the ropes. That had been a juddering blow. He looked down at his lap. He was becoming agitated. Saunders decided that he and Grant had revealed just enough information for now. He thought that it would be a good idea to get Mr Wilson into a cell, and let him stew for a few hours. Let him work out for himself that he was absolutely fucked.

But before he did that, Saunders wanted to prod him again. This was going to be the head-wobbler.

"Can you tell me why this CCTV camera has footage of Curtis Kennedy getting out of your vehicle on Wednesday night, in Shaw?"

Wilson's head definitely wobbled.

"And why this footage shows him getting back in, forty-five minutes later?"

There was no reply. Saunders placed the photograph on the table.

"This footage was captured from CCTV at the Spar store on Oldham Road. That is your car, isn't it Mr Wilson?"

"Nah, listen, this is a fit-up. I'm not saying anything else, it's a fucking stitch up. You lot have been gunning for me for years. Now you're trying to blag some bullshit murder bollocks on me. It's not going to stick, I'll tell you now."

Saunders smiled. "I'm not happy with what you are telling me Mr Wilson. Your story just doesn't add up. We have reason to believe that you went up to Sheffield after dumping a suitcase which contained the Curtis Kennedy, into a stream, and that you somehow guessed that there would be a heavy police presence in Glossop, so you went back via Barnsley in order to evade the police. But you didn't count on us giving the police in Sheffield a buzz, did you?"

"Yeah, whatever you say officer."

"Right, I'm going to carry out a few more enquiries to see if that is the case. Interview suspended at zero eight forty-five hours. Okay, let's get you in a cell for a bit while we check your story out. You might want to think again about not having a solicitor present when we reconvene."

Wilson was led out of the interview room. He looked considerably less confident than he had done when he'd entered, and the flirtatious manner that he'd displayed for Grant had vanished completely. It was as though a different man was leaving the room.

*****

Rudovsky and Kenyon had been asked to hang fire with their interview until Miller gave the nod. They were sitting in the interview room at Longsight police station, desperate for the go ahead. It was frustrating for the two detectives who were absolutely pumped up and ready to get going with Daniel Hart.

Miller had wanted to see how the other three interviews panned out first. He suspected that Daniel Hart was the weak link, and he wanted the chain breaking at the earliest stage.

Just after nine, Rudovsky's phone finally started ringing.

"It's the gaffer. Hi Sir," she said.

"Hi Jo, thanks for hanging back. Is your phone on loudspeaker?"

"Yep."

"Cool. Hi Pete."

"Hello Sir." Said Kenyon.

"Right, quick heads up. I'm glad you're going in after the rest of us. Saunders and Grant have given Simon Wilson a judder."

"Oh?"

"Yes, he started off being a bit cock-sure of himself, but

they've dropped a few hints that he's in deep shit. They've suspended the interview, and now I want us all to play a game of chess between these two."

"Go on."

"Well, there's nothing too dramatic going on at this stage, but Wilson's been banged up for a bit of a stew, so there'll be fireworks when he goes back in."

"Interesting. Sounds positive."

"Yes, well, we'll see. But I want you to add a few more questions to your list."

"Go on, I've got my pen."

"I need to know if Hart denies working with Wilson. For some reason, Wilson has denied it. Also, I want you to start a psychological game on Hart, asking how much he trusts Wilson. You know the drill, start getting in his head, make him paranoid. Finally..."

"Yes?"

"It'll be a bit later in the interview, but, we need to know where the suitcase came from. We'll see if the answers match up."

"No worries."

"Great. Okay Jo, you know why I've chosen you and Pete for this one. If anybody is going to crack, it'll be this whopper you're going to be interviewing. So, do your usual assessments at the start Jo, let Pete do the introductions and the first few questions, and then once you know how you're going to pursue it, play him like a fucking harp."

"No problem Sir. Oh, before you go, how did we get on with the Cole brothers?"

"No comment."

"Ah."

"But at least Wilson's been talking. It was mostly a load of shite, but its more use than no comment."

"Right. Speak soon."

"Good luck."

*****

Ten minutes later, Daniel Hart was led into the interview room by a custody officer.

"What the fuck is all this about?" He asked as he entered the room.

"Take a seat please, Mr Hart." Kenyon didn't look at the suspect, he was staring down at the information that Miller had provided.

Rudovsky was looking at him, she was staring directly at Daniel Hart, trying to read his body language, his mental state, and his general demeanour. She quickly assessed that he was worried.

"You better tell me what the fuck this is all about. I'm not even joking."

"Were you read your caution when you were arrested?" asked Kenyon, looking up for the first time at Hart.

"Yeah."

"Well, that's what it's all about."

"Well it's dog shit."

"Okay, well, let's just read your rights and start the interview, and you can have your say."

Hart sat down, and started staring straight at Kenyon. He was going for the hard-man routine, staring Kenyon out. The DC read out his rights for the interview, before starting with very general questions.

"Where were you on Friday evening?"

"When was that?"

"Two nights ago."

"I was in my mate's car, went for a drive."

"Your mate, that'll be Simon Wilson?"

"What if it is? We haven't done anything."

Rudovsky felt that she had the measure of this bloke already. She decided to start her work.

"Well you have done something, haven't you Daniel?" She was smiling in a sarcastic way, and Kenyon knew straight away how she was going to play this. She was going to piss Daniel Hart right off. Her instincts for how to conduct an interview were legendary around the department.

"Ain't done jack-shit ma'am!"

"Okay, fair enough. But that's not what your mate is saying."

"Yeah, whatever." Hart blew a raspberry.

"Seriously. When we told him about the discovery of your blood at the scene of a murder near Sheffield, he's definitely put some distance between you both. He's not describing you as a mate, let's just put it that way." Rudovsky was grinning.

Hart looked down at the table-top. That was a pretty devastating comment. It was obvious that Hart's world had just started spinning, very quickly.

"Blood. What you chatting?"

"Where you fell over a big rock, it had come away from the dry-stone wall. We assume that you tripped over it when you were carting the suitcase containing Curtis Kennedy in the dark." Boom. Rudovsky wasn't messing about, and Kenyon looked excited about Rudovsky's fiery line of questioning.

"Nah…" Hart looked like his whole plan was scuppered. He continued staring down at the table-top.

"Have you got any fresh injuries on your person. Anything that has bled in the last few days?"

"You what… chatting shit."

"Your mate, Simon Wilson claims that it was you threw the suitcase into the water." It was a lie. But fuck it.

"You fucking what?" Hart looked furious.

"He says that you lost the plot. And with your blood at the crime scene, you're absolutely buggered here mate. So, I suggest you ask your family and friends for twenty calendars for Christmas, right up to the year 2037. That's when you'll be getting out of Strangeways mate."

"This is total…"

"Did you not feel evil, throwing that lad into the water, knowing he was going to die in that suitcase?"

"IT WASN'T ME!" Hart leapt to his feet and shouted at the top of his voice.

That looked like a major breakthrough, from where Kenyon and Rudovsky were sitting. Four minutes in. This was a personal best for Rudovsky and she looked suitably chuffed.

"Sit down please, Mr Hart."

"The only people there were you, Curtis Kennedy and Simon Wilson. I'm pretty sure it wasn't Curtis who chucked the suitcase into the stream, although I must admit, I've not checked to see if he was a practising magician."

There was no response to Rudovsky's cheerful sarcasm.

"So, if it wasn't you, it was Simon Wilson. Is that what you're saying?" asked Kenyon.

Hart was staring down at the table-top again. He started beating out a rhythm with his fingers. Rudovsky wasn't letting long silences hang. She was determined to capitalise on Hart's outburst. She thought she knew exactly where Hart's button was, and she was happy to give it another push.

"It takes a sick bastard to do that. Killing somebody like that, a slow, torturous death."

"It wasn't fucking me."

"We know that you were there. Got your blood...."

"Where are you getting this twenty-stretch from?" asked Hart. He seemed to have regained his composure a little.

"Well, murdering Curtis Kennedy."

"Which I didn't do... go on..."

"And causing grievous bodily harm to four DWP workers..." Rudovsky was razor sharp. Her answers were lightning fast.

"What the... you trying to pin that shit on me as well?"

"Er, yeah. Obviously. You were in the car outside the DWP worker's address in Shaw, you went in the Spar for... what was it again DC Kenyon?"

"Two bottles of Lucozade Sport, and a packet of Doritos. The spicy ones."

"Aw God! Can't stand them, give me raging heart-burn."

"I like 'em. Packet of them with a tub of salsa. Can't beat it."

As Rudovsky and Kenyon talked shit, it was extremely clear on the face of Daniel Hart that he was feeling completely demoralised. He was starting to realise that the police knew for a fact that he was up to his neck in this.

"I think we'll suspend the interview now, at nine-thirty-seven." Said Kenyon, aware that Hart needed a bit of thinking time, to wind him up further.

*****

"Sir, Hart is close to tears. He's denying that it was him. He's not denying that it was Wilson. So, we've banged him up for a bit of me time. I'm pretty sure he'll be singing like a canary when we get him back in. Any news from the other suspects?" Rudovsky sent her text message. She hadn't tried phoning in case Miller was back in an interview with Lenny Cole.

A couple of minutes later, Miller had text back. "No updates from other interviews. The Cole boys know the score, so they'll be giving us plenty more no comments. Our only hope of a break-through is with your guy, and Wilson cracking. Good work guys."

"Cheers. Keep us informed please Sir."

Rudovsky and Kenyon decided to pass the time discussing the facts of the information that was available to them. They could both sense that Miller's instinct regarding Hart had been right. He was very capable of cracking, he was the weakest link. They just needed to know how to make it happen.

"He's sat in there now torturing himself, his head will be full of panic, and anger, feelings of betrayal. We need to know how to push him up to the cliff edge, and then give him the idea that he might be able to have a safe landing if he plays ball." Rudovsky was writing notes as she talked.

"Yeah, but the trouble is Jo, there's not going to be a safe landing. He's fucked, and he knows it. We can't promise him anything, because he's not going to be able to get away from the murder scene. He's had it."

"Unless..."

"What?"

"He didn't seem keen on the idea of taking responsibility for the DWP attacks, did he? What if we make heavy weather of the attacks, and take Curtis Kennedy out of the picture for a bit, that might be a way of figuring out whether he's the attacker, or if its Wilson."

"It's neither of them, Jo. Think back to the CCTV footage of the attacker running through Hyde bus station Jo. Neither Wilson, or Hart are the correct physical profile. Neither are tall and thin."

"Good point. Hmmm." Rudovsky thought long and hard about her colleague's comment. After a minute or so, she spoke. "That's still the way in. Let's tell him that we believe he is the DWP attacker, and that Wilson is going to be released, as are the Cole brothers. That's going to totally blow his mind."

"Yes, that's a good shout Jo."

"If we keep on and on and on about the DWP attacks, and the fact that he's facing all this shit on his own, he might just 'fess up."

"Yes, totally support you Jo. Good shout."

Kenyon and Rudovsky set about building a series of questions regarding each DWP attack. They both felt a great amount of pressure, but there was also an element of excitement, too. They both felt that Hart was there for the taking.

Chapter Thirty-Eight

Daniel Hart looked like he had been crying in his cell. That was the impression he gave the detectives as he was led back into the interview room just after 2pm. This image was completely at odds with the hard-man persona that he wanted so desperately to portray.

"Right, listen to me yeah? I'm being stitched up here, and I'm not having it. I swear down, I've done fuck all wrong."

This was a good start. But Rudovsky wasn't about to let Hart call the shots. She was as sharp as ever.

"Yes, well, they all say that Daniel. Come on and sit down, we've got some more questions to ask."

"Nah man, listen to me. This isn't on. I'm looking at twenty years for sitting in a fucking car!"

Kenyon restarted the recording unit, and reminded Daniel Hart of his rights.

"Okay, so off tape there, you made a comment. Would you like to repeat what you said?" Rudovsky was staring straight through Hart, determined to make him feel as though she considered him nothing more than a piece of murdering scum.

"Yeah, I just said, this is fuck all to do with me. I said I'm not doing twenty years for sitting in a car!" His face was red, and he was angry. The anger wasn't aimed at Rudovsky and Kenyon though.

"Daniel, as I explained earlier on this morning. Your blood was discovered at the crime-scene, and we have CCTV footage of you and Kennedy together. If you were indeed sat in a car, as you claim, how could your blood have got a quarter of a mile away from the car, in the middle of a farmer's field, close to where we discovered Kennedy's body?"

"I can explain that."

Both Rudovsky and Kenyon laughed. It was part of the game, but Hart didn't appear to be thinking of the police strategy. He was completely absorbed by a sense of self-preservation.

"Listen to me, if I said that I did help to pull the suitcase, but that was all. That was all of my involvement, what am I looking at?"

"That depends entirely on the jury." Said Kenyon. "And whether you could prove that what you are claiming, is true."

"Here's what I want. You give me full protection, new identity and everything, and I'll tell you everything."

"What do you mean by everything Daniel?"

"I'll tell you everything, about that kid Kennedy, and what happened. I'll tell you what these DWP attacks were all about. I'll even tell you who did them. But I'm not going down on my own for all this shit. No way."

"How do we know that you're not just talking a load of rubbish?"

"You don't. But when you hear what I've got to say, and you look into it, you'll know it's right."

"You want to go on Witness Protection?" asked Kenyon.

"Yes."

"Do you fully understand the implications of that?"

"Yeah, well, sort of."

"Well let me just make something clear. If you sign up for WP, it means that your life as you know it is over. It will mean moving away to a new place, most likely in another country. Usually America."

"Yeah, well, I'm up for that. I'm telling you, I've been sucked into all this by mistake, and I want out."

"I can't promise you anything. But I'll go and speak to my boss, and see what he thinks."

"Thinks about what? I've just told you, I'll tell you the whole story. Everything."

"Okay, but can I just remind you that as things stand, you are going to be facing four charges of GBH, plus one charge of attempted assault against the DWP workers, although I think the CPS would agree to attempted murder charges under the circumstances. Plus, you are going to be charged with the murder of Curtis Kennedy. So just don't start trying to call the shots in here Sonny Jim. It's you who needs this deal, not us. Do you understand?"

"Yes, just hurry up."

Kenyon suspended the interview. Rudovsky left the room and called Miller.

"Jo!"

"Hi Sir."

"How's it going?"

"Very well. Hart is denying any involvement other than pulling the suitcase."

"Oh, let him go then..."

"No, seriously. He's asking for a deal."

Miller's voice changed in an instant. "What sort of deal?"

"Basically, he's going to blow the whole thing up if we agree to stick him on WP."

"Seriously?"

"Yes Sir. Seriously. He's shitting himself at the prospect of twenty years. He says if we do this for him, he'll tell us everything, about Kennedy, about the attacks. The lot."

"What does he want it return?"

"Not sure. I think he just wants to be charged with helping to pull the suitcase."

"Okay, deal. But wait for me, I'm on my way over now."

*****

Miller was out of breath as he reached the corridor where Kenyon and Rudovsky were waiting for him. He was red in the face, and he looked like he'd jogged here from his car.

"Where is he?" Asked Miller, leaving the pleasantries out.

"He's sat in there Sir, with a custody officer." Rudovsky pointed at the interview room door.

Miller walked straight in, he gestured Kenyon and Rudovsky to follow.

"Alright?" said Miller, nodding at the would-be gangster who looked more like a scared, nervous year eight who'd been caught with a rucksack full of stolen mars bars.

"Not really." Said Hart. He looked back down at the table-top which he'd been concentrating on before Miller burst in.

"This is DCI Miller," said Rudovsky.

"Yeah, I know who he is…" Miller assumed that Hart was referring to the fact that the DCI was a recognisable face, from all of the high-profile cases that he'd investigated through the years. But he'd be wrong, as he found when Hart continued talking.

"…he's the reason that we're in this fucking mess."

This comment made Miller raise his eyebrows. That was pretty random.

"Interview reconvenes at fourteen forty hours, now present in the room is DCI Andrew Miller."

"What's happening about this witness thing?"

"Witness Protection?"

"Yeah."

"Well, I can sign that off. And if you're genuine about only pulling the suitcase, and no other involvement, I can probably convince the CPS that you were made to do that under duress. There probably won't be any charges, if you can provide quality information."

This news visibly lifted Hart's mood.

"I'm telling you now, I've got the full story."

"Okay, well let's hear it."

Part Four

"Fuck's sake! It's getting on top."

Simon Wilson was sitting in his Range Rover, the engine was running. Both he and Daniel Hart were keeping an eye on Curtis Kennedy. It was dark, but there was just enough light coming through from the garage at the other end of the street, to see what he was up to. Kennedy had been standing in the ginnel behind one of the DWP worker's houses. All he'd had to do was keep an eye on the occupants of the house, especially the woman. And now it looked like he'd messed it all up, as he came sprinting up the ginnel towards Wilson and Hart.

"What the fuck is going on?" said Hart as Kennedy raced towards them. There was a guy chasing him with a baseball bat, he was swinging it, battering Kennedy as he ran.

"Aw fuck it!" said Wilson as he stepped on the accelerator and drove the car forward, moving the vehicle out of sight of the ginnel.

"Stop! You need to wait for him or Marco will blame us!" Pleaded Daniel Hart.

Wilson slammed on the brake. The Range Rover screeched to a halt.

A couple of seconds later, Kennedy had jumped in and was sat on the back seat. He was crying.

"You fucking tube!" said Hart, as Wilson set off at speed. He raced around the junction at the bottom of the street, and then pressed his foot hard against the accelerator. The Range Rover was moving at speed, heading up the hill past Manor Park.

"What the fuck!" shouted Wilson as the full power of the Range Rover was tested. Within minutes, the car was high above Glossop, ascending the Pennines, negotiating the sharp bends of the Snake Pass at speed.

"What happened?" said Wilson.

"Dunno, some guy just came and started shouting, he twatted me round the head with a bat. My heads killing!"

As the road straightened out a bit, Wilson pulled the car over. It was pitch-black up there, and the twinkling orange lights of Glossop looked a long way away. Wilson got out.

"Come on," he said to Hart as he jumped out of the vehicle. He went to the boot and pulled out a large plastic suitcase. Wilson then opened the back door and grabbed Kennedy.

"Get out!"

Kennedy did as he was told. He was scared, confused, and in a great deal of pain. Dawson led him to the rear of the vehicle. Hart was standing there, illuminated by the red brake lights.

"Get in here. In case we get stopped by police."

"What?" Kennedy looked petrified.

"Stop being a dick, just get in. If the police catch you, you're going down for a ten stretch. We're trying to help you, you butt-plug."

"Ten-stretch?" Kennedy was holding his head. It was streaming with blood where the baseball bat had connected.

"JUST GET IN!" Snapped Wilson. He was conscious of the fact that a car could come along at any minute and illuminate the three men, and Kennedy's blood-soaked head, and the suitcase.

Curtis Kennedy did as he was told, and curled up into a ball as he struggled to fit into the suitcase. Wilson snapped the lid shut, and he and Hart lifted it back into the boot.

"Now stay silent!" said Wilson as he slammed the boot shut.

The two men got back into the Range Rover, and pulled off, continuing towards Yorkshire. As they reached the first bend, another car came towards them from the opposite direction and illuminated the two occupants faces.

"That was close!" said Hart.

There was a long, tense silence as Wilson continued driving.

Eventually, Wilson spoke. "I'm going to have to ring Marco."

Hart was looking out of the back window.

"Chopper's up!"

"Fuck."

Hart was right. In the distance behind them was the unmistakable sight of the police helicopter. It had its gigantic torch on, the glow looked like a huge white floodlight, and the thick white beam of light that it generated was strobing around the town.

Wilson dialled Marco.

"Whassup?"

"Aw Marco, it's all going tits up. Someone's chased the kid, he's had his head twatted in."

There was a silence. It was intimidating, and it lasted way too long.

"Marco?"

"Yeah, yeah, I heard you. Where's the kid?"

"In the suitcase, in the boot."

"Where are you?"

"On the tops, going over the Snake Pass."

"Right..."

"The chopper's up in Glossop. Just seen it."

"Fucks sake. Right, you need to lose the suitcase. Somewhere it won't be found."

Now the silence was in the car. Neither Wilson or Hart spoke. This was suddenly becoming a lot darker than the original plan, which was to gather a bit of intelligence from outside a house.

"Did you hear what I said?"

"Yes." Said Wilson, though he sounded extremely unhappy as he said it.

"Find a river or summat, check for one on Google maps. As soon as you find one, chuck him in."

There was another uncomfortable silence.

"Inside the case?"

"Yes. Then stay the fuck away from me until further notice. Text me when you've finished." Marco hung up.

"What the..." said Hart.

"Shut up. Right, open Google maps on there. Find a river." Wilson passed his phone to Hart.

Hart started scanning the local area on the map. They were coming towards several reservoirs, just a few miles up the road. But Hart couldn't bring himself to point them out.

"Got summat?" asked Wilson after a minute or two.

Hart showed him the phone, and the huge areas of water that the blue dot of their vehicle was moving towards on the map.

A heavy silence hung, as the blue dot continued to move slowly towards the vast expanse of water which the road seemed to go through the middle of.

"It's Ladybower Res. That's perfect. They'll never find him in there." Said Wilson.

"This is fucked up." Said Hart. He felt sick. This wasn't his cup-of-tea at all.

"Shut up Dan. We've had our orders. Deal with it."

Hart began to think that Wilson was getting something of a perverse buzz out of all this.

Soon, the blue dot was in the centre of the water on the map. There was nowhere to pull over, and there was a constant flow of traffic coming in the opposite direction, and from the junction which was controlled by traffic lights. It felt like a very vulnerable spot, and a very risky place to throw a suitcase into the reservoir, over the side of a dry-stone wall.

"We can't do it here. It's on top." Said Wilson. "Look for a river. We'll get spotted here."

"We, what's all this fucking we shit? I'm having jack-shit to do with this."

"I don't think Marco will buzz off that Dan. You'll be working in his factory if he hears you saying shit like that."

"This is messed up. He hasn't done owt wrong."

"Marco's orders."

There was another frosty silence.

The car continued to hurtle towards Sheffield. Soon, they'd reached a stream on the map.

"This'll do, look, its at the top of that hill." Wilson was pointing to a blue line on the map which was running parallel to the road, about half a mile up the hill to their left. "We'll chuck him in there, then carry on to Sheffield, and we're home and dry.

Hart just stared at the road ahead. He remained silent.

"Don't start taking your ball home now. We've got no choice, it's us or him."

"We don't need to fucking kill him. Jesus."

"Seriously Dan, you need to have a chat with yourself. Ask yourself why the chopper was up so quick? Ask yourself why that guy came running after the kid. They obviously know the score. We can't drive around with him in the boot. We'll be getting sent down ourselves mate. Marco's right. We need to lose the suitcase."

Hart remained silent. It had never been his intention to get this heavily involved. All he wanted was to make some easy money, punch a few bad people, dish out a few punishments. But not this. This was going way too far.

"Right. Come on." Wilson pulled the car into the car park of a derelict old church. "Come on!" He raised his voice slightly the second time.

Both men pulled the suitcase out of the Range Rover. Wilson was fidgeting around in the small compartment in the boot of the car. He pulled out some bungee straps.

"Here, wrap these around it." Wilson started fastening the straps around the suitcase, pulling them as tense as he could before coupling the two hooks together.

"Nah mate. I'm not doing fuck all."

This comment made Wilson snap at the younger man. "Dan, you better fucking grow a pair. I can't be doing with you pussying about."

"Let me out now, I can't breathe," shouted Kennedy from inside the suitcase.

Wilson crouched down. "Shut up, you. We'll let you out in a minute."

"Better had do!" was Kennedy's reply.

"Fucking hell, I'm completely surrounded by bell-ends," muttered Wilson as he attached the final bungee strap around the case. Two minutes later, the pair had tipped the case over a dry-stone wall, and were clambering over it. Kennedy was crying loudly inside the suitcase.

"You go on that side, drag that handle." Ordered Wilson.

The two men pulled the retro old suitcase up the field in the pitch black, as cars continued to drive along the A57 just beneath them at the bottom of the hill. As well as the cars, they could hear cows mooing, owls hooting, alongside the constant flow of water in the distance, and Kennedy's muffled pleas for help from inside the case.

Wilson was checking the map on his phone. "There's a bridge just up here. We'll chuck the case in there, then get the fuck out of here."

As Wilson said it, Hart tripped over. He hit the ground with a thud.

"Get up you fucking Dime bar."

"Shut up, I've done my ankle in," snapped Hart. He was wincing in pain.

"Oh, fuck you Dan. You're acting like a baby."

Wilson left Hart in a heap on the ground, and pulled the suitcase along the grass, continuing up the slope with the crying youth inside the well-sealed luggage container. Eventually he reached a stone bridge that went over the stream. He hoisted the suitcase up onto the wall.

"Let me out!" shouted Kennedy from inside. He must have sensed that something wasn't right. At that moment, Wilson shoved the suitcase off the wall, and it crashed into the water and rocks below with a loud splash. He clicked on the torch function on his phone, and checked that the suitcase was fully submerged in the flowing water. It was. Bubbles were coming up from the orange plastic object.

"Right." He said as he started walking briskly, back down towards where he had left Hart.

There was no sign of his colleague as he reached the spot where they had split up.

"Dan!" he shouted. "Dan! Dan!"

But there was no reply. Hart had cleared off.

Wilson continued down the hill, back towards the eerie, abandoned church. As he reached the Range Rover, he saw that Hart was standing by the passenger door.

"Get in," was all he said as he unlocked the vehicle. "I need a shit."

Hart got into the car, and he saw Wilson disappear into a bush near the back of the church, the headlights of a passing car had illuminated him as he disappeared into the foliage.

Hart felt as though he was about to have a heart-attack. Wilson was gone for about a minute, but it felt like an hour. As each second passed, the tighter his chest became. He couldn't breathe all the way in, he could only take shallow, panting breaths.

Hart was snapped out of his anxiety attack by Wilson opening his door and jumping in.

"That's better. Always need a shit when I kill someone."

Wilson started the engine and seconds later the Range Rover was back in motion on the road, hurtling towards Sheffield at 70mph.

Nothing was said until ten minutes later, when Wilson spotted a police car, and a police officer gesturing him to stop. The thought crossed his mind to step a little harder on the gas, and zoom through the road-block. But he quickly came to his senses and slowed down. He said "fuck" under his breath as he started rolling the window down.

"Hi,"

"Hello," said the policeman. "Where have you come from?"

"Oh, er, Manchester."

"And where are you heading?"

"Sheffield, Sir."

"Do you mind if I ask why you are travelling tonight?"

"Oh, er, just going to pick the daughter up, she's at Uni."

The policeman was making notes in his pocketbook.

"Is this your vehicle?"

"Yes."

"And your name and address please Sir?"

"Listen, what's all this about? I've never had anything like this?"

"We're checking all vehicles coming over the tops, in relation to an incident that has taken place in Manchester."

"Oh right, well, er my name is Simon Wilson, my

address is four-one-one Hyde Road, Gorton, Manchester."

Another set of car headlights pulled up behind Wilson's car, and the policeman gestured the driver to stay put.

"Do you have any form of identification with you this evening, Sir?"

Wilson pulled the visor flap down from above his head, and pulled out his driving license photo-card.

"Thanks, and what's your name Sir?" asked the officer of Hart.

"Daniel Hart, fifty-nine Whitehead Road, Gorton." Hart flashed his own driving license from his wallet.

"Thank you, and what's your business in Sheffield?"

"Oh, er, nowt, just come along for the drive."

"Okay. I just need to check your vehicle. Can you step out please?" The policeman was talking to Wilson. Hart was relieved, he was covered in mud, from where he'd fallen in the field.

"Open the rear door please Sir," said the policeman. Wilson did as instructed and the officer shone his torch into the car. Wilson was praying that the beam of the torch didn't hit the blood stains on the head-rest. He seemed satisfied. "Can I look in your boot please?"

"Of course officer, no problem." Wilson walked around to the rear of the vehicle and opened the boot. It was empty. The policeman then pulled up the flap where the tool compartment sits. It was also empty.

"Okay, sorry for your trouble. Have a safe journey."

"Yeah, yeah, no worries officer."

Wilson got back into the car and started the ignition as the policeman wandered on to the car which was waiting behind.

"See? Marco was right." Said Wilson as he drove away. Hart said nothing.

In fact, nothing else was said for much of the one hour and fifteen-minute journey back to Manchester, via Barnsley and the Woodhead Pass. As Wilson's Range Rover approached Hyde, Hart realised that he had to try and offer some kind of olive branch to the other man, if only for his own preservation.

"Sorry, I freaked out back there. You're right, it was the best thing to do." Hart made it sound genuine. At the back of his mind was the prospect of Marco punishing him for dissent.

"Was that your first one?" asked Wilson, coldly.

"Yeah. Yeah, soz. I know it was the right thing to do, just freaked me out. That's all."

"Don't worry about it Dan. First ones are the hardest. You've just got to remember, it's us or them. It's a doggy dog world. You'll be alright in the morning."

"Yeah, no, I mean, I'm alright now. Just thought it was a bit tight, but we'd be banged up ourselves now if we'd not done it. I'm cool."

"Nice one, good. I'm glad you understand."

"Listen, you won't say out to Marco will you, about me panicking?"

"Nah man, will I fuck. Jesus, it'll be you next if he heard about that. Trust me mate, I won't say a word."

"Cheers. No, I appreciate that. I owe you one."

Not long after the two men had made their peace, Wilson pulled up outside Hart's house.

"Right, go and get your head down. See you later. And seriously, don't worry about Marco. What he doesn't know can't hurt him, yeah?"

"Yeah. Thanks again." Hart got out and closed the car door. Wilson pulled away immediately.

What followed was the longest night of Daniel Hart's life. He tried to sleep, tried desperately to erase the vision of Curtis Kennedy curling up in a ball in that suitcase under the red glow of the rear lights. The mental vision of Kennedy curled up in that enclosed space, as the water started rushing into the suitcase haunted him.

As though this wasn't torturing him enough, he was also plagued by images of Marco coming after him, sending the Cole brothers, or some other heavies to take him out of the picture. Would Simon Wilson keep his word, or was he headed straight over to Marco's, to tell him about Hart's reaction to the bosses order? These thoughts torturing Daniel Hart all night, and continued to do so throughout the following day.

But as each long hour drew to a close, Daniel Hart began to think that Simon Wilson had kept his word. Marco wasn't aware of the tantrum, if he had of been, he would have made it known by now. But even with this relative peace-of-mind, Hart couldn't erase the mental imagery that he had conjured up, the visions of the freezing cold water filling that hard, bound-up suitcase, and the absolute terror of Kennedy's final moments of life.

In one sense, Hart was glad when he heard the police smashing his front door open. It was over.

Part Five
Chapter Thirty-Nine

Rudovsky, Kenyon and Miller listened quietly, somewhat sympathetically to Daniel Hart's story. He wasn't a nice man, that much was clear. But at the same time, he wasn't a cold-blooded killer, that much was becoming obvious as he retraced his steps on that bizarre, unplanned night. He kept breaking down, lots of tears and soggy handkerchiefs followed. The detectives sensed that the tears weren't just for him. He seemed genuinely gutted about what had happened to Curtis Kennedy.

Once the story was told, Miller had a few questions about a number of matters which didn't quite stack up.

"You seemed to imply that this was a freak occurrence, and that Kennedy was killed in the spur of the moment?"

"Yeah, he was."

"So why then was Simon Wilson carrying an enormous plastic suitcase in his boot?"

"I don't know."

"You don't know, or you don't want me to know?"

"Swear down, I have no idea."

"Do you not think that's a pretty random item to have in one's boot?"

"Yeah, well, I don't know."

"I think that it was planned all along, and I think you bottled it, and came up with this story to cover your arse."

"I didn't."

"Did you not ask him why he had a massive suitcase, big enough for a body, in his boot?"

"No."

"But you do admit that it's a pretty amazing coincidence, that Wilson just so happened to have this item at the precise moment that he needed to dispose of a person?"

"Listen, right, I've told you what happened. I don't fucking know why he had the suitcase. He never mentioned it, and I've never looked in his boot before. He might have had it in there for years."

"Okay, well I'll have to take your word for it. On another matter, who carried out the attacks on the DWP workers?"

Hart didn't hesitate in answering. "It's a guy called Miggy. He's one of Marco's psycho boys. He carries out random attacks, two-grand a pop."

"Miggy?" Miller had an eye-brow raised.

"His real name is Jamie Miggins. Miggy for short, but he's known to you lot, he's in and out of Strangeways."

"And so this Miggins character just attacked the DWP staff on Marco's orders, and then what?"

"And then he gets his money."

"Two grand?"

"In twenty-pound notes, as soon as it's been mentioned on police radio, we go and deliver payment. Me and Simon were the ones who dropped it off for him."

"How does Marco have access to police radio?"

"Marco can get his hands on anything he wants. He's got loads of police radios. Every time one of your officers claims they've lost one, you can pretty much guarantee that Marco ends up finding it."

"What's Miggy's address?"

"I'm not sure, we never went to his address. We'd meet him at bus stops or in ginnels and stuff around Haughton Green. Always somewhere low-key, no witnesses."

Miller was writing pages of notes as Hart spoke. It was all starting to sound a bit unlikely, and he was beginning to think that he was being led up the garden path with this.

"We have a significant problem with your story Daniel. We only have evidence placing *you* at the murder scene. When this comes to court, Wilson's defence team are going to argue that you were the one who dumped the suitcase, and their argument will be strong, because there is evidence linking you to the location. There's nothing connecting your mate to that place, other than being in the car, seven miles up the road at the roadblock. I need you to think hard, and give me something that proves Simon Wilson was there. We're going to interview him again in a bit. I need something that will trip him up, without mentioning that we know the full story."

"Okay, well, he took a shit at the church, just in the bush near the back door."

"Are you kidding me?"

"No, seriously. Go and check."

"We will, well, I won't but I'll send someone along. My days of looking in bushes for turds are behind me."

"Don't look at me!" said Rudovsky. There was a brief halt to the tension in the room.

Miller had been desperate to ask his next question, but had decided to hang-fire until the end.

"When I came in here, you made a rather strange comment, you said that this was all my fault. Would you like to expand on that?"

Hart blew out a big breath. This was going to be the moment of truth. The point of no return.

"You were seen looking around outside Marco's mill, a couple of weeks back. Then Marco heard that you were asking a few people a few awkward questions."

Miller looked surprised. He'd always taken a great pride in how discreetly he conducted his enquiries. He had been at the mill, trying to figure out a way in, for the forthcoming raid on the address. That was true. But he'd stayed well out of sight, hidden at all times by shrubbery and foliage. It wasn't as if he'd been pulling on the gates or climbing over the barbed-wire topped, steel-spike fence.

"That's true, I have been carrying out certain enquiries. But I'm surprised that it came to Marco's attention."

"Nothing gets past Marco. He's got the whole building locked down, there's CCTV in the fucking bushes outside. He's obsessed."

This really was a surprise. Miller looked mildly embarrassed by the announcement.

"Okay, so, I hold my hands up, I have been investigating Marco MacDowell, and his illegal cannabis farm. We've known about it for several months, every time the helicopter goes up, they joke about the building being on fire because of the effect the place has on their thermal imaging kit."

"He's always wondering about that..."

"The thermal imaging?"

"Yeah, he's put loads of heat-reflective sheets all around the walls and windows. But he was always paranoid that it would still leak past."

"Oh, it leaks out alright. The building glows up orange because of the heat that's in there, it would be less obvious if he erected a two-hundred metre-high arrow with the words "cannabis factory" written on the side in illuminous yellow glitter."

Hart grinned. It was the first sign of him relaxing since Miller had entered the room half-an-hour earlier.

"So, anyway, back to me. How the hell are my investigations into Marco MacDowell linked to the murder of Curtis Kennedy, and the DWP attacks?"

Hart breathed in sharply. This was another difficult moment. "Well basically, the whole point of it was to get you off his case."

"Are you seriously suggesting that Marco MacDowell has organised the attacks on the DWP staff in order to stop me investigating his drug factory?"

"That's exactly what I'm saying."

Miller exhaled loudly. This was becoming more and more bizarre by the minute. He looked at Rudovsky and Kenyon. They too seemed to be struggling to follow the logic.

"But surely, he mustn't have thought that I'd just forget about him. He can't seriously believe that he can get rid of me just like that?"

"Well, yes, he did do, didn't he?"

Miller smirked at Rudovsky and Kenyon. This was completely insane. After a minute of thought, he decided to speak again. "Well, he's got a shock coming now, hasn't he? Because I'm back on his tale, so it was all completely pointless, wasn't it?"

"No, it wasn't. Can't you see. He's done this to distract you, while he dismantled the factory. He's sold all the growing kit, he's sold all the weed. He's even sold the fork-lift trucks and the vans. Seriously, he's closed it down, he's made millions in the last week. His factory doesn't exist anymore."

The look on Miller's face said it all. He had been well and truly mugged off. He felt as though he'd been winded.

"Where is he now?" asked Rudovsky, filling in for her boss as he tried to come to terms with that devastating announcement.

"Marco? He's dust. His plan was to make as much cash as he could, and as soon as it looked like the factory was coming on top, he planned to cause a massive diversion, and set off into the sunset, early retirement. Why else do you think he was so obsessed with running such a small team, and putting thousands of CCTV cameras up? He's had something like this planned for years. It was originally going to be prison officers that were going to be attacked, but when he saw the shit that the DWP were doing to people, he thought they'd be an easier target, and it would really push you lot off his back."

Miller looked like he had dealt with the initial shock, but he hadn't really. His head was spinning, he couldn't believe it. He wasn't upset that Marco had disappeared, that wasn't the issue at all. His thoughts were on Kath Palmer, and Jason Brown, and Gary Webster, and Margaret Wilkins. And Curtis Kennedy. He was struggling to comprehend that the trail of unspeakable violence, against some really lovely people, was not about the DWP cuts and sanctions at all.

Marco MacDowell had just hijacked a cause, in a bid to divert attention away from himself for a while. It was evil, and Miller really couldn't remember feeling so appalled by such selfish and heartless behaviour. The crime gangs generally kept their nasty activities amongst themselves, it was rare that an innocent member of the public became a victim. The idea that the DWP staff had been injured so seriously, so mercilessly, as part of a stunt, really didn't sit well with Miller. He felt as though he was going to be sick.

"I need a break." Said Miller. Stop the tape."

"DCI Miller is leaving the room. Interview suspended at 15.25."

Chapter Forty

Miller had been standing outside the interview room for several minutes when Rudovsky came out to see where he was. He was stood, holding the wall in a standing push-up position. When he saw Rudovsky, he quickly dropped his arms and began wiping his face. Miller had been crying.

"Alright boss?"

He wasn't alright, that much was obvious.

"Come on Sir. You alright?"

Miller resumed his standing position, leaning against the wall as though he was trying to push it down. He didn't speak, and Rudovsky felt hugely uncomfortable in this awkward, thick silence.

Eventually, he spoke. "How am I going to break this to Kath? How the f... how the hell am I going to go in there and explain that she's going to be staring at the ceiling for the rest of her life, because some evil little cunt wanted to get one over on me and sell all his drugs?" The tears were forming again in Miller's eyes. He continued talking. "He could have just gone. He didn't need to do this."

"Sir, I...."

"Kath's of the view that this was down to a mental illness problem. She's trying to find peace in that, trying to tell herself that it wasn't malice, it wasn't personal, it was just one of those things. It was bad luck. This is going to kill the woman, Jo."

Rudovsky was speechless. She couldn't think of anything to say to comfort her DCI.

Miller stayed like that for a moment, before pulling himself together. "I promised her that I'd catch the bastard that did it, and that's what I'm going to do. Go in there and find out when MacDowell left town. I also want you to find out what the Cole brothers involvement was in all this. Finally, get some info that is going to upset Wilson, details of crimes he's committed. He'll know something, they can't help themselves from bragging."

"Sir."

Miller wiped his eyes and his face and looked at

Rudovsky.

"Hay-fever." He said.

"Bullshit."

Miller didn't smile, where normally he would at one of his DC's cheeky remarks. "See you in a bit. Got to make some calls."

*****

One hour after Miller had learnt the truth about the sadistic crimes he'd been investigating, he'd managed to rationalise his feelings, and get his head around the vile trap that he'd fallen into. Those initial feelings of outrage, humiliation and guilt were now receding. He knew that he had plenty of time to indulge himself in those feelings, but that would have to wait for the time being. Miller had his work cut out. His first task was to contact the Home Office's Border Force, and request a database search for Marcus MacDowell on the exit check records.

This database contains the names, addresses and travel documentation details of all passengers leaving the UK. He also needed the man behind the attacks, Jamie Miggins, aka "Miggy" bringing in as a matter of the utmost importance and DI Saunders had been given his instructions to find out every detail about the man, and organise his detention at the earliest opportunity.

Miller had contacted his opposite number, the DCI in Sheffield, and requested his CSI officers go and search for Wilson's excrement in the bushes around the back of the church. The DCI was happy to oblige, which pleased Miller. There was a very good chance that DNA typing could be obtained, linking Wilson to the exact location where the suitcase trail began. It was fingers crossed on that, and there was a good bit of relief that Miller and his team wouldn't be required to get "hands on" with that aspect of the investigation.

Miller was about to contact Dixon to provide an in-depth update on the day's developments, when his phone rang.

"DCI Miller."

"Ah, good afternoon, its Brian Oldham, Border Force."

"Hiya Brian, got anything?"

"Yes, it looks like good news for you."

Miller felt his heart-beat quicken. He felt his face tighten.

"Yes please!" said Miller with a smile.

"Marcus MacDowell has nor presented himself at any British port since 2015, his last recorded journey leaving the border was Manchester to Amsterdam, and he returned three days later. There are no records of him leaving the UK since that time."

Miller punched the air, and said "yes" through clenched teeth. It meant that MacDowell was still in the UK, and could be put on an international travel ban immediately.

"That's amazing. Unless..."

"Unless he's sneaked out with fake ID?"

"Precisely."

"That's probably not the case DCI Miller."

"I know, I know, but we can't be 100% sure, can we?"

"Well no, but we can be 99.9% sure."

"How come?"

"He's booked on the 19.50 flight from Liverpool John Lennon airport to Marrakesh, flight number FR3028, this evening."

Brian Oldham, the Border Force officer had just given Miller the best news that he had heard for years.

"You absolute beauty Brian. Thank you so much!"

"It's alright, happy to be of assistance."

"Is he travelling with any companions?"

"No, it doesn't look like it, just one ticket was booked on the flight. The booking was made online, last night at 23:18."

"And was that the first available flight to Marrakesh."

"I'll just check..." There was a moment of silence as Brian checked his system logs. "Yes, there is one flight a day to Morocco out of Liverpool."

"Are there any flights from Manchester to Marrakesh?"

"Yes, several a day."

"So, he's specifically chosen to fly from Liverpool, thirty miles away." Miller was thinking out loud.

"That's often the case. They seem to think that smaller airports have smaller security systems. Most northern criminals choose flights from Liverpool, or Leeds Bradford. It always makes us laugh."

"Excellent. That's so good, well done mate."

"I hope it goes well."

"Oh, it will. Just do me a favour, put Marcus MacDowell on your watch list, he's wanted for murder and several violent crimes. It's just as an added layer of insurance."

"No problem. That's done now for you. As soon as MacDowell presents himself at any UK Border Control, the officers will see that he can't travel, and they'll detain him."

"Excellent. Thanks a lot Brian."

Miller was confident that with MacDowell on the Border Force's watch list, he wouldn't be able to slip through the net. It occurred to the DCI that if MacDowell was prepared to go to such sickeningly violent lengths to divert attention away from himself, it was perfectly reasonable that this scum-bag was capable of booking a flight that he had no intention of catching, to distract any police that might be waiting to ambush him.

*****

"Keith, alright?"

"Oh hi Sir. I've got all the info on Jamie Miggins. Just setting up an armed response and tactical aid team now, Tameside are getting back to me in the next few minutes."

"And there's nothing on radio?"

"Nothing Sir, it's strictly off-air."

"Okay, good."

"Is that why you phoned?" Saunders could tell that Miller's mind was on something else.

"No, as soon as you've got that boxed off, I want you and Grant back in the interview room."

"Oh? Developments?"

"Oh yes. Lots."

Miller spent five minutes bringing Saunders up-to-speed with everything that had turned-up since the two had last spoken. Saunders was impressed. Things were moving at the pace he liked.

"Okay, I'll chase Tameside up now, and see what's what."

"They need to take the prisoner to North Manchester Custody Suite."

"No problem."

"Okay, get the rest of the interview done, then get Wilson in bed for the night, and call me. We've got a big night on."

"Sir."

*****

Simon Wilson had been going over things in his mind. It was made obvious by the stressed, jaded look on his face as he was led into the interview room. Grant and Saunders could not mistake the change in his demeanour from the last time they'd met seven or so hours earlier, in this same room.

"Okay, we'll start the interview now, if that's okay?"

Wilson nodded to DC Grant, and she read him his rights and explained the interview procedure again.

Once the official stuff was done, Saunders launched straight in. "We think you were talking a lot of shit to us this morning. But it's okay, because its shit we want to talk."

Wilson looked confused.

"You do know that we've got your DNA on file from the last time that you were arrested?"

Wilson nodded.

"Do you understand the implications of that?"

He nodded again.

"And do you understand that it is possible to take DNA traces from human excrement?"

He didn't nod this time. He looked confused again.

"Mr Wilson, did you have a plop anywhere on Friday night?"

"What?" It looked as though the penny was starting to drop.

"Did you get caught short?"

"What...I..."

"You see, we've found a poo that contains your DNA profile. It was discovered remarkably close to the location where Curtis Kennedy's body was discovered."

"Plus, Forensics have found traces of Curtis's blood in your vehicle, along with small traces of his urine in the boot."

"Are you still suggesting that this is a stitch up?"

There was no reply. Wilson was just staring impassively at the table-top.

"It's quite ridiculous saying that we're stitching you up, when we have your car's tyre marks at the church car park. We also have your turd at the church. We have your travelling companion's blood on the stone in the field, plus the victim's blood the rear-seat upholstery in your car. Let's see, what else, do we have?" Saunders looked at Grant with a wide smirk on his face.

"Don't forget the bungee tie that was found by the spare wheel. Looks identical to the ones which were used to wrap the suitcase, the one which was used to kill Curtis."

Wilson didn't respond. He was stressed, no doubt about it, but it seemed as though he wasn't prepared to allow these two coppers to see him cave in. There wasn't a hint of remorse.

"Would you like to try and explain why we have these major pieces of evidence which link you to the murder of Curtis Kennedy, beyond all reasonable doubt?"

"No comment." Wilson was staring down at his lap now.

"Well, I think that's enough for now." Said Saunders.

Wilson looked up. "Am I being charged?" he asked.

"Not yet. We're confident we'll get even more conclusive evidence from your car. I'm surprised that you've allowed yourself to take the blame for all this on your own, though."

That comment got through. Wilson suddenly had a look of anger. "What's that supposed to mean?"

"No comment. Come on, let's get you back to your cell.

We'll pick this up again in the morning."

"No. You've got to charge me or let me go..." said Wilson, as though desperate to hear his fate. The two detectives smiled slyly at one another. Saunders threw his eyes over at Grant, then back at Wilson, creating a "what's he like?" look, which amused Grant.

"Under the circumstances, I'm confident we've enough to secure the maximum ninety-six hours to detain you. But you're right, after that time is up, we will have to decide whether we are going to charge you, or release you. I mean, if you can come up with a plausible explanation for all of the evidence against you, you'll be out of here by Thursday."

"Interview suspended at sixteen-fifty." Said Grant, delighted that Saunders had managed to wrap this up with plenty of food-for-thought for Wilson to sleep on. It was going to be a long, long night.

Saunders requested a custody officer to come and escort Wilson back to his cell. As soon as he was led away, Saunders and Grant raced out of the police station, and into Saunders' car.

Chapter Forty-One

Tameside Division were delighted to be involved in the arrest of Jamie "Miggy" Miggins. He was known to several of the CID officers based at Ashton police station, and had his own revolving door at Strangeways prison. At least it felt like that. He'd go in for a year, sometimes two, for violent crimes. But somehow, he always managed to wriggle out of the most serious charges, and received far more lenient sentences than the Ashton officers had been hoping for.

With hindsight, it came as no surprise that Miggins was the chief-suspect for the DWP attacks. Several of the CID staff in Tameside were annoyed with themselves for not suggesting his name. As soon as it had been relayed to them by their DCI, the room erupted with the sound of discontent. The DWP attacks meant a lot to the Tameside officers, they'd attended the attack in Hyde the previous week, and Stockport is only up the road from their patch. These attacks had been very close to home for all of them. Too close to home.

Ashton's DCI addressed his officers. "There is a total radio ban on this job. We have reason to believe that Miggins, and others, have been eaves-dropping our radio network for some time. So, there will be absolutely no airtime until further notice in relation to the DWP attacks. If you do hear any talk on police radio about the DWP attacks, ignore them, these are decoy remarks being made by DCI Miller's team, and they will be completely irrelevant to the inquiry. It's just to give the impression that its business as usual if the attackers are monitoring. Is that understood?"

"Yes Sir!" said the group of twenty-six detectives in the incident room at Ashton police station.

"Thank you. Right, down to business. We currently have several patrols out looking for Miggins's vehicle. As soon as it is seen in transit, we are going for a hard stop, led by armed-response officers."

The tension rose in the room. Suddenly, things had become very serious.

"At this moment in time, we have not made eye-ball on

the suspect's car. However, he was caught in an ANPR log, driving through Denton at eleven o'clock this morning, headed in the direction of Stockport, possibly Brinnington estate, he is known to spend a lot of time in that area. We have to make the assumption that he is still local to that district, or the Denton, Hyde, Haughton Green or Bredbury areas at this moment in time, as these are his most frequented districts. As soon as one of our patrols spots him, we will engage in Operation Imbellis."

*****

Operation Imbellis was named after the Latin word for coward, and the major operation got under way shortly after 5pm. It was dark, and raining in Manchester. Miggins's car had been spotted headed towards Denton, coming from Bredbury. Unmarked police cars quickly made discreet pursuit, and within minutes of the initial sighting of Miggins' dark blue Ford Focus, there was a convoy of unmarked vehicles on his tail, with many more units headed his way.

Communications between the police teams involved in this pursuit, were not as straight-forward as usual. Each car was in contact with the control room via open-line mobile phone, which was being managed as a conference call by the Detective Superintendent at Ashton. This unique form of communication was limited, but effective enough to keep a running commentary with the police vehicles, and to feed-back key intelligence from the ground to the control room. The information that the officers all heard was that Miggins was alone in the vehicle, and he seemed to be quite relaxed, smoking a cigarette and singing along to the radio. He hadn't appeared spooked by any of the trailing cars, as he continued to play the air-drums against his steering-wheel.

Miggins's car continued into Denton, passing the turn-off for his address in Haughton Green. It had been hoped that he would head back towards his home, and that the arrest could be made as he got out of his vehicle at his address, on the council estate. That had been the plan that the officers had hoped for, and the fact that it wasn't now an option was disappointing, although it wasn't a major problem. There were plenty of officers on hand to make the arrest, wherever the opportunity presented itself.

By the time that Miggins' car had travelled through the traffic lights at Crown Point, turning left and headed towards Manchester, the Armed Response Unit had arrived on the opposite side of the junction, and was ready to join the convoy.

Now came the tricky part, which was to decide where the ambush, or "hard-stop" was going to take place. At this juncture, the Superintendent relayed the commentary from the ARU, whose officers would dictate the ultimate decision on how the arrest was going to pan out.

Less than a mile down the road from Crown Point, close to the motorway junction at Denton Rock, Miggins's car began slowing down for traffic lights, and he hit his indicator, telling the trailing officers that he was about to pull into Sainsbury's supermarket. The Superintendent's voice suddenly lifted a few octaves as he relayed the message from the ARU officers.

"Standby Operation Imbellis. Suspect's vehicle is about to turn left into Sainsbury's. Armed Response want a hard stop outside the car park. Repeat, all units, hard stop OUTSIDE the car park entrance, do not allow the suspect to enter the car park. Over."

The Superintendent had clearly forgotten that his radio language wasn't required over mobile phone, but none of the awaiting officers noticed. They were too absorbed in what was happening. This was it.

The traffic lights changed to amber, then to green, and Miggins's car pulled forwards, turning into the road which led to the supermarket. Four unmarked police cars suddenly hit their sirens and blue lights, the first one accelerating past, and then in front of Miggins's Focus, while the others surrounded the vehicle at either side, and behind. The front car slammed on the brake, forcing Miggins to stamp hard against his own foot-brake. The rear car nudged Miggins's car forward, as the other two unmarked police vehicles wedged him in at either side, leaving him with no escape route, not even through the door, as it wouldn't open widely enough to allow him out. As all of this was happening, the ARU Range Rover had swooped around the side, and pulled up in front of the diamond-shape formation. It was a text-book hard-stop.

In the blink of an eye, the armed response officers were out, and had their weapons trained on Jamie Miggins.

"Armed police!"

"ARMED POLICE! PLACE YOUR HANDS ON THE STEERING WHEEL!"

There were four armed officers standing in front of the vehicle, all of them had the barrels of their Heckler and Koch G36 assault rifles pointed directly at Miggins. His face confirming the fear and surprise. This high-adrenaline encounter had taken him completely unawares.

"MOVE THIS VEHICLE!" Shouted one of the ARU officers, pointing at the car which was blocking the driver-side door. Within seconds the vehicle had zoomed out of position and the car door was pulled open. The coward who had crept up behind innocent people, viciously attacking them and causing them horrendous injuries, was crying like a terrified toddler, snot and all.

Footage was being recorded of this arrest via the ARU officer's body-cams. For the twenty officers that stood around the scene as Miggins was cuffed and placed in the back of a police van, there was a sense of relief that this awful week of terror was over, and a sense of morbid delight that this whimpering, snivelling little bastard would long be remembered for this pathetic, debasing body-cam footage, above all else.

Chapter Forty-Two

At 5.20pm, the SCIU team members were sitting in the incident room, waiting for Saunders and Grant to get back from interviewing Wilson. All four of the suspects that had been picked up in that morning's dawn-raids had now been informed that they were having a sleep-over. The Cole brothers were the only ones who made a fuss. Wilson had been quite subdued throughout the second part of his interview, and the stark reality of the situation was dawning on him as he settled down to a night locked up with nothing but his own thoughts for company. Hart knew what side his bread was buttered, and headed back to the custody cells looking quite relaxed.

"Sorry, sorry!" said Saunders as he burst through the doors, with DC Grant just a few footsteps behind.

"Every red light! We tried the blues and twos, but the amount of pillocks that won't let you through is getting worse!" added Grant.

"Okay, no problem. Sit down, we need to get started. It's been an eventful few hours, there's no time to discuss all of this now. But here's an overview of the day's developments. We know who killed Kennedy, we know what his involvement was, we know who carried out the attacks. We also know that the man who organised all of this horror in our city is booked on a flight out of Liverpool John Lennon airport at 19.50, headed for Marrakesh."

"Fucking Norah! That's a hell of a day of developments!" Chapman looked stunned by the extraordinary progress which had been made over the course of just one day of questioning. He and Worthington had endured the day from hell, sitting around and receiving "no comment" replies from Linton Cole.

"Yes, it gets better. I'm just waiting for a call to tell us that the actual attacker has been apprehended, the arrest operation is live as we speak. Once we have him, a cheap little hitman from Haughton Green, we just need to apprehend MacDowell at the airport, and it's all over."

These words were comforting to the SCIU staff. This

case had been deeply disturbing, and extremely troubling for every one of them. The prospect of it all being concluded tonight was an incredibly welcome proposition.

"However, we need to keep a sense of reality. We have to assume that the arrests of the Cole brothers, and of Hart and Wilson won't have escaped his attention. Wives and girlfriends have probably been in touch with him by now, if not other gang members who've heard the news. So, let's be clear... this is not a done-deal. Not by any stretch of the imagination."

This comment took the wind from under the SCIU officers wings slightly. But they understood it was a sensible suggestion. Miller continued, "we have organised a major police operation in conjunction with border force and Merseyside police. The airport is going to be inundated with undercover and armed officers, and as soon as MacDowell presents himself at the airport, he's going in a police van. I've taken the decision that we will stay away, as there is a very high probability that MacDowell will have some eyes and ears at the airport prior to him making an appearance, just to check that nothing is untoward. We have to remember that we're all familiar faces to him and his team of scumbags, so I'm not prepared to risk anything going tits-up at this late stage in the proceedings."

There was an air of disappointment. None of the team liked to sit it out when a major arrest was imminent. Especially when the stakes were this high, and the crimes involved were so repugnant. But it did make sense.

Miller held his hand up as his phone started ringing.

"Miller!" he said, the expectancy in his voice was unmistakable. He smiled as he listened to the DCI in Ashton break the news. Miller raised his thumb to his team. There was an audible sigh of relief from all of the detectives.

"Brilliant, okay, nice one, nice one, cheers." Miller hung up.

"We've got the fucking bastard!"

*****

At exactly the moment that Miller was talking to his

team, and celebrating the arrest of Jamie Miggins, the check-in desk was opening at Liverpool John Lennon airport, processing passengers for flight FR3028, scheduled to depart two hours later, at 19.50.

There were no obvious signs around the entrance, or in the vast reception of the huge, glass-fronted building that anything untoward was going on. It looked like business as usual in the main lobby, which resembled an enormous bus station. Hundreds, if not thousands of excited, and anxious looking passengers and giddy kids were queued in long lines, waiting for their turn at the check-in desks. They were all eager to get this boring part done, so they could get through customs, and buy a drink at the bar, ready to kickstart their holiday.

But unbeknown to the holidaymakers, all around the airport were dozens upon dozens of plain-clothed officers. Some were armed, some were not, and they blended into the queues extremely well. Many of the police officers were waiting in the Ryan Air queue, the queue for the 19.50 flight to Morocco. The plan was to make a very peaceful, very quiet arrest, the moment that Marco MacDowell presented himself.

The apprehension amongst the police officers was high, and the longer the wait went on, the greater the tension became. After forty minutes, the Ryan Air queue was dwindling, and it was starting to look like this had been a red-herring. It looked as though MacDowell had pulled another stunt, diverting the police's attention, while he did something else. But what?

Miller was in the SCIU incident room, with his team, anxiously following progress thirty-five miles away, via a mobile phone conversation with the Merseyside Chief Superintendent who was Gold Commander of the operation.

"It looks as though your theory was correct, DCI Miller. As each minute passes, it looks more and more unlikely that MacDowell is going to show up here tonight."

Miller's mind was racing. "Okay, well, let's see if that flight leaves without him. If it does, I'll call an urgent press conference and we'll make him Britain's most wanted man before that plane is over the north-sea. He's not leaving the country via any other port, his name will flag up on the watch-list as soon as his details are entered into any airport or seaport check in desk..."

Suddenly, the Chief Super in Liverpool sounded tense. "Sorry, er, standby." The phone crackled. Miller felt his insides somersault. Something had happened, and he had no idea what it was. His team were sat before him, glaring back. They all felt the sense of apprehension.

*****

The Ryan Air queue was much shorter now than it had been when check-in had opened. A young family from Runcorn were getting near to the front, and the children, a boy and a girl aged about eight and ten, were becoming more and more excited with each passing minute. Their parents looked stressed, the kids were driving them nuts with the constant talking and giggling and ducking under the ropes which separated the queues.

"Mum, I'm thirsty, can I get a drink?"

"Can I go to the toilet?" They asked, repeatedly.

"Amber! Leon! Just simmer down."

"I'm bursting though!" pleaded Leon to his mother.

"No. Its nearly our turn now. Just wait quietly, how many times have I got to say it?"

"Just calm down, will you both?" said the dad. He was beginning to dread this holiday, and they'd not even dropped off their suitcases yet. Amber and Leon looked down at the floor, looking sad for being told off.

A couple of minutes later, the two youngsters had got over it, and started bobbing under the ropes once again, and were giggling as they tried to pop up at the same time on either side. Their parents were relieved to see that they were now finally at the front of the queue.

Marco MacDowell's appearance had changed from the photographs that all of the Merseyside and border force officers had. He'd managed to disguise his bald, shiny head under a baseball cap, and he had a deep stubble that was almost a beard. He was wearing a dark blue Nike tracksuit and white trainers. His eyes were covered by sunglasses. He was near the front of the queue, just behind the young family, when a border force officer walked over to him and politely asked to see his passport.

MacDowell smiled politely, and dropped his rucksack off his shoulder. He started unzipping the back-pack.

"Yeah, no problem mate," he said as he rummaged inside. "It's here somewhere, I just had it ten minutes ago." He put the bag on the floor and knelt down, and as he did so, he yanked the little girl, Amber, by her hair and dragged her towards him. She screamed loudly.

It had all happened so fast. MacDowell was stood again, and he had the little girl's head gripped between his hand, and his other arm. "You try anything, and I'm going to break her fucking neck. Do you understand?"

The border force officer stepped backwards, slowly, his hands raised before him.

Amber's mum was at the check-in desk, but heard her daughter screaming. She saw what was happening and screamed herself. Amber's dad started walking towards MacDowell.

"Stay there! DON'T MOVE!" He shouted. "I will snap her neck. One twist that way." He demonstrated with his arm and twisted the little girl's head slightly. "Do you understand me?" He asked. He was very calm, and Amber's dad stopped dead in his tracks. His daughter was screaming, staring at him, pleading to her dad to help her.

"RIGHT! LISTEN!" MacDowell was shouting at the top of his voice, his voice was so loud that it reverberated all around the building. "YOU PUT ME ON THAT FLIGHT, AND IT LEAVES RIGHT NOW, OR I WILL KILL THIS KID. IS THAT CLEAR?" He shouted.

Panic swept through the airport, as hundreds of families dumped their belongings, grabbed their loved ones and began running away from the danger. There was screaming and crying and shouting. It was total chaos. The airport staff had all hidden beneath their check-in desks. The only people remaining in the airport lobby were the undercover police officers and

MacDowell, and Amber's family. The young girl was still screaming and wriggling and trying to kick the man who had her in a head-lock. Her little brother was crying uncontrollably.

The Merseyside DCS was hearing all this on his radio, and he had video from CCTV. He recognised that this needed a swift conclusion. "This is Gold Command. Do we have a clear shot of the hostage-taker, over?"

The radio crackled. "This is Firearms Sergeant Wilson. We have a clear shot, head area only, over."

"This is Gold Command. The girl must not be placed in any danger. Permission to fire when absolutely safe to do so."

"Received over." Said the Firearms Sergeant. He then spoke to his officers. "Who has the cleanest head shot, as far away from the hostage, over?" The officer sounded calm, and collected. There was no hint of panic present in his voice.

"This is Firearms Officer 232, Sir. I have a clear shot, estimating forty, that's four-zero centimetres clearance from hostage. Over."

"Permission to fire when confident to do so."

On the airport floor, MacDowell was still shouting his orders. "OPEN THESE DOORS, AND NO TRICKS. I WANT TO BOARD THAT PLANE R...."

The shot had been silent. The top of MacDowell's head exploded, and he fell to the floor. The nearest police officer ran towards him and grabbed Amber, scooping her up and sprinting away from the dead man, shielding her face so that she couldn't see what had just happened.

Within seconds, a dozen police officers were surrounding the body, assessing whether CPR was required. It was very quickly established that this gunshot wound was not consistent with life. As the pool of dark red blood expanded over the polished floor, it was soon apparent that MacDowell's brains had just been blown out of the back of his skull, a necessary, emergency course of action to protect the little girl.

It was all over.

Chapter Forty-Three

Rudovsky arrived home just after 9pm. She was tearful.

"Hiya love," said her girlfriend, Abby.

"Alright?" Rudovsky sounded flat.

"I've had Sky News on all night. Bloody amazing work! Well done!" Abby sounded excited. But her excitement soon changed to concern when she saw Jo's face.

"Love, what's up?"

Rudovsky sat down and pressed mute on the remote. The Sky News reporter was standing outside Liverpool John Lennon airport. The reporter looked excited, waving her arms around as she spoke to the camera, describing the drama that had occurred just a few hours earlier. Soon, the screen changed, and Rudovsky was looking at herself, and her boss DCI Miller as they presented an emergency press conference to reveal the news that the DWP attacks were finished.

"What's up Jo, come on love."

Rudovsky felt emotional, and her eyes were welling up. Abby's affectionate concern had tipped her over the edge. She started rubbing Jo's arm. "S'up love? You should be buzzing, from everything that was said at the press conference. I thought you'd be buzzing, love."

"I'm just... I'm feeling pretty shit."

"Why?"

"Because it was all for nothing. Obviously, we didn't say nowt in the press conference, because it's all got to be a secret until the court case. But, basically, it was just a piss-take. The guy who was shot, he set it all up to get Miller off his tail. He knew that if somebody started attacking DWP workers, Miller would be put on that case. It gave him enough time to clear out his weed factory." A tear rolled down Jo's face, and Abby wiped it away with her thumb.

"And now, I just can't stop thinking about the victims. Especially Kath. She's a gorgeous woman. And... aw God, I just can't cope with it..."

Abby hugged Jo, and held her close. It wasn't like Jo Rudovsky to get emotional, but Abby could see that she was really feeling this case. And it was raw.

"Come on Jo, it's not your fault. At least you got it all sorted pretty quickly. It's an amazing result."

"I know, I know." Jo laughed nervously. It wasn't amusement, she just felt very embarrassed and vulnerable, crying openly like this. She took the tissue that Abby had offered her and blew her nose.

"Don't feel stupid Jo. Not in front of me."

"Do you know what the worst thing is?" She asked, dabbing her eyes with the tissue.

"No, what?"

"Well, not only was it all for nothing, but it's all just going to carry on. That's the end of the story now. But the fucking horrible bastards who run this country will carry on treating the poor just as badly, and the public will go back to pretending they can't see it. I feel so fucking conned, and let down, and confused." Rudovsky started crying again.

"Nah. The government haven't long left now, Jo. They're as much use as a one-legged man in an arse-kicking contest, mate."

"Yeah, I know. But they'll still sanction the one-legged man and everybody will just ignore it again. They'll say it's his own fault for only having one leg. I fucking hate what half of the people have become in this country. Self-righteous, self-obsessed freaks with their 'I'm alright Jack' attitude."

"Well, do what I do, Jo."

"What's that?"

"Start a petition on Change."

Epilogue

The crimes which shocked the nation were soon forgotten about by the media, as other news stories about sleazy politicians, tax avoidance schemes, insane Presidents, cowardly acts of terrorism and Brexit once again took over the front pages and the top-of-the-hour headlines.

But life would never be the same again for Kath Palmer, or for Jason Brown, Gary Webster and Margaret Wilkins. They were left to face a life of misery and disability, and were sadly, very quickly forgotten about by the general public, with the exception of Stewart Grimley, the man who had escaped serious injury thanks to his IKEA chopping board. He went on to appear in Celebrity Big Brother, and with his dog Barney, began a lucrative career advertising insurance policies for pet and personal injury cover, using his catch-phrase "As luck would have it." He no longer works for the DWP.

The Crown Court in Manchester heard the case against Simon Wilson and Jamie Miggins. Wilson was found guilty of the murder of Curtis Kennedy, and was also charged for his involvement in the DWP attacks. He was sentenced to a minimum of twenty-seven years.

Jamie Miggins pleaded guilty to all five charges of attempted murder against the DWP staff, and was sentenced to a minimum of seventeen years in prison. With the death of Marco MacDowell, his side-kick, Simon Wilson and Jamie Miggins became the living faces of the atrocious crimes.

Daniel Hart was cleared of all counts. The jury accepted Hart's version of events, that Hart was only there for a drive out, and had pleaded with Wilson not to kill the young man. The Witness Protection deal which had been organised enabled Hart to present evidence against Wilson, via video-link. Hart denied all charges of being complicit in the DWP attacks. He is now settling into a new life working as a postman in Springfield, Missouri.

The Cole Brothers never faced any charges for their involvement in the disappearance of Curtis Kennedy. There was insufficient evidence to build a case, as Kennedy's mother and sister refused to give evidence against the two gangsters.

The British government continue to torment and attack the poor and vulnerable, ramping up their hatred to a new level with the roll-out of Universal Credit, which is creating even more misery and homelessness, more addiction and ultimately more death amongst the poorest, and neediest. The government maintain that their benefit reforms "are working." The people that they are designed to "help" are not working, and you can find them in most city-centre doorways, soup kitchens and food-banks.

Many people look back on Britain's recent history with a sense of utter disbelief. One example being the general election of 1964. Just a few weeks before the Supremes were topping the UK charts with their best-known track "Baby Love," the Conservatives were running an election campaign with the slogan "If you want a nigger for a neighbour, vote Labour."

Now, some fifty or so years on, most rational thinking people genuinely cannot comprehend this type of language or attitude as ever being acceptable in Great Britain, let alone an election slogan. It is right that society now looks back on that time with a great deal of shame and embarrassment.

In a similar way, fifty years from now, when the true scale of the horror is reported as fact, and all of the data has been collated, people will not be able to comprehend the despicable way that Britain, one of the richest countries on earth, treated its frailest, poorest and neediest citizens between 2010 and ????

The End